Jane, Unlimited

KRISTIN CASHORE

KATHY DAWSON BOOKS

KATHY DAWSON BOOKS
PENGUIN YOUNG READERS GROUP
An imprint of Penguin Random House LLC
375 Hudson Street
New York, NY 10014

Text copyright © 2017 by Kristin Cashore
Maps copyright © 2017 by Ian Schoenherr

Printed in the United States of America
ISBN 9780803741492

1   3   5   7   9   10   8   6   4   2

Design by Jennifer Kelly
Text set in Adobe Garamond Pro

for all aunts,
especially mine

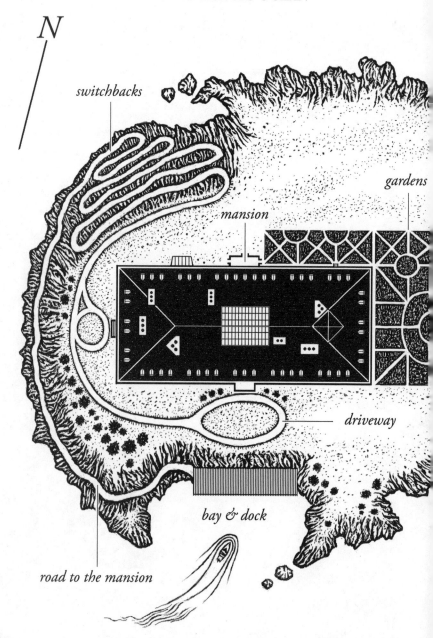

ATLANTIC OCEAN

N

switchbacks

gardens

mansion

driveway

bay & dock

road to the mansion

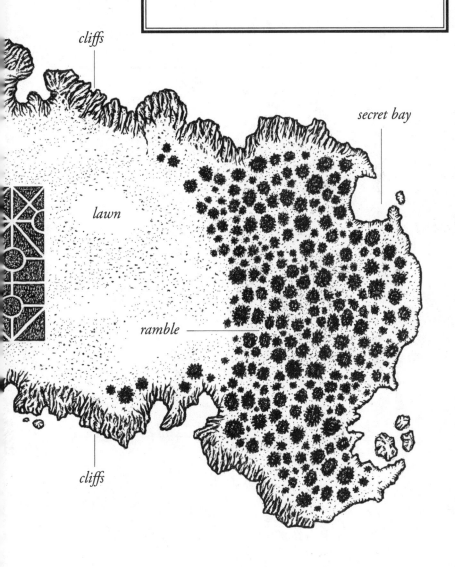

TU REVIENS
Island and Grounds

cliffs

secret bay

lawn

ramble

cliffs

ATLANTIC OCEAN

TU REVIENS
Mansion Interior

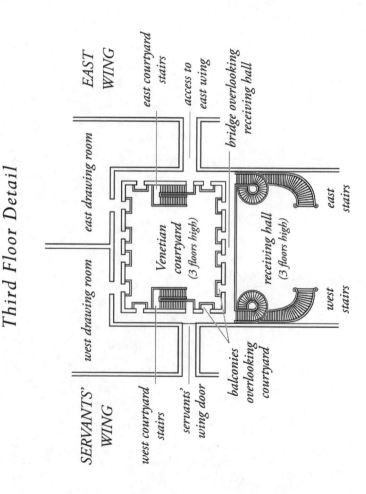

Third Floor Detail

EAST WING

east courtyard stairs

access to east wing

bridge overlooking receiving hall

east drawing room

Venetian courtyard (3 floors high)

receiving hall (3 floors high)

east stairs

west drawing room

west stairs

SERVANTS' WING

west courtyard stairs

servants' wing door

balconies overlooking courtyard

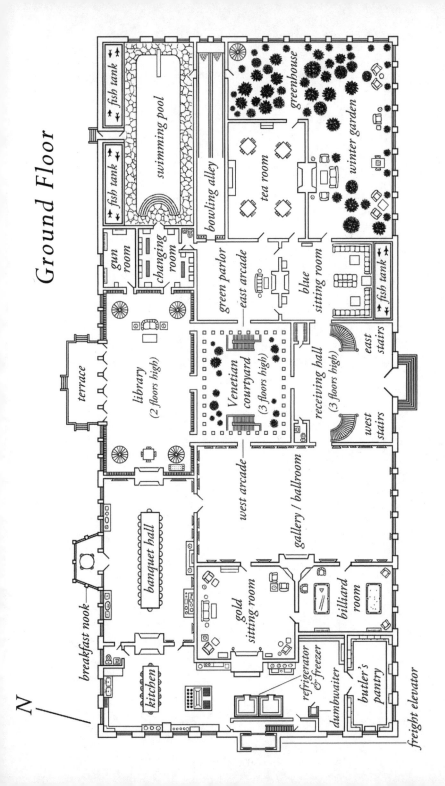

Ground Floor

N

fish tank

fish tank

swimming pool

fish tank

greenhouse

winter garden

gun room

changing room

bowling alley

tea room

green parlor

east arcade

blue sitting room

fish tank

terrace

library
(2 floors high)

Venetian courtyard
(3 floors high)

receiving hall
(3 floors high)

east stairs

west stairs

west arcade

gallery / ballroom

banquet hall

breakfast nook

gold sitting room

billiard room

kitchen

refrigerator & freezer

dumbwaiter

butler's pantry

freight elevator

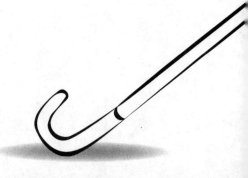

CONTENTS

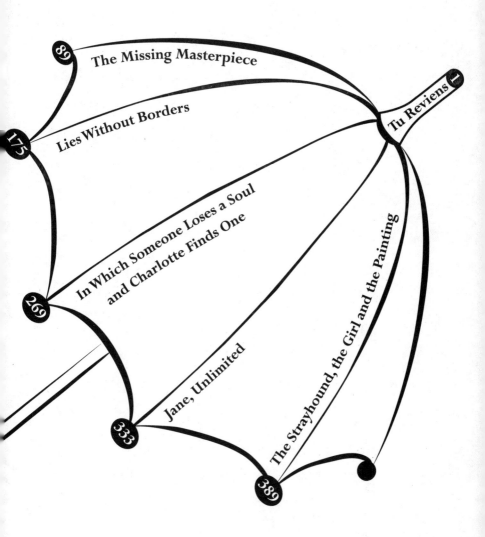

Tu Reviens 1

The Missing Masterpiece 89

Lies Without Borders 175

In Which Someone Loses a Soul and Charlotte Finds One 269

Jane, Unlimited 333

The Strayhound, the Girl and the Painting 389

Tu Reviens

The house on the cliff looks like a ship disappearing into fog. The spire a mast, the trees whipping against its base, the waves of a ravening sea.

Or maybe Jane just has ships on the brain, seeing as she's inside one that's doing all it can to consume her attention. A wave rolls the yacht, catches her off balance, and she sits down, triumphantly landing in the general vicinity of where she aimed. Another wave propels her, in slow motion, against the yacht's lounge window.

"I haven't spent a lot of time in boats. I guess you get used to it," she says.

Jane's traveling companion, Kiran, lies on her back in the lounge's long window seat, her eyes closed. Kiran isn't seasick. She's bored. She gives no indication of having heard.

"I guess my aunt Magnolia must have gotten used to it," says Jane.

"My family makes me want to die," Kiran says. "I hope we drown."

This yacht is named *The Kiran*.

Through the lounge window, Jane can see Patrick, who captains the yacht, on deck in the rain, drenched, trying to catch a cleat with a rope. He's young, maybe early twenties, a white guy with short dark hair, a deep winter tan, and blue eyes so bright that Jane had noticed them immediately. Someone was apparently supposed to be waiting on the dock to help him but didn't show up.

"Kiran?" says Jane. "Should we maybe help Patrick?"

"Help him with what?"

"I don't know. Docking the boat?"

"Are you kidding?" says Kiran. "Patrick can do everything by himself."

"Everything?"

"Patrick doesn't need anybody," Kiran says. "Ever."

"Okay," Jane says, wondering if this is an expression of Kiran's general, equal-opportunity sarcasm, or if she's got some specific problem with Patrick. It can be hard to tell with someone like Kiran.

Outside, Patrick catches the cleat successfully, then, his body taut, pulls on the rope, arm over arm, bringing the yacht up against the dock. It's kind of impressive. Maybe he *can* do everything.

"Who is Patrick, anyway?"

"Patrick Yellan," Kiran says. "Ravi and I grew up with him. He works for my father. So does his little sister, Ivy. So did his parents, until a couple years ago. They died in a car accident, in France. Sorry," she adds, with a glance at Jane. "I don't mean to remind you of travel accidents."

"It's okay," Jane says automatically, filing these names and facts away with the other information she's collected. Kiran is British American on her father's side and British Indian on her mother's, though her parents are divorced and her father's now remarried. Also, she's revoltingly wealthy. Jane's never had a friend before who grew up with her own servants. *Is Kiran my friend?* thinks Jane. *Acquaintance? Maybe my mentor?* Not now, maybe, but in the past. Kiran, four years older than Jane, went to college in Jane's hometown and tutored Jane in writing while she was in high school.

Ravi is Kiran's twin brother, Jane remembers. Jane's never met Ravi, but he visited Kiran sometimes in college. Her tutoring sessions had been different when Ravi was in town. Kiran would arrive late, her face alight, her manner less strict, less intense.

"Is Patrick in charge of transportation to and from the island?" asks Jane.

"I guess," Kiran says. "Partly, anyway. A couple other people chip in too."

"Do Patrick and his sister live at the house?"

"*Everyone* lives at the house."

"So, is it nice to come home?" asks Jane. "Because you get to see the friends you grew up with?"

Jane is fishing, because she's trying to figure out how these servant relationships work, when one person is so rich.

Kiran doesn't answer right away, just stares straight ahead, her mouth tight, until Jane begins to wonder if her question was rude.

Then Kiran says, "I guess there was a time when seeing Patrick again, after a long absence, made me feel like I was coming home."

"Oh," says Jane. "But . . . not anymore?"

"Eh, it's complicated," Kiran says, with a short sigh. "Let's not talk about it now. He could hear us."

Patrick would have to have superpowers to hear a word of this conversation, but Jane recognizes a dismissal when she hears one. Peering through the window, she can make out the shapes of other boats, big ones, little ones, vaguely, through the downpour, docked in this tiny bay. Kiran's father, Octavian Thrash IV, owns those boats, this bay, this island off the eastern seaboard, those waving trees, that massive house far above. "How will we get to the house?" she asks. She can see no road. "Will we ascend through the rain, like scuba divers?"

Kiran snorts, then surprises Jane by shooting her a small, approving smile. "By car," she says, not elaborating. "I've missed the funny way you talk. Your clothes too."

Jane's gold zigzag shirt and wine-colored corduroys make her look like one of Aunt Magnolia's sea creatures. A maroon clownfish, a coral

5

grouper. Jane supposes she never dresses without thinking of Aunt Magnolia. "Okay," she says. "And when's the spring gala?"

"I don't remember," Kiran says. "The day after tomorrow? The day after that? It's probably on the weekend."

There's a gala for every season at Octavian Thrash IV's house on the sea. That's the reason for Kiran's trip. She's come home for the spring gala.

And this time, for some inexplicable reason, she's invited Jane along, even though, until last week, Jane hadn't seen Kiran since Kiran's graduation almost a year ago. Kiran had stumbled upon Jane at her job in the campus bookshop, because, like many visiting alumni, Kiran had remembered it had a public restroom. Trapped behind the information desk, Jane had seen her coming, an enormous handbag on her arm and a harassed expression on her face. With any other ghost from her past, Jane's first instinct would have been to turn her shoulder, hide behind her dark curls, and make herself into a statue. But the sight of Kiran Thrash brought Jane instantly to the strange promise Aunt Magnolia had extracted from her before she'd gone away on that last photography expedition.

Aunt Magnolia had made Jane promise never to turn down an invitation to Kiran's family estate.

"Hey," Kiran had said that day, stopping at the desk. "Janie. It's you." She'd glanced at Jane's arm, where tattooed jellyfish tentacles peeked out from under her shirtsleeve.

"Kiran," said Jane, instinctively touching her arm. The tattoo was new. "Hi."

"Do you go to school here now?"

"No," Jane said. "I dropped out. I'm taking some time. I work here. In the bookstore," she added, which was obvious, and not something she wanted to talk about. But she'd learned to chat, to fill the silence with false enthusiasm, and to offer her failures as conversational bait, because sometimes it enabled her to head off the very next question Kiran asked.

"How's your aunt?"

It was like muscle memory now, this steeling herself. "She died."

"Oh," Kiran said, narrowing her eyes. "No wonder you dropped out."

It was less friendly, but easier to bear up against, than the usual reaction, because it brought a flare of annoyance into Jane's throat. "I might have dropped out anyway. I hated it. The other students were snobs and I was failing biology."

"Professor Greenhut?" Kiran asked, ignoring the dig about snobs.

"Yeah."

"Known school-wide as a pretentious douche," said Kiran.

Against her better instincts, Jane smiled. Greenhut assumed his students already knew a lot about biology, and maybe the assumption was just, because no one else in the class had seemed to struggle like Jane had. Aunt Magnolia, who'd been an adjunct marine biology teacher, had spluttered over the syllabus. "Greenhut's a superior, self-righteous donkey," she'd said in disgust, then added, "No offense to Eeyore. Greenhut is trying to weed out students who didn't go to fancy high schools."

"It's working," Jane had said.

"Maybe you'll go to school somewhere else," Kiran said. "Somewhere far away. It's healthy to get away from home."

"Yeah. Maybe." Jane had always lived in that small, upstate university town, surrounded by students whenever she'd stepped outside. Tuition was free for faculty kids. But maybe Kiran was right, maybe Jane should have chosen a different school. A state school, where the other students wouldn't have made her feel so . . . provincial. These students came from all over the world and they had so much money. Jane's roommate had spent her summer in the French countryside and, once she'd learned that Jane had taken high school French, wanted to have conversations in French about towns Jane had never heard of and cheeses she'd never eaten.

How disorienting it had been to attend the classes she'd watched enviously through the windows her whole life, and wind up miserable. In the end, she'd spent most nights with Aunt Magnolia instead of in her dorm room, feeling like she was living a parallel version of her own life, one that didn't fit her skin. Like she was a puzzle piece from the wrong puzzle.

"You could be an art major somewhere," Kiran said then. "Didn't you used to make cool umbrellas?"

"They're not art," said Jane. "They're umbrellas. Messy ones."

"Okay," said Kiran, "whatever. Where do you live now?"

"In an apartment in town."

"The same apartment you lived in with your aunt?"

"*No*," Jane said, injecting it with a touch of sarcasm that was probably wasted on Kiran. Of course she hadn't been able to afford that same apartment. "I live with three grad students."

"How do you like it?"

"It's fine," Jane lied. Her apartment-mates were a lot older than she and too pompously focused on their abstruse intellectual pursuits to bother with cooking, or cleaning, or showering. It was like living with self-important Owl from *Winnie-the-Pooh*, except that their hygiene was worse and there were three of them. Jane was hardly ever alone there. Her bedroom was a glorified closet, not conducive to umbrella-making, which required space. It was hard to move around without poking herself on ribs. Sometimes she slept with a work in progress at the end of her bed.

"I liked your aunt," Kiran said. "I liked you too," she added, which was when Jane stopped thinking about herself and began to study Kiran, who had changed somehow since she'd last seen her. Kiran had used to move as if she were being pushed by at least four different urgent purposes at once.

"What's brought you to town?" Jane asked Kiran.

Kiran shrugged, listless. "I was out driving."

"Where are you living?"

"In the city apartment."

The Thrashes' city apartment was the top two floors of a Manhattan mansion overlooking Central Park, quite a distance away for someone who was just "out driving."

"Though I've been called home to the island for the spring gala," Kiran added. "And I may stay awhile. Octavian is probably in a mood."

"Okay," said Jane, trying to imagine having a gazillionaire father, on a private island, in a mood. "I hope you have a nice time."

"What is that tattoo?" asked Kiran. "Is it a squid?"

"It's a jellyfish."

"Can I see it?"

The jellyfish sat on Jane's upper arm, blue and gold, with thin blue tentacles and spiral arms in white and black reaching all the way down below her elbow. Jane often wore her shirtsleeves rolled up to show a glimpse of the tentacles because, secretly, she liked people to ask to see it. She pushed her sleeve up to the shoulder for Kiran.

Kiran gazed at the jellyfish with an unchanging expression. "Huh," she said. "Did it hurt?"

"Yes," said Jane. And she'd taken on an extra job as a waitress at a diner in town for three months to pay for it.

"It's delicate," said Kiran. "It's beautiful, actually. Who designed it?"

"It's based on a photo my aunt took," said Jane through a flush of pleasure, "of a Pacific sea nettle jellyfish."

"Did your aunt ever get to see your tattoo?"

"No."

"Timing can be an asshole," Kiran said. "Come get drinks."

"What?" said Jane, startled. "Me?"

"After you get off work."

"I'm underage."

"So I'll buy you a milkshake."

That night, at the bar, Jane had explained to Kiran what it was like to budget for rent, food, and health insurance on a part-time bookstore salary; how she'd sometimes believe in absentminded moments that Aunt Magnolia was just away on another of her photography trips; about the detours she found herself taking to avoid the apartment building where they'd lived together. Jane didn't mean to explain it all, but Kiran was from the time when life had made sense. Her presence was confusing. It just came out.

"Quit your job," Kiran said.

"And live how?" Jane said, irritated. "Not everyone has Daddy's bottomless credit card, you know."

Kiran absorbed the dig with disinterest. "You just don't seem very happy."

"Happy!" said Jane, incredulous, then, as Kiran continued to sip her whiskey, seriously annoyed. "What's your job, anyway?" she snapped.

"I don't have a job."

"Well, you don't exactly seem happy either."

Kiran surprised Jane by shouting a laugh. "I'll drink to that," she said, then threw back her drink, leaned over the bar, reached into a container of paper umbrellas, and selected one, blue and black to match Jane's shirt and her tattoo tentacles. Opening it carefully, she twirled it between her fingers, then presented it to Jane.

"Protection," Kiran announced.

"From what?" Jane asked, examining the umbrella's delicate working interior.

"From bullshit," said Kiran.

"Wow," Jane said. "All this time, I could've been stopping bullshit with a cocktail umbrella?"

"It might only work for really small bullshit."

"Thanks," said Jane, starting to smile.

"Yeah, so, I don't have a job," Kiran said again, holding Jane's eyes briefly, then looking away. "I apply for things now and then, but it never comes through, and I'll be honest, I'm always kind of relieved."

"What's the problem? You have a degree. You had really good grades, didn't you? Don't you speak, like, seven languages?"

"You sound like my mother," said Kiran, her voice more weary than annoyed. "And my father, and my brother, and my boyfriend, and every damn person I talk to, ever."

"I was only asking."

"It's okay," she said. "I'm a spoiled rich girl who has the privilege to mope around, feeling sorry for herself for being unemployed. I get it."

It was funny, because those were Jane's thoughts exactly. But now, because Kiran had said it, she resented it less. "Hello, don't put bullshit in my mouth. I'm armed," Jane said, brandishing her cocktail umbrella.

"You know what I liked about your aunt?" Kiran said. "She always seemed like she knew exactly what she was going to do next. She made you feel like that was possible, to know the right choice."

Yes. Jane tried to respond, but the truth of it caught in her throat. *Aunt Magnolia,* she thought, choking on it.

Kiran observed Jane's grief with dispassion.

"Quit your job and come home with me to Tu Reviens," she said. "Stay awhile, as long as you like. Octavian won't mind. Hell, he'll buy your umbrella supplies. My boyfriend is there; you can meet him. My brother, Ravi, too. Come on. What's keeping you here?"

Some people are so rich, they don't even notice when they shame others. What value was there in all the deliberate, scrabbling care Jane put into her subsistence now, if a near-stranger's indifferent invitation, born of boredom and a need to pee, made Jane more financially comfortable than she could make herself?

But it wasn't possible to say no, because of Aunt Magnolia. The promise.

"Janie, sweetheart," Aunt Magnolia had said when Jane had woken extra early one morning and found her aunt on the stool at the kitchen counter. "You're awake."

"*You're* awake," Jane had responded, because Jane was the insomniac in the family.

She'd balanced her hip on the edge of Aunt Magnolia's stool so she could lean against her aunt's side, close her eyes, and pretend she was still asleep. Aunt Magnolia had been tall, like Jane, and Jane had always fit well against her. Aunt Magnolia had put her cup of tea into Jane's hands, closing both of Jane's palms around its warmth.

"You remember your old writing tutor?" Aunt Magnolia had said. "Kiran Thrash?"

"Of course," Jane had responded, taking a noisy slurp.

"Did she ever talk about her house?"

"The house with the French name? On the island her dad owns?"

"Tu Reviens," Aunt Magnolia had said.

Jane had known enough French to translate this. "'You return.'"

"Exactly, darling," Aunt Magnolia had said. "I want you to make me a promise."

"Okay."

"If anyone ever invites you to Tu Reviens," she'd said, "promise me that you'll go."

"Okay," Jane had said. "Um, *why?*"

"I've heard it's a place of opportunity."

"Aunt Magnolia," Jane had said with a snort, putting her cup down to look into her aunt's eyes. Her aunt had had a funny blue blotch staining the otherwise brown iris in one of her eyes, like a nebula, or a muddy star, with little spikes, spokes.

"Aunt Magnolia," Jane had repeated. "What the hell are you talking about?"

Her aunt had chuckled, deep in her throat, then had given Jane a one-armed hug. "You know I get wild ideas sometimes."

Aunt Magnolia had been one for sudden trips, like camping in some remote part of the Finger Lakes where overnights weren't exactly permitted and where cell phones didn't work. They would read books together by lantern light, listen to the moths throw themselves against the canvas of the tiny, glowing tent, then finally fall asleep to the sound of loons. And then a week later Aunt Magnolia might go off to Japan to photograph sharks. The images she brought back amazed Jane. It might be a photo of a shark, but what Jane saw was Aunt Magnolia and her camera, pressed in by water, silence, and cold, breathing compressed air, waiting for a visit from a creature that might as well be an alien, so strange were the inhabitants of the underwater world.

"*You're* wild, Aunt Magnolia," Jane had said. "And wonderful."

"But I don't ask you for many promises, do I?"

"No."

"So promise me this one thing. Won't you?"

"All right," Jane had said, "fine. For you, I promise I won't ever turn down an invitation to Tu Reviens. Why are you awake anyway?"

"Strange dreams," she'd said. Then, a few days later, she'd left on an expedition to Antarctica, gotten caught too far from camp during a polar blizzard, and frozen to death.

Kiran's invitation brought Aunt Magnolia near in a way that nothing else had in the four months since.

Tu Reviens. You return.

It's unsettling, to be so far from home—all her usual anxieties lifted, only to be replaced with new ones. Does Kiran's father even know Jane is coming? What if she's just a third wheel once Kiran meets up with her boyfriend? How does a person act around people who own yachts and private islands?

Standing in the lounge of *The Kiran,* the rain falling in sheets outside, Jane tells herself to breathe, slow, deep, and even, the way Aunt Magnolia taught her. "It'll help you when you learn to scuba dive," Aunt Magnolia had used to say when Jane was tiny—five, six, seven—though somehow, those scuba lessons had never materialized.

In, Jane thinks, focusing on her expanding belly. *Out,* feeling her torso flatten. Jane glances at the house, floating above them in the storm. *Aunt Magnolia never worried. She just went.*

Jane suddenly feels like a character in a novel by Edith Wharton or the Brontës. *I'm a young woman of reduced circumstances, with no family and no prospects, invited by a wealthy family to their glamorous estate. Could this be my heroic journey?*

She'll need to choose an umbrella appropriate for a heroic journey. Will Kiran think it's weird? Can she find one that isn't embarrassing? Teetering across the lounge floor, opening one of her crates, Jane lights upon the right choice instantly. The petite umbrella's satin canopy alternates deep brown with a coppery rose. The brass fittings are made of antique parts, but strong. She could impale someone on the ferrule.

Jane opens it. The runners squeak and the curve of the ribs is warped, the fabric unevenly stretched.

It's just a stupid, lopsided umbrella, Jane thinks to herself, suddenly blinking back tears. *Aunt Magnolia? Why am I here?*

Patrick sticks his head into the lounge. His bright eyes flash at Jane, then touch Kiran. "We're docked, Kir," he says, "and the car is here."

Kiran sits up, not looking at him. Then, when he returns to the deck, she watches him through the window as he lifts wooden crates onto his shoulder and carries them onto the dock. His eyes catch hers and she looks away. "Leave your stuff," she says to Jane dismissively. "Patrick will bring it up later."

"Okay," Jane says. Something is definitely up with Patrick and Kiran. "Who's your boyfriend, anyway?"

"His name is Colin. He works with my brother. You'll meet him. Why?"

"Just wondering."

"Did you make that umbrella?" asks Kiran.

"Yes."

"I thought so. It makes me think of you."

Of course it does. It's homemade and funny-looking.

Kiran and Jane step into the rain. Patrick holds a steadying hand out to Jane and she grabs his forearm by accident. He is soaked to the skin. Patrick Yellan, Jane notices, has beautiful forearms.

"Watch your step," he says in her ear.

Once on land, Kiran and Jane scurry toward an enormous black car on the dock. "Patrick's the one who asked me to come home for the gala," Kiran shouts through the rain.

"What?" says Jane, flustered. She's trying to shield Kiran with her umbrella, which sends a rivulet of icy water down the canopy straight into the neck of her own shirt. "Really? Why?"

"Who the hell knows? He told me he has a confession to make. He's always announcing shit like that, then he has nothing to say."

"Are you . . . good friends?"

"Stop trying to keep me dry," Kiran says, reaching for the car door. "It's only making both of us more wet."

There is, it turns out, a road that starts at the bay, continues clockwise around the base of the island, then enters a series of hairpin turns that climb the sheer cliffs gradually.

It's not a soothing drive in a Rolls-Royce in the rain; the car seems too big to take the turns without plummeting off the edge. The driver has the facial expression of a bulldog and she's driving like she's got a train to catch. Steel-haired and steel-eyed, pale-skinned with high cheekbones, she's wearing black yoga clothes and an apron with cooking stains. She stares at Jane in the rearview mirror. Jane shivers, tilting her head so her boisterous curls obscure her face.

"Are we short-staffed again, Mrs. Vanders?" Kiran asks. "You're wearing an apron."

"A handful of guests just arrived unannounced," says Mrs. Vanders. "The spring gala is the day after tomorrow. Cook is having hysterics."

Kiran throws her head against the back of the seat and closes her eyes. "What guests?"

"Phoebe and Philip Okada," Mrs. Vanders says. "Lucy St. George—"

"My brother makes me want to die," Kiran says, interrupting.

"Your brother himself has made no appearance," says Mrs. Vanders significantly.

"Shocking," says Kiran. "Any bank robbers expected?"

Mrs. Vanders grunts at this peculiar question and says, "I imagine not."

"Bank robbers?" says Jane.

"Well," Kiran says, ignoring Jane, "I announced my friend ahead of time. I hope you've set aside space; Janie needs space."

"We've set aside the Red Suite in the east wing for Jane. It has its own morning room," Mrs. Vanders says. "Though regrettably it has no view of the sea."

"It's nowhere near me," Kiran grumbles. "It's near Ravi."

"Well," says Mrs. Vanders with a sudden softening of expression, "we still have sleeping bags if you want to have sleepovers. You and Ravi and Patrick liked to do that when you were young and Ivy was just a baby, remember? She used to beg to be included."

"We used to toast marshmallows in Ravi's fireplace," Kiran tells

Jane, "while Mr. Vanders and Octavian hovered over us, certain we were going to burn ourselves."

"Or set the house on fire," says Mrs. Vanders.

"Ivy would make herself sick and fall asleep in a sugar coma," Kiran says wistfully. "And I would sleep between Patrick and Ravi on the hearth, like a melting s'more."

Memory comes on sharply; memory has its own will. Sitting with Aunt Magnolia in the red armchair, beside the radiator that clanked and hissed. Reading *Winnie-the-Pooh* and *The House at Pooh Corner*. "Sing Ho! for the life of a Bear!" Aunt Magnolia would say as Christopher Robin led an *expotition* to the North Pole. Sometimes, if Aunt Magnolia was tired, she and Jane would read silently, wedged together. Jane was five, six, seven, eight. If Aunt Magnolia was drying socks on the radiator, the room would smell of wool.

The car approaches the house from behind, roars around to the front, and pulls into the drive. It's not a ship anymore, this house, now that Jane sees it up close. It's a palace.

Mrs. Vanders opens a small, person-sized door set within the great, elephant-sized door. There is no welcoming committee.

Jane and Kiran enter a stone receiving hall with a high ceiling and a checkerboard floor on which Jane creates small puddles everywhere she steps. The air whooshes as Mrs. Vanders closes the door, sucking at Jane's eardrums and almost making her feel as if she's missed a whispered word. Absently, she rubs her ear.

"Welcome to Tu Reviens," says Mrs. Vanders gruffly. "Stay out of the servants' quarters. We don't have room for visitors in the kitchen, either, and the west attics are cluttered and dangerous. You should be content with your bedroom, Jane, and the common rooms of the ground floor."

"Vanny," says Kiran calmly, "stop being an ogre."

"I merely wish to prevent your friend from skewering her foot on a nail in the attic," says Mrs. Vanders, then stalks across the floor and disappears through a doorway. Jane, unsure if she's meant to follow, takes a step, but Kiran puts a hand out to stop her.

"I think she's going to the forbidden kitchen," she says, with half a smile. "I'll show you around. This is the receiving hall. Is it ostentatious enough for you?"

Matching staircases climb the walls to left and right, reaching to a second story, then a third. The impossibly tall wall before Jane almost makes her dizzy. Long balconies stretch across it at the second and third levels, archways along them puncturing the tall wall at intervals. The balconies might serve as minstrels' galleries, but they also serve as bridges connecting the east and west sides of the house. The archways glow softly with natural light, as if the wall is a face with glowing teeth. Straight ahead, on the ground level, is another archway through which greenery is visible and the soft glow of more natural light. Jane hears the sound of rain on glass. Her mind can't make sense of it, in what should be the house's center.

"It's the Venetian courtyard," Kiran says, noticing Jane's expression, leading her toward the archway. She sounds defeated. "It's the house's nicest feature."

"Oh," says Jane, trying to read Kiran's face. "Is it, like, your favorite room?"

"Whatever," Kiran says. "It makes it harder for me to hate this place."

Jane studies Kiran instead of the courtyard. Kiran's pale brown face is turned up to the glass ceiling, the pounding rain. She is not beautiful. She's the kind of plain-looking that a good deal of money can disguise as beautiful. But Jane realizes now that she likes Kiran's snub nose, her open face, her wispy black hair.

If she hates this place, Jane wonders, *why does she consent to come when Patrick calls? Or does Kiran dislike every place equally?*

Jane turns to see what Kiran sees.

Well. What an excellent space to stick in the middle of a house; every house should have one stuck in its middle. It's a glass-ceilinged atrium, stretching fully up the building's three stories, with walls of pale pink stone and, in the center, a forest of slender white trees; tiny terraced flower gardens; and a small waterfall shooting from the mouth of a fish. At the second and third levels, long cascades of golden-orange nasturtiums hang from balconies.

"Come on," Kiran says. "I'll show you to your room."

"You don't have to," says Jane. "You can just tell me where to go."

"It'll give me an excuse not to go looking for Octavian yet," Kiran says. Laughter erupts from a room not too distant. She winces. "Or the guests, or Colin," she adds, grabbing Jane's wrist and pulling her back into the receiving hall.

It's strange to be touched by someone as prickly as Kiran. Jane can't tell if it's comforting or if she feels a bit trapped. "What's Colin like?"

"He's an art dealer," Kiran says, not directly answering Jane's question. "He works for his uncle who owns a gallery. Colin has a master's in art history. He taught one of Ravi's classes when Ravi was an undergrad; that's how they met. But even if he'd studied, like, astrophysics, he'd probably have ended up working for his uncle Buckley. Everyone in that family does. Still, at least he's using *his* degree."

Kiran has a degree in religion and languages she's apparently not using. Once, Jane remembers, Kiran wrote a paper on religious groups working with governments to encourage environmental conservation that fascinated Aunt Magnolia. She and Kiran had talked and talked. Aunt Magnolia had turned out to know a lot more about politics than Jane had realized.

Kiran backtracks through the receiving hall and takes the east staircase on their left. The walls going up are covered with a bizarre collection of paintings from all different periods, all different styles. On every landing is a complete suit of armor.

Dominating the second-story landing is a particularly tall realistic painting done in thick oils, depicting a room with a checkerboard floor and an umbrella propped open as if left to dry. Jane feels she could almost step into the scene.

A basset hound, coming down the steps toward them, stops and stares at Jane. Then he begins to hop and pant with increasing interest. When Jane passes him, he turns himself around and follows eagerly, but his long radius makes for slow turning, and basset hounds aren't designed for steps. He treads on his own ear and yelps. He's soon left behind. He barks.

"Ignore Jasper," Kiran says. "That dog has a personality disorder."

"What's wrong with him?" asks Jane.

"He grew up in this house," Kiran says.

Jane has never had a suite of rooms to herself.

Kiran's phone rings as they step through the door. She glances at it, then scowls. "Fucking Patrick. Bet you anything he has nothing to say. I'll leave you to explore," she says, wandering back out into the corridor.

Jane is free now to examine her rooms without needing to hide her amazement. Her gold-tiled bathroom, complete with hot tub, is as big as her bedroom used to be, and the bedroom is a vast expanse, the king-sized bed a mountain she supposes she'll scale later, to sleep in the clouds. The walls are an unusually pale shade of red, like one of the brief, early colors of the sky at sunrise. Fat leather armchairs sit around a giant fireplace. Jane opens her umbrella and sets it to dry on the cold hearth, noticing logs stacked beside the fireplace and wondering how one goes about lighting a fire.

The morning room, through an adjoining door, has eastern walls made of glass, presumably to catch the morning sun. The glass brings her very near the storm, which is nice. A storm can be a cozy thing when one isn't in it.

Outside, formal gardens stretch to meet a long lawn, then a forest beyond, disappearing into fog, as if maybe this house and this small patch of land have floated out of normal existence, with Jane as their passenger. Well, Jane and the mud-soaked child digging holes with a trowel in the garden below, short hair dripping with rain. She's maybe seven, or eight. She raises her face to glance up at the house.

Is there something familiar about the look of that kid? Does Jane recognize her?

The little girl shifts her position and the sensation fades.

After surveying her morning room (rolltop desk, striped sofa, floral armchair, yellow shag rug, and a random assortment of paintings), she returns to her bedroom, wrapping herself in a soft dark blanket from the foot of the bed.

A small scratching noise brings her to the hallway door, which she opens a crack. "You made it," she says as the dog barrels in. "I admire your persevering spirit."

Jasper is a classic basset hound in brown, black, and white; his nose is long, his ears are longer, his legs are short, his eyes sag, his mouth droops, his ears flop. He is a creature beset by gravity. When Jane kneels and offers a hand, he sniffs it. Licks it, shyly. Then he leans his weight against her damp corduroys. "You," Jane says, scratching his head in a place she suspects he can't reach, "are perfect."

"Oh," says a voice at the door, sounding surprised. "Are you Janie?"

Jane looks up into the face of a tall girl who must be Patrick Yellan's little sister, for she's got his looks, his coloring, his brilliant blue eyes. Her long, dark hair is pulled back in a messy knot.

"Yes," says Jane. "Ivy?"

"Yeah," says the girl. "But, how old are you?"

"Eighteen," says Jane. "You?"

"Nineteen," she says. "Kiran told me she was bringing a friend but she didn't tell me you were my age." She leans against the door frame, wearing skintight gray jeans and a red hoodie so comfortably that she might have slept in them. She reaches into her hoodie pocket, pulls out a pair of dark-rimmed glasses, and sticks them on her face.

In her gold zigzag shirt and wine-colored cords covered with dog hair, Jane feels awkward suddenly, like some sort of evolutionary anomaly. A blue-footed booby, next to a graceful heron.

"I love your outfit," Ivy says.

Jane is astonished. "Are you a mind reader?"

"No," says Ivy, with a quick, wicked grin. "Why?"

"You just read my mind."

"That sounds disconcerting," says Ivy. "Hmmm, how about zeppelins?"

"What?"

"Were you thinking about zeppelins?"

"No."

"Then that should make you more comfortable."

"What?" says Jane again, so confused that she's laughing a little.

"Unless you *were* just thinking about zeppelins."

"It's possible I've never thought about zeppelins," says Jane.

"It's an acceptable Scrabble word," says Ivy, "even though it's often a proper name, which isn't allowed."

"Zeppelins?"

"Yeah," she says. "Well, *zeppelin,* singular, anyway. I put it down once on two triple-word scores. Kiran challenged me, because zeppelins are named after a person, Count Ferdinand von Zeppelin or somebody, but it's in the Scrabble dictionary anyway. It earned me two hundred fifty-seven points. Oh god. I'm sorry. Listen to me."

"Don't—"

"No, really," she says. "I swear I'm not usually afflicted with verbal diarrhea. I also don't usually brag about my Scrabble scores two minutes after meeting someone."

"It's okay," says Jane, because people who talk so easily make her comfortable, they're less work, she knows where she stands. "I don't play much Scrabble, so I don't know what it means to earn two hundred fifty-seven points. That could be average, for all I know."

"It's an amazing fucking score for one word," Ivy says, then closes her eyes. "Seriously. What is wrong with me."

"I like it," says Jane. "I want to hear more of your Scrabble words."

Ivy shoots her a grateful grin. "I did actually have a reason for coming by," she says. "I'm the one who got your room ready. I wanted to check if everything's okay."

"More than okay," says Jane. "I mean, there's a fireplace and hot tub."

"Not what you're used to?"

"My last bedroom was about the size of that bed," Jane says, pointing to it.

"The 'cupboard under the stairs'?"

"I guess not that bad," says Jane, smiling at the Harry Potter reference.

"I'm glad," says Ivy. "You're sure you don't need anything?"

"I don't want you to feel like you have to take care of me."

"Hey, it's my job," says Ivy. "Tell me what you need."

"Well," says Jane. "There are a couple things I could use, but I don't really *need* them, and they're not normal things I would ask you for."

"Such as?"

"A rotary saw," says Jane. "A lathe."

"Uh-huh," says Ivy, grinning again. "Come with me."

"You're going to bring me to a rotary saw and a lathe?" says Jane, tossing the blanket back onto the bed.

"This house has one of everything."

"Do you know where everything is?"

Ivy considers this thoughtfully as the dog follows them out into the corridor. "I probably know where *almost* everything is. I'm sure the house is keeping some secrets from me."

Jane is tall, but Ivy is taller, with legs that go on forever. Their strides are well-matched. The dog clings close to her feet. "Is it true Jasper has a personality disorder?" she asks. "Kiran said so."

"He can be quirky," Ivy says. "He won't do his business if you're watching him—he glares at you as if you're being unforgivably rude. And there's a painting in the blue sitting room he's obsessed with."

"What do you mean?"

"He sits there gazing at it, blowing big sighs through his nose."

"Is it a painting of a dog or something?"

"No, it's a boring old city by the water, except for the fact that it's got two moons. And sometimes he disappears for *days* and we can't find him. Cook calls him our earthbound misfit. He's our house mystery too—he appeared one day after one of the galas, a puppy, as if a guest had brought him and left him behind. But no one ever claimed him. So we kept him. Is he bothering you?"

"Nah," says Jane. "This house," she adds as Ivy walks her down the hallway toward the atrium at the house's center. A polar bear rug, complete with head and glassy eyes, sits in the middle of the passageway. It looks like real fur. Wrinkling her nose, Jane makes a path around it, then rubs her ears again, trying to dislodge a noise. The house is humming, or singing, a faint, high-pitched whine of air streaming through pipes somewhere, though really, Jane's not totally conscious of it. There's a way in which background noises can enter one's unconscious self, settle in—even make changes—without tripping any of one's conscious alarms.

Ivy slows as she nears the center of the house. They are on the highest level, the third, and Ivy takes the branch of the hallway that goes to the left. Jane follows, finding herself on one of the bridgelike balconies she saw from the receiving hall. The bridge overlooks the receiving hall on one side and the courtyard on the other.

Ivy stops at one of the archways overlooking the courtyard. Someone's left a camera here, perched on the wide balustrade, a fancy one with a big lens. Picking it up, Ivy hangs it around her neck. When Jane steps beside her, breathing through the heady feeling of vertigo, Jasper does too, shoving his head between two balusters.

"Jasper," Jane says in alarm, reaching for his collar, then realizing he's not wearing one. "Jasper! Be careful!"

Jasper demonstrates that he cannot possibly fall, by straining with all his strength to push himself through the balusters, failing, then looking up at Jane with an "I told you so" expression. It's not a comforting demonstration.

"Don't worry," Ivy says. "He won't fall. He's too big."

"Yeah," Jane says, "I see that, but I still wish he'd stay back. Respect the heights, you long-eared bozo!"

At this, Ivy lets out a single, small laugh. "Quixotic," she says.

"What?"

She shakes her head at herself. "Sorry. It just occurred to me that if I'd been able to play the word *quixotic* in that spot instead of the word *zeppelin,* I'd have scored even more points. Because of the combined power of the *x* and the *q*. They're valuable letters," she adds apologetically, "because they're rare. You make me want to talk. It's like a compulsion. I could go get a muzzle."

"I told you, I like it," says Jane, then notices, suddenly, the words on Ivy's camera strap: *I am the Bad Wolf. I create myself.*

It's a reference to the TV show *Doctor Who.* "Are you a sci-fi fan?"

"Yeah, I guess so," says Ivy. "I like sci-fi and fantasy generally."

"Who's your favorite Doctor?"

"Eh, I like the companions better," says Ivy. "The Doctor's all tragic and broody and last of his kind, and I get the appeal of that, but I like Donna Noble and Rose Tyler. And Amy and Rory, and Clara Oswald, and Martha Jones. No one ever likes Martha Jones but I like Martha Jones. She's an asskicker."

Jane nods. "I get that."

"Were you going to say something about the house?" says Ivy. "Before?"

"The decorative stuff," Jane says. "The art. Isn't it kind of . . . random?"

Ivy leans an elbow on the balustrade. "Yeah, it's definitely random," she says. "*Officially* random, really. A hundred-some years ago, when the very first Octavian Thrash was building this house, he, um, how should I put it, he . . . *acquired* parts of other houses, from all over the world."

"Acquired?" says Jane. "What do you mean? Like, the way Russia acquired Crimea?"

Ivy flashes a grin. "Yeah, basically. Some of the houses were being remodeled, or torn down. Octavian bought parts. But in other cases, it's hard to say how he got his hands on them."

"Are you saying he stole?"

"Yes," Ivy says. "Or bought stuff that was stolen. That's why the pillars don't match, or the tiles, or anything really. He collected the art the same way, and the furniture. Apparently ships would arrive full of random crap, maybe a door from Turkey, a banister from China. A stained-glass window from Italy, a column from Egypt, a pile of floorboards from some manor kitchen in Scotland. Even the skeleton is made of the miscellaneous crap he collected."

"So . . . the house is like Frankenstein's monster?"

"Yup," she says, "speaking of sci-fi. Or like some kind of cannibal."

"Will it eat us?"

Her smile again. "It hasn't eaten anyone yet."

"Then I'll stay."

"Good," she says.

"Some of the art seems newer."

"Mrs. Vanders and Ravi do the buying these days. Octavian gives them permission to spend his money."

"What things do they buy?"

"Valuable stuff. Tasteful stuff. Nothing stolen. Ravi works as an art dealer in New York now, actually, with Kiran's boyfriend, Colin. It's like his dream job. I think he cries with happiness every morning on his way to work. Ravi is bananas about art," she adds, noticing Jane's puzzled expression. "He's been known to sleep under the Vermeer. Like, in the corridor, in a sleeping bag."

Jane is trying to imagine a grown man sleeping on a floor beneath a painting. "I'll try to remember that, in case I'm ever walking around in the dark."

"Ha!" says Ivy. "I meant when he was a little kid. He doesn't do it now. We used to play with some of the art too, like, pretend-play around it. The sculptures, the Brancusi fish. The suits of armor."

While Jane tries to file all this information away, rainwater pounds on the glass ceiling of the courtyard. "What about the courtyard?" she says, taking in the pink stone, the measured terraces, the hanging nasturtiums. "It isn't unmatching. It feels balanced."

"Mm-hm," says Ivy with a small, crooked smile. "The first Octavian rescued the entire thing from a Venetian palace that was being torn down, and brought it over on a boat in one piece."

There's something preposterous about a ship carrying three stories of empty space around the Italian peninsula, through the Mediterranean, and across the Atlantic.

"This house kind of gives me the creeps," Jane says.

"We're about to go into the servants' quarters," Ivy says. "It's nice and simple in there, with no dead polar bears."

"Does that bother you too?"

Ivy gives a rueful shrug. "To me, he's just Captain Polepants."

"Huh?"

"That's what Kiran and Patrick called him when we were little. They thought it was hilarious, because Kiran's half British, and in the U.K., *pants* means underpants. Mr. Vanders had a name for him too," Ivy says, screwing her face up thoughtfully. "Bipolar Bear, I think it was. Because he likes psychology. Funny, right?"

"I guess," Jane says. "My aunt was a conservationist. She took pictures of polar bears instead of making rugs out of them."

"Speak of the devil," Ivy says, looking down to the courtyard below. An elderly man darts across the floor. He's a tall, dark-skinned black man in black clothing, with a ring of white hair. He carries a small child on one hip, maybe two or three years old. All Jane can see of the child from above is wavy dark hair, tanned skin, flopping arms and legs. "Why?" the toddler yells, squirming. "Why? Why!"

"Kiran never mentioned there'd be so many kids here," Jane says, remembering the little girl digging in the rain outside her window.

Ivy pauses. "That was Mr. Vanders," she says. "He's the butler, and Mrs. Vanders is the housekeeper. They manage a pretty big staff. He's always in a hurry."

"Okay," Jane says, noticing that Ivy's said nothing about the child, and that her face has gone measured, her voice carefully nonchalant. It's weird. "You said we're going into the servants' quarters?" she adds. "Mrs. Vanders actually told me I'm not allowed there."

"Mrs. Vanders can bite me," says Ivy with sudden sharpness.

"What?"

"Sorry." Ivy looks sheepish. "But she's not in charge of the house. She just acts like she is. You do whatever you want."

"Okay." Jane wants to see the house, every part of it. She also wants to not get yelled at.

"Come on," Ivy says, pushing away. "If we see her, you can just pretend you don't know which part of the house we're in. You can blame me."

She's backing away across the bridge while facing Jane, willing Jane to follow her. Then she shoots Jane her wicked grin again, and Jane can't say no.

"Every time I step into a new section, I feel like I'm in a different house."

Jane spins on her heels, examining the unexpectedly serene, unadorned, pale green walls of the forbidden servants' quarters, in the west wing of the third story. All the doors are set into small, side hallways that branch off the main corridor.

"Wait till you see the bowling alley downstairs," Ivy says, "and the indoor swimming pool."

Jane realizes she's been breathing the faint, rather pleasant scent of chlorine ever since Ivy joined her. "Are you a swimmer?"

"Yeah, when I have time. You can use the pool whenever you want. Tell me if you want me to show you the changing rooms and stuff. That's my room," she adds, pointing down a short hallway to a closed door. "Hang on, let me put my camera down."

"What are you taking pictures of?"

"The art," she says. "Be right back." She leaves Jane in the main corridor, where Jasper leans against her legs, sighing. Jane's clothing has dried, mostly; at any rate, she no longer feels like a soggy, cold stray. She's exposed out here, though; she imagines Mrs. Vanders peering at her disapprovingly around corners, and she also wishes she could see Ivy's room. Do the servants have hot tubs and fireplaces too? Is Ivy always on the clock? Does she get to travel to New York like Kiran does? If she's nineteen, will she go to college? How did she go to high school? For that matter, how did Kiran go to high school?

Ivy emerges.

"Do you have a hot tub in there?"

"I wish," says Ivy, grinning. "Want to see?"

"Sure."

Jane and Jasper follow Ivy into a long room with two distinct realms: the bed realm, near the door, and the computer realm, which takes up most of the rest of the space. Jane never knew one person could need so many computers. A jumble of ropes is propped beside one of her keyboards, along with two of the longest flashlights Jane's ever seen. Large, precise drawings—blueprints, sort of—cover the walls. Jane realizes, looking closer, that they're interior maps of a house that are so detailed that they show wallpaper, furniture, carpets, art.

"Did you make these?" asks Jane.

"I guess," says Ivy. "They're the house."

"Wow." Jane sees familiar things now: the Venetian courtyard, the checkered floor of the receiving hall, the polar bear rug.

Ivy seems embarrassed. "Patrick and I share a bathroom in the hall," she says. "Mr. and Mrs. Vanders have their own suite, though, and it has a hot tub."

"You could use my hot tub."

"Thanks," says Ivy, pulling the tie out of her messy bun, shaking her hair out, and winding it back up again. The air is touched with the scent of chlorine, and jasmine.

"Marzipan," Ivy says randomly, giving her hair a final tug.

Jane is used to this by now. "Yeah?"

"Another great word to play in that same spot, because of the position of the *z*."

"Are you always thinking up good eight-letter Scrabble words?"

"Nope. Only since you came along."

"Maybe I'll be good for your Scrabble game."

"It's looking that way. Brains are bizarre," says Ivy, going back into the corridor and leading Jane and Jasper past more hallways and doors.

"If you grew up here," says Jane, "how did you go to school?"

"We were all homeschooled," says Ivy, "by Octavian, and Mr. Vanders, and the first Mrs. Thrash."

"Was it strange? To be homeschooled, on an isolated island?"

"Probably," says Ivy with a grin, "but it seemed normal when I was a kid."

"Will you go to college?"

"I've been thinking about it lately," Ivy says, "a lot. I've been saving up, and I took the SATs last time I was in the city. But I haven't started applying."

"What will you study?"

"No clue," she says. "Is that bad? Should I have my whole life plotted out?"

"You're asking a college dropout," says Jane, then isn't sure what affect to adopt when Ivy looks at her curiously. *I'm okay? I'm not okay? I feel stupid? Back off, my aunt died?*

"I didn't mean to put you on the spot," says Ivy. "There's nothing wrong with being a college dropout."

"It doesn't feel very good, though," says Jane.

"That doesn't mean it's wrong," says Ivy thoughtfully.

That sounds like something Aunt Magnolia would say, though she'd say it in ringing tones of wisdom, whereas Ivy says it as if it's a new possibility she's considering for the first time. They've come to a door at the end of the corridor, made of unfinished planks, with a heavy iron latch instead of a knob. Ivy pulls it open to reveal a landing with elevator doors straight ahead and stairs leading up and down. She flicks a switch on the landing and the room above brightens. "West attics," she says before Jane can ask. "The workshop is up there."

"Mrs. Vanders said I wasn't allowed in the west attics, either," says Jane. "She said it's dangerous."

Ivy snorts, then starts up the steps. "Come see for yourself. If it looks dangerous, we won't go in."

"Okay," says Jane, pretending to be the rule-breaker she isn't, because she doesn't want to lose Ivy's respect. "Wow," she adds as her climb brings an enormous room into view. It's filled with neat rows of worktables, almost like a shop class. With tall windows and high, wooden rafters, it's as big as the entire west wing, rich with the smells of oil and sawdust. Rain drums against the roof. Through the windows Jane can just barely make out the spire on the house's east side, puncturing the storm clouds.

It's a tidy, open, barn-like space, with no loose nails or shaky beams. Jane wanders, Ivy following. An unfinished chest draws her attention. It's walnut—Jane knows her woods. It has a carved top depicting an undersea scene of sperm whales (Jane also knows her whales). Above the whales, a girl floats in a rowboat, oblivious to the creatures below.

"Who made this?" Jane asks.

"Oh," says Ivy, looking embarrassed but pleased. "That's mine."

"Really? You make furniture too? It's beautiful!"

"Thanks. I haven't touched it in forever. I don't get time for the big projects. Though my brother and I did finish a boat recently."

"You and Patrick made a boat up here?"

"Yeah. A rowboat. We had to lower it to the ground on ropes through a window. There's a freight elevator to the outside, and a dumbwaiter," Ivy says, waving a hand back toward the stairs, "but it was a boat, after all."

A DIY rowboat. Jane tries to make her umbrellas watertight, but it's not like anyone's going to drown if she screws something up. "Do you take the boat out?"

"Sure," says Ivy. "It's a great little boat."

Who builds a boat, in her spare time, with her own hands, then slaps it onto the ocean and rows around in it successfully? Probably while announcing winning Scrabble words and being bold and daring.

"There's a rotary saw in the back somewhere," Ivy says, "and we have a few different lathes."

"Thanks," says Jane, feeling a bit desolate.

"You should help yourself to whatever you need."

"Thanks," Jane says again, hoping Ivy won't ask her what she needs them for.

The house moans and grumbles, almost as if in sympathy with Jane's feelings. *As old houses do,* Jane thinks to herself. She imagines this house curled up with its back to the sky, shivering around the center it must keep warm, holding its skin against the driving rain.

A tiny, self-contained glass room sits near the stairs. There's a table inside, on which is propped a large painting of a white man with sloping shoulders, wearing a beret with a great, curling feather. Brushes, bottles, and light fixtures surround the painting.

"Is someone a painter?" Jane asks, pointing.

"Rembrandt's a painter," Ivy says, grinning. "That's a Rembrandt self-portrait. It's one of the house's pictures. Mrs. Vanders is cleaning it. She has a degree in conservation, among other things. Maybe you can smell the acetone—sort of a sharp smell? She uses it sometimes."

"Oh," Jane says, feeling silly for not recognizing a Rembrandt. "Right."

"That room is her conservation studio," Ivy says. "It's sealed, so the art is protected from sawdust, and the glass is a fancy kind that shields it from outside light."

"Wow."

"Yeah," says Ivy, understanding. "This is a house of serious art lovers. And Octavian has more money than God."

A door at the back end of the attic opens with a scraping sound, startling Jane. Spinning around, she sees a flash of yellow wallpaper in a bright room beyond. A man with a pert mouth steps from the room, notices Jane, and clicks the door shut quickly. He has dark hair and East Asian features and wears a navy blue suit and orange Chuck Taylors.

Pulling latex gloves from his hands and shoving them into his pockets, he walks across the room toward them both. "Hello," he says.

"Hi," says Ivy, her voice carefully nonchalant again. "This is Philip Okada," she tells Jane. "He's visiting for the gala. Philip, this is Kiran's friend Janie."

"Nice to meet you," says Philip, speaking with what sounds like an English accent.

"You too," says Jane, glancing at the gloves dangling from his coat pocket.

"Forgive me," he says. "I'm something of a germophobe and I often wear them. How do you know Kiran?"

"She went to college in my hometown."

"Ah." He smiles a polite smile, his face creasing into lines that make Jane think he must be at least thirty. Thirty-five? Even older? When do old people get laugh lines?

"How do you know the Thrash family?" asks Jane, deciding to be nosy.

"The New York party scene," says Philip, his expression pleasantly bland.

"I see," says Jane, wondering what that means, exactly, and how a germophobe manages a crowded party "scene." Is there more here than meets the eye?

"Well," he says, "see you later, no doubt." He bends down to give Jasper a vigorous rub behind the ears. Then he descends the stairs, sliding his hand along the metal railing.

"You'd think a germophobe would avoid dogs and railings," says Jane.

Ivy's face is expressionless. "Take whatever you need," she says, turning away. "Our attic is your attic."

Definitely more here than meets the eye.

In the end, Jane borrows a rotary saw, a small lathe, a tarp, some beautiful birch rods, a can of stain, a can of varnish, and a worktable that's a good height for her sewing machine. The workshop contains a thousand other things she could use, but she's already embarrassed enough by her riches, especially when she needs to take two trips to get them downstairs.

While Jane is balancing her first armload, Ivy's phone makes a noise like one of the horns in *Lord of the Rings*. "Sorry," she says, glancing at it. "That's Cook. You'll be okay? Leave the worktable. Someone'll bring it to you later."

"Okay," Jane says, "thanks," wondering when she'll see Ivy again, but too shy to ask.

Jasper follows Jane back and forth from the attics to her rooms, stumping along cheerfully behind her, waiting patiently at the base of the attic steps each time. "I like you, Jasper," says Jane.

Her suitcase and crates arrived while she was gone. Dinner is hours away and the storm is still raging on the other side of the glass. At her morning room windows, Jasper beside her, Jane gazes out at the drenched world. She supposes it's an appropriate day, an appropriate setting, to consider the making of umbrellas.

It wasn't the colors that had first drawn Jane to umbrellas, it wasn't the mechanics.

It was Aunt Magnolia.

On rainy days, when Jane was a child and Aunt Magnolia was away on a deep-sea photography trip, Jane would build an umbrella fort on the campus green and hide inside. The sound of rain thudding against a taut piece of fabric stretched above her was like being underwater. Jane could crawl into her umbrella fort and imagine herself where Aunt Magnolia was.

The elderly neighbors, who cared for Jane when Aunt Magnolia was gone, were warm and attentive and kind, but they were old, and Jane was generally left to play alone. Aunt Magnolia had given her an old scuba helmet to wear inside her umbrella fort, so that her own breathing sounded strange. Sometimes, depending on the weather, a chorus of tiny frogs joined the other noises. Jane would lie on her back in the wet grass, breathing through the nozzle, listening, pretending the umbrellas were giant jellyfish.

And once when she was in high school, when Aunt Magnolia had been taking pictures in the oceans of New Zealand for what felt like an eon and Jane had been staying in the apartment alone, she'd found herself in art class building an umbrella sculpture. Her art teacher had opened a closet full of miscellaneous junk and told everyone to go scrounging and make something. The closet had contained birch rods, various wires and metal fixings, and a huge piece of dark fabric spread across with fireflies. It had been raining that day, water coursing down the art room windows. It wasn't really what the art teacher had meant by "art," but it had somehow found Jane, this lopsided, water-absorbent thing with an open canopy like a real umbrella. It had been a mess, really. Made of lucky discoveries and countless mistakes. But tears stung her eyes when she looked at it.

Who can say how we choose our loves? After that first attempt, she'd rifled through the coat closet, snatched up the two bedraggled umbrellas she'd found, then applied herself to taking them apart.

Their tension came from branches that reached away from a central trunk and from each other—as far from each other, in fact, as they could get. The reaching away was what held the domed canopy taut and stretched in place. Why had Jane loved this, that the reaching away held it together? Who knows. But she had, and she'd taken apart every umbrella she could find, and experimented with waterproofing, and built rickety frames Aunt Magnolia would stumble over, or find piled in corners. She became particular about small variations in color and shape. She worked on them a little bit every day back then, almost compulsively.

"There is nothing wrong with impractical loves," Aunt Magnolia had responded whenever Jane had apologized for spending so much time on them.

And then college had started up and she'd had no time for anything, except schoolwork that had felt like a hill of sliding rock.

"Janie-love," Aunt Magnolia would say sometimes. "When did you last work on an umbrella?"

Jane's grades had been passing when Aunt Magnolia had been around to help, but her aunt had had a lot of travel that fall and Jane found herself failing biology. And then Aunt Magnolia had died. Jane had dropped out of school. And umbrellas were all she could face, almost as if one perfect umbrella might make Aunt Magnolia come back.

Jane sits on the striped sofa in her morning room, holding her stomach. Jasper comes and leans against her legs.

Christopher Robin and Winnie-the-Pooh set out to sea once in an umbrella, Jane remembers. *During a flood, to save Piglet.*

Maybe, she thinks to herself, she should take her umbrellas down to the water, turn them upside down like boats, and send them off on the waves, carrying nothing. Maybe if they carried away all the nothing, she'd be left with something.

"Ocean pollution, hm?" Aunt Magnolia would say to that. "That's your big solution, is it?" Or, "All right, allow yourself a good wallow, then get up from that sofa, stop feeling sorry for yourself, and do something useful."

All right, fine, Aunt Magnolia, Jane thinks. *For you, I'm getting up.*

With a great breath, she pushes herself to her feet and surveys the morning room.

She lays the tarp down to protect the middle of the shag carpet, where she plans to do the most heavy-duty work, then begins pulling umbrellas out of her crates and opening them. There isn't room for them all, so she stacks some unopened on the floor and leans some in corners while Jasper watches appreciatively. She's brought every one. She has no other place to store them; Jane brought everything she owns to this house. She has thirty-seven completed umbrellas. Some of them aren't even so bad. They transform the room into an odd landscape of colorful, spiky hills.

Opening the rolltop desk, she finds it has small docketed drawers. "Letters Unanswered," "Letters to Keep," "Postage," "Photographs," "Addresses" and so on. She removes the tickets one by one, turns them over, and creates her own labels: "Glues," "Nickel Silver Wire," "Tying Wire," "Pins," "Ferrules," "Brass Runners," "Wire Cutters," "Hinges," "Tips." It's satisfying to drop each item into its proper drawer. Jane piles an assortment of steel ribs and canopy fabric atop the desk chair and the side tables nearby. She leaves her sewing machine on the floor for the time being, then washes her hands in the gigantic gold-tiled bathroom.

The last things Jane removes from her crates are five large framed photographs, four of them taken by Aunt Magnolia and one by a colleague. A rose-colored anglerfish in Indonesia with skin filaments that make it look like it's carrying a forest on its back. The big, dark eyes of a Humboldt squid in Peru. An underwater photo of falling frogs in Belize, their arms and legs grasping at the water for purchase, their eyes panicked. A Canadian polar bear, happily suspended underwater, resting, untroubled by the cold.

These photos had required great patience and serendipity. Aunt Magnolia had never done anything that would scare the animals; she hadn't pursued them or tried to manipulate them. Mostly, she'd waited. She'd been a spy of the underwater world, where things are silent and slow.

She'd loved the freezing, polar underwater landscapes best. The strangeness, the harshness, the sense of isolation. She'd written under the polar bear photo in scratchy pencil, "Sing Ho! for the life of a Bear!"

Finally, there was a photograph of Aunt Magnolia herself, standing, in scuba gear, on a New Zealand seafloor, touching the nose of an enormous southern right whale who peered at her with quiet dignity. Aunt Magnolia had been so encouraged by her visit to New Zealand, where the sea life is fiercely protected by law. "It gives me hope for the world," she'd said. She'd been that way. Hopeful. Aunt Magnolia had believed there was a point.

Jane takes a few paintings off the walls to make room for Aunt Magnolia. Once she's hung the final photograph, she hears the radiator clang in a lonely, "pay attention to me" way. It's a sad sound, but cozy too. Jane is content with what she's made of this room. *Maybe,* she thinks, *good things will come of this odd adventure after all.*

She has one work in progress. It's almost done, only needs the appropriate ferrule to crown it and a tie and button to hold it closed. It's an alternating blue and violet pagoda umbrella with a red shaft and handle. The pagoda-shaped canopy had presented a satisfying challenge, but the result feels fussy and over-the-top.

"Honestly, I kind of hate it," she tells Jasper, opening it for him. "And the colors don't suit you," she says as he walks under the canopy. "The red in your brown clashes with its reds. Oh dear. Dreadful."

Jasper seems depressed.

"It's not you, Jasper," says Jane. "There are reds that suit you dazzlingly. Here." She wades through umbrellas to fetch the brown-rose-copper satin that's still drying from its earlier use. "Sit under this one. Beautiful," she says with a rush of pleasure as she appraises the effect.

"I could have made that one just for you." She reaches for her phone. "Should I take a picture?"

Jane's afternoon is contentedly spent photographing Jasper under every umbrella that suits him, finishing up the pagoda piece, and allowing ideas for the next umbrella to bump against her thoughts.

Jane is lying on her back on the rug in the morning room, thinking about umbrella-shaped things for inspiration, when Ivy comes to collect her for dinner. Mushrooms, lampshades, jellyfish. Bells? Mixing bowls. Tulips. The tapping on her outer door finally reaches her consciousness. "Come in!" she yells.

Ivy enters the morning room, a warm, tall rush of red that pushes itself into Jane's umbrella thoughts. What would an Ivy umbrella look like?

Ivy stops in astonishment, surveying the room. "Holy crap," she says. "Why do you have so many umbrellas?"

"I make them," Jane says from the floor. "Don't ask me why."

"Maybe because they're awesome?" she says, stepping into the umbrella landscape, moving among them, looking closer.

Jane sits up, straightens her shirt, and peers around the room, trying to imagine it through Ivy's eyes.

Ivy crouches down and reaches a finger to touch Jane's bird's egg umbrella, which is oblong and pale blue, with irregular brown spots. The oblong shaping of it had been a nightmarish task, because the ribs had needed to differ in length and shape while it was open, but lie flat and neat while closed. There'd been a moment when Jane had wanted to break the whole damn thing over her knee. She's glad she didn't. This is one of her better umbrellas.

Ivy is running a finger along the open edge of the canopy, with a touch so gentle and tentative that Jane can feel it, like a hum under her skin.

"Can you tell what it is?" Jane asks.

"Of course," says Ivy. "It's a bird's egg."

Jane's happiness is complete.

"It's dinnertime for the family and guests," Ivy adds. "That means you."

"Aye aye, Captain Polepants," Ivy says as she leads Jane down the corridor, past the polar bear.

"Is he military, then?"

"I don't really remember," says Ivy, "but I think we pretended he was a polar explorer who would bring his discoveries back to the queen."

"Who was the queen?"

"Not me," says Ivy.

She leads Jane down the stairs to the receiving hall, then into the single most enormous room Jane has ever seen inside a private house. "What is this?" Jane asks, trying not to squeak. "The throne room?"

Ivy makes a little *heh* sound and says, "The ballroom. But now you've got me trying to decide which room Octavian would choose as his throne room. Probably the library."

Jane is barely listening. Deep and high-ceilinged, the ballroom shines with burnished dark mahogany wood. "The Thrashes have *balls?*"

"The galas are basically balls," Ivy says. "People dressing up and dancing waltzes in fancy rooms, et cetera." Then she leads Jane through a doorway into another long room, bright with chandeliers and containing a table that could seat thirty. Four people, two men and two women, are assembled at the far end, their voices sharp, cutting across one another. Kiran isn't there.

As Ivy leads Jane toward them, Jane asks, "Will you eat with us?"

"No," says Ivy. "I eat in the kitchen." But she seems to interpret something in Jane's expression, something Jane herself probably couldn't articulate, for she takes Jane's arm above the elbow and squeezes it, then touches one of the empty chairs so Jane will know the right place to sit. Then, flashing her another small, wicked grin, she pushes through a swinging door beyond the table.

Jane sits down. No one seems to notice her. She tries to blend in and absorb the rapid-fire conversation, which appears to be an argument about a family they all know personally.

"You don't seriously think they did something bad to their own kids?" says an English-sounding black woman who has a heart-shaped face and short, curly dark hair. A shimmering star sits in each of her earlobes, maybe made of tiny, sparkling diamonds? She's next to Philip Okada, the germophobe from the attic. She's wearing a lot of foundation and eye shadow.

"No, I'm only saying they've clearly flipped out," says the other woman, white, rosy-cheeked, with honey-brown hair and two rows of pearls at her throat. She's got an American accent and a deep voice. "People do unpredictable, bad things when they flip out, so how can we know what they've done, really?"

"Is that a medical term?" Philip Okada asks her, teasing. "To 'flip out'?"

"Philip," says the pearl-necklace lady forcefully. "The Panzavecchias are our friends. They left their lab one day and *held up a bank*. Why would they choose to do that?"

"Well," says the star-earring lady beside Philip, "you've heard the rumors about Giuseppe's gambling problem and the Mafia."

"Okay, but have any of you ever known Giuseppe Panzavecchia to so much as bet on a dog race?" says pearl necklace.

"But people hide habits when they become problems," says star earrings. "We might not know what Giuseppe's really like."

"But we *do* know what he's like," says pearl necklace. "Don't we? All Giuseppe ever does is brag about his kids. I mean, have you heard him talk about Grace and her amazing mnemonic memory devices? Grace is a little eight-year-old computer. Giuseppe could just die of pride. Maybe I'll believe he's got a touch of a gambling problem somewhere that he's hiding from everyone. But to choose to get mixed up with the Sicilian Mafia when his life revolves around those three little kids? Why should we believe that? Just because he has an Italian name? It's offensive."

"Do you have another theory, then?" asks star earrings.

"No," says pearl necklace. "I only reject that the Panzavecchias chose an affiliation with organized crime. Either something else we haven't thought of is going on, or they both inhaled some toxic gas in that lab of theirs and flipped out."

Mrs. Vanders pushes through the swinging door, making Jane jump. Laden with serving plates and bowls and followed by Ivy, she glares at Jane in a way that makes Jane feel guilty, instantly, before she's even had time to consider what she might be guilty of. As she delivers to the table what looks like a giant pot roast, roasted vegetables, and an enormous pear salad, then exits abruptly through the swinging door, Jane struggles to assimilate all that's happening—for she knows the name Panzavecchia. Not personally, like these people, but from the news.

It's been headline news for a few days, in fact, maybe a week. Victoria and Giuseppe Panzavecchia, married microbiologists from two wealthy New York families, left their university lab in Manhattan at lunch one day; made a bank robbery attempt that failed when a particularly courageous bank teller challenged them to produce weapons they didn't have; ran from the bank; rounded the corner; and promptly vanished into the ether. At practically the same moment, their daughter, Grace, went missing from her private school, and their sons, little Christopher and Baby Leo, were snatched from the arms of their nanny in Central Park. Baby Leo was ill. The nanny had only just noticed spots forming on his skin when he'd been taken.

The news has also reported that Giuseppe had been warned by the Mafia that if he didn't pay his gambling debts, his family would be made to disappear. And now they have.

All these people at this table *know* the Panzavecchias? Do all rich New Yorkers know one another? The whole story seems suddenly absurd, in the very moment it becomes real. It sounds like some silly mobster movie. But if these people know the Panzavecchias, then Grace and little Christopher are real. Baby Leo is a real baby. Their lives changed suddenly, crazily, in one day. Just like Jane's did the day her parents died in a plane crash when she was a baby. And the day she got the call about Aunt Magnolia.

Jane realizes now that Kiran and Mrs. Vanders's comment about bank robbers, in the car on the way up to the house, had been a Panzavecchia joke.

"You all *know* the Panzavecchias?" she says aloud, then immediately regrets it, because now everyone is looking at her and she can hear the naïve wonder in her own voice.

"We do," says the pearl-necklace lady crisply. "I'm Lucy," she says, holding out a hand. "Lucy St. George. Ravi's girlfriend, so to speak."

"I'm Janie," she says, shaking Lucy's hand awkwardly, and adding, unsure that it's even true, "Kiran's friend."

"I met Janie earlier," Philip Okada announces to the table. "Upstairs. Janie, this is my wife, Phoebe."

Star-earring lady holds out a perfectly manicured hand, nails turquoise. "Nice to meet you," she says.

"And I'm Colin," says the fourth person, reaching a long arm toward Jane. Kiran's boyfriend. Jane supposes she was expecting someone boring, or bland, or generically rich-looking. But he's a skinny, pale guy with sandy hair, gentle eyes, and a soft scattering of freckles that make him look young, sweet.

Heels strike on the wooden floor and Kiran strides into the room.

At the sight of her familiar, irritable face, something in Jane's chest loosens.

She slumps into the chair between Jane and Lucy. "Sorry," she says shortly. "Phone call with bad reception. It's raining frogs. What are we talking about? Janie, did you meet everyone?"

"We were very polite and introduced ourselves, sweetheart," says Colin.

Kiran doesn't look at Colin or indicate that she's heard. "Do you have everything you need?" she asks Jane. "Is everyone being nice to you?"

"I'm fine," says Jane.

"And how are you, Kiran?" asks Phoebe Okada. "What are you doing these days?"

"Is that code for 'Do you have a job yet?'" asks Kiran.

Phoebe raises one perfectly groomed eyebrow. "Why? Do you have a job?"

"I think you know the answer to that."

"Don't you speak a lot of languages, Kiran?" says Philip Okada. "You could help Colin when his work takes him abroad. Don't you sell to a lot of foreigners, Colin?"

Kiran speaks distinctly to the salt shaker she holds in her hand. "You want me to join my boyfriend on his work trips. So I can make it my life's purpose to help him with his work."

"He didn't mean it that way, Kiran," says Phoebe. "It would just be nice for you to have something to *do*."

"Everyone wants to tell me what to do," says Kiran.

Philip's wife smoothes her expression, looking carefully neutral. Her makeup seems hard, masklike; Jane gets the feeling that tapping on her face would sound like hail hitting a window. Beside her, Philip seems limited to a small range of friendly expressions. The more belligerent Kiran becomes, the more unoffended he looks. *They're false,* Jane realizes. *They're pretending at something.*

"Kiran will be ready for the right work, when it presents itself," Colin says firmly. "And she'll be brilliant at it."

Kiran doesn't look at Colin. Her shoulders remain hard and straight. "Does anyone know when Ravi's coming?" she asks.

"Tonight, late," says Lucy St. George. "He texted me this afternoon. He had an auction in Providence, then headed to the Hamptons on his bike. He said someone was picking him up there."

"Someone? Patrick?" says Kiran.

"I think so."

Jane is boggled at the notion of Ravi bicycling from Providence to the Hamptons. It must be a hundred miles at the least.

"And where are you from, Janie?" Phoebe asks. "What kind of people are your parents?"

Jane is caught unawares. *What kind of people are my parents?* "Dead," she says. "Yours?"

"Oh, I'm sorry," says Phoebe. "My parents run a refrigeration corporation in Portsmouth, in the south of England. Did you grow up in an orphanage?"

"Did you grow up in a refrigerator?"

This surprises a choked laugh out of Kiran. Jane flushes, shocked at herself, but Phoebe merely focuses imperturbably on her salad. When she drops a slice of pear onto the table, Philip says "Oops," picks it up with his fingers, and feeds it to her, in plain view of everyone. It's slightly embarrassing. Not to mention that he's a very strange germophobe.

"My mother's sister adopted me," Jane tells Lucy St. George and Colin, since they seem more . . . genuine. "My parents died when I was too young to remember them. My aunt taught marine biology at the college where Kiran went. She was also an underwater photographer and a conservationist."

"Is your aunt retired?" asks Colin.

"Colin!" says Kiran with sudden indignation.

"What?"

"You're being intrusive! Leave her alone!"

"I'm sorry," says Colin, honestly confused. "Did I say something bad?"

"It's okay," Jane says, embarrassed by Kiran's burst of protectiveness. "She died, in December, in an expedition to Antarctica. She was going to photograph humpback whales."

"Oh," Colin says. "That's awful. I'm sorry."

"I tutored Janie in writing," Kiran says, "when she was in high school and I was in college."

"Christ," Colin says. "You're a child."

If only, Jane thinks. *If I were still a child, I'd be having dinner with Aunt Magnolia right now, instead of with these people.* On special nights, they would eat at the diner in town. Aunt Magnolia had owned a beautiful long coat, a dark, iridescent purple with a lining that shifted from silver to gold depending on the light. She'd often left it unbuttoned, knowing that Jane loved the glimpses of the secret shimmer inside. It had made Aunt Magnolia look like some of her own photographs of squids in the deep. It had made her look like outer space.

"Has anyone spoken to my mother?" Kiran asks, which strikes Jane as a strange question for her to ask this group. Kiran's mother divorced Octavian Thrash IV a long time ago.

"You mean your mother, or your stepmother?" Colin asks her. "Charlotte," he explains, looking at Jane.

"My own mother, of course," Kiran says. "Why? Have you seen Charlotte?"

"Of course not, sweetie. I would've told you if I'd seen her," Colin responds, which makes no sense to Jane. The wedding was recent and Charlotte, Octavian's new wife, lives in this house. Where is she, anyway? Where is Octavian? Don't they eat dinner? The air is moving against Jane's eardrums. Whispering a word? Has someone at the table whispered "Charlotte"? Kiran absently rubs one of her ears and Jane does the same, then notices herself mirroring Kiran. She wonders, *Isn't that kind of peculiar?*

Then she forgets.

"My mother is a scientist too, like Janie's aunt," Kiran says to Phoebe, "as I think you know. A theoretical physicist. She could tell you things about the universe that would show you how small you are. And my *step*mother is an interior designer who always worked for a living before she married my father, and she's damn good at it. Remember whose house you're in, if you're going to be snotty to my friends."

There is a pause. "Kiran," Colin says, "would you please pass me the salt?"

It's the first time Jane has seen Kiran and Colin look into each other's faces since the dinner began. Colin wears the expression of a man determined not to frighten a trapped creature. Kiran looks as if she might throw the salt at his face. She hands it to him silently.

Jane feels a bump against her leg and spends the rest of the meal passing tidbits down to Jasper.

Later that night, a sound wakes Jane, pulls her out of a dream about Baby Leo Panzavecchia. He's wailing, he's feverish. His angelic face is covered with angry welts and pustules; he's dying. "Silly Baby Leo," Jane mutters. "Everyone gets chicken pox. You're not going to die."

Through her bedroom window, the moon gleams low in the sky, a slice of orange. The storm is over. What woke her? The house has made a noise, like an annoyed grumble at being pulled out of its repose. Or did that noise come from Jane herself? It's hard to tell.

It's past four, which is unfortunate, because Jane can never fall asleep again once she's awake. When she was little, Aunt Magnolia would stroke her hair, telling her to pretend that her lungs were a jellyfish, slowly swelling and emptying as they moved through underwater space. "Your body is a microcosm of the ocean," she'd used to say. Jane would fall asleep with Aunt Magnolia's hand in her hair, imagining herself the entire ocean, vast and quiet.

Now Jane sleeps with a blue wool hat of Aunt Magnolia's that she'd unfailingly packed on her polar expeditions but left behind on that last Antarctic trip. This hat has only ever known Aunt Magnolia alive and well. It's scratchy and springy. Jane reaches around under the covers for it, finds it, balls it up, pulls it close to her face, and breathes. Jellyfish are ancient creatures. Jane can be ancient and silent too.

No. Sleep is impossible. Pushing out of bed, Jane finds a hoodie to wear over her *Doctor Who* pajamas. *What is this house like,* she wonders, *in the middle of the night?*

Her curiosity outweighs her trepidation.

As she steps out of her rooms, she decides that the house *is* making protesting noises. Rumbles and groans, and something unplaceable, like the underwater echo of the laughter of children. But after all, a large old house would make strange noises, so she dismisses it. And she doesn't notice herself cringing as the sound hurts the back of her teeth. She doesn't feel her breath catching.

Motion-sensor spotlights hit each painting, one by one, as Jane progresses down the corridor toward the atrium, then turn off again once she's passed. Forgetting about Captain Polepants, she trips over his head. Softly swearing, she continues on.

The house's grumbles give way to actual human voices, distant and angry. Someone is having an argument in the courtyard. Jane begins to notice the scent of a pipe. Cautiously, she moves into one of the balustered archways and peers down.

A young man in black leather gesticulates with a motorcycle helmet at an older man, maybe in his fifties, who wears a silk, paisley bathrobe and bites down on the pipe Jane smelled. Their coloring is different, the elder man is white and the younger is brown, but Jane can see the father-son resemblance in the way their faces flash with anger. She can hear it in their voices. This is Octavian Thrash IV and Kiran's twin brother, Ravi, who, Jane now realizes, did not ride a bicycle today from Providence to the Hamptons.

"Silly boy," Octavian is saying. "Of course I didn't sell your fishy."

"Why do you do that?" Ravi says in disgust. "Why do you make a point of talking to me like I'm a child?"

"Stop behaving like a pollywog and I'll stop treating you like one," Octavian says. "Waking Patrick up in the middle of the morning to fetch you. Waking me up with your indignation when you get here and a sculpture's not where you've left it."

"Excuse me for being concerned about a missing Brancusi. And I didn't wake Patrick up," Ravi says. "He met me for a drink on the mainland and it got late, as it always does with Patrick. I didn't wake you up either. You're a creature of the night."

"Not an excuse for you to stumble in drunk and raving."

"I'm not drunk," Ravi says distinctly. "And I merely want to know why the Brancusi fish isn't in the receiving hall. No, forget that—I want to know why you don't *care* it's not in the receiving hall. You understand the piece I'm talking about? The one Ivy used to build an underwater kingdom for out of Play-Doh? You let her keep it in her bedroom for weeks, surrounded by Loch Ness Monster LEGOs."

"I know the piece," says Octavian wearily.

"Jesus, Dad, it's worth millions. It was your own acquisition! Where the hell is it?"

"I expect Mrs. Vanders thought it would look better somewhere else," Octavian says. "Or maybe she's studying it for provenance. Between you and Vanny, it's a wonder there's any art left in the house. She made me return a seventeenth-century tapestry to some old geezer in Fort Lauderdale."

"Right," says Ravi testily. "Because she figured out it was Nazi plunder, acquired by your esteemed grandfather during the Holocaust. How dare she."

"It's damned amusing, you getting all huffy about provenance," says Octavian. "I know what you're up to with your mother. How do you explain the provenance of the art she supplies you with?"

Ravi peers at Octavian without expression. Crosses his arms. "There's no reason to do a provenance study on the Brancusi," he says coolly. "Vanny and I know everywhere it's been since Brancusi created it."

"Well, surely you don't think someone stole it?"

"I don't know what to think," Ravi says, swiping a hand through wet hair and turning away from his father. "It's not like you not to care. You used to be a normal person, who slept normal hours, and had normal conversations, and loved the art as much as I do, and gave a shit."

"Watch your language," says Octavian sharply.

"Whatever," says Ravi. "At least you give a shit about something. I'm tired and cold. I'm going to bed."

The courtyard has its own matching interior staircases, on the east and west sides, that rise to the top floor. Ravi chooses one and begins to climb.

After a moment, his father takes the pipe from his mouth and says, "Welcome home, son."

Ravi stops climbing. He doesn't turn around to face his father, but he says, "How's Mum?"

"Your mother is tiptop, of course," says Octavian. "She always is. What did Patrick need that kept you out so late? Brooding again? Affairs of the heart?"

Ravi breathes a laugh and doesn't answer. "He's a silent brooder, you know that. How's Kiran?"

"Your sister has not yet deigned to visit me."

"Well, you don't make it easy, you know, with your vampiric hours. And Charlotte?"

A draft touches Jane's throat, making her shiver. "Your stepmother is still away," Octavian says sadly, glancing up at the glass ceiling and showing Jane, suddenly, where Kiran gets her snub nose, her broad face. Then Octavian turns and wanders through the north arches into a part of the house Jane hasn't seen yet.

Ravi continues to climb, his footsteps echoing. The house seems to settle into a sigh around the aloneness of the two men. A long, deep breath.

Jane knows Ravi's rooms are near hers on the third floor, but he stops at the second floor and disappears into the bowels of the house. *Interesting*, thinks Jane, remembering that Lucy St. George introduced herself as Ravi's girlfriend, "so to speak." Whatever that means.

She's trying to decide where to go next when Jasper appears, making small whining noises at her and hopping.

"Shush," Jane whispers to him, bending down to soothe him.

He moves closer to the main staircase that leads down to the receiving hall, and whimpers again. He seems to be trying to lure her to those stairs. "Do you need to go outside, Jasper?" she whispers, going with him, beginning to follow him down the stairs.

The spotlights are no longer turning on as Jane moves. It's quite dark. She follows Jasper's low, black, descending shadow, clings to the banister, and wishes she'd paid more attention to the location of light switches earlier.

Jasper stops on the second-story landing so suddenly that she walks into him and loses her balance, tumbling against the banister, grabbing on to it with a gasp. When she pushes herself back toward the nice, solid wall, Jasper trots around behind her and begins to head-butt her calves over and over.

Everyone is bonkers, Jane thinks. "Jasper," she whispers, swatting at him. "What the hell are you doing?"

Before her, dimly, Jane recognizes the huge oil painting she was admiring earlier, the painting of the house interior with the umbrella left open to dry on the checkered floor. Jasper is still head-butting her. "Enough!" she whispers. "Knock it off, screwball!" She starts down the next flight of steps, but he makes an urgent yipping noise behind her. She turns back. "What? What is it?" but she can barely see him, and when she climbs back up to the landing, he's gone.

Jane turns up the steps, wondering if maybe he's returned to the third floor. But she doesn't find him again. She's just decided to return to her rooms when a figure appears across the way, gliding past the opposite archways, then out of sight.

Ravi again? Or maybe Octavian the Fourth?

No. It looked like Philip Okada, Phoebe's germophobic, Chuck Taylors–wearing husband. Jane hears a door swing open and closed and recognizes it as the door to the servants' wing.

What business does Philip Okada have going into the servants' quarters at four-something in the morning?

On impulse, she rounds the perimeter of the courtyard and slips silently into the servants' wing. There's no sign of Philip. She'll be spotted if anyone comes out of a room, unless she manages to dive into one of the small side hallways in time. Holding her breath, she tiptoes along and sets herself to the lunatic task of resting her ear against doors.

Nothing. Door after door after door, the only thing she hears is nothing. The servants of Tu Reviens are enviable sleepers. She puts her ear to the door she knows is Ivy's. Also nothing. She's as relieved as she is ashamed of herself. *I hardly know her. It's none of my business what she does or whom she does it with and I shouldn't be sneaking around spying on her. What is wrong with me?* She moves back into the main corridor, determined to return to bed.

Suddenly, a door opens and light spills out from a small hallway near the end of the main corridor. Jane freezes, then jumps into a nearby side hallway and flattens herself against the wall where she can't be seen.

"You'll have to stay there until the final phase," says a deep voice Jane recognizes. Patrick Yellan.

"While not knowing where I am?" says the English-accented voice of Philip Okada, dryly. "Won't that be lovely."

"Be grateful for it," says Patrick. "The less information you have, the safer you are."

"Yes, yes," says Philip. "Who doesn't like a mystery holiday in a room with no windows?"

"Not everyone is swallowing the story you're putting out," says a third voice, female, brusque, English-accented. Phoebe Okada.

"Don't worry about it," says Patrick.

"When it involves the safety of my husband?" says Phoebe sharply. "Go to hell, Patrick."

"We'll handle it," says Patrick roughly.

The voices are receding. Jane, not entirely in her right mind, can't help herself: She edges out of her hiding place and directs one eye into the corridor. The three conspirators are at the far end, passing through the big wooden door that leads to the west attics. Patrick is in front. Phoebe is next, wrapped in a pale green, silky robe. Philip Okada brings up the rear, still wearing his blue suit, carrying a plush white bag with orange ducks on it, and holding a gun.

The door closes behind them. Jane turns and dashes out of the servants' quarters, heart racing. While she was in the west attics earlier, she saw a spire through the big windows, somewhere in the east wing. She wonders now if she might be able to see into the west attics from that spire.

Starting around the atrium, Jane barrels headlong into the dog, then falls over him, trying not to cry out or crush him. Scrambling to her feet, she tries to get around him, push him away, but he's head-butting her again and his low center of gravity makes him stick in place like a tree stump.

"Jasper! Move!" Jane whispers, then accidentally steps on one of his toes. He squeals.

"Sorry!" Jane whispers. "Sorry!"

He barks.

"Jasper-Bear?" rises a voice from below. "You okay? Come here, boy."

It's Ravi, climbing the courtyard steps from the second level. "Yes," Jane whispers to Jasper, "go bark at someone who's not trying to be stealthy. Hey!" she cries as the dog takes her pajama leg in his mouth and starts pulling. Jane grabs her waistband as it slides down her hip. "What are you trying to do, pants me?"

"Who the hell are you?" says Ravi, behind Jane, out of breath from running the rest of the way up the stairs. "And what are you doing to my dog?"

"Your precious dog is mauling my pajamas," Jane retorts, not even looking around. "Jasper! Stop it, or I won't take any more pictures of you with the umbrellas!"

"Oh, hell," Ravi says, "a weirdo. My mother didn't bring you here, did she? Oh, god, I don't even want to know where you're from."

"Your sister brought me here," Jane says, "and your dog is the weirdo."

Jasper, who's finally released Jane, now stares at her reproachfully. Then he turns and marches away.

"That dog may be weird," says Ravi, "but he's still my dog."

Turning to Ravi, Jane finds that shadowy, predawn light suits him. Spectacularly. Ravi is tall and solid, electric, with scowly eyebrows and a face that flashes with feeling. He's got dramatic white streaks in his hair too, surely premature, since he's Kiran's twin.

"You're sure my mother didn't bring you here?" Ravi says. "You look like you'd be one of her projects, not Kiran's."

"I'm my own project, thank you very much," Jane says coldly.

This startles a smile onto his face. "Ravi," he says, holding out a hand. He's shivering, but his hand is warm.

"Janie," she says. She decides not to tell him about Patrick and the Okadas and the gun. She has no idea where anyone fits in here.

She falls into step with him, walking down the east corridor. He has a grin that's never more than a few words away and eyes that are careful to catch hers frequently. He carries his motorcycle helmet under one arm. He smells like wet leather.

"You haven't seen a fish sculpture anywhere, have you?" he says. "Looks a little like a squashed bean, on a mirrored pedestal?"

"Doesn't sound familiar," Jane says.

"I like your *Doctor Who* pajamas," he says. "Which Doctor do you favor?"

"I like the companions," says Jane automatically.

"Sure," says Ravi, "who doesn't? But I think I'd go for Ten. Ten is yummy. And youthful."

"The Tenth Doctor was nine hundred and three years old," says Jane loftily.

"Well, yeah, but Ten was youthful in spirit," Ravi says. "Yeesh. Do you let anything past?"

Before they get to their rooms, he stops at an unusual door Jane hasn't yet noticed. It's wooden and arched, with a doormat that reads WELCOME TO MY WORLDS. It has a mail slot and a bellpull and it occurs to Jane that it may be the entrance to the east spire.

"I feel like I'm in a Winnie-the-Pooh story," Jane says.

Ravi grins again and says, "Those are favorites of mine. Someday, somewhere, I'll meet a Heffalump." Then he slips his hand inside his coat and pulls out one perfect nasturtium blossom. He pushes it through the mail slot and lets it fall through.

Together, Jane and Ravi walk on. "G'night then," he says, retreating into the room right before hers, yawning mightily.

"G'night," she responds, as much to Captain Polepants as to Ravi, who's already gone.

There's no point trying to get any more sleep now that she's seen what she's seen. Philip with a gun. Patrick, who's Ivy's brother. Patrick, who keeps telling Kiran he has something to confess, but never confesses. Ivy, who clammed up yesterday whenever Philip was around, or whenever Jane asked her what should have been innocuous questions.

Jane finds a clear wedge of yellow shag carpet near the morning room windows and lies down. She needs to think. The moon is smaller now, higher, paler than it was before, a slice of apple. Slowly it slides out of her view. The sky lightens and dissolves the stars.

No matter how many times she goes over the conversation, she can't make sense of it. Philip is going somewhere and it's dangerous. Philip is going somewhere, but he doesn't know where? Patrick and someone else have put out a story that not everyone's buying. Okay. A story about *what?*

Phoebe and Philip had been playacting at dinner; Jane had suspected it, and now she's sure of it. Pretending to care about Kiran and her job. Pretending to care about the Panzavecchias. Pretending to be snobbish about Jane and her aunt.

Is the Panzavecchia story the one that not everyone's buying? It's true that Lucy St. George isn't buying it. But what could Patrick and the Okadas have to do with a bank robbery, the Mafia, and a pair of missing socialites?

There's the missing Brancusi too. How does that fit in?

Jane wonders, suddenly, if she's being naïve; if it's normal for rich people in fancy houses to walk around with guns. This is the USA, after all; judging by the news, doesn't every third person have a gun? Maybe what's remarkable is that she's never seen anyone casually carrying a gun before this.

Then again, aren't the Okadas British? Do Brits wander around with guns?

Why would Patrick, who's a servant, be in charge of whatever's going on? And if Patrick is in charge of something underhanded . . . does Kiran know? And what does it mean about Ivy? About all her strange moments of deliberate nonchalance?

It depresses Jane to think about that. She doesn't want reasons not to trust Ivy.

Breathe, Aunt Magnolia would say. *Wait. Let it settle. The pieces will start to fit together in a way that makes sense. And be careful, my darling.*

What would an umbrella look like if it were a mystery? Jane wonders suddenly. *Even better, what if it were a weapon of self-defense?*

The ferrule, the tips, and the rod would be sharp. The springs would be tightly wound so that the canopy opened hard and fast like a blow from a shield.

"And I'll choose shades of brown and gold that suit Jasper," Jane mutters as she rolls up onto her feet.

An hour later, she's trimming down the diameter of a birch rod using the lathe, wearing goggles and a heavy canvas apron, when she hears someone explode through her outer door. She pushes her goggles up into her dark curls.

Ravi looms in the morning room doorway, wearing black silk pajama bottoms and nothing else. It's impossible not to stare.

"What the hell are you doing?" he yells, wincing at the light. "Do you know what time it is? Do you appreciate that I'm sleeping on the other side of the wall? My mother brought you here from a hell dimension!"

"You seem obsessed with your mother," says Jane. "Have you considered therapy?"

He moans, rubbing his face. "No one would believe the truth about my mother."

"Mm-hm," says Jane. "Is that because it's your own special truth?"

"What the hell are you building?"

"An umbrella," says Jane.

"Are you kidding me?" he says, then sweeps his hand out in a gesture that encompasses the entire room. "You aren't satisfied that there are enough umbrellas?"

"I make umbrellas," Jane says, shortly. "It's . . . what I do."

Wearily, he rubs his head. His white-streaked hair must've been wet when he lay down, for it's dried in a funny orientation, flat and sticking out to the right, like it's secretly trying to point Jane in that direction without him knowing. "You know, I think Patrick mentioned you last night," he says.

"Patrick talks about a lot of things," says Jane significantly.

Ravi scrunches his nose. "Maybe to you," he says. "He's the strong, silent type to me."

"He's never . . . *confessed* anything to you?"

"That's a really odd question," says Ravi. "Why, did he confess something to you? Didn't you literally just meet him, like, yesterday?"

"Yeah. Never mind."

"I think Kiran mentioned you too."

"Wow, you must know everything about me," Jane says, with a touch of sarcasm that alarms her. Ravi is a college graduate, an heir to the Thrash fortune, but he doesn't make her feel like a child. He makes her feel like she might be about to do something unwise.

"Do you hate me or something?" he says, grinning.

"I'm working," says Jane.

"Yes," he says. "On umbrellas, at five thirty in the morning."

"You're interrupting."

He's looking around the room now with curiosity. "You made all these umbrellas?"

"Yes."

"How?"

"What do you mean, how?"

"Well, how does one build an umbrella? What's the first step?"

"I don't know," says Jane. "You could start a few different ways. I'm not, like, an expert."

"As an art appreciator," he says, "I'm curious."

"Well," Jane says in confusion, "I mean, you can watch if you want."

He sighs, then yawns, then marches out, then marches back in again, wrapping the blanket from Jane's bed around himself. He weaves his way through the saws, umbrella parts, and umbrellas to the striped sofa Jane has pushed against the back wall, then settles himself down. For the next couple of hours, he alternates sleeping on her sofa with waking grouchily to the noises of her saws and asking intelligent questions about umbrella-making. "How do you keep the ribs from rubbing through the canopy after repeated openings?" he mumbles, then grasps his hair. "Christ. I keep dreaming about that damn Panzavecchia baby. Little Leo, you know?"

"I insert a small piece of fabric between the joints and the canopy as a buffer," Jane says, focusing hard on the work of her fingers. "It's called a prevent."

He's already half-asleep again. Jane notices, through her absorption, that his cleverness fades from his face when he's sleeping. She wonders if she's wrong to believe that he's ignorant of the Patrick stuff.

"And yeah," she says, speaking to herself. Speaking to the house, which groans back at her. "I dreamt about him too."

* * *

Ravi is still asleep on Jane's sofa when her stomach informs her that it's time for breakfast.

Not knowing the breakfast routine in this house, and not really wanting to come face-to-face with someone alarming like Patrick or Philip, she texts Kiran, who's likely to be protective. "Breakfast?"

Kiran texts back. "Be there soon. Go to banquet hall."

Jane closes Ravi into the morning room so she can get changed. *Aunt Magnolia? What do I wear on a day like this?*

She pulls on a ruffled dress shirt the red-orange color of a weedy sea dragon, black-and-white-striped jeans like a zebra seahorse, and her big black boots. She rolls her sleeves up to the elbows so her tattoo tentacles are visible. Feeling a bit more courageous, but with fists clenched tight, she heads down to the banquet hall.

Colin, Lucy St. George, and Phoebe Okada sit at the far end of the long table, silently drinking coffee and eating poached eggs and toast. Jane slides into an open seat, studying Phoebe, who's heavily made-up again, her eyes rimmed with smoky grays and her lips a deep purple. Phoebe stares back at Jane with an aggressively pleasant expression, until, losing her nerve, Jane's eyes drop to her plate.

Colin reads a newspaper, an actual, physical newspaper that makes Jane wonder how newspapers are delivered to this house. Behind the smooth curtain of her honey-brown hair, Lucy reads a book, *The House of Mirth,* with occasional glances at her phone whenever it vibrates. Various strangers keep stomping through the banquet hall, shouting to each other, carrying cleaning supplies, buckets and vases, stringed lights, a ladder, dropping things. The gala is tomorrow. She's surprised that the houseguests seem limited to this small group.

"Who comes to these parties?" Jane asks. "Rich New Yorkers?"

Colin looks up from his newspaper. "Yes," he says with a sympathetic smile. "But not just from New York. Up and down the eastern seaboard, and always people from abroad too."

"How do they get here?"

"In their own boats, mostly, though Octavian also charters a couple of boats for any of the guests who need it. There's a seasonal staff too, as you can see."

"Where's Octavian, anyway?" Phoebe asks, turning her implacable gaze on Colin. "We haven't seen him once since we arrived. He wouldn't go away on a gala weekend, would he?"

"I think he's lurking around," says Colin. "Ravi said something about him being depressed."

"Ah," says Phoebe. "That's too bad, though not surprising, with Charlotte missing."

"Charlotte's missing?" says Jane, startled.

"I thought you were Kiran's friend?" says Phoebe, raising one eyebrow. "She didn't tell you her stepmother is missing?"

"We talk about other things," Jane says defensively.

"Kiran can be very closemouthed," says Colin, "even with those she's closest to. Charlotte went away unexpectedly about a month ago. She left a cryptic note for Octavian, but then she never wrote again, and no one's heard from her."

"But, where was she going?" asks Jane. "Hasn't anyone searched for her?"

"She didn't say," says Colin. "Octavian hired investigators and everything, once a few days had gone by and it started to seem like she'd truly vanished. But they didn't turn up much, just some discrepancies about her background and the suggestion that her mother might have been a crook."

Jane's ears are uncomfortable. "What kind of crook?" she asks, swallowing hard.

"Some sort of con artist," says Colin.

Jane, rubbing her ears, is trying to figure out how this might connect to the weirdness from last night. A missing stepmother and Philip going on a mystery journey. The Panzavecchias, also missing, and the sculpture missing too. And a con artist in the family?

"How did you sleep?" Jane asks Phoebe abruptly, willing her to say something about nighttime parlays, and guns.

"Badly," Phoebe says as a flash of some feeling—unhappiness, or worry—crosses her face. Very suddenly it makes her softer, accessible, and Jane sees that her makeup is a camouflage so she'll seem bright and awake. In fact, her eyes are lined, her face heavy with exhaustion.

"I slept badly too," says Lucy St. George, looking up from her book. "This house wakes me up. I hear it moaning and sighing, as if it's lonely here on this island, far away from other houses."

Yes, Jane thinks. *Someone else here has an imagination.*

"My Lucy is ever a poet," says Colin.

"*Your* Lucy?" Jane says. "I thought you had a Kiran, not a Lucy."

"I'm pleased to report that I have one of each," says Colin, smiling. "Kiran is my girlfriend and Lucy is my cousin."

"Oh! Are you a St. George, then, too?"

"Alas," says Colin, "I'm a Mack. The poor Irish relation."

"Oh, Colin," says Lucy St. George. "Please don't start talking about the potato famine."

"And why shouldn't I talk about the potato famine?"

"It's tacky," says Lucy. "You went to all the most expensive boarding schools and universities."

"My education was financed by Lucy's father, my uncle Buckley," Colin says to Jane with a smirk. "He was training me up to be useful."

"Oh, here we go." Lucy rolls her eyes.

"I see," says Jane. "Are you useful?"

"Very," Colin responds. "At least to Uncle Buckley. He's a fine art dealer. I find him art to buy, and then I find him rich people to sell it to. It's Ravi's job too."

Jane wonders how much training is needed for a job like that, if it's something any person could do, if they learned enough. "I think I'd like a job that relates to art," she says cautiously, "someday."

"Would you?" says Colin. "Do you have an eye for art, or for design?"

"I guess."

"Are you artistic?"

"I guess," Jane says again.

"You could focus it in some practical direction, like architecture," says Colin. "Have you ever taken a drafting class? I hope you're thinking about ways to differentiate yourself from everyone else. Are you being strategic about it? Do you have any unique interests or skills? What's your brand?"

Jane feels a sudden compulsion to shield the existence of her homemade umbrellas from Colin's questions. "I'm not that artistic," she lies.

"Too bad. No new news about the Panzavecchias," Colin says, turning another page in his newspaper.

"Nothing online either," says Lucy. "I wonder if any of my contacts know anything."

"Contacts?" Jane says.

"Lucy's a private art investigator," says Colin.

"What's private art?"

"She's a private investigator," Colin says with a small smile. "Collectors hire her to find their stolen art when the cops come up empty. She's very good, despite anything you might hear about a recent mishap with a Rubens."

"Oh, Colin," says Lucy calmly. "Do I have to listen to stories of my own mishaps at breakfast? Besides, Jane doesn't want to hear about chasing art thieves."

"I kind of do," says Jane, thinking of the missing Brancusi sculpture, and wondering if this might elucidate anything.

Lucy looks at Colin with a weary indulgence, then returns to *The House of Mirth*. It's a clear dismissal.

"In the movies," says Colin, turning back to Jane, "it's always some rich collector who wants to steal the *Mona Lisa* or something. Right?"

"Or a famous Monet," says Jane, "or a Van Gogh or Michelangelo's *David*. Maybe they even steal it for fun."

"Exactly," he says. "But in real life, the smart, professional art thief steals a lesser work, less famous, by a lesser master. Preferably a piece nobody's ever heard of, by an artist nobody knows, worth forty thousand dollars instead of forty million dollars. Something that doesn't have a well-documented past, so that it can be reintroduced back into the market without raising suspicions, and sold to someone who has no idea it's stolen."

"Oh. I guess that makes sense."

"When a famous masterpiece is stolen," Colin says, "like the Van Dyke or the Vermeer that makes front-page news, there's little hope of finding a collector who'll buy it. That picture usually ends up being passed from one criminal to another as collateral in the drug trade."

"Really?" says Jane, startled.

"Really."

"But, do drug traffickers care about art?"

"They care about cash alternatives," Colin says matter-of-factly.

"I don't understand what that means," she says.

Colin smiles. Jane senses he's enjoying being the one in the know. "Money laundering is a tricky business," he says. "It's harder and harder for criminals to move cash around without getting caught. But art is easy to move, and when it's stolen, it's all over the news how much it's worth. Very convenient for me, if I've got a famous, stolen Rubens and want to trade it for a lot of drugs. Or if I need a loan to buy the drugs, but my lender requires collateral. A famous picture makes great collateral."

"Do you think you've explained it in enough detail, Colin?" says Lucy sweetly, her nose still buried in her book. "Perhaps you'd like to take Jane on a field trip?"

"You're the one who should do that, cuz," says Colin. "It's your world, not mine." He cocks a significant eyebrow at Jane. "Don't tell anyone," he says, "but sometimes Lucy has to go undercover into the drug world."

"Voluntarily?" Jane says, staring at Lucy, who calmly reads her book, looking, for all the world, like someone who belongs in an armchair crocheting doilies and eating crumpets. She's wearing pearls again this morning, around her neck and in her ears.

"Mm-hm," says Colin. "Often, the only way to recover a master-piece is to set up a sting."

"You do that?" Jane says to Lucy. "What do you pose as? A drug dealer? What do you *wear?*"

"Colin," says Lucy, putting her book down and fixing her cousin with quiet eyes. "I'm going to invoke my position as family badass and tell you it's time to shut up now."

"But, Lucy," Jane says, "does this mean that last night at dinner, when you said you couldn't picture the Panzavecchias getting involved in organized crime, you knew what you were talking about? Like, from *experience?*"

"Yes," says Colin, looking upon his cousin with amusement. "Lucy knows what she's talking about. She's met some of those people."

"Colin," says Lucy. Her voice is a warning.

"Well, *I* don't see any reason not to believe it," Phoebe puts in. "If Lucy poses as drug dealers and executes undercover stings, why shouldn't Giuseppe owe money to mobsters?"

"Sure," says Lucy, frustrated and sarcastic. "Why not."

"Lucy recently managed to intercept a stolen Rubens," Colin says pleasantly, "in the Poconos. She traded a big pile of heroin for it and, once she had the Rubens in hand, called in the FBI, who arrested all the bad guys. It was a great triumph. Then some random carjacker stopped her and stole the Rubens before she could pass it on to the

FBI. Very embarrassing. It's made her a bit touchy. Has Ravi met you yet?" Colin asks Jane, transitioning subjects abruptly. "He's going to like you."

"What? Why should Ravi like me?" Jane responds, confused, then suddenly mortified, remembering that Lucy is Ravi's girlfriend and Ravi is sleeping, shirtless, on her sofa.

"Oh, he likes variety," says Colin.

"Variety!" says Jane as Lucy claps her mouth shut and sits there looking startled and stung. Why is Colin taking digs at Lucy?

"I'm sure Ravi will barely notice me," says Jane. "I'm nobody."

"We'll see," says Colin.

Lucy rises to her feet, closes one hand around her book and the other around her phone, and stalks from the room.

"Why did you do that?" asks Jane.

"Do what?" asks Colin.

"Try to make your cousin jealous of me."

"It's family stuff," he says with a benevolent expression. "Don't worry about it."

"Okay, but don't use me as one of your weapons."

"Good girl," says Phoebe crisply, nodding at Jane, surprising Jane so much that she can only stare back.

"I can see I'm being ganged up on," says Colin. "Where's Philip this morning, Phoebe?"

"Philip was called out in the night," says Phoebe, a crease of worry appearing in the center of her forehead.

Jane's eyes are riveted to Phoebe's face. "Out?" she says. "Out where?"

"For his work," Phoebe says.

"What did he do, swim to the mainland?" Jane asks.

"Philip knows how to operate a boat. The Thrashes have lots of boats. It happens. He's a medical doctor."

"Oh," says Jane, picturing Philip Okada again with latex gloves on his hands. "His germophobia must make his job difficult," she adds, fishing.

Phoebe blinks. "His germophobia," she repeats.

"Yes," Jane says. "He mentioned his germophobia."

"It's a recent development," says Phoebe.

"Since when?" says Colin. "I didn't know he was germophobic."

"It's not unusual for medical doctors," says Phoebe. "He doesn't like to talk about it."

"What kind of doctor is he?" asks Jane.

"A GP," says Phoebe.

"I see," says Jane. "Doesn't that mean general practitioner?"

"Yes. Why?"

"No reason," says Jane. "I'm just sorry there isn't another doctor who can fill in for him while he's on vacation. I mean, it'd be one thing if he were the only doctor in the world who could attach someone's brain back to their spinal cord, but lots of people are GPs."

"My husband is very devoted to his patients," says Phoebe. "Are you belittling his work?"

"Oh, Phoebe," says Colin. "I'm sure she wasn't. Have you eaten enough? Here. Have some fruit."

"I'm sorry," says a new voice, speaking with a mild accent Jane can't particularly place.

They all turn to stare at the East Asian man with salt-and-pepper hair who's stepped in from the kitchen and stopped just inside the doors. "I forget the way to the receiving hall," he says, clutching a bucket to his chest. Jane assumes he's one of the seasonal staff, cleaning for the gala.

"It's that way," says Colin, pointing to an exit at the other end of the room. "Pass into the ballroom, then choose the second doorway on the left."

"Thank you," says the man. He disappears through the exit.

At that moment, the door to the kitchen swings open to reveal Mrs. Vanders, who pointedly locks eyes with Phoebe.

"Well then," says Phoebe. "I've finished my breakfast."

She crosses the room with loud claps from her high-heeled boots and takes the same exit the cleaner took.

Mrs. Vanders stays in the kitchen doorway and directs another impenetrable expression at Jane. Then she swings away.

Kiran never showed up for breakfast at all. Colin is being insensitive to Lucy. Phoebe is lying about her husband and almost seemed as if she intentionally followed that cleaner. Jasper's got nothing on these people.

Jane finishes her breakfast. Then she goes straight through the adjoining door into the kitchen. It's time to ask Mrs. Vanders what's behind that stare.

But Mrs. Vanders is gone.

Mr. Vanders is there, sitting in the enormous kitchen, his back to Jane, bent over messy piles of blueprints at a long table. Regular blueprints, not Ivy's detailed ones. He's muttering angrily.

Patrick mans a mountain of eggs and a pot of boiling water at an oversized stove with about a dozen burners. He's rubbing his eyes and yawning, no doubt because first he and Ravi had a late night together—brooding, wasn't it?—on the mainland, then he snuck around the house with the Okadas until dawn, being mysterious. Patrick's jaw, Jane notices, is strong and elegant. He probably looks like a Brontë hero when he broods.

"Out until four in the morning with Ravi, two nights before the gala," grumbles Mr. Vanders, "and all of us scurrying to find that damn thing. You owe Cook, young man."

"How about I pay him back by cooking breakfast this morning," says Patrick sourly. Then he notices Jane near the door. "Janie. Are you looking for Kiran?"

When Mr. Vanders hears Patrick's words, he turns, pushes up from the table, and stares at Jane exactly the way his wife does, except that he does it from a dark face and under shaggy white eyebrows. Jane can just imagine their wedding photo, the two of them glaring out of it with withering expressions. Next, his gaze takes in Jane's eclectic outfit.

"I'm looking for Mrs. Vanders," says Jane.

"You might have some of your aunt Magnolia's style," Mr. Vanders announces gruffly, "but she had a subtlety you lack."

Jane is thunderstruck. "You knew my aunt Magnolia?"

He waves a pen in an impatient gesture. "My wife wishes to explain it herself," he says. "I think she went up to our rooms. Fourth door on the right. Either that or she's on the third floor, east wing, beginning her daily inventory of the art. Or she's dealing with the day staff, which would place her anywhere in the house."

"How helpful," says Jane.

"Hmph," he says. "Your aunt was not sarcastic."

Distantly, a noise begins, like a shrilling teakettle. It stutters, fluctuates so that it's hard to tell where it's coming from—the vents in the walls? The burners of the stove? In the very moment Jane recognizes it as a wailing child, it turns to a wild sort of laughter and she clenches her teeth. "What *is* that?"

"I should think it's obvious that it's a child," says Mr. Vanders.

"Are there many children here?"

"It's a large staff," he responds. "Most people in life have children."

"I saw a little girl digging in the garden yesterday," says Jane.

Mr. Vanders freezes. Astonishment lights his face, then vanishes so quickly that Jane wonders if she imagined it. What could possibly be so significant about a little girl digging in the garden?

Pointing his pen at the exit, he practically commands, "Talk to Mrs. Vanders!"

"Well, geez. I hope she's a better conversationalist than everyone else in this house," Jane mutters as she turns away, amazed with the way some of the people she's encountered here—Mr. Vanders, Ravi, Phoebe, Colin—provoke her most sardonic but also her most honest self. Jane may not be comfortable in this house, but she wonders if maybe this house makes her comfortable in herself. She feels almost as if she's meeting herself again after a long absence. *Aunt Magnolia?*

"By the way," Jane says louder as she reaches the door, "I'm the sultan of subtle."

"I don't think there's a sultan of subtle," Patrick remarks absently behind her. "It's more an office for ministers and spies."

In the receiving hall, a team of women drag lilac branches around, cutting and arranging them in pots. Jane climbs the steps quickly, trying to reach an altitude where the scent is less overwhelming. Every spring her campus town is choked with the smell of lilacs. It's impossible to separate that smell from Aunt Magnolia.

She stops on the second level, noticing that someone's given the suits of armor big bouquets of daffodils to hold in their arms. Jasper is on the opposite landing again. He stands in front of that tall painting of the room with the umbrella, watching Jane, whimpering. Thinking to give him a scratch, she moves onto the bridge above the receiving hall, but then the sound of a camera shutter echoes somewhere above.

Jane knows who it is. Leaning out, she cranes her neck to find Ivy on the bridge above. Her stomach is propped against the railing and she seems to be photographing the receiving hall.

For a split second, Jane considers pretending not to see her. If she doesn't talk to Ivy, she won't have to think about whether Ivy's mixed up in something bad.

Then Ivy lowers her camera and sees Jane. She leans over the railing, smiling. "Hi," she says.

"Hi," says Jane cautiously. "What are you doing?"

"Taking pictures."

"Of what?"

"Wait there," Ivy says, then straightens and walks out of Jane's sight.

A moment later, she steps onto Jane's bridge. She's wearing a ratty blue sweater and black leggings and she smells like chlorine again, or maybe like the sea. She looks like the sea. Beautiful, and unconcerned, and full of secrets.

"What are you up to?" she asks Jane.

"I'm looking for Mrs. Vanders," Jane answers. "Why are you taking pictures of the receiving hall?"

"Didn't I tell you? I'm photographing the art," Ivy says, then opens her mouth to say more, then closes it, looking carefully casual, and Jane knows, immediately, through some instinct that touches the skin of her throat, that whatever's going on, Ivy is involved.

"Ivy?" she says, with a sinking heart. "What is it?"

"What's what?" says Ivy. "Look." She shows the camera to Jane, scrolling through the last dozen or so shots. Every picture contains one or another piece of art in the house, though much of the art is obscured by members of the gala cleaning staff. Jane sees the women arranging lilacs, and the bucket-carrying man who walked through breakfast this morning. Several of the pictures feature this man, the art fading into the background.

"It must be hard to focus on the art when the house is so full of people," Jane says, fishing again.

"Yeah."

"Why are you taking pictures of the art?"

"For Mrs. Vanders," Ivy says in that fake, nonchalant voice. "To help her catalog it."

"Ivy?" says Jane, dying to ask her if she's really taking pictures of the art, or if she might, for some reason, be taking pictures of the people.

"Yeah?"

"Nothing," says Jane, biting back frustration. "It just seems to me like some of the people in this house are acting weird."

"Really? Like who?"

Like you, with that fake innocent voice, Jane wants to reply. She wonders, what if she told Ivy about seeing Patrick and the Okadas? "Mrs. Vanders, for one," she says. "She keeps giving me weird looks."

"She does that to everyone," says Ivy.

"Right," says Jane with a touch of sarcasm she can't hide. "I'm sure everything's completely normal."

Now Ivy's studying Jane with wide-eyed surprise. "Janie?" she says. "Did something happen?"

"Morning, you two," says a voice behind Jane.

Kiran's on the landing, about to descend the steps to the receiving hall. "Sorry, Janie," she says. "Did you get breakfast?"

"Yeah."

"Hey, hon," Kiran says, flashing a quick smile at Ivy. "How are you this morning?"

"Good," says Ivy distractedly, still watching Jane with puzzlement. "Patrick's back. He's probably looking for you."

"Mm?" says Kiran, inflecting the monosyllable with disinterest. She starts down the steps. Just as her feet touch the hall's checkerboard floor, Ravi appears at the very top of the stairs.

One after another, the servants in the receiving hall turn to look up at him, then smile. He's showered, shaved, barefoot, and dressed in black, and up there on his stage, with those white streaks in his hair that make him look older than he is, sophisticated. He's hard not to smile at. Kiran cranes her neck to him, her face suffused with light. When he sees her, he starts down the steps, singing her name, skipping, rushing. Reaching her, he enfolds her in a hug that makes Jane wish she had a twin brother.

Then Ravi's eyes take in the entire hall, find Jane and Ivy standing on the bridge.

"I like your friend," he says to Kiran, loudly enough for Jane to hear.

"Behave yourself, Ravi," Kiran chides him.

"Hey, Ivy-bean," Ravi calls up to Ivy, flashing her a grin.

"Hey, Ravi," Ivy calls down, her smile big and real. She adds, in a tone of mischief, "How's your girlfriend?"

"Perfectly aware that I'm a sexual magnet," he says.

Ivy snorts. "Just don't forget about my powers." She adds sideways to Jane, "Ravi and I have a joke that I'm a witch."

"I thought you only used your powers for good," says Ravi.

"*Good* is such an enigmatic word," says Ivy.

"Oh my god!" Ravi says. "Someone's corrupted you! Hide the grimoires!"

"Let's take a vote of the house and see who people think is more corruptible, me or you."

"Oh, hell," Ravi says. "You know, just because the majority believes it doesn't mean it's true."

"*Majority?* Pah. It's going to be unanimous."

"That doesn't make it true, either."

"Listen, all I'm saying is, Lucy seems like a nice lady. So don't forget about my powers."

"Got it. When my testicles dry up and drop off, I'll know who—"

"Oh, god," Kiran interrupts. "Please don't make me picture your testicles, Ravi."

"Come see Mum," says Ravi to Kiran.

"Oh *god!* You switch from your testicles to our mother?"

74

"She's the other woman most likely to threaten my testicles," says Ravi. "Come have breakfast, then come visit Mum with me."

"I'm not in the mood for her various realities," says Kiran. "She makes my head spin."

"You can't avoid her forever," says Ravi. "or Dad either. From the sound of things, you're avoiding him too."

"Well," says Kiran sweetly. "Then you should consider yourself flattered that I'm not avoiding you."

"I was born irresistible," says Ravi. "I can't take credit for it." Then his eyes slide to a place under the bridge Jane and Ivy are standing on. His face grows quiet. "Hey, man," he says to someone Jane can't see. He kisses his sister on the cheek, then passes through one of the doors that lead, among other places, to the banquet hall.

The person Ravi has greeted has fine shoulders Jane recognizes from above. As Patrick walks into the receiving hall toward Kiran, his broad, T-shirted back is to Jane, so she can't see his expression, but she can see Kiran's. It's one with which Jane is becoming well-acquainted: a measured hardness. Kiran's wall. *And she's right to protect herself,* Jane thinks. *Patrick lies.*

Patrick stops before Kiran. "Hey," he says. "Are you okay?"

"Yes," Kiran says, then flicks her eyes toward Jane and Ivy as a signal to Patrick. Patrick glances over his shoulder and sees them on the bridge.

Jane studiously pretends to look elsewhere for a moment, then, as soon as Patrick looks away, returns to watching them.

"So," Patrick says, turning back to Kiran. "On your way to breakfast?"

"Yes," says Kiran.

"Say hi to your fancy boyfriend for me," he says.

"Patrick," Kiran says. "Stop it."

"Imagine if I could say that to you," Patrick says, "and you did what I asked. 'Kiran, stop it.'"

"I'm not having this conversation here."

"All right," Patrick says sharply, then spins around and strides away into the east wing.

Kiran looks after him, fists closed hard. Her brittle mask is slipping. Suddenly she bursts across the checkerboard floor after him, her heels slapping on marble, like gunshots. She passes out of sight.

Jasper, still on the second-story landing, starts hopping and yipping in front of that tall painting. It's like he's channeling a rabid kangaroo.

"What is going on in this weirdo house?" Jane ask Ivy.

"Why, whatever do you mean?" says Ivy. Her tone is tongue-in-cheek.

"Do Kiran and Patrick have some sort of history?" says Jane.

"Sort of," Ivy says. "I mean, they love each other. But it's messy. At the moment, I'd say they have fundamental incompatibilities."

"You mean, like, that Kiran has a boyfriend?"

"No," says Ivy, her voice inflected with a kind of certainty. "I think the issues are mainly on Patrick's side."

"You mean because he sneaks around and lies," says Jane.

Ivy's alarm is physical, her body tensing and her eyes rushing to Jane's. Then she starts talking, filling the silence, as if to keep Jane from saying anything else. "I think Kiran's with Colin because she's trying to move on, actually. He's kind to her—he looks out for her. Like, once, before Colin and Kiran started dating, Octavian was criticizing Kiran at dinner for being sad and mopey and unemployed. Colin looked right at him and told Octavian there was no shame in being sad or mopey or unemployed, if that's what you happened to be. He said it in this completely reasonable voice that sort of made you feel like you'd be an asshole to argue. Octavian shoved his pipe in his mouth and left the table."

"Huh," says Jane, trying to focus on the conversation, rather than on her misery. "I take it most people don't talk to Octavian like that?"

"Octavian can be hard on Kiran and Ravi," says Ivy. "Colin found the way to put him in his place without actually being rude. Kiran's never been able to do that for herself."

"And what about Ravi and Lucy? How did they ever end up together?"

"They've sort of had a thing since they met, maybe two or three years ago," says Ivy. "They're really close, then they fight, then they're close again. It's hard to tell how serious it is."

"He doesn't seem like a guy who's serious about anyone."

"Oh, he always puts on that act."

"Is it an act?"

"I guess I can't be sure," says Ivy. "But I don't think he'd actually cheat. Ravi is pretty loyal."

"Isn't he young for her?"

"Yeah," says Ivy. "He's twenty-two, and emotionally he's about twelve. She's thirty."

"Does Ravi like older women?"

"Ravi is attracted to everyone," Ivy says, "panoptically."

Jane doesn't know that word. "Panoptically?"

"All-inclusively," Ivy says with a grin.

Jane gets being attracted to different kinds of people. To men and women, to people of different shapes and sizes, looks, personalities; she gets not having one type. But there are certainly qualities she prefers. Like, for example, the knowledge of big words she doesn't know; that's an attractive quality. "Really, everyone?" Jane says. "Everyone alive?"

"Well. He's not a pedophile. And he's not into incest," Ivy says. "And he knows I'd castrate him if he ever came near me. But he has this way of seeing what's beautiful about everyone."

"Is he even attracted to, like, Mrs. Vanders?"

"I'm hoping his feeling for her is more of a mother-son thing," Ivy says with a chuckle. "Beyond that, I'm not going to think about it."

"Well, what about your brother?"

Ivy purses her lips. "In the case of Patrick, we have to make a distinction between attraction and intention. I mean, Ravi has principles. He wouldn't consider Patrick that way, not seriously. Not that it would ever happen anyway, because Patrick is straight. But regardless, Ravi wouldn't go there, because Ravi thinks Kiran should be with Patrick."

There's a lot to file away here, and questions Jane wants to ask but can't, quite, because they're not really relevant. Like, is *Ivy* straight? And why is she so easy to talk to? Even when she keeps switching over, intentionally, to a different, insincere version of herself?

"Ivy?" Jane starts.

Then, when Ivy responds with an appreciative *Hm?*, she sighs and says, "Never mind."

"Is that a jellyfish?" says Ivy. "Showing under your sleeve?"

"Yes," Jane says, growing warm, and suddenly shy.

"Can I see it?"

Carefully, Jane rolls her sleeve up to her shoulder. The jellyfish's long, detailed arms and tentacles, then its golden body, come into view, anchored on her skin.

"Holy shit," says Ivy, in a voice of awe. She reaches out and traces the bottom of the bell with a finger. "That is *gorgeous,*" she says. "Did you design it?"

Why does Ivy's admiration make Jane so sad about Ivy lying? "It's based on a photo my aunt took," she says. "My aunt Magnolia. She raised me. Then she died. Maybe you knew that? She was an underwater photographer. She used to teach me to breathe the way a jellyfish moves." It's a ridiculous mouthful, but Ivy is still touching Jane, and Jane needs her to know all of it, all the parts of it.

Ivy's finger drops. She frowns.

"Ivy?" says Jane.

"Ivy-bean," says a deep, scratchy voice. It's Mrs. Vanders, taking big, hurried steps toward them. "Where's Ravi?"

"I think he's having breakfast," says Ivy thickly, her eyes on her camera.

"I need him," says Mrs. Vanders. "I need to position him in front of the Vermeer."

"Why?" says Ivy. "Is something wrong with the Vermeer?"

"I just want him to stand in front of it," says Mrs. Vanders, "and not notice anything wrong about it, so that I can stop worrying about the damn thing and apply myself to the million tasks surrounding a gala. Send him to me, but don't tell him anything! You," she says, narrowing eyes on Jane. "I have things to say to you."

"I've been getting that impression," Jane responds. "Can we talk now?"

"I'm busy," says Mrs. Vanders. "Find me! And say nothing to anyone!" She spins around and heads back the way she came.

"Ivy?"

"Yeah?"

"Earlier, in the kitchen, Mr. Vanders said that he knew my aunt Magnolia."

"Yeah?"

"Did *you* know my aunt Magnolia?"

Ivy opens her mouth to answer. Before she can say anything, Mrs. Vanders pops her head around the entrance to the bridge again and yells, "Ivy! No more dawdling! Find Ravi!"

Ivy takes hold of Jane's arm right where the jellyfish tentacles reach to her elbow. She grips so hard that it hurts. "Talk to Mrs. Vanders," she says. "Please?" Then she turns away and heads down the stairs, leaving Jane to rub her arm and nurse her resentment.

The moment Ivy disappears, Ravi enters the receiving hall. He's carrying two pieces of toast in one hand and a bowl of fruit in the other.

Taking a bite of toast, he jogs up the western stairs and crosses onto Jane's bridge.

"Breakfast too sedentary for you?" asks Jane wearily.

"I wanted to say hi to you again," says Ravi.

"Ravi," says Jane, ever so slightly turning a shoulder to him, "aren't you with Lucy?"

"On and off," he says. "Off at the moment."

"Oh," says Jane, confused that this information pleases her. "I'm sorry."

"Well," he says, "to answer your question, yes. Every meal in this house is too sedentary for me."

"Then," says Jane, "that means you'll want to keep moving."

Ravi chuckles, then surprises Jane by doing just what she suggests. He doesn't even crowd her too much as he passes. "I'm sorry to say that another soul awaits me this morning," he says as he walks away. "What about you, do you have any interest in the universe's multiple realities? Or are you like my twin, opposed to cosmology?"

"What are you talking about?"

"Come with me," he says.

"Where?" Jane asks, thinking partly of Mrs. Vanders, but mostly of this strange little interplay she seems to have going with Kiran's panoptically attracted brother.

"You do know what cosmology is, right?" Ravi says. "The study of the cosmos? You're not confusing it with cosmetology? The application of makeup?"

"Condescending donkey," says Jane, then adds, "No offense, Eeyore."

Ravi chuckles as he steps away. "Your choice."

Jane watches him move gracefully up the stairs. She's completely forgotten to tell him that Mrs. Vanders is looking for him.

"Oh," she says, meaning to call out to him. But in that moment, a kid darts into the receiving hall below her. This house is like Grand Central Station.

Jane has seen this girl before: She's the one who was digging up the garden yesterday in the rain. Carrying something close to her chest, she goes to a side table, pushes some lilacs aside, and slides the thing onto the empty space. Jane can't see it properly; there are too many lilac branches in the way.

It seems almost to Jane as if this little girl waited until the lilac ladies left, then snuck into the hall just when she wouldn't be seen. The girl darts out again, taking the path under Jane that leads into the Venetian courtyard—spots Jane up on her perch, and freezes. She glares at Jane for a millisecond before continuing on, leaving Jane wondering if it's utterly irrational to imagine that she looks like the news pictures of the oldest Panzavecchia child, Grace. The one who vanished from her school the same day her parents tried to rob a bank. The one with the mnemonic memory devices.

Ravi is long gone. Mrs. Vanders is long gone. Kiran is long gone and that child is just gone; only Jasper remains, still hopping and wiggling and occasionally whining on his landing. Piles of lilac branches litter the checkerboard floor below, like berries on ice cream.

The house is suddenly still, like it's holding its breath.

Then the gunshots of Kiran's boots touch Jane's ears once more and Kiran stalks into the hall.

She walks to the pile of lilac branches on the floor. She picks one up, shakes the water out of it, then throws it back down again, seemingly just for the violence of it. Then she wraps her arms around her chest, hugging herself, pressing her chin to her collarbone. She doesn't see Jane. Jane's ability to see Kiran is an intrusion into Kiran's personal pain; Jane knows this. Still, Jane reaches out, unable to stop herself. She wants to help.

"Kiran?"

Kiran's mask slides into place. She raises her eyes to Jane. "Oh," she says. "Hi, Janie."

"Are you okay?"

"Why does everyone keep asking me that?" she says. "Do I seem so *not* okay?"

"You seem sort of . . . missing."

"Missing!" Kiran says. "That's just lovely. Why did I even come here if people are going to accuse me of being missing?"

"Did Patrick confess to anything yet?"

Kiran's face flickers with irritation. "I forgot I'd told you about that. No. He's said nothing. You're sweet to remember."

"What do you think it's about?"

"I don't know," Kiran says, "and I'm trying not to care."

The lilac ladies come trooping back into the hall with more armfuls of empty vases. Kiran swings her back to them so they can't see her expression.

"Do you ever feel," she says to Jane, "like you're trapped in the wrong version of your life?"

This extraordinary question fixes Jane in place. She's felt exactly that way, ever since Aunt Magnolia died and the wrong version of Jane's life wrapped its arms tight around her, dove into the water, dragged her to the bottom, and held her there while she drowned.

"Yes," says Jane.

"People tell you that what happens to you is a direct result of the choices you make," Kiran says, "but that's not fair. Half the time, you don't even realize that the choice you're about to make is significant."

"That's true," says Jane. "My parents died in a plane crash when I was one. Most everyone on the left side of the plane lived and most everyone on the right side died. My parents picked seats on the right, randomly, for no reason."

Kiran nods. "Octavian went to an art auction in Vegas but his flight was delayed. He got in so late that he missed breakfast, so he caught a cab, and told the cabbie to find him a restaurant out in the desert, where he could drink a Bloody Mary and eat eggs while surrounded by flowering cactuses. The cabbie told him forget it and drove him to the Bellagio, where he got lost trying to find the restaurant and ran into a lady drawing sketches of the layout of the casino. He asked her if she was planning a heist. She told him her name was Charlotte, she was an interior designer, and she was redesigning the casino floor. Now she's my stepmother. Could that be more random?"

"On the other hand," Jane says, "they did *decide* to get married. Some things happen because we choose them."

"Right," says Kiran. "Go ahead, say it. I've chosen to be unemployed and useless."

"Kiran," Jane says, remembering Colin's words to Octavian. "You're not useless. You just haven't found your path. I mean, welcome to my world. I don't have a path either. I'm a way bigger moper than you are."

"You're not moping," Kiran says. "You're grieving."

Kiran has a way of saying words that send a beam of light through the bullshit. *I'm grieving. It's like pushing my will through molasses.*

"Come walk with me," Kiran says, "and I'll tell you the mystery of Charlotte."

A heating pipe clangs somewhere and the air moves in the hall, whispering a word that she doesn't quite catch. *Charlotte.*

Jane rubs her ears, trying to decide. She wants to know more about Charlotte, sure.

But she also needs to ask Mrs. Vanders about Aunt Magnolia—though it's not as if finding out that her aunt was best buddies with Mrs. Vanders will bring Aunt Magnolia back. Jane suspects that beyond her urgency to *know* lies a crash into disappointment.

So maybe Jane should follow that Grace Panzavecchia look-alike who vanished into the depths of the house? What if that girl really *is*

Grace Panzavecchia? And what if that's the answer to the Okadas and Patrick, to the gun?

Of course there's a part of Jane that wants to follow Ravi wherever he's gone; really, wherever he goes. Ravi makes Jane feel like she's been asleep and she might finally be able to wake up.

And what's going on with the dog? The ridiculous dog, who's whining on the second-story landing, watching Jane with the single most tragic expression ever seen on the face of a dog.

A bell rings somewhere in the depths of the house, almost too distant to hear, but sweet and clear, like a wind chime. "Choose, choose," it seems to say.

Mrs. Vanders, the little girl, Kiran, Ravi, or Jasper?

The left side of the plane or the right.

Aunt Magnolia? Jane thinks. *Where should I go?*

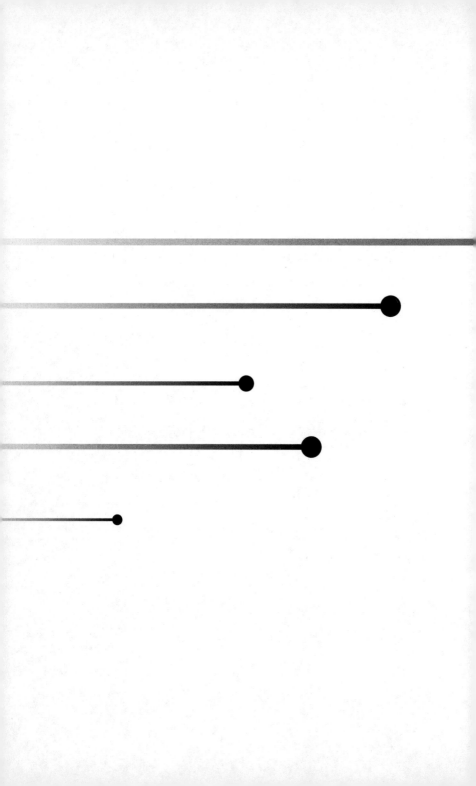

The
Missing
Masterpiece

Jane decides.

"You know what, Kiran?" she says. "I need to talk to Mrs. Vanders first. I think she knew my aunt. I'll catch up with you later, okay?"

"Okay," Kiran says, shrugging, disappointed. "Text me."

"I will."

Kiran wanders away.

When Jane reaches Jasper on his landing, he jumps up, circles around her, then runs at the back of her legs in his usual way. She scrambles past. "Geez, Jasper!" she says. "Come with me, you're invited," but when she turns back to check on him, he's gone.

Jane finds Mrs. Vanders at the far end of the second-story east corridor, standing on one leg, studying a painting. The flat of Mrs. Vanders's bare foot is balanced against her inner thigh and her hands are in a praying position. Jane assumes it's some sort of yoga pose.

"Hello, Mrs. Vanders," she says as she approaches.

"You," says Mrs. Vanders, not looking at her, not moving. She's got a walkie-talkie clipped to the back of her black yoga pants.

"Yes," says Jane. "I heard that you knew my aunt."

"You're not Ravi," she says.

"No," says Jane. "Ravi went to visit someone. His mother, I think? Is she in the house somewhere?"

Mrs. Vanders's response is a dismissive *humph*. "You've been spending a lot of time with Ivy," she says. "What have you two been discussing?"

Jane is fed up. "Did you *not* know my aunt, then?" she says, choosing sarcasm. "Am I wasting my time?"

"My question about Ivy is relevant to your question about your aunt."

"How could that possibly be? Did they know each other?"

"Do you travel much?" counters Mrs. Vanders.

"No!" says Jane. "Why? Did you travel with her or something?"

"We have one of your aunt's travel photographs," Mrs. Vanders says. "A little yellow fish, peeking out of the mouth of a bigger fish. Your aunt had a way of . . . finding what was hidden."

"Oh," Jane says, astonished. One of her photographs, here? Jane begins to swell with pride. How appropriate that Aunt Magnolia's work should make its way into the artistic jumble of this house. "So, is that how you knew her? Did you buy the print from her?"

Mrs. Vanders sighs shortly. "Yes. That's it."

"I see," says Jane, feeling that this makes sense, except—except for the parts that don't. "But what does that have to do with Ivy?"

"I only wondered how much she'd told you."

"Right, but why would it matter? Is the photo a secret?"

"Of course not. It's hanging in the west wing," says Mrs. Vanders, flapping one hand toward the west wing and finally stepping out of her one-footed stance. She brings her face very close to the painting before her.

"Did she come here?" says Jane. "My aunt? Did you know her?"

"We communicated about the photo," says Mrs. Vanders.

"In person? Mr. Vanders seemed to know things about her, like, how she dressed."

"Oh, hell," says Mrs. Vanders, her nose only inches from the painting.

"What?"

"Forgive me," she says. "Does this picture look right to you?"

Jane, who couldn't care less about the picture, bites back an impatient retort and takes a look. It's a lovely, smallish painting of a woman writing at a desk. A frog sits on the checkerboard floor behind the woman, its dusty blue skin touched by sunlight coming through the window. The frog has a secretive expression on its face and the woman is quite intent on her work.

"Right, in what way?" says Jane.

"Like the Vermeer it is," says Mrs. Vanders. "*Lady Writing a Letter with Her Frog.*"

"I have no idea what that painting is supposed to look like."

"Johannes Vermeer," Mrs. Vanders says. "A woman with a pearl earring? A woman with her frog?"

"I know about Jan Vermeer," Jane says. "He's famous and all that. But how am I supposed to know if this one looks right? I've never seen it before."

"Well, what do you think of the light?"

Jane peers again at the painting, which has soft, bright parts and deep, dark parts that she can, in fact, appreciate. The scene seems lit with true sunlight. "Incandescent?" she ventures.

"Hm," says Mrs. Vanders. "I'm telling you, that lady looks peaky to me. She's not as incandescent as usual."

"Are you saying someone's altered the painting?"

"Altered it or forged it," says Mrs. Vanders.

"Forged it!" says Jane. "Seriously?"

"Or replaced it with a version by a different Jan Vermeer," Mrs. Vanders adds darkly.

Jane is beginning to wonder if Mrs. Vanders's physical balance is inversely proportional to her mental balance. "How much is the painting worth?" she asks.

"Vermeers are rare, and rarely change hands," says Mrs. Vanders. "It could certainly fetch a hundred million dollars at auction."

"Good *grief*," says Jane. How strange that a painting can be more valuable than the entire house it hangs in. Like a wooden box containing a diamond ring, or a ship containing Aunt Magnolia.

"Listen, I can see it's important," says Jane. "But you should talk to Ravi about it, or Lucy St. George, not me. Can you tell me more about my aunt?"

At that moment, Ravi appears at the top of the hall, walking toward Jane and Mrs. Vanders with his remaining slice of toast in one hand.

"I'll thank you to say nothing outright about the Vermeer to Ravi," Mrs. Vanders mutters sidelong to Jane.

"Why?"

"Because *I* want to handle it," says Mrs. Vanders.

Ravi carries a framed painting of lily pads under the other arm. It's recognizably impressionistic, certainly a Monet. Except that as he approaches, Jane notices that there's something . . . *off* about the frogs sitting on the lily pads. Their eyes are intelligent, but . . . dead. And the lily pads seem like they're hovering, like, actually floating around the painting. Almost. It's pretty strange.

"Have a minute, Vanny?" Ravi asks cheerfully. "I've brought you something."

Mrs. Vanders glances at the freaky Monet Ravi's carrying and comes over with a look of pure disgust. "Oh, honestly, Ravi," she says. "Please tell me you're not going to ask me to help you find a buyer for *that*."

"Please, Vanny?" Ravi says.

"You try my patience. You and your mother!"

"Yeah, yeah," says Ravi. "But you know all the specialized collectors."

"I'll think about it," says Mrs. Vanders, then adds significantly, "As we stand here in front of the Vermeer."

"Yes," Ravi says, resting his eyes placidly upon the Vermeer. Jane watches Mrs. Vanders watching Ravi.

"It's always been my favorite," says Ravi.

"Yes," says Mrs. Vanders, "it's incandescent, isn't it?" then says no more.

Jane looks from Mrs. Vanders to Ravi, still waiting for Mrs. Vanders to ask Ravi if anything seems strange to him about the Vermeer.

"I don't understand," she says.

"Mind your own business, girl," says Mrs. Vanders sharply. "I do things in my own time."

Something inside Jane snaps. "So you don't actually care if something's wrong with the Vermeer?" she says. "Was it just a convenient topic of conversation to keep you from having to answer my questions about Aunt Magnolia?"

"Something wrong?" Ravi says. "What are you talking about?"

"She thinks the lady looks peaky," Jane says, then adds belligerently, when Mrs. Vanders directs a look of fury upon her, "She used the word *forged*."

Ravi freezes. He squeaks out, "Forged?"

"I didn't want to trouble you, Ravi," says Mrs. Vanders. "Particularly just before a gala. I'm sure it's nothing."

Ravi reaches out and lifts the frame from the wall. "Screwdriver," he says with what sounds like controlled panic.

"Ravi, I think it's apparent I don't carry a screwdriver on my person."

"I do," says Jane, reaching into her pocket for the small folding knife she keeps next to her phone. It has a tiny screwdriver extension that she snaps into place, then hands to Ravi.

A moment later, Ravi is crouching on the floor, ever-so-carefully taking the frame apart. With an intense focus, he separates the canvas from the frame, then holds it up against the light. Then he reaches his fingertip toward the face of the writing lady, almost, but not quite, touching her eye.

Mutely, he sets the canvas on the floor, then hides his face in his hands.

"So, I was right," says Mrs. Vanders, sounding defeated.

"Where's Lucy?" is Ravi's muffled response.

"We'll get her immediately," says Mrs. Vanders. "Jane, do you think you could find her?"

"Happy to," she says, but before she can move, Lucy herself appears in the corridor, walking toward them.

Lucy picks up her pace, looking puzzled, when she sees Ravi kneeling on the floor. "Ravi?" she says. "Why do you have that picture out of its frame?"

"It's a fake," says Ravi, gripping his white-streaked hair.

"What?" Lucy exclaims. "How can that be?"

A tear runs down Ravi's face, then another. It's so odd to Jane, that she should be standing here while someone as rich as Ravi kneels on the floor and *cries* about the theft of a painting of unimaginable value.

"It's a perfect fake," Ravi goes on. "Perfect except that it's missing the pinprick in the lady's eye. The pinprick is family knowledge. We've never told anyone."

"What?" Lucy takes the canvas into her hands. "Give me this thing. What on earth are you talking about?"

"The lady's eye is the vanishing point of the picture," says Ravi. "Vermeer stuck a pin in the canvas. He attached a string to work out the perspective. That's why the scene is so well-balanced. Mrs. Vanders discovered the hole, years ago."

Lucy stares, incredulously, at Ravi. "You had knowledge of the way Jan Vermeer worked?" she says. "And you've never shared it with the art establishment? When we know so little about how Vermeer worked!"

"Someone has our Vermeer, Lucy!" cries Ravi in an explosion of passion. "I don't care if he painted it with a brush stuck up his ass!"

"This is unbelievable," Lucy says, holding the painting close. "It's a remarkable forgery."

"Even the cracks in the paint look right," says Mrs. Vanders grimly. "At a quick glance, anyway."

"And the edges," Ravi says, reaching up for it, taking it back from Lucy. "The edges are a match. Someone took it out of its frame and photographed them."

"It's bad this has happened now, the day before a gala," Lucy says. "The gala preparations only widen the spectrum of suspects."

"Well, it's not anyone in the Thrash family," Ravi says. "Or the Yellan family, or the Vanders family. We all know about the pinprick."

"Except that an argument could be made that you'd leave the pinprick out," Lucy says. "If the forgery had the pinprick, but was discovered, in some other way, to be a forgery, we'd know the forger was a Thrash, Vanders, or Yellan."

"Well, I know it wasn't," Ravi says stubbornly.

"Yes, all right, Ravi," says Lucy, with a sudden flash of impatience. "I'll be sure to include your sophisticated analysis in my investigation. Honestly, I still can't believe it. You're absolutely certain this is a forgery?"

Ravi answers her with a wet sniffle, then picks the folding knife up and returns it to Jane. "Where's Kiran?" he says. "Have any of you seen her?"

"She's in the winter garden," Lucy says, "playing cards with Phoebe and Colin."

Leaving the forgery and its frame strewn on the floor and his freaky Monet propped against the wall, Ravi stands. "I have to tell her," he says, gliding toward the service staircase. The door swings shut behind him.

After a moment's silence, Jane says, "Wow."

Lucy's eyes narrow on Mrs. Vanders, then on Jane, sharp and dark. In that moment, Jane can imagine Lucy sitting down with drug dealers and duping them into handing over a priceless masterpiece.

She knows it's Lucy's job, but really, it's too absurd, that Lucy could imagine *she* has anything to do with it.

Still, Jane gets it, because her view on every other person in the house has also changed. Until she can work her mind through every possibility, she's not going to trust anyone either.

Since that includes Mrs. Vanders and Lucy, Jane says, "Good-bye, then," and goes to her rooms.

Jasper is waiting outside her door. When she lets him in, he burrows under the bed. Soon his soft snores emerge, which is cozy, and helpful somehow, like fuel.

Outside the morning room windows, she sees Mr. Vanders digging in the gardens in the same area the little girl was digging yesterday. He works with a trowel in a slow and graceful manner, as if the act of digging is the point, rather than achieving holes. He stops for a moment to sneeze. Jane wants to lean out and yell at him that nothing's ever going to grow out there if everyone keeps hacking at it.

She turns back to the room of umbrellas, not really looking at them, her thoughts circling the forged Vermeer. On the one hand, it's a relief that a house mystery is coming into the light, for everyone to know and to talk about. On the other hand, the more she learns, the less things make sense. And she really doesn't want all of this to lead to the revelation that Ivy's mixed up in art theft somehow.

Though if Ivy, or anyone, is mixed up in art theft, Jane supposes it's better to know.

Dammit.

She snatches up a sketchbook, flips past umbrella sketches to a blank page, and begins a list, starting with the most blatantly suspicious.

Patrick Yellan
Philip Okada
Phoebe Okada
— *Philip sneaking around with a gun. All three of them talking about the Panzavecchias? Philip seen in a back room in the attics, now gone someplace mysterious, lying about being a germophobe. Phoebe lying about Philip. Patrick "has something to confess" to Kiran but never actually confesses. Broods. Has easy access to boats. Was out late with Ravi.*

Gritting her teeth, Jane adds the next name.

Ivy Yellan
— *Keeping something from me. Says she's taking photos of the art but is she? Has blueprints of the house including the art and decoration. Says she knows all the house's secrets. Is "saving up" for college. Seems to resent Mrs. Vanders.*

Now she decides she may as well round out the servants.

Mrs. Vanders
— *Total control freak. Likes to control what everyone does and doesn't know, where everyone goes, whom everyone talks to, and what they talk about. She's Patrick's boss. Was being cagey about admitting her forgery suspicions to Ravi. Why?*
— *On the other hand, she's the one who pointed the forgery out to me, making her an unlikely suspect.*

Mr. Vanders

— *Seen with a small child yesterday. Seen with blueprints today. Evasive. Currently digging in the garden. (Can a painting be buried safely?)*

Cook

— *Never around.*

Random gala staff

She moves on to the other residents and guests.

Lucy St. George

— *Art PI, so she knows a lot about how heists work. Her father, Buckley, is an art dealer (as are her cousin and boyfriend). Recently lost a Rubens. On-again, off-again with Ravi. (Any bad feelings there? Revenge?)*

Colin Mack

— *Also knows a lot about the art world/art theft. Buckley is his uncle. Kiran doesn't seem to like him even though they're dating (but Kiran doesn't seem to like anyone else either). Was being a jerk to Lucy, his cousin, at breakfast.*

Kiran Thrash

— *Unhappy. Mad at everyone. Hates the house, hates the art. Would she do something to act out?*

Ravi Thrash

— *Loves the art. The Vermeer is his favorite, he slept under it as a* kid. Loves it enough to steal it? Is he a good actor? Why was Mrs. Vanders being evasive around him—does she suspect him?

Octavian Thrash
— *Doesn't seem to care about the missing Brancusi.*
[NOTE TO SELF: The missing Brancusi! Surely this matters more now that the Vermeer is gone too!]
— *His wife has disappeared. Seems depressed and antisocial. Mad at Ravi. Keeps vampiric hours. Are the Vermeer and the Brancusi insured? Don't rich people fake thefts sometimes to collect on insurance?*

Charlotte Thrash
— *Mother may have been a con artist. Was drawing floor plans of a Vegas casino when Octavian met her—suspicious? Has been missing for a month, which is super-weird. When was the Vermeer forged? Could she have taken it with her? (When was the Brancusi last seen?)*

Jane chews the end of her pencil, contemplating her list, trying to decide if anyone in the house is safe for her to talk to. Jasper, droopy-eyed and curious, waddles into the room.

Jane adds:

Jasper Thrash
— *The only individual in the house (besides me) who's definitely innocent.*

She turns to a new page. She writes:

What to do?

Possibilities:

— Talk to Mrs. Vanders, who's got to be innocent. Find out whom she suspects. Ask her probing questions about Ivy.

— Talk to Lucy St. George, who probably has inspirations about what's going on.

— Confront Ivy.

"What do you think, Jasper?" she says.

He comes closer and leans against her boots, gazing up at her with what Jane decides is resolution.

"Personally," she says, "I like the first two ideas better than the third."

Jasper leans harder.

"Ready?" Jane says. "Let's go."

She heads toward the center of the house, figuring she'll check the kitchens for Mrs. Vanders.

As she approaches the stairs, she hears voices in the receiving hall, then sees Kiran and Colin standing together. Kiran has her arms crossed tight, as if in self-defense.

Jane starts down toward them.

"I don't know," she hears Kiran say. "It sounds like Mrs. Vanders was looking at it and got a funny feeling."

"Have you seen it?" says Colin. "It's beautiful."

"Yeah, I wouldn't have been able to tell it's a fake," says Kiran. "But the art is Vanny's thing, after all."

"Don't you think it's interesting that Philip left last night?" says Colin. "I was just pressing Phoebe about it and she told me he'll be moving to a different remote location every day with some rich patient of his who's on some trip. Doesn't that sound convenient?"

"Except that I know plenty of rich people who'd think it was completely reasonable to expect their doctor to fly in to treat their tummyache," says Kiran. "Imagine the retinue Buckley would bring if he went on some complicated trip."

"Oh, come on. Buckley's not that bad."

"God, you suck up to him," says Kiran.

Jane has reached the second-story landing, where Jasper blocks her like a short, hotdog-shaped linebacker, growling when she tries to sidestep him.

Sighing, Jane pauses to scribble in her sketchbook, turning to face the wall so it'll look like she's taking interested notes on the art rather than on the private conversations of people nearby.

Buckley St. George, she writes. *Rich and spoiled.* Then she draws an asterisk next to Philip's name, because Phoebe's explanation sounds ridiculous to her; then she writes, *Why is Colin dating Kiran when she's so awful to him?*

Someone coughs behind her.

It's Colin, standing a few steps below, looking up at her with raised eyebrows. "Hi," he says.

"Hi," says Jane, closing her notebook.

"What are you doing?" asks Colin. "Taking notes on that painting?"

Jane glances at the painting she's supposedly taking notes on. It's the tall oil of the room with the drying umbrella. "I was taking notes on the umbrella," she says reasonably, then remembers that this won't signify anything to Colin, who doesn't know she makes umbrellas.

"Sure," he says. "I'd suspect you of planning a heist, except no one would steal that picture."

He's teasing; or at any rate, Jane can tell he's not seriously accusing her of anything. "Why not?" she says, seeing an opportunity to learn more about heists. "It's nice."

"It's too big to move and it's not worth anything."

"Maybe I'm stealing it because I like it."

"It's by a painter of unremarkable talent," Colin says.

"Do you think so?" Jane says, looking closer. "I mean, I guess it's not amazing—"

"It belongs to no particular school, either," he says. "Knowing Octavian, I bet it was a flea market purchase."

"Well, but it has its charms, especially for fans of umbrellas. Why are you so determined to convince me it's worthless?"

"Because," says the voice of Lucy, who rounds the corner from somewhere or other, "if Colin sees someone focused on a picture he thinks is worth nothing, he begins to worry that he's missing something."

This surprises a grin onto Jane's face, which makes Lucy laugh. "He's my cousin," she says. "I know him."

"So, Colin," says Jane, "you're trying to convince me you're right because you're afraid you're wrong?"

A crash below interrupts whatever indignant thing Colin's about to say. The crash is followed by a series of yells. Jane, Lucy, and Colin look at one another in astonishment. Then, together, they rush to the railing, Jasper crowding Jane's feet.

"Octavian!" Ravi screams, standing in the receiving hall and waving something around in his hands. "Octavian!" On the checkerboard floor, beside him, a vase lies shattered. Water and lilacs are strewn about. "Octavian!" he screams again, his voice straining out of his throat, tearing at the ceiling.

"Colin," says Lucy breathlessly. "Is that the bottom half of the Brancusi sculpture? The pedestal for the fish that always sits in the receiving hall?"

"Yes," says Colin in wonderment.

"But where's the top half? Where's the fish?" says Lucy.

"How should I know?"

"Colin," Lucy says, in a voice suddenly made of steel. *"Where is the fish?"*

"I don't know!" Colin says. "You're the detective, not me! What do you think, *I* broke it off?"

Lucy waves a dismissive hand at her cousin and starts down the stairs toward Ravi. Cleaners and decorators are lining up at every level to stare down at Ravi's fit. Ivy is also down there now, standing next to Kiran and Phoebe, all of them gaping at Ravi.

A strange sense of panicked relief fizzes through Jane. Now the missing Brancusi is coming out into the light too. And Jane remembers seeing the Grace Panzavecchia look-alike girl bringing something into the receiving hall, leaving it on one of the side tables. Had that been the pedestal?

Jane realizes suddenly that the white plush bag with ducks on it that Philip Okada had been carrying was a *diaper* bag. Baby Leo Panzavecchia is sick; Baby Leo is missing; Philip Okada is a doctor.

What's going on here? Some sort of complicated conspiracy involving the Panzavecchias, their doctor, the servants, and art theft? Jane studies Ivy, who's watching Ravi with calm concern but who doesn't look particularly surprised. Patrick, she notes, isn't here.

"Let me see that," Lucy says to Ravi, trying to take the pedestal from his hands, but Ravi won't give it to her. He yells over her, barely noticing her, "Octavian! Octavian!"

Finally, Mrs. Vanders sweeps into the hall. "Be quiet!" she says. "What in the name of all that's reasonable is the matter with you?"

"This," Ravi yells, shaking the pedestal at her. "This is what's the matter with me!"

When Mrs. Vanders sees the pedestal, she freezes. Jane can't see her face from the landing, but when Mrs. Vanders reaches a hand out to Ravi, he passes the pedestal to her. With one finger, Mrs. Vanders touches a spot in the middle of its flat, mirrored surface, then exhales as if in relief.

"Let me see it," Lucy says. Mrs. Vanders passes the pedestal to Lucy.

Lucy touches the same spot, then nods at Mrs. Vanders, who's watching her closely.

"Ravi?" Lucy says. "The sculpture was removed cleanly from the base. Assuming the sculpture itself is unbroken, it should be easy to reattach it, once it's found."

"Once it's found?" Ravi says. "Once it's found!?" he shouts.

"Calm down," Mrs. Vanders says to him. "Ravi, take a breath. Tell me where you got this pedestal."

Ravi points to a row of side tables. "It was sitting there," he says. "Someone—put—a vase of lilacs on it—as if it were a party decoration!" he screams.

"All right," Mrs. Vanders says. "Take another breath."

"It wasn't there last night," he says. "Someone took the whole thing away, broke off the fish, then put the pedestal back. What kind of lunatic would do that? And if this is what they've done to the Brancusi"—his voice grows almost hysterical—"what have they done to the Vermeer? I want a list of everyone who's come and gone in this house. Now!"

"Very well," Mrs. Vanders says sarcastically. "That would be the caterers, the musicians, the extra cleaning staff, the actual residents of the house, and your guests. Shall we start the interrogations now or later?"

"Why do you sound like that?" cries Ravi. "Don't you appreciate what's happened here?" He turns suddenly on Phoebe Okada. "Where's your husband?" he spits at her. "He's gone off the island, hasn't he?"

Phoebe stares back at Ravi, her face made of stone. "I'm going to pretend you didn't just imply that Philip stole from you," she says. Then she strides out of the room, disappearing into the Venetian courtyard, her face closed and intense.

"Truly, listen to yourself, Ravi," says Mrs. Vanders. "Philip Okada is a physician who answered an emergency call."

"Have you contacted the FBI?" says Ravi.

"How?" exclaims Mrs. Vanders. "Telepathically, while we've been standing here enjoying your tantrum?"

"Wait, you *haven't* contacted the FBI?" cries Ravi. "Do you even *remember* about the Vermeer?"

"Ravi, of course I'll call the proper authorities," says Mrs. Vanders. "But you need to take a breath and realize that this thing with the Brancusi is very different from a fine forgery of a Vermeer. This has the indications of an accident, or a prank."

"Who would play a prank with an irreplaceable work of pure genius?" Ravi says, his voice rising again. "Call the FBI, the CIA, and Interpol! My art could be in Hong Kong by now! Lucy!"

"I'm right here, Ravi," says Lucy, standing beside him, still holding the pedestal to her chest. Her face is white and she actually looks a little nauseated.

"Lucy," Ravi says, grabbing on to her shoulders, practically shaking her. "Lucy. Will you find my art?"

"Ravi, sweetie," she says, "I'll do all I can."

"Thank you," he says. "Thank you." When he lets Lucy go, she stumbles, which he barely notices, because he's swung back on Mrs. Vanders.

"We should cancel the gala," he tells her.

"We're not canceling the gala," she responds.

"The gala is the perfect distraction if someone is trying to slip out with stolen art," Ravi says.

"Ravi Thrash," Mrs. Vanders says. "There has been a gala in this house every season for over a hundred years. Neither war nor the Great Depression nor Prohibition nor the death of three Octavian Thrashes has stopped the gala from taking place."

Ravi glares at Mrs. Vanders. Then he takes a step away from her, raises his face to the upper levels, and roars, "Octavian! Wake up and get the hell down here!"

"Go to his room, Ravi," Ivy says quietly. "You know he won't get out of bed in the daytime."

Ravi turns to Ivy then, his shoulders slumping. "Maybe you should come with me, Ivy-bean," he says. "Will you come with me and keep me calm?"

"I'll come with you if you keep yourself calm," says Ivy.

"I'm sorry we lost your fish," Ravi says, sounding like a little boy.

"It's not my fish," Ivy says, gently. "It's your fish."

"But you're the one who's always loved it most," he says, then reaches to put an arm around Ivy. They walk together toward the stairs and begin to climb.

Mrs. Vanders stares at them as they go, a wary expression on her face. Then she holds a hand out to Lucy without even glancing at her. Lucy passes the sculptureless pedestal back to Mrs. Vanders. Lucy's eyes flicker upward once, to Colin, who's still standing beside Jane, white-faced. Lucy pulls her phone from her pocket.

"Are you okay?" Jane asks Colin, because he doesn't look well.

"It's hard to see Ravi so upset," Colin says.

"He sure knows how to make a scene," Jane says, wondering if this is why Mrs. Vanders didn't want to put ideas in Ravi's head about the Vermeer.

But why is she being so cagey about calling the FBI?

"The truth is, I'm worried about Lucy too," Colin says. "It's a humiliation for something like this to happen right under her nose, especially on the tail of losing that Rubens."

"Right," Jane says.

"It's as if the thief is making a public point of not taking Lucy seriously as a private investigator," says Colin. "It's very personal."

"Who do you think did it?"

Colin breathes a laugh, then shrugs. "Someone foolish."

"Isn't it scary?" says Jane. "To think there's a thief in the house?"

"Sure," he says. "But don't worry too much. We've got Lucy on the case."

"Do you know who Lucy suspects?"

"She doesn't share that stuff with me," says Colin, with a sharp little resentment that makes Jane curious. She badly wants to get back to her rooms, where she can think through all these new developments in peace. But as she turns to go, Colin says, "Kiran mentioned you make umbrellas. Is that what you meant earlier when you said you were artistic?"

Jane is startled. "It's nothing," she says, trying to build a dam that will hold back Colin's interest. "Just a hobby."

"I appreciate that," he says. "Still, it's a pretty cool hobby."

"Thanks," Jane says, turning to go again, but finding that he moves with her. Jane doesn't want Colin to go with her. She stops again.

"I'm sorry," he says immediately. "I swear I'm not stalking you. I'm just interested in the umbrellas."

"I don't really want to talk about them," Jane says, "and I definitely don't want to show them to you."

"Fair enough," Colin says. "Forgive me—I can't help myself, really. It's my job to be nosy whenever I hear about some new, interesting kind of art."

"I'm only a beginner!" Jane says. "They're a mess! They're not art!"

Colin is all outstretched, surrendering hands and a smiling, open face. "I know," he says. "Again, I'm sorry. Forget I brought it up. Here, I'll prove it to you by walking you to your rooms and whispering not a single word about umbrellas. Okay?"

"I suppose," Jane says.

As they walk up the stairs, Jasper follows.

"The Brancusi is an odd choice for a thief," Colin says. "It's not small. It'd be hard to sneak it out."

"What does the fish look like?" asks Jane. "Will I know it if I see it?"

"It looks like a long, flat, ovalish, white sliver of marble," Colin says. "Very abstract, as fish go."

"Is it—beautiful?"

"It's not really my taste," he says, "but it's certainly valuable."

"Is the fish worth anything without its pedestal?"

"Sure, it's worth something," says Colin. "But Brancusi's pedestals are critically important to his sculptures. That fish is meant to balance on that particular pedestal. They go together. Really, it would be ridiculous to display them separately."

"So, then, this is a pretty strange theft."

"Yes," says Colin. "It's a kind of vandalism, really. Will you just look at this crazy kitsch?" he says, tapping the head of Captain Polepants with his foot as they go by. "Uncle Buckley loves this stuff."

"Really?" says Jane, wanting to know more about the spoiled and famous Uncle Buckley. "I guess I've been imagining someone very . . . sophisticated."

"Oh, he's got eclectic tastes too. Actually—oh, never mind," says Colin, raising another yielding hand. "I forgot I'm not allowed to say anything about umbrellas."

He's baiting Jane. It's working too. Now Jane really wants to know what Colin was going to say about Uncle Buckley and umbrellas. "As long as it's not about *my* umbrellas, I don't mind."

"Well," he says, grinning, "I was only going to say that Uncle Buckley collects umbrellas. He practically has one for every outfit."

"He does?"

"Oh, yes. Polka dots, stripes, floral prints. He's always wishing more people did representational things too, like, making the canopy look like the head of a frog, or a Volkswagen Beetle, or whatever."

"Really!"

"He's the sort of person who could help you someday," Colin says, "if you ever decided you were ready to show anyone your umbrellas. But now I've probably crossed the line again, right?"

"What do you mean, help me?" Jane asks, because she can't stop herself. She makes representational umbrellas; her eggshell umbrella is representational. It's one of her best, really, one of the few she might be willing to show someone.

"Well," says Colin, "he finds buyers for art. I understand that you think your umbrellas aren't art. But if you keep working at it, maybe someday they will be, and a partnership with someone like Uncle Buckley is the sort of thing that could make an artist's life explode. Like, in a good way."

Jane has stopped in her tracks once again. *Aunt Magnolia? Is this why you wanted me to come here? So that someone would see my umbrellas, and make my life explode?*

Colin is lingering beside Jane awkwardly, scratching his head, swinging himself around to look at the art on the walls while Jane stands there having her interior monologue.

"Are you okay?" he finally asks.

"If I show you my umbrellas," Jane says, "will you remember that I'm only a beginner?"

"Of course I will," Colin says, smiling broadly. "I'm not an asshole, you know."

Jane has a feeling that whether or not Colin is an asshole, this is exactly the result he hoped for when he promised to walk her to her rooms and not whisper a word about umbrellas.

Nonetheless, Jane opens her door, takes a deep, jellyfish breath, and ushers him in.

In Jane's morning room, Colin weaves among her umbrellas, making thoughtful noises, lifting them to the light, and testing the tension of each one. He opens them with rough, swift movements that make Jane nervous that he'll hurt them.

"Hey!" she says. "Gentle! They're handmade!"

Jasper comes and leans against Jane's feet, watching Colin anxiously. Bending, twirling, studying each creation fiercely, Colin reminds Jane of Sherlock. "It couldn't be more obvious," Jane expects him to say as he lifts her ivory and black lace spiderweb specimen to the light, thrusting it upward like a saber. "The butler did it, in the library, with the spiderweb umbrella."

What he actually says is, "You know, until this moment, I've never understood my uncle's fascination with umbrellas. Some of these are really something."

To Jane's alarm, her eyes fill with tears. She immediately turns away from him and touches her sleeve to her face.

"Why a spiderweb?" he says.

"We had a spider," says Jane, sniffling, "one winter, living in our kitchen window. My aunt wouldn't let me kill it. We named it Charlotte, of course."

"And this one?" he says, lifting one up that seems red, until the light hits it and it turns various shades of purple.

Jane is rubbing her ears. "It's made of two translucent fabrics," she says, "red on the outside and blue inside, so it seems like it's glowing different purples, depending on the light. I tried a yellow and blue one too, to make green, but the green gave people a sickly pallor."

"Uncle Buckley would appreciate that you consider those factors," says Colin. "Do they work? I mean, are they waterproof?"

"A few of them have little leaks at the seams," Jane says. "Some of them open more smoothly than others. Some of them are a little too heavy, as you probably noticed."

"Yeah, some of them are heavy."

"But I use them when it rains," says Jane. "They work well enough."

"You'll get better at the engineering," says Colin. "It's clear you have the talent, and the drive."

Jane can't respond to this without more tears, so she keeps her mouth shut.

"Will you let me take one to Uncle Buckley?" Colin says. "I think he might like to deal them."

"After what I said about them leaking?"

"Well, not the leaking ones, obviously."

"But, don't you see how crooked they are? Can't you see the uneven seams?"

"They're handmade," he says. "That makes them charming. There are people who would pay hundreds of dollars for these umbrellas."

"Oh, get out," Jane says.

"Rich people love to spend money," Colin says. "If you let me show one to Uncle Buckley, we may be able to help you take advantage of it. It'll make his day, which will make my day. I haven't found anything interesting for him in a while."

"Well," Jane says, flabbergasted. "Sure, I guess."

"I should really take a few," he says. "Three or four, to show your brand."

My brand? Jane can't begin to think what her brand is. But as Colin makes his selections, she can see that he's choosing some of her favorites. The copper-rose and brown satin that she held on the boat because it seemed appropriate for a heroic journey. The oblong, deep-canopied bird's egg umbrella that's pale blue with brown speckles. The dome umbrella, designed, both inside and out, to look like the dome of the Pantheon in Rome.

"I've never been there," Jane says, "but Aunt Magnolia would talk about it as if it was a magical place. She said it rains right through the hole at the top of the dome, straight down into the building, but I didn't think that would make for a practical umbrella design, so from the outside I show the view inside, and from the inside I show a view of the night sky. It's painted silk, with glitter glued on for stars."

"What are you working on now?" he asks.

"I'm—not sure," Jane says. "I had an idea this morning, but now I'm getting a different idea."

"Excellent. You artists must follow the muse," he says, his arms full of Jane's umbrellas. She follows him into the bedroom, wanting to touch them again, to say good-bye. Her babies.

"When will I hear back about them?" she asks anxiously.

"I'll send them today on the mail run," Colin says. "Uncle Buckley's in the city. He'll probably get in touch in the next couple days."

After Colin leaves, Jasper goes into the bedroom and burrows under the bed.

"Fat lot of help you are," Jane calls after him.

At her worktable, she absently strokes a dusty blue fabric at the top of her pile, noting an unevenness in the dye, like a watermark, all across it. It reminds her of something. What? It's a flaw in the fabric, but there's something familiar about it.

Using her waterproof fabric glue, Jane begins to glue points of glitter in various blues, sparingly, with no particular pattern, across the fabric, to accentuate the unevenness. She still wants to make the brown-and-gold self-defense umbrella, but right now, this uneven blue seems the right backdrop to her thoughts. Jane does some of her best thinking while she's making umbrellas, if she's working on the right umbrella.

As she slices the uneven blue fabric into gores, Jane comes up with one possible story that makes sense of everything. Sort of. What if the Panzavecchias, in addition to being microbiologists, are art thieves, in cahoots with the servants at Tu Reviens, and together they staged a disappearance, so that no one would suspect them when they subsequently stole the Vermeer? And their little daughter Grace wants to be an art thief like her parents, so she stole the Brancusi? But since she's eight, she did it badly? Like, maybe she broke the fish part off by accident, then, in regret, returned the pedestal?

Or—maybe she *doesn't* want to be an art thief, maybe she hates that her parents are art thieves, and maybe her *parents* stole the Brancusi. Then, in rebellion, she returned whatever part of it she could get her hands on?

Jane can see the glaring holes in these theories. They don't explain the Mafia, the involvement of the Okadas, or why Mrs. Vanders would have drawn attention to the forgery in the first place, among other things.

Jane might think that there were two *separate* mysteries in the house, one about the servants, Okadas, and Panzavecchias, and one about art theft—if only she hadn't seen that girl putting something on one of the tables in the receiving hall.

She fashions a rosette for the place at the top of the canopy where the gores meet. *If I were a better detective,* she thinks, *I would've thought to check the receiving hall to make sure she didn't actually put something else there, not the pedestal at all.*

I suppose I should check it now.

Jane pushes her gores back, sets her glue down, and wipes her hands on her work apron, leaving a tiny constellation of stars. As she stands, she notices little carvings on her worktable: a blue whale and its calf, swimming along the corner of the table's surface. Moving her supplies aside so she can search the rest of the table, she also finds a shark and its shark babies along the top edge.

Ivy made this worktable, then. Jane traces the carvings with her finger, wishing she didn't like them so much.

"Jasper?" she calls out, pulling off the apron and grabbing her sketchbook. His nose emerges from under the bed as she passes through the bedroom. Together they leave the rooms.

"Aye, aye, Captain Polepants," Jane says.

Flipping open her sketchbook as she walks, she glances through her list of names, again wondering whom to trust. It's amazing, really, how easy it is to imagine a story around each and every person, turning that person into a con artist. Lucy, for example, is perfectly positioned to steal art. No one would suspect her, and she could frame someone else for the crime. Kiran has nothing but free time, goes wherever she wants, whenever she wants, and doesn't exactly put out a vibe of beneficence. Mrs. Vanders and Ravi could be in on it together, staging tragic discoveries of missing art to deflect attention from their involvement. After all, isn't Ravi apparently known for acquiring peculiar Monets from someone, probably his mother? Couldn't the Monet be a forgery? And didn't he bring it straight to Mrs. Vanders?

With a weary sigh, Jane flips her sketchbook closed.

On the second-story landing, before Jasper can begin his usual blockade, she takes the initiative and crosses the bridge to the opposite landing. With a protesting yip, Jasper hesitates, then sits his rump in place, apparently deciding to wait there.

Taking the west stairs down to the receiving hall, Jane wanders around the room, her big boots echoing on the checkered floor. The air reeks of lilacs. The various side tables are crowded with vases but also contain a few small, stark, modern-looking sculptures. A big family photo sits on one, Octavian with one arm around Ravi and his other arm around a blond, white, youngish-looking woman. The blond woman has an arm around Kiran, who doesn't look happy, exactly, but nor does she look like she wants to stab someone, which might be the most one can expect from a family photo of Kiran. Ravi is beaming out of the frame. Octavian too has an aspect of pleasure, maybe also of quiet pride. The blond woman, who must be Charlotte, is smiling, but with a touch of confusion, or distraction. Her eyes are focused on something far away.

Jane picks it up, looking closer. Golden-orange nasturtiums hang on pink walls in the background of the photo. Jane wonders, could this be what the little girl delivered to these tables? Why not? It makes no less sense than anything else.

She's trying to rub away a strange, bloated sensation in her ears when she hears the closing of a camera shutter.

With a grim unwillingness, Jane looks up at the third-story bridge. Ivy stands there, her camera raised to her face. She's aiming it at a woman on the west landing who's dusting a suit of medieval armor with a big, pink feather duster.

If I asked, Jane thinks, *she'd tell me she's taking a picture of the suit of armor.* But Jane doesn't ask. She just watches Ivy, until Ivy lowers her camera and sees her.

At the sight of her, Ivy flushes. Then her eyes drop and her mouth hardens with something like resentment. She turns and strides away.

Jane feels as if someone has punched her lungs. *Okay,* she thinks. *Ivy is mad at me for some reason. Whatever,* she thinks, clapping the photo back onto the table and standing tall. *I'm going to solve this mystery.*

Marching up the east staircase, she prepares herself for an altercation with Jasper, but this time he's just watching her with a sad, droopy face. When she passes into the second-story east wing, he quietly follows.

She stops at the end of the corridor, where a single empty bracket on the wall marks the Vermeer's previous home.

"You again?" says a faraway voice.

Jane turns to find Lucy St. George walking down the corridor toward her.

"And you again," Jane says.

"Yes," Lucy says. "I wanted another look. Or maybe I'm just wandering. I do my best thinking when I'm moving around."

"I get that."

"What are you up to?"

"Something drew me here."

"Not the weird house noises, I hope," says Lucy.

"I don't think so," says Jane. "I think I was hoping to see the painting again. The copy, I mean. I guess I should've known it wouldn't be here, on public display."

"Mrs. Vanders put it in the house safe, for the police," says Lucy dryly. "She won't even let me see it unless she's hovering over me the whole time."

"Has she called the police, then?"

"So she says."

"You don't think she has?"

"Well, I have contacts with the police, and the FBI and Interpol," says Lucy. "I've asked a couple of deliberately vague leading questions, but no one's mentioned it, even though I would've thought this would be big news."

"Do you suspect her?" says Jane. "I mean, she's the one who called attention to the forgery in the first place."

"Let's just say I don't suspect her for the Vermeer," says Lucy.

A new understanding of things begins to touch Jane's mind. "Wait. Do you mean you think there are two different thieves?"

"A thief with the expertise to forge the Vermeer would never perform a hack job on a Brancusi," says Lucy. "So, yeah. Two separate thieves. One with a lot of knowledge, time, and resources, and another—" Lucy pauses, shaking her head in disbelief. "Who's arrogant and foolish."

Staring at the blank space on the wall, Jane thinks about this. She wouldn't have called Mrs. Vanders arrogant and foolish. She's bossy and controlling, but not foolish. Neither is Patrick, nor Ivy. It sounds more like . . . Lucy's idea of Colin, or of Ravi.

"I wonder which thief Ravi will hate more," says Lucy, "the competent one or the incompetent one."

"So, you don't suspect Ravi?"

"Didn't you see his histrionics?"

"Couldn't that have been an act?"

Lucy twists her mouth. "Ravi is a child. What you see is what's there. Apparently the art, at least, is capable of breaking his heart."

She says this with an interesting bitterness. Jane finds herself wondering if Lucy is jealous of the art, but it's hard to figure out how to ask. "What do you mean?"

"Oh, nothing," says Lucy. "Forget it. It's interesting Philip took off last night, isn't it? He and Phoebe are always showing up for the galas early, eager as beavers to spend time in this house. They could've had time to plan the forgery of the Vermeer."

"You're connecting them to the Vermeer? Not the Brancusi?" says Jane, with mild disappointment, because it's the Brancusi that's connected, possibly, to the little girl, and the little girl who's possibly connected to the Okadas. Then again, Lucy St. George doesn't know about the late-night secrets of the Okadas. And the little girl might've just been carrying that family portrait. "What's Phoebe Okada's job, anyway?" Jane asks.

"Oh, she's a mathematician," Lucy says, "in the computer science department at Columbia. People talk about her as if she's a genius."

This doesn't fit in anywhere, and Jane is getting frustrated. "I saw the Okadas sneaking around last night," she blurts out. "With Patrick."

Lucy's eyes narrow on her. "What do you mean? Where?"

"In the servants' quarters," says Jane. "Just after four in the morning."

"I think that's when Philip was called away," says Lucy. "Patrick was probably just helping him organize a boat."

Jane almost says something, then stops. She doesn't mention the girl, the diaper bag, the puzzling conversation, the gun. It's not that she doesn't trust Lucy; it's that she doesn't trust anyone. She needs to keep thinking.

"What's wrong with that dog?" Lucy asks.

Jane looks down to see Jasper with his head tilted sideways, cradling her ankle gently in his long mouth. He's not biting; until she sees him there, she doesn't even feel it, although now she's conscious of his drool soaking through her jeans leg.

"Jasper!" she says. "What are you doing? You look like you're waiting for the right moment to eat me whole!"

"Maybe you taste good," says Lucy with a chuckle.

Jane extricates her ankle and says, "The dog is the only person not on my list of suspects."

"I noticed you seem to be detecting," says Lucy with a grin. "Are you interested in a career like mine? Chasing down thieves, finding forgeries, recovering originals?"

Jane has been thinking about this; about copies of precious things, in particular. What if it turned out that there were copies of Aunt Magnolia? Like a Cylon, or a cloning project in some sort of sci-fi story? What if Jane's personal copy wasn't the original? Would that make Jane's aunt Magnolia less precious? Wasn't Jane's copy precious *because* she was Jane's? Jane isn't trying to solve this crime because of forged art. She's trying to solve it because she wants to understand the *people*. Ravi, Mrs. Vanders, Ivy. She wants to know why Aunt Magnolia sent her here. She wants to know what everything *means*.

"Not really," Jane says. "The truth is, I don't really care about the art being forged, not personally. I mean, I *liked* the forgery. I thought it was beautiful. Everyone's said so, everyone's been talking about it all day. And hardly anyone even noticed it was forged. Who cares if it's the one worth a hundred million dollars or not?"

Lucy is watching her with a small, wistful smile. "A lot of people care."

"Well," says Jane, "I hope Ravi gets his painting back."

"You hope that out of niceness," Lucy says. "Not because you're concerned about the money. It's for the best. My job isn't all it's cracked up to be, and Colin showed me your umbrellas. Anyone with half an artistic eye can see that that's meant to be your career."

A small implosion of happiness roots Jane to the floor. Then Lucy's phone rings. Mouthing the word *Dad*, she steps away to answer it.

Jane goes back to her rooms, still glowing from Lucy's words. There, her eyes fall upon her uneven blue umbrella in progress.

She realizes, suddenly, what the unevenness of saturation in the fabric has been reminding her of. It's the discoloration in Aunt Magnolia's eye, the blue blotch inside her brown iris. Aunt Magnolia's muddy star, with its spikes, its spokes, like a broken umbrella.

Jane is going to make an umbrella that looks like a broken umbrella, but isn't. It will be a working umbrella, but uneven and blotchy, a blue splotch umbrella that looks like Aunt Magnolia's eye. Jane's heart holds the idea, and her hands know what to do.

Sometime later, Ravi knocks on Jane's bedroom door, comes into the morning room, and stands there, glaring.

"Yes?" Jane says, the word muffled around a bite of trail mix she's found in one of her bags. She's missed lunch.

"Octavian has forbidden me from searching anyone's private property," Ravi says.

Jane's hands are measuring umbrella ribs against each other. The ribs of this umbrella will be unmatching, varying in length, which means that the canopy will be an odd, uneven shape, not round. "You're welcome to look through my things," she says.

"That's what a thief would say," Ravi says captiously. "Knowing I never would."

"I don't think, if I were a thief, I'd be the type to take that kind of chance."

Ravi's still glowering, but seems interested in this. "I think I would, if I were a thief."

"That doesn't particularly surprise me," Jane says with a grin. "You like games."

"That's true," he says, then softens his eyes on Jane. "You should play with me."

It's such an abrupt change of focus, and such an unmistakable invitation, that Jane bursts out laughing from the shock of it.

"Ravi," she says. "No, and stop it."

"Lucy and I are off again," he says. "I told you."

"I don't care."

"Okay," he says with a shrug. "Just being frank about what I like."

Just being Ravi, Jane thinks to herself.

"I keep picturing Ivy," says Ravi.

"What?" Jane says, startled.

"She used to stand in front of the Brancusi, jumping up and down, singing it a song about tuna fish. She was three."

"Oh," Jane says. "That's adorable."

"I remember her in pigtails, wearing little saddle shoes."

Jane can imagine this too, though the three-year-old she's picturing has a big camera around her neck and smells like jasmine and chlorine, which is surely ridiculous. Jane can't really picture the fish. "The way Colin described it to me," she says, "it's pretty abstract, for a fish."

"Right, but that's the beauty of it," Ravi says. "It's the human experience of a fish. There isn't a single scale or fin. It's just an oblong sliver of marble. But it has such a sense of movement." He waves a hand, beginning to move around the room in his enthusiasm, finding the spaces that are clear of umbrellas. "It practically disappears from a certain angle, like a fish flashing through water. It's a perfect representation of what you really see when you see a fish in water, before your brain tries to fill in all the things you know about what makes a fish a fish. And no one but Brancusi could capture it that way. I expect it's the reason he mounted it on a mirrored base, for the movement and the flashing."

"I'm sorry it's missing," Jane says, partly because at this point, she wants to see it for herself. "How much is it worth?"

"I don't care," Ravi says. "That's not what this is about."

Jane suspects he isn't trying to be endearing; he's just being honest. And of course he can afford not to care about the money.

It's endearing anyway. "I get that," Jane says. "But it'll matter to the investigation. I'm sure it matters to the thief."

"Yes," Ravi says, wiping his eyes tiredly with a hand. "Lucy will need to know. Lucy is going to find our fish and our Vermeer, and when she does, I'm going to tell the whole world. This is going to redeem her from the Rubens she lost."

"It's nice of you to think of your loss that way," says Jane. "As Lucy's redemption."

"I'm a nice person," Ravi says miserably. Then he picks up an umbrella, a closed one that's propped in a corner. It's not one Jane has given much thought to recently, one of her simpler, smaller affairs, with pale gores of various complementary yellows and a varnished mahogany rod and handle. With careful fingers, Ravi caresses the umbrella's ferrule and its notch, its hand spring, for all the world looking as if he appreciates the care with which Jane created it.

"May I open it?" he asks her.

The only person who's ever asked Jane's permission before opening an umbrella is Aunt Magnolia. "Yes," she says breathlessly. It really is one of her more decent umbrellas; as Ravi slides it open, she warms with sudden, unexpected pride.

"It's elegant," Ravi says. "You're talented."

"Thank you," Jane manages to say.

"For a teenager," he says with a cheeky grin.

"You were a teenager not that long ago."

"True. It makes me think of Kiran," Ravi says. "The soft colors. She should have it. Can I buy it from you?"

"Seriously?"

"Of course."

Jane almost tells him he can have it, as a gift. But, rich people love to spend money, says Colin. "It's a thousand dollars," she says, obeying a slightly hysterical whim.

"Done," Ravi says. "Can I give you a check later?"

"Ravi," Jane says, stunned. "I was kidding."

"Well, I'm not. I'll leave it here until I've paid you."

"You can take it with you! I trust you not to steal!"

Ravi's grin flashes bright. "That's something, I guess."

"Not to steal the *umbrella*," Jane amends.

"Good to know I'm on your list of suspects," he says. "You may as well know you're not on mine. I wouldn't even know about the forgery if you hadn't blurted it out about Mrs. Vanders's suspicions."

"I guess that's true," says Jane, alarmed to realize her role.

"I could see people paying thousands for some of these umbrellas, you know," he says. "Have you thought of working with a dealer? I could show a few to Buckley."

"Colin has already offered," Jane says, "and I think you're both delusional."

"Damn Colin," Ravi says cheerfully. "He'll get the credit, and the commission."

"I'm sure you'll miss that ten dollars. You say thousands, but Colin says hundreds."

Ravi shakes his head. "Buckley will value them higher. Not all of them, but a few of them. And he'll want to see what you do in the future."

He leaves with the yellow umbrella under his arm.

* * *

At dinner, Colin is the only person who seems to want to talk. Ravi isn't even there. Phoebe frowns at her plate and Lucy glances up from her phone now and then to pretend she's paying attention. Kiran looks tired, flinching every time Colin begins to speak, as if listening is an unbearable strain.

It's hard to watch, but Jane hopes Colin will keep talking nonetheless, because he's asking some of the very questions she wants to know the answers to.

"Is either piece insured?" he asks the table.

When no one else responds, Kiran finally stirs herself and says, "No."

"Why not?" asks Jane, who can't fathom why anyone wouldn't insure art that's so valuable.

Lucy speaks absently, as if bored, not raising her eyes from her phone. "Insurance on pieces like that, especially a Vermeer, is prohibitively expensive."

"None of the art is alarmed, either," says Kiran. "Octavian trusts people. I've never understood it," she adds sadly.

"Well, at least that rules Octavian out as a suspect," says Colin. "He'd gain much more by selling them than by stealing them."

Kiran's face hardens. "No one in my family stole the fucking art," she says in a low voice.

"Sweetheart," says Colin in amusement. "I just said he didn't."

"Maybe you think I took it?" says Kiran. "Or my brother, or my mother, or my stepmother?"

"Darling," Colin says, in a deliberately soothing voice that makes Kiran's shoulders stiffen more. "Of course I don't, but you know it had to be *someone*. We figure it out by eliminating people."

"Yes," Kiran says, "I'm not twelve years old, I understand how it works. But since it has to be *someone,* let's not talk about it at dinner. There's no way to consider any of the suspects without getting someone's back up at this table."

Phoebe frowns extra hard at this. Jane wonders then if Kiran might suspect anything about Patrick. Could that be why she seems so miserable?

"Would you feel better if I spoke more generally?" asks Colin, in an avuncular tone that's starting to grate on Jane's nerves. "Do you know much about Vermeer?" he asks, startling Jane by addressing the question to her. "Did you know there are few Vermeers in existence? Another of them is missing too, stolen from a Boston museum in 1990. It's probably being passed around as collateral in the drug world, maybe at seven or eight percent of its market value. That's the going rate at the moment for a stolen picture."

"Colin," says Lucy, emerging from her phone and speaking sharply. "We don't want to talk about it. Just shut up."

At that moment, Ravi comes exploding into the banquet hall. "Lucy," he says, swooping down on her. "Colin. I'm taking another look at the fake. I want you both to look at it too and give me your thoughts on the forger."

"Right now?" Lucy says, not even glancing up, her fingers moving furiously across her phone keyboard. "I'm eating."

"Right now," Ravi says.

"I'll come later."

"You're not actually eating, Lucy," Ravi says. "Anyone can see that."

"Ravi—"

His voice changes, to something quiet, and forlorn. "Luce. Please?"

Lucy looks up, into Ravi's face. Then, sighing sharply, she pushes herself back from the table.

Colin, watching these proceedings, speaks in his careful, singsong voice. "Kiran," he says, "do you mind if I go with Ravi?"

"No, it's fine," she says. "You should help."

It's a relief to watch him go. A minute later, Phoebe finishes her food and also excuses herself. Jane is alone with Kiran, who picks up her fork and stabs a green bean, then stabs it again.

"Kiran?" Jane says, then stops when Kiran flinches. It occurs to Jane that Kiran doesn't want another person asking her if she's okay. "Is there—anything I can do to help with the missing art?"

Kiran coughs a laugh, then stabs a different green bean. "It's not funny, of course," she says. "It's awful. Or anyway, Ravi feels awful, which makes me feel awful. And I feel awful speculating about who might have done it too." She shakes her head briefly, as if clearing it. "Ravi gave me the yellow umbrella," she says. "It's lovely. Thank you. I hope you charged him lots of money."

"I did, actually," says Jane, surprised that Kiran remembers that money matters to Jane in a way it doesn't to her.

"It's really special," Kiran says. "I'd like to see the rest of them."

"I'd be happy to show them to you," Jane says, "anytime," realizing she means it, because Kiran feels different from everyone else. Kiran is careful. She'll be respectful. She understood Aunt Magnolia, and she'll understand the umbrellas.

"Do you want to go into business with them?" she says. "Ravi could help you."

"Actually, Colin has taken a few to show to his uncle."

Kiran eats a green bean, then stares at her fork. "I don't know why I'm dating him," she says.

She's voiced Jane's own question, but Jane isn't sure how to respond.

"I mean," Kiran says, "he seems like a fine person and all. Doesn't he?"

"Uh-huh," Jane says, "most of the time."

"Ravi likes him."

"But, do *you* like him?"

"I like having sex with him," she says.

"Really?" Jane says, then, realizing how she sounds, flushes with embarrassment.

Kiran laughs. "He probably doesn't seem the type, huh? Let's just say there are benefits to him feeling like he needs to be an expert on everything."

Jane once kissed a boy from her high school at a party, and a girl in her dorm who was pretty drunk. And she thinks about sex. But she hasn't even come close. Not really.

"I feel like I *should* like him," Kiran says.

"Aunt Magnolia used to tell me to be careful not to *should* all over myself," Jane says, which makes Kiran glance at her in surprise, then chuckle.

"But, really," Kiran says, with a strange, stubborn kind of earnestness. "I *should* like him. The funny things he says should make me laugh. The conversations we have should interest me. He's smart, he's educated, he never does anything objectively wrong. And yet I can't relax around him, and I can't tell whether it's actually something about him, or if it's just that I can't relax anywhere, about anything." She blinks fast, looking away from Jane.

"Oh, Kiran."

"It sucks," she says. "And trying to figure it out makes me really tired."

"Is Patrick part of it too?" Jane asks.

Kiran makes a hopeless, impatient noise. "No. He doesn't get to be part of it. At least Colin is an open book."

"Well," Jane says, feeling distinctly useless. "I wish I knew how to help. I don't have much experience. Mainly what I know how to do is drop out of college and make umbrellas."

A smile touches the corner of Kiran's mouth. "What would your aunt tell me to do?"

Jane takes a careful breath. "She'd probably tell you to breathe like a jellyfish."

"Do jellyfish breathe?"

"I mean, imagine your lungs are moving the way a jellyfish moves," Jane says. "Breathe deliberately, deep and slow, into your belly."

"Okay," Kiran says, focusing on her next breath. "And this will solve my problems?"

Now Jane is smiling. "It will, if your problems relate to breathing."

"Aunt Magnolia was a wise woman."

Yes, Jane thinks. *She was.*

That night, Jane's rooms feel cavernous and dark, the ceilings too high, the air too chilly. In her morning room, the darkness presses in. So she works, moving her hands steadily across the skeleton of her umbrella, trying to be patient with all the questions that don't have answers.

There's a stage in umbrella-making when the umbrella is little more than a rod and eight ribs. If Jane opens and closes it, it moves like a jellyfish made of wires, like an undersea creature in the world's creepiest ocean.

Since she's using ribs of different lengths for this umbrella, the frame makes a particularly strange and unbalanced jellyfish. It's hard to know if this will have the effect she's going for. She'll have to wait and see. But she thinks she might want this umbrella to be like a secret. When other people look at it, they'll see something broken-looking and weird. Only Jane will know that it's the blue splotch in Aunt Magnolia's iris.

Once again, the groaning house wakes her before dawn, this time from a dream about Ivy stealing a fish. The dream becomes a voice—a house voice—with moaning walls and rattling windows that tell Jane to look outside, and before she's entirely awake, she's stumbled out of bed and pressed herself against the glass in the morning room. The night is clear, the moon is just rising, and the garden is knit like black lace.

Jasper blunders into the room from the bedroom and stands beside her at the window. He presses his nose to the glass.

Beyond the garden, movement. A dark shape. No—two dark shapes. One of the shapes switches on a flashlight. The other person is illuminated briefly, not enough to make out any features, but enough to show that this person is carrying a flat, rectangular package. They cross the lawn and disappear into the trees.

Patrick and Ivy, Jane thinks, struck by a certainty she can't justify. Her heart begins to beat in her throat. "Jasper?" she says. "Does that package seem the right size for the Vermeer?"

Jasper sneezes.

"Yeah," Jane says. "So, what do we do?"

Jasper sets his paw on Jane's foot. It's a gesture Jane isn't certain how to interpret. Is he trying to keep her here, or is he expressing team solidarity in the face of adventure?

Or maybe he's a dog, Jane says to herself, *he doesn't understand language, and he likes how your foot feels.*

"Well, Jasper," says Jane. "I guess we need a flashlight. An ally would be nice too."

Finding her hoodie and socks and slipping into her big black boots, checking the time—it's not even 5:15 yet—Jane goes out into the corridor. After considering things for a split second, she knocks on Ravi's door. Jasper leans on her ankles. When there's no answer, she knocks harder, and when there's still no answer, she takes a conscious risk of discovering him having sex with someone and barges right in. It's not like he hasn't barged in on her, and there's no time to waste here.

Ravi's bed is palatial, and empty.

Interesting. She tries to conjure up the mental image of the two figures entering the forest again, to see if she can turn one of them into Ravi, but it's really no use; she didn't see enough.

"I wish I knew which room is Lucy's," she says to Jasper as they proceed down the corridor. "I wish—" She trips over Captain Polepants.

"Ack! I wish I knew who to trust." Where is she likely to find a flashlight? The kitchen? The servants' quarters?

Jane has a sudden vision of the two long, powerful flashlights propped on Ivy's computer desk.

If Ivy's in the forest now, there's nothing to stop Jane from going into her room and "borrowing" a flashlight. And if it turns out that Ivy *is* in her room . . .

Jane heads toward the servants' quarters. As she and Jasper round the courtyard, she hears music in the house somewhere. A Beatles recording, which strikes her as odd at this hour.

In the servants' wing, she starts to lose her nerve. If Ivy's in her room, then Jane's appearance at five-something in the morning is going to be pretty unexpected. And Ivy hasn't been too friendly lately. She stops outside Ivy's door.

"Jasper?" she whispers. "What do I do?"

Jasper looks back at her with a blank expression appropriate to a dog.

With one big breath, Jane knocks.

After the briefest pause, Ivy's door swings back sharply, Ivy's face alert and interested behind it, her glasses in place. Behind her, one of her computers is on, fans whirring and lights flashing like a little spaceship in the darkness. "What do you want?" she demands in alarm, glancing past Jane into the corridor. "Why are you here?"

She's still wearing the ratty blue sweater and black leggings from yesterday and her dark hair is unbound, falling down her shoulders messily to the middle of her back. And she looks so unhappy to see Jane that Jane is stung.

"I need a flashlight," Jane says.

"What for?"

"I just need one."

"Tell me what for."

"Why should I?"

Ivy speaks roughly. "Because if you need a flashlight, that tells me you're going outside, and it could be dangerous."

"You mean because of the Panzavecchias," Jane says, "and Philip Okada sneaking around with a gun?"

Ivy seems stunned into silence.

"Are you going to give me a flashlight or not?" says Jane. When Ivy still doesn't respond, she turns on her heel and stalks out into the corridor.

"Wait," Ivy calls after her. "Janie, wait."

Jane doesn't wait. When she turns down the corridor toward the center of the house, Jasper, behind her, yips and whines, then emits one short bark that finally gets Jane's attention. She turns back to him impatiently. "What!"

Jasper is backing down the corridor toward the big plank door with the iron latch at the far end, the door that leads to the west attics. He's whining as he moves, clearly begging her to follow.

With a frustrating sense of futility, Jane gives in. "Goddammit, Jasper," she says, turning to follow. "You're lucky I've watched so many dog movies."

Jasper leads her through the wide plank door, then straight ahead to a sliding metal door that Jane realizes must be the freight elevator, and the fastest route to the outside. She presses the button. When the door slides open, she and Jasper step in.

As it slides closed, a hand reaches in and stops the door.

Jane is hyperventilating as Ivy pushes herself through the crack. She's dressed in tight black from head to toe and she's wearing a backpack and checking the light on her flashlight, which is big enough to bludgeon someone with. It shines like a beacon. Briefly, it illuminates the bulge of a gun holster under Ivy's hoodie, below her left breast. The elevator doors slide shut.

"Ivy?" Jane says, her voice cracking.

"I'm going to stick to you like shit on your shoe," says Ivy, "until you tell me where you're going."

Jane figures that if she's stuck in an elevator with Ivy and a gun, there's no point in holding back what Ivy's going to learn eventually anyway. "I saw two people outside with a flashlight and a Vermeer-sized package," she says. "They crossed the lawn and went into the trees."

"Got it," says Ivy.

"I assumed it was you and Patrick," Jane adds nastily.

Ivy's face is expressionless. "We have nothing to do with the Vermeer."

"No, just the broken Brancusi," Jane says. "And the bank robbery, and the kidnapping of children."

Saying nothing, Ivy fishes a dark balaclava out of a pocket and pulls it down across her face, over her glasses. The contrast between her and Jane, who's still in her hoodie and *Doctor Who* pajamas, borders on the absurd. The elevator screams as it descends, then lets them out into a blasting wind and the sudden noise of the sea far below.

Ivy grips Jane's wrist, hard.

"Let go," Jane says. "You're hurting me."

Ivy says, "We have to move fast," then begins to pull Jane across the lawn. Jane scrambles along beside her, still hurting, amazed at how strong Ivy is and how fast she's moving.

"Where are you taking me?"

"There's a bay in the ramble," Ivy says. "A hidden one, on the island's northeast edge. A great place for sneaking art off the island."

"You would know," Jane says, then focuses on being dragged toward the trees without falling.

The ramble is a steep, rocky, hillocky forest of scrub pines. There are no trails and Jasper is pushing himself to his limits to keep up with the downhill sliding and jumping Ivy and Jane are doing. He disappears occasionally, then reappears, presumably finding alternate, more basset-hound-friendly routes of passage. The rattling wind covers whatever noise he's making. Ivy continues to move with assurance, familiar with the forest. Daybreak is coming on fast.

Ivy grips Jane higher on her arm and jerks her to a stop.

"What—" Jane begins, then shuts her mouth as she sees what Ivy's seeing. A man sits on a rock with his back to them, not ten feet away, surrounded by trees. His hair is clipped close and his body is hefty, sturdy; he has a red beard. His pants legs are soaked through, as if he's been wading through water. Beside him on the rock is a small pile of orange slices. He reaches to the pile and eats one occasionally. A gun sticks out of the back waistband of his jeans.

Ivy pulls Jane away.

"Let's go back to the house," Jane whispers as Ivy tugs her down the slope, out of range of the man. "Please, Ivy, stop. Let me go." But Ivy suddenly pulls her down behind a shrub and puts an arm around her, whispering *Shhhh* urgently in her ear, and Jane freezes, no idea what's happening. Where's Jasper? Jane begins to panic about Jasper. What if the horrible man sees—

Jasper presses against Jane's leg on the side opposite Ivy. Pushing away from Ivy, Jane buries her face in his neck, breathing into his fur. "Oh, Jasper."

But Jasper's attention seems fixed on a point through a hole in the shrubbery. Ivy is holding some of the branches back and staring out into the growing light.

Jane moves some branches aside and looks where they're looking.

It's the bay of which Ivy spoke, some twenty yards away, a place where the forest gives way and the land slopes down to a small, crescent-shaped inlet of dark sand. Lucy St. George stands on the shore in all black, holding a gun. She's pointing it at a very tall white man in a speedboat moored to a single wooden post in the water.

"Lucy," Jane whispers. "Lucy! What is she doing?"

What Lucy seems to be doing is arguing with the man. He's at the motor, one hand grabbing it as if he's ready to take off at any moment. He keeps waving his other hand around and yelling things at Lucy that Jane can't hear. His words have the tone of angry, passionate questions.

"Whatever," Jane hears Lucy shout back in a derisive voice. "I'm not doing it anymore. It's a waste of my talents. Yours too, J.R."

J.R. reaches into his coat and Jane is frightened; she thinks, from the expression on his face, that he's reaching for a gun. Instead he pulls out a whistle. He blows into it with a shrill blast. He's the tallest man Jane has ever seen, thin as a reed.

A moment later, branches crack and leaves rustle and the red-bearded man who's been eating oranges comes through the brush onto shore. Without even a sidelong glance at Lucy or her gun, he wades directly into the water, unmoors the boat, and climbs in. J.R. brings the boat to life like the waking of a thousand bees. Then the boat zips away, J.R. looking back at Lucy balefully.

"Who were they?" Jane whispers to Ivy. "Where's the painting? Why did she let them go? Is it an undercover sting?"

"No," says Ivy grimly, pulling off her balaclava. "I'm not getting 'undercover sting' from this."

"Do you mean—"

"Shh!"

Still on shore, Lucy wraps her arms tight about herself, one hand still clutching her gun. Then she turns abruptly to scan the trees. Is she waiting for something? Someone? Finally, she makes a small, impatient gesture, sticks her gun inside her jacket, and begins to walk away from shore, directing herself not precisely toward the spot where Jane and Ivy are hiding, but near to it. She wears a fuzzy black knit hat that makes her look big-eyed and young. She seems very alone to Jane somehow, as if Jane is looking into a View-Master at the only woman in the world. As Lucy approaches, she wipes her cheeks with the back of her hand and Jane sees that she's crying.

Ivy reaches under her hoodie toward the gun holster and makes a move to stand up.

"What the hell are you doing?" Jane whispers fiercely, grabbing on to Ivy's arm and yanking her back down.

"I'm going to stop her!" says Ivy, struggling to break free of Jane's grip.

"Stop her doing what?" Jane says. "We still don't know what's going on!"

"Don't be so naïve!" says Ivy. "She's an art thief!"

"Fine, but I won't let you shoot her!"

"What?" says Ivy, staring at Jane with an incredulous expression. "I'm not going to shoot her!"

"Then why do you have a *gun?*"

"Okay," says Lucy's voice, rising, cold and careful, from a place very near. "Who's there? I can hear voices. Come out slowly."

Ivy is so startled that she drops back down, gasping, eyes wild. She reaches under her hoodie. "Stay hidden," she whispers. "Let me handle this, please."

Before Jane can even begin to try to figure out what to do, Jasper barrels around the shrubbery toward Lucy. Jane stands up, crying out, and watches the dog ram into Lucy. Unprepared, Lucy topples, cursing, struggling with her gun. The dog climbs on top of her and closes his mouth on her gun, growling, flailing to and fro. Everything is happening so fast. Jane runs to them, terrified that the gun will go off in Jasper's mouth. Lucy struggles, her fingers bleeding and trapped; she understands too.

"Stop him," Lucy sobs. "Stop him. Pull him away. He'll blow my head off!"

"Jasper," Jane says, wrapping arms around his middle and trying to pull. "She's not going to shoot us!"

"I'm not," Lucy gasps. "Of course I'm not going to shoot you. I swear!"

Jasper's grip slips. The sudden release sends Jane falling down sideways with the dog in her arms. She and Jasper struggle and roll, then she finds her feet and rights herself.

When she stands, Lucy is on her feet again too. Lucy holds her gun, trained on Jane.

"Lucy," Jane says, confused.

Lucy's eyes are steady and hard behind the barrel of the gun. Blood runs down her hands. "So," she says. "You're charmingly trusting, aren't you?"

Not really, no, Jane thinks, her thoughts taking sluggish steps, *but there's a world of difference between not trusting someone and believing they're actually capable of shooting you. This is my fault,* Jane thinks. *Ivy is here. Jasper is here. I brought them here and put them in danger.* "Jasper," she says to the dog, who's emitting a low growl beside her that terrifies her because of how Lucy might react. "Be quiet, and still."

Ivy's strong voice rises behind Jane from the bushes. "I've got a gun too," she says. "Drop yours, Lucy, or I'll shoot you."

Lucy snarls. "You don't have a gun."

"Don't I?" says Ivy. "If you hurt Janie, I'll make your knees explode. Now drop it. I'm going to count to one."

What happens next happens so fast that Jane can barely follow it. Jasper launches himself at Lucy. Lucy tries to shoot him. Jane screams and runs at them, Lucy's gun goes off, and Jasper's teeth are clamped around Lucy's knee. Lucy goes down again, Lucy is screaming in pain, and Jasper is bleeding. Jasper is bleeding! Jane falls on Lucy and wrests the gun from her hands. She doesn't know what to do with it once she has it, but then Ivy is beside her, taking it away. Ivy trains Lucy's gun on Lucy, who's still screaming, still struggling to escape the grip of Jasper's teeth. Jasper is holding on hard.

"Brave dog," Jane says, grabbing on to him. It's just his ear. Lucy's shot a hole through the flap of his big, floppy ear. Tears stream down Jane's face. "Jasper, you brave, brave dog. I'm so sorry. Are you okay? Let go. Let me look at your ear."

Jasper lets Lucy's knee go. Jane hugs him and he licks her face, bleeding all over her. She cries into his fur. It's a big wet mess. His ear is bleeding copiously and Jane presses on it with her sleeve, not really sure how to help him, until Ivy suggests Jane remove one of her layers and use it to tie the ear tightly to his head.

"I'd give you one of my layers," Ivy says, "except that I'm not taking my eyes off this asshole."

"It's lovely, your concern for the dog," snarls the asshole in question, rocking over her injuries, moaning. "I'm in bad shape here."

Jane can't stand the sound of Lucy's voice in her airspace. "If she talks again," she says to Ivy, "shoot her."

"Changed your mind, then?" asks Ivy in a gently teasing tone.

Jane is too ashamed to look at Ivy. She tries to fashion a bandage for Jasper with her hoodie. It's not going well. She's still crying, and frightened, and shaking too hard.

She takes a deep, steadying breath.

"Hey, Janie," Ivy says quietly. "You know we're all going to be okay, right? We've got this."

The three women and one dog make an odd procession back to the house. Jane is still in her *Doctor Who* pajamas, she's covered in Jasper's blood, and her face is tear-stained. Her hoodie is wrapped twice around Jasper's head, its sleeves tied in a bow. Jasper doesn't seem to mind looking silly. His head is high and he walks with a spring in his step.

"Jasper," Jane says to him, "you are the picture of heroism."

Several feet ahead of them, Lucy snorts. Lucy is bloody, bedraggled, and limping, her wrists locked together with restraints Ivy pulled out of her backpack.

Ivy walks behind her, Lucy's gun held coolly in her hands, like some sort of ninja wondergirl.

"Who were you waiting for back on shore, Lucy?" Ivy asks. "After your friends in the boat left and before you heard us talking? Who were you expecting?"

"No one."

"Bullshit," Ivy says. "Who did you leave the house with early this morning, carrying a flashlight and the Vermeer? Janie saw you."

"You'll never link me to the Vermeer," Lucy says. "Janie must've seen the guys from the boat."

"No," Ivy says, "she didn't. Only one of those guys had wet pants legs."

"So maybe the other one changed into dry pants when he got back to the boat."

"What happened," says Ivy, "is that you and an accomplice carried the Vermeer from the house to the forest this morning and passed it to the guy in the boat. The guy with wet pants was a lookout for the other one. We saw him sitting in the ramble. The person you left the house with acted as your lookout. I want to know who it is."

"I don't have an accomplice," Lucy says in a bright, musical voice.

"Right," says Ivy sarcastically. "Whoever your accomplice is, I expect all your wailing chased him neatly away, so, well done with that." Then Ivy reaches an arm around to her backpack again, pulls out a walkie-talkie, and speaks into it. "Hello," she says. "Somebody pick up. Mrs. V? Mr. V?" No one answers.

Jasper, struggling his way up the hill beside Jane, slipping on leaves and beginning to pant, makes Jane's tears rise again. "Are you okay, buddy?" Jane asks him. "Do you want to be carried?"

"Almighty god," says Lucy. "Maybe we should stop so you can build a shrine to the dog."

"The dog is the reason we're safe and you're in trouble," Jane says coldly to her back. "That's why you keep making snide remarks about the dog. The dog kicked your sorry ass."

Now Ivy is chuckling. Reaching once more into her backpack, she pulls out a chocolate bar and hands it to Jane. Jane tears it open, amazed at how hungry she is.

Again Ivy tries the walkie-talkie. Finally, as they break out of the trees onto the lawn, Mrs. Vanders's voice comes crackling through. *"Ivy-bean?"* she says. *"Where are you?"*

Moments later, calls have been made and a contingent of New York State troopers is on its way.

"They'll also search the waters between the island and the mainland, with the hopes of intercepting that boat," says Mrs. Vanders's scratchy voice. *"And I'll send a couple people into the ramble to look for the accomplice."*

"And a vet," Jane says to Ivy. "Jasper needs a vet."

"Yes," says Ivy into the walkie-talkie. "Jasper needs a vet. Lucy shot him. He's got a bleeding hole in his ear flap."

"My god!" says Mrs. Vanders. *"How unnecessary! Patrick!"* Jane hears her bellow. *"The dog needs a vet!"*

"Has anyone snuck into the house in the last few minutes?" Ivy asks.

"Ivy," says Mrs. Vanders's voice, *"are you forgetting it's a gala day? The doors have been wide open and people have been streaming in and out since the sun came up."*

"Damn," says Ivy. Then she says to Lucy, "Your accomplice is having one hell of a lucky day. Kind of makes you jealous, doesn't it?"

"No doubt it would," says Lucy, "if I had an accomplice."

"You do realize you'll go down for the Brancusi too, don't you, Lucy?" says Ivy.

Lucy's only response to this is a tight mouth and a closed face.

"Maybe they'll even reopen the case on the Rubens," says Jane.

"Yeah," says Ivy. "Good point, Janie."

When the group reaches the house, they're met on the back terrace by Mrs. Vanders, who comes forward to clap a hand on Lucy's shoulder and lead her inside, face grim. Octavian the Fourth, looking sallow in his paisley dressing gown, is also standing on the back terrace, as is Ravi, who is wide-eyed and speechless. Ravi's eyes on Lucy are disbelieving. He looks like a hurt little boy. Lucy stares back at him. When a tear slides down Ravi's face, Lucy begins to cry silent, angry tears of her own.

The police divide into two groups, one searching the forest for Lucy's accomplice, the other commandeering the billiard room, because it has only two doors, and they both close. They've made clear their intention to talk to the entire household, one by one, starting with Lucy, then Jane, then Ivy, then Ravi. Then everyone who was awake when Jane and Ivy brought Lucy back to the house, which includes Octavian, Mr. and Mrs. Vanders, Cook, Patrick, all the regular staff, and all the temporary staff hired for the party. Then everyone who was asleep, or claimed to have been, and wandered downstairs after the fact: Phoebe Okada, Colin Mack, Kiran.

The vet has also arrived, a big bear of a woman who's in the kitchen making a gentle fuss of stitching Jasper's ear. She says Jane did well with the improvised bandage and shouldn't be alarmed by the blood. "Ears bleed like that," she says, "but it looks worse than it is. This dog is going to be just fine." Nonetheless, every time Jane looks at Jasper, tears start sliding down her face. When he gazes back at her lovingly, it only makes the tears come faster.

The police, armed with the basic story, talk to Lucy alone for a very long time.

Jane and Ivy wait their turns in the gold sitting room, which adjoins the billiard room. Ivy sits quietly, watching Jane sniffle and rip her cuticles until they bleed. Jane looks back at Ivy once and notices that her irises turn purple at the edges. She doesn't look at Ivy again.

Finally, Ivy speaks. "Are you mad at me?"

Jane finds some dirt under a fingernail and digs at it, only managing to lodge it deeper. Ramble dirt, no doubt. Crime-fighting, mystery-solving, confusion dirt.

"I've been trying to imagine what this is like for you," says Ivy. "Especially since it sounds like—you know about some things. Like, you saw something, or overheard something, with Philip? Maybe with Patrick?" She pauses. "Anyway, I'd be mad."

"I don't see why I should tell you what I saw or heard," Jane says simply, "when you haven't told me anything."

"You're right."

"And I don't know why you're asking me if I'm mad," Jane continues in an even tone, "when you're the one who's been acting like you're mad at me."

"I'm not mad at you," says Ivy dismally.

"Well, you've been wandering around with your camera," says Jane, "making that shutter noise, pretending to take pictures of the art, and then, when you see me, you act like you're mad."

"I'm not mad at you," Ivy repeats. "I'm mad that I'm not allowed to tell you what's going on."

"Well," says Jane. "You need to improve your directionality."

This almost elicits a surprised smile from Ivy.

"I've been failing lately," Jane says, "pretty hard, at figuring out who to trust."

"That's partly my fault," says Ivy, leaning toward her. "It's Lucy's fault too. She tricked you. She took advantage of your better nature. She's the sucky, faily one, not you."

"I should've known," Jane says. "*You* knew right away."

"Yes, well," says Ivy with a wry expression, slumping back in her seat. "Not trusting people isn't something to be proud of, either."

"But you were right," Jane says. "You got it right."

"Only because I have more experience with untrustworthy people," Ivy says. "Janie, seriously. You were brave out there. You tried to keep everyone safe, even Lucy, all while not knowing what was going on. You got the gun away from Lucy, for god's sake."

Smoothing the sleeves of her pajama top, Jane lets this praise lap against her, cautiously. Then one of the police officers sticks his head through the billiard room doorway, glares all around, retreats again, and slams the door.

"I'm nervous," says Jane.

"Why?"

"I don't know," Jane says. "I've never been questioned by the police before."

"Ah," says Ivy. "Well, all you have to do is tell the truth."

"That's just it," says Jane. "What if I incriminate someone innocent by accident?"

"I think that in this sort of situation," Ivy says, "you can't help what you do by accident. And you're much less likely to hurt innocent people if you tell the truth."

Jane studies Ivy's calm face. "The truth is that you told Lucy you had a gun," she says.

"Ah," says Ivy again. "But did you ever actually see that gun?"

"No," Jane admits, "not exactly."

"The police will ask you what I said *and* what I did," Ivy says. "Just tell them the truth. They'll conclude that I was only pretending to have a gun, for leverage."

Jane swallows. "That does make me feel better. A little. Except that I saw the shape of the gun under your hoodie."

Ivy glances down at her hoodie, which is flat now, with no gun-shaped bulges. She's wearing canvas sneakers now too, and her hair is tied back in a messy knot. While Jane was fussing over Jasper and the household was waiting for the police, Ivy must have returned to her room and made a few changes. "Then you should tell them that too," she says simply. "A shape under a hoodie is pretty inconclusive."

"I want to know what's really going on," Jane says, holding Ivy's eyes. "Personally, for myself."

Ivy's eyes are a soft, worried blue behind her glasses. "Is it okay with you if we have that conversation later? After the police go?"

"Will we actually have it?"

"Yes," says Ivy. "I swear it."

"Will you tell me everything?"

"Everything."

"Is it going to upset me?"

Ivy takes a slow breath. She seems very tired suddenly, blinking eyes that look like they sting with exhaustion. "I don't know," she says. "The truth is, I've lost perspective."

"I can help you with that," Jane says. "If it's upsetting, I'll make sure to get *really* upset, so you can't miss it."

Ivy laughs. "You think you're joking, but that probably would be helpful. That's how much I've lost perspective." Then she yawns. "Yeesh, sorry. Are you less nervous now?"

"Well," Jane says, pausing. "I went to Ravi's room first before I came to yours. He wasn't there."

"He wasn't?"

"No."

"Well," Ivy says, "I can see why you wouldn't want the police to know that, but Ravi can take care of himself. He'll tell the police where he was. You could complicate things for him if you say he was where he wasn't."

Ivy is right. Jane's best course is to tell the truth.

"Thanks," she says.

"Sure," says Ivy. "It's normal to be nervous."

"You're not."

"I am," she says. "I'm like a duck on the water. I look calm but my feet are working a mile a minute underneath. And I haven't slept yet, so I'm basically a mess."

"Are you sure Lucy has an accomplice?"

"I don't know," says Ivy. "She definitely seemed to be expecting someone besides us on the beach. She must be going crazy trying to figure out who took the Brancusi, and I was hoping she suspects her own accomplice. Because could she really believe that there could be *three* art thieves in the house at once? Lucy, Lucy's accomplice, *and* someone else? Wouldn't she think that's too much of a coincidence?"

"You're certain Lucy didn't take the Brancusi?"

"Yeah," Ivy says. "I'm sorry it keeps coming back to the things I can't tell you."

"But that's why you taunted her, saying she'd go down for the Brancusi?" Jane says. "You were hoping it would convince her to name her accomplice?"

"Yeah," Ivy says. "If she has one. It could be that the guy with the wet pants came to the house to meet her, and you saw the two of them entering the forest. But I doubt it."

Suddenly Jane realizes something. "Ivy," she says. "The police are going to ask *you* about the Brancusi. And they're going to ask if you really had a gun. Are *you* going to lie?"

Ivy pauses, glancing into the light coming from the ballroom doorway. The ends of her hair glow gold. "I'm going to do what I think is right," she says. "And after all this is over, I swear to you I'm going to tell you all the things I can't tell you right now."

Jane sits quietly with this for a moment, until she realizes two things. One, that she believes Ivy. Two, that she really can't believe, despite guns and missing children and stolen art, that anything Ivy's doing is truly bad.

"You know there's a word for that shutter sound?" says Ivy.

"Huh?"

"That sound a digital camera makes. The fake shutter sound."

"It's fake?"

"Well, think about it. A digital camera doesn't have a shutter. It's just designed to make the noise cameras used to make, back when they did have shutters."

"I never thought about that!"

"There's a word for a design choice that incorporates a feature that's now obsolete. I can't remember what it is."

"Think it's a Scrabble word?"

Ivy grins. "I certainly hope so."

Jane can't explain it, but she feels more ready for the police now. She feels like she can handle whatever comes. "I'd like to know what word that is."

"I promise that when I think of it," says Ivy, "I'll tell you."

When the police yank Lucy St. George out of the billiard room, she trips over the molding, remaining upright only because one of the officers is gripping her arm hard. It seems to Jane that they're being unnecessarily rough. Jane wants to be glad, but Lucy's not a big person. As they haul her through the gold sitting room, she winces in pain.

She catches Jane's eye. "Is Ravi in the receiving hall?" she asks.

Jane can't imagine why she should answer. "I don't think so."

Lucy seems relieved. "Thanks," she says as the police drag her away.

Jane wants to yell after her that she didn't arrange it for Lucy's convenience. That she would never do anything for a person who lies and pretends, then shoots a dog.

A surly policeman who smells like the sea comes to the billiard room doorway and calls Jane's name.

The police officers, two men and one woman, have impassive faces, sharp voices, and a lot of questions. Jane tells the truth, and most of the time, her honest answer is, "I don't know."

"The man in the forest was eating an orange," she offers at one point.

"Eating an orange," her interrogator repeats in an expressionless voice, not writing this illuminating piece of evidence down. Jane and the police officers are sitting, a bit awkwardly, around one end of the fanciest billiard table she's ever seen, with dusty blue felt and lions carved into the wooden legs.

"Did Lucy St. George say anything to the men in the boat?" asks an officer whose mouth is hidden by a bushy white mustache.

Jane tries to remember. "Yes," she says. "I think Lucy said, 'I'm not doing it again, it's a waste of my talents, and yours too, J.R.' Or something like that. I was pretty far away and the water was noisy."

"Not doing *what* again?" asks the mustached officer. "And who's J.R.?"

"He's the man who drove the boat away," Jane says.

"Hmm," says the officer. Jane can hear worlds of communication in that "hmm." In these officers' long careers, she's the most useless witness they've ever questioned.

They ask her questions about her own history and her reasons for being in the house. They seem bored by her answers. She tries to sound casual when she tells them about never actually having seen Ivy's gun. She aims for a blasé tone when she tells them about Ravi not having been in his bedroom too. They perk up a little at that, which deflates her. Ravi could be the accomplice, couldn't he? Couldn't his tantrums be an act? If they are, he deserves to be caught. Right?

No. Jane can't believe Ravi is involved. Then again, she once thought the same about Lucy. "Do the police give medals to dogs?" she asks.

"Thank you for your time," they respond grimly, then sweep Jane back into the gold sitting room.

"How was it?" asks Ivy, who's still sitting there.

"I have no idea," Jane says.

Toenails scrape and ring on tile as Jasper comes barreling into the room. His ear is bandaged and attached loosely to his neck with tape. When he sees Jane, he throws himself at her. Jane drops down to the floor, takes him into her lap, pets him, and, naturally, begins to leak tears again. He pants hotly into her face.

"I've never seen that dog behave toward anyone the way he behaves toward you," says Ivy, searching through her many pockets, finally unearthing a tissue. She brings it to Jane, crouches down, and, while Jane's still hugging the dog, touches the tissue, gently, to Jane's face.

For a moment, Jane feels that everything is right.

"Ivy Yellan," says an officer who appears in the billiard room doorway, in a tone of acute boredom. "And you," he says, jutting his chin at Jane.

"What?" Jane says. "Me? You just talked to me."

"Yes," he says. "I haven't forgotten your scintillating testimony. Do us a favor and go find Ravi Thrash, will you? He's next."

"I'm right here," Ravi says, appearing in the ballroom doorway.

"Good," the officer says to Ravi. "Kindly stay."

The officer and Ivy disappear into the billiard room, leaving Jane and Ravi, who studies Jane's face. She sniffles hard, wiping her eyes on her pajama sleeve.

"What are you crying about?" asks Ravi.

"The dog," Jane says, which is true, if an understatement.

"Yeah," he says grimly.

"You look tired," she says.

"The FBI should be handling this case," Ravi says. "If our artwork is still in New York State, it's a miracle. Vanny is literally trying to give me an ulcer, calling in the state police instead of the FBI. How was it, talking to them?"

Jane pauses, then speaks in a particular tone. "I answered all their questions honestly."

He rubs his neck, sighing. The white streaks in his hair suddenly make him seem old, tired. "Is there a reason you shouldn't have?"

"I went looking for you first," Jane says. "This morning. I went to your room first, before going outside. It was just before dawn and you weren't there. I told them."

Ravi's eyes linger on Jane. "And now you're telling me you told them," he says, "so I'll know not to tell them I was safely tucked up in bed the whole time?"

"Yeah," says Jane. "I guess so."

The corner of Ravi's mouth turns up. "You're a puzzle."

"Ravi, if that's a segue to flirting, I'm literally going to lose it."

This elicits a sad smile, then a weary shake of the head. "I spent the night with my dad in the library," he says, "listening to the Beatles."

"The Beatles!" Jane exclaims. "I forgot to tell the police about the Beatles." Placing Jasper on his four feet, she stands, turns, and barges through the billiard room door. Four surprised faces swivel up to look at her.

"I forgot to tell you that as I was crossing the atrium on my way to the servants' quarters," Jane announces, "I heard someone playing the Beatles."

The faces stare at Jane in bewilderment. She leaves the room and shuts the door before things deteriorate any further.

"I'm pretty sure I'm their least favorite witness ever," she tells Ravi.

"Don't worry," he says. "Patrick will brood, Kiran will be silent and depressed, Colin will be condescending, and Phoebe will say something snobbish and defensive."

"Thanks," Jane says. "That makes me feel better."

His half grin again. "Keep me company while I'm waiting?"

Jane has sympathy for Ravi, who's had a rotten morning. But she's still dressed in her *Doctor Who* pajamas, she's run through the ramble, fallen over, rolled around, had a gun pointed at her, been bled on by a dog, bawled her eyes out, and been interrogated by the police. She needs a shower, and a deep, dark nap with Jasper snoring into her ankles. "I need to get cleaned up," Jane says.

"Yeah, okay," he says. "Send me Kiran if you see her, will you? I'm worried about her."

"Why?"

Ravi throws himself into an armchair and closes his eyes. "Nothing to do with any of this. Let's just call it twin stuff."

One moment, Jane is passing through the ballroom with Jasper at her heels, weary and spent, dodging gala staff whose voices are too sharp and bright. The next moment, she's ravenous. This is why Jane does, indeed, cross paths with Kiran, who's with Colin in the breakfast room, a little nook off the banquet hall, poking at a poached egg with a spoon.

"I just wish I was more surprised," Jane hears Colin say. "Who's your guess for her accomplice? Someone in the house? A servant?"

"I don't have a clue," says Kiran.

"She could have an entanglement with the guy who mans your boats," says Colin. "One of those secret relationships across class."

"Patrick?" says Kiran, sounding thoroughly confused, and rubbing her temples as if they hurt. "Where are you getting this from?"

"They look pretty cozy together. I can't see him turning her down," says Colin.

There's a smugness to his tone, subtle, indefinable; he's pleased with his own speculations.

Something inside Jane mutinies. "Colin," she says. "Why do you keep pushing her into conversations she doesn't want to have?"

"What?" Colin says, looking up at Jane. His hair is damp. He's showered and bright as a daisy. "Pushing who?"

"Kiran!" Jane exclaims. "You keep badgering her."

Colin sits back, offended. "I love Kiran," he says. "What do you know about anything? You're a child, and a stranger here."

"She doesn't want to talk about it," says Jane. "She wants to be alone."

"She's depressed!" Colin says. "I'm getting her interested in something!"

"You bully her!"

"You have a lot of nerve," Colin says, then turns to Kiran. "Sweetheart, do I bully you?"

Kiran is holding her spoon so tightly that her fingertips are white. "Colin," she says to her plate, "I think it's time we broke up. In fact, I'm sure of it. I'm sorry, but it's over."

Two spots of red grow in Colin's cheeks. After a moment, he pushes his chair back quietly, and stands. "Very well," he says stiffly. "By the way," he adds, flashing hot eyes into Jane's, "you're wrong. She doesn't prefer to be alone. She's quite fond of a certain one of her servants. I used to think she could be happy with me, but now I'm not sure she's capable of happiness."

"Don't talk about me as if I'm not here," Kiran says, "you patronizing prick."

Colin opens his mouth to speak, then claps it closed tight. He turns to go. As he's walking away, he spins back suddenly and addresses Jane.

"Incidentally," he says, "I hate to tell you, but there was an accident with your umbrellas. They fell into the street in Soho and got run over by a truck. I'm awfully sorry. I don't suppose they were insured?"

Her Pantheon dome umbrella. Her eggshell umbrella. Her brass-handled, brown-and-copper-rose umbrella. Jane is choking over her own astonishment.

"How horrible," Kiran says.

Jane looks into Kiran's face and finds that all of Kiran's warmth and feeling for her is real and surging.

Then she looks into Colin's face, which contains the most perfect balance of sorrow, solicitude, and regret. Also something else. The tiniest gleam of something childish. Triumph.

An instinct pricks her.

Turning without a word, Jane passes through the banquet hall into the kitchen, stopping only to hold the door for Jasper. Mr. Vanders and Patrick are huddled together at a table, muttering to each other.

"Who did the mail run yesterday?" Jane asks them.

They barely glance at her. "Cook," says Mr. Vanders.

"And where's Cook right now?" Jane asks.

"Down at the dock," says Mr. Vanders.

"I need to ask him a question."

Mr. Vanders eyes Jane then, with curiosity. He reaches into a drawer behind him, pulls out a walkie-talkie, presses a button, and says, "Son."

A moment later, a raspy voice answers. *"Dad?"*

Mr. Vanders hands the walkie-talkie to Jane. She's never used one before. She presses the button and says, "Hello?"

"Yeah?"

"Cook?"

"Yeah?"

"Did Colin Mack give you a long, narrow package yesterday for the mail run?"

"Yeah," says Cook. *"Umbrellas."*

"How were they packaged?"

"With about a mile of bubble wrap around them," he says, *"and nailed into a crate. I helped him pack them."*

"Who was it addressed to?"

"Buckley St. George, at his Soho offices. I private-messengered it in Southampton with the guy the family always uses."

"The family? Which family?"

"The Thrash family!" he says. *"What family do you think? Octavian transports art from time to time. We always use this guy."*

"Is he clumsy?" asks Jane. "Does he drop things? Is he a bike messenger who's always in peril?"

"Of course not! He's a professional art courier! He drives a specialized truck!"

Jane hands the walkie-talkie back to Mr. Vanders and marches off, Jasper at her heels. *"Hello?"* says Cook's voice behind her, somewhat irate. *"Who is this? Dad? Is that Magnolia's niece?"*

Jane pushes back through the swinging door, amazed at her own certainty.

This time, when she barges into the billiard room, the surprised faces contain a touch of annoyance. Ivy has gone; the police are talking to Ravi. He brightens a notch at the sight of Jane. Ravi expects entertainment.

"Colin Mack is the accomplice," Jane says, "or at any rate, he's a jerk who stole from me. The proof is that you'll find three umbrellas in the offices of Buckley St. George, who, frankly, I don't trust either. Maybe St. George is behind the whole thing. Maybe he positioned his daughter and his nephew here so they could steal the art, and Colin, being an arrogant ass, couldn't resist stealing my art too. Please note," Jane adds with desperation, determined to tell the whole truth, "that all of this is conjecture, based on a look in Colin's eyes and possibly also my inability to accept the slaughter of my umbrellas. But I think I'm right," she finishes.

One of the police officers clears her throat. "We are investigating the theft of two pieces of art, worth, on the underside, over a hundred million dollars," she says. "You're talking to us about umbrellas."

"Colin just told me that the umbrellas were destroyed," says Jane. "That means that if those umbrellas are in Buckley St. George's offices, then Colin lied to me so he could steal them. Are you looking for a thief or not?"

The police are at the house most of the day, despite the fact that it's gala day. Jane plays some distracted chess with Kiran in the winter garden, and waits.

In late afternoon, the news comes through that the umbrellas have been found. Two are smack in the middle of Buckley St. George's desk and Buckley himself is discovered walking through Soho with the third, the speckled eggshell, in the rain. According to the police, Buckley is charmed by Jane's umbrellas. The pale blue with brown speckles matches his bow tie. He's intended to purchase that one from Jane personally. He's astonished to learn that Colin's made up a story about them having been destroyed; he insists Colin never told him. "Damn stupid boy!" he says, and then, when he hears the part about Lucy and the Vermeer, he stops talking.

The police lead Colin away. He tries to look dignified and amused by this turn of events, but his face is bloodless, his eyes frightened. Jane watches him go with Kiran at her side. There is contempt in Kiran's expression that could freeze a star.

But still there's no sign of the missing Vermeer.

Later that day, the police ask Jane to come to New York to identify her umbrellas. Kiran comes too. The police don't need her, but she wants

Jane to have access to the Thrashes' city apartment while she's there, and Jane senses that she'd rather be anywhere than at the gala.

The light is falling as they board the boat. The gala is beginning; incoming boats sparkle on the water like stars.

Kiran unfurls a little, like a fern, as the police boat enters Long Island Sound and the Manhattan skyline appears. The city night fills her eyes, makes them clearer. Soon, the New York State Police barracks appear, on a strange, wooded patch of land in the East River called Ward's Island.

Inside the noisy, yellow-lit building, an officer named Investigator Edwards places the umbrellas on a desk and asks Jane if she recognizes them. He has a voice like a man stranded in a desert and a face like John Wayne. It seems silly to Jane, this emergency nighttime journey to the city to identify umbrellas she could easily have identified by photo or even by description. But, with her umbrellas before her, Jane is relieved she came. He lets her pick them up, touch them, inspect them, even hand them to Kiran, who tells Jane that each one is beautiful. They're in the same condition they were in when Jane saw them last.

"When can I have them back?"

"When we're done with the investigation," Investigator Edwards rasps, then adds, not without sympathy, "They're evidence. That means we'll take good care of them." His eyes, Jane notices, gray and clear, are surrounded by fine laughter lines. Then she notices a slight brown discoloration in one of his gray irises and even though she knows it's irrational, she trusts him with her umbrellas, implicitly.

"Your positive ID of the umbrellas will justify a search warrant of Buckley St. George's office," Investigator Edwards says as Jane hands the umbrellas back to him. "And his correspondence and his financials too. If he's got other stolen property, we'll find it."

Kiran's eyes slide to the investigator and lock on his face. Buckley St. George, Jane remembers, isn't just Colin's uncle and Lucy's father.

He's Ravi's boss. Ravi is going to lose his job. "You're sure Buckley St. George is involved?" Kiran asks.

"Not sure of anything," says Investigator Edwards. "We don't think Buckley St. George knew that Colin Mack intended to steal the umbrellas. But we did find those two perps and the boat, entering the East River from the Sound. They could've been on their way to Buckley St. George, intending to deliver the Vermeer."

"You said you found the guys," Kiran says, "but you didn't say if you found the Vermeer."

His face splits into a grin. "Yeah."

"That's funny?" says Kiran.

Reaching down, Investigator Edwards retrieves something from a drawer. "The chief petty officer did find a parcel on board," he says, "just the right size for the picture. But when he opened it, there was a blank canvas inside, and this." He lays a flat, transparent plastic bag on the desk before Kiran and Jane. It contains a paper napkin on which someone has written, with a felt pen in block letters, the words *BITE ME, YOU DESPOT.*

"Huh," Kiran says. "That *is* funny."

"Yeah," says Investigator Edwards.

"You think Lucy or Colin wrote that?"

"It appears to be Lucy St. George's handwriting."

"And you think it's a note to her father?"

"Possibly."

"So, what? You think Lucy stole the Vermeer at her father's instruction, kept the Vermeer for herself, then sent that napkin to her father as a message?"

"It's a theory."

"And where's the Vermeer?"

"No idea. Lucy's not saying. Neither is Colin, who, by the way, still insists he's got nothing to do with any of it. Unfortunately for him, we found the prints of his boots in the ramble. Stepped in mud from the recent rain, we assume, while serving as Lucy's lookout this morning."

Kiran rolls her eyes dismissively at this mention of Colin. "What about the two guys in the boat?" she asks. "You couldn't arrest them. It's not illegal to carry a paper napkin wrapped up to look like a stolen Vermeer."

"You're quick, Miss Thrash," he says. "You might like detective work. You're right, it's not illegal. But guess what else?"

"You want to play a guessing game?" Kiran asks mildly.

Investigator Edwards smiles a dazzling smile. "Guess," he says. "It's about one of the guys, the tall, skinny one called J.R. Turns out the *J* is short for Johannes."

"Johannes?" says Kiran. "Is that really his name? Like Johannes Vermeer?"

"Johannes Vermeer Rutkoski is his name," says Investigator Edwards. "His parents hoped he would aim high."

"He's the forger?"

"Yup."

"Here's his workshop," Investigator Edwards says, then shows Kiran and Jane a big, glossy photo of an easel in a cluttered room. On the easel is an unfinished painting. Jane has seen it before, in the west attics of Tu Reviens, where Mrs. Vanders is cleaning it.

"That's our Rembrandt self-portrait," Kiran says. "Or, it's going to be!" She clutches her temples. "Octavian has never done a thing about security," she says. "No alarms, no cameras. Ever since Charlotte disappeared, he doesn't even lock the doors. He can't bear to."

"Well, it is an island," the investigator says. "But that doesn't make it inaccessible, and you do have all those parties."

Inspector Edwards shows Kiran and Jane one more big photo: a whole row of canvases, leaning against a dirty wall, all painted to look like the Vermeer picture *Lady Writing a Letter with Her Frog*. "His practice attempts," says the inspector.

"Johannes Vermeer Rutkoski is a prodigious talent," says Kiran tiredly. "Makes me think there should be a museum somewhere of all the finest forgeries."

By the time Jane and Kiran get to the Thrash family apartment, Jane is so exhausted that she collapses onto the proffered bed without even removing her clothes. It seems impossible that her scramble through the forest was only this morning.

Kiran comes to her doorway. "Good night, sweetie," she says.

"Kiran?" says Jane. It's the first time they've been alone all day. "Are you okay?"

"I've been better," she says. "But I've been worse. Don't worry about me, just get some sleep. You're the hero of the day, after all . . ."

Jane falls asleep before she can hear Kiran's reflections on heroes.

Her dreams are deep and wild. Ivy is running through a forest dressed in black. She's in danger. She's running away from Jane, vanishing behind tall, dark, slender trees. No. She's turned. She's running back toward Jane. As Ivy nears Jane, she slows, reaches out, hands Jane something. It's an umbrella, and Jane realizes she's not Ivy. She's Aunt Magnolia, in the purple coat with the silver-and-gold lining.

The umbrella Aunt Magnolia hands Jane is the one she's been working on, the one that looks lopsided and uneven, like the blue splotch in Aunt Magnolia's eye. "It's broken, darling," she says, pressing it into Jane's hands. "But it can still keep you safe."

Jane wakes with a fuzzy-feeling mouth from not brushing her teeth the night before, and pins and needles in her legs from sleeping in jeans. The dream feels very near. She tries to hold on to it.

She emerges from her bedroom to find Kiran staring over Central Park through the glass walls of the penthouse, a coffee cup in her hands. When Jane joins her, the two of them witness a rare New York frogstorm. More of a drizzle, really, but enough to muck up the traffic and give the surface of the park the appearance of water, moving with hopping specks and waves of blue.

"How did you sleep?" asks Kiran.

"I had a wonderful dream," says Jane.

It's strange to step back into the receiving hall of Tu Reviens having missed the gala. It's empty, stale; no musicians, caterers, or cleaners. No buzz of activity. The lilacs in the vases look, and smell, bruised somehow.

Kiran goes off to find Ravi and give him the news that the Vermeer is still well and truly gone.

Upstairs, Jasper lies outside Jane's door with his nose to the crack. Seeing her, he leaps to his feet and comes running at her, lopsided and bandaged. As Jane kneels to receive his ecstatic, slobbery greetings, she has a startling sense of coming home. "Ow!" she cries as he scrambles into her lap, his claws digging into her thighs. "Jasper! You're not small!"

In her rooms, she waits for a few moments, looking around, not sure what she's waiting for. Then she sets off to find Ivy.

But when she encounters Mrs. Vanders in the kitchen, Mrs. Vanders tells her that Ivy's gone away.

"Gone away!" says Jane. "Where? Is she coming back?"

Mrs. Vanders is tapping the keys on a laptop at one of the kitchen tables. Patrick stands at the stove sautéing garlic. "Of course she's coming back!" says Mrs. Vanders. "Good god, girl. Don't look so forlorn."

"She didn't tell me she was going."

"Nor should she have," says Mrs. Vanders crisply. "I strictly forbade it."

"She was sorry to leave without explaining," Patrick adds, glancing at Jane over his shoulder.

"This reminds me," says Jane, in increasing annoyance. "I want to know about my aunt Magnolia."

"Ivy asked me if she could be the one to tell you everything," says Mrs. Vanders. "I said yes. It seemed important to her. So you'll just have to wait."

"Well, when's she coming back?"

"In a few days," says Mrs. Vanders.

For a couple of seconds, Patrick goes very still, staring at the wooden spoon in his hands. Then he lays the spoon on the stovetop carefully, switches the burner off, and says to Mrs. Vanders, "I'm done lying to Kiran." He walks into the back of the kitchen and disappears through a door.

"Oh, god help us," Mrs. Vanders says in alarm, springing up from the table, rushing off to follow him, then coming back, glaring in Jane's general direction, slapping her laptop closed, and rushing off again.

"Jasper," says Jane, focusing on the canine at her feet, who gazes up at her with his tongue hanging out. "I literally give up. None of them will ever make any sense. Well. As long as we're waiting for Ivy, we should finish up the umbrella, don't you think?"

The Aunt Magnolia umbrella is waiting for Jane, sitting in the middle of Ivy's worktable, washed in the fading light of the morning room windows.

As her fingers move along its parts, fitting the uneven canopy against the mismatched ribs of the frame, Jane is thinking about broken things. She's proud of herself, for stumbling and making mistakes but still, in the end, putting together the broken pieces of the mystery.

She wonders if she could fit the pieces of her life back together too. *Aunt Magnolia?*

When the canopy is attached to the frame with that particular balance of not-too-loose, not-too-tight, Jane slides the runner up and props the umbrella open, then places it on Ivy's worktable. She stands back. It's crooked and inelegant, just as she meant it to be. It looks like one of those umbrellas you see sticking out of trash bins on rainy days. Except that its crookedness, if you look close, has a kind of balance that Jane has achieved with careful deliberateness, and it's a good umbrella, an unusual umbrella that will protect her from rain. It's also Jane's secret, because when she looks at it in her peripheral vision, it becomes the spiky, spoky, foggy blue splotch of Aunt Magnolia's eye.

I'll never sell this umbrella, Jane thinks. *This one's for me.*

"Jasper?" she says. "Want to go look at Aunt Magnolia's photo?"

There's some activity in the west wing of the second story. As Jane and Jasper walk down the corridor inspecting the art, Patrick comes out of a bedroom with a pile of sheets and blankets and dumps them on the floor. Mrs. Vanders follows with a vacuum cleaner.

"We're clearing out the bedrooms that were used for the gala," Patrick says, in response to Jane's questioning glance. "This was Lucy St. George's room, actually."

Jane only manages a half-interested grunt, because she's just discovered Aunt Magnolia's photo on the wall across from Lucy's room. It's a big print. Backing away to get a better vantage point, Jane breathes it in.

A tiny yellow fish—that's a goby—peeks out from inside the cavernous, sharp-toothed maw of some great gray fish with a bulbous nose. Jane remembers this photo; Aunt Magnolia took it in the waters near Japan. It's always left Jane wondering. Has the big fish captured the small fish as food? Or, is the small, bright fish hiding inside the mouth of the big fish?

Jane is bursting with heartache and pride.

Then her perspective shifts and she notices a problem with the matting behind the photo. Something is creating an uneven bulge, as if the framer carelessly placed a thick rectangle of cardboard behind the print.

A framing mistake like that will ruin the print, and Aunt Magnolia's photos deserve better care. "Mrs. Vanders?" Jane begins with mild indignation, and then, understanding, goes rigid and electric, like a bolt of lightning.

Jane reaches for the screwdriver in her pocket. Wordlessly, she lifts the frame from the wall. Laying it on the floor with the back facing up, she works at the screws that hold the frame in place.

"What on earth do you think you're doing?" says Mrs. Vanders in an outraged voice, appearing beside her. "Just because that's your aunt's photo doesn't give you license to take it apart! That's an expensive frame!"

With trembling fingers, Jane removes the backing of the frame. Protective tissue-like paper lies under it, and through the tissue, Jane can see the outlines of what she knew she would find. Carefully, she takes hold of the edges of the thin paper and pulls it away.

Jane and Mrs. Vanders are looking down, astonished, at *Lady Writing a Letter with Her Frog.* Jane studies it. There's something quieting, even awesome, about the fine web of cracks across the canvas, and its clean, soft light. It's as if the lady, intent on her writing while sitting in a bath of light, is made of soft marble. As if marble can be a warm, living thing.

"Hold it up to the ceiling lamps!" says Mrs. Vanders.

Ever so carefully, Jane lifts the canvas by the edges and holds it up to the light. The lady's eye glows like a tiny star.

"How on earth did you know?" says Mrs. Vanders.

Jane's eyes are full of tears. Frightened she'll drip on Vermeer's masterpiece, she hands the canvas to Mrs. Vanders and says, "Aunt Magnolia led me to it."

A week and a half after the gala, they finally get word from Investigator Edwards. Kiran tells Jane over a game of chess in the winter garden. "Turns out Buckley St. George has some interesting offshore accounts, and some irregular financials that possibly link him to a New Jersey heroin cartel."

"Really?"

"The police raided the cartel and found a Delacroix that belongs to some friends of Ravi's." Kiran tilts her head to indicate Ravi, who's sprawled in a nearby armchair, pretending to read an art magazine with a Rembrandt seascape on the cover.

"Delacroix?" says Jane.

"French painter," offers Ravi in a grouchy voice, not looking up from his magazine. "Nineteenth-century Romantic. Influenced the Impressionists. I could take him or leave him."

"Oh, stop it," says Kiran. "You love Delacroix."

"Nothing compares to the theft of a Vermeer."

"It's all over now, Ravi," says Kiran. "Janie found your Vermeer. You can stop acting like you, personally, were the target of an outrageous conspiracy."

"I'll put it on my to-do list for the day after tomorrow," says Ravi grumpily.

Kiran half grins at Jane. "Anyway," she says, "Ravi's friends didn't even know the Delacroix was missing. They've had a forgery hanging on their wall, and they had no idea. Ravi introduced Colin to those friends."

"That self-righteous shithead," offers Ravi.

Kiran chuckles.

Raindrops ping like pebbles against the windows. Jane moves one of her rooks back and forth, idly. Kiran is a better chess player than she is.

"Did Colin really think that was going to work," Jane says, "lying about my umbrellas? Out of spite? How much money could he possibly have made from them?"

"You humiliated him," says Kiran. "He struck out to make you small again."

"It's kind of pathetic."

"Yeah, well," says Kiran. "It was stupid too, given what was at risk. I don't think he's the master manipulator he thinks he is. I'm really glad I broke up with him *before* we figured out he's an art thief. Thanks for your help with that."

"I helped too!" says Ravi.

"How did you help, exactly?"

"General moral support!" he says. "Through our psychic twin link!"

"Right," says Kiran. "How could I forget."

Their teasing is like the rain—gentle, and washing Jane with a kind of comfort, and a wistfulness too. Ravi pretends to be a child because it makes Kiran smile, which in turn gives Ravi the look of someone who's made his favorite person happy.

"And you," says Ravi, clapping his dark eyes upon her. "I have some ideas about you and your umbrellas."

"Okay," says Jane. "Anything specific?"

Jane has started a new umbrella, and Ravi knows all about it. It's something to do with a house of mystery and intrigue. Jane hasn't worked out the details yet, but she thinks this new umbrella might have windows made of clear plastic and doors that open and close, and art on the walls, and a freight elevator, and a basset hound. Ravi has taken to visiting her from time to time while she's working on it. He asks questions about fabric tension and the placement of springs and inspects Jane's inventory. He's held her Aunt Magnolia umbrella out at arm's length, trying to get some distance from it in order to understand it better. This hasn't seemed to work for him.

"It's the color of a frogstorm," Jane has told him, not telling him all the rest.

He's scrunched up his face, then put the lopsided umbrella back on the floor, muttering, "I guess every artist goes through a Frog Period."

"You really think I'm an artist?" Jane has responded. But Jane is coming to know the answer to that question on her own. She's seeing her umbrellas differently now. People other than she might love those umbrellas someday, probably not for Jane's reasons, but for their own reasons—reasons Jane won't know or understand. Jane is beginning to appreciate this wonderful, surreal fact about the creative process.

"You could start a business," Ravi says now, stretching his legs out before him in the armchair and regarding Jane balefully. "I could help."

"That's not very specific," Jane says.

"You're young," Ravi says. "You've got all the time in the world to establish yourself. And I bet we could get some millionaire designer to send you to college."

"College?" Jane says. "Is there a college where I could make umbrellas?"

"Probably," Ravi says, shrugging. "There's a college for everything. How about a shop someday? I've been to an umbrella shop in Paris where each umbrella is different, and designed by the owner. Your umbrellas will be good enough for that."

"Paris?"

"Or wherever," he says. "The world is your rainstorm."

He juts his chin at the windows and Jane smiles, because it's pouring now, just like the day she arrived. Water streams down the glass and makes her feel safe, contained in a bubble. It's a lot to think about. College, Paris, shops. *Aunt Magnolia? Is this why you made me promise to come here? So the world would be my rainstorm?*

"Do you think someday, when I'm rich and famous, my umbrellas will be used in the drug world as currency?" Jane says.

Ravi flashes her a grin. "Did you know that drug dealers who use art as currency are considered classy?"

"Classy? Seriously? How do you know that?"

"Lucy told me, of course."

"If she's the one who told you, how do you know it's true?"

"I guess I don't," Ravi says. "But I expect most of what she told me was true. Really, there were only a few details she needed to lie about."

The police are saying that Buckley St. George placed his daughter not just in the path of the Thrashes to steal, but straight into the drug underworld, where it was her job to pretend to be an undercover investigator pretending to be a crook. It's difficult for Jane to wrap her head around. All that pretending and manipulating seems an odd direction to focus one's passions.

"I wonder if she enjoyed it," Ravi says. "It must feel amazing to get away with a theft like that." He adds, with some bitterness, "And to fool people."

"I'm not sure she enjoyed fooling you, Ravi," Jane says. "I think she cared about you."

"Don't defend her to me," Ravi says heatedly. "No one who cared about me and knew me at all would steal my art."

"That's true," says Jane, "but I think she was surprised, and upset, by how much it hurt you."

The charges against Lucy now include the theft of the Rubens she "lost," although apparently Lucy blames that theft on pressure from Buckley, just as she blames the Brancusi incident on Colin. Lucy seems to have entered some sort of delayed adolescent rebellion. When the police put her in the same room with her father, she began to scream at him for pressuring her about whom to date.

In another part of the house, the Brancusi is back. It appeared, complete and undamaged, in its usual spot on a side table in the receiving hall, six days after the gala. No one in the house can explain it to Ravi, who's alternately elated and furious. Mrs. Vanders had been keeping the pedestal in the west attics, storing it safely until the fish was found, and one day, when she'd gone up there, it—the pedestal—was gone. Then she'd found it, to her amazement, in the receiving hall, the fish perched atop the pedestal once again, complete and as it should be, or so she says.

Still scowling in his armchair, Ravi says to Kiran abruptly, "What's going on with you and Patrick?"

Kiran takes one of Jane's pawns with her knight and shrugs.

"Oh, come on, sis," says Ravi.

Kiran sits back in her chair, looking untroubled, acting like she didn't hear. Jane wonders how far to push.

"Did Patrick ever confess to you?" Jane asks, not glancing at Ravi, but feeling his hearty approval of her interference. "I saw him the other day, the day we got back from New York. He seemed . . . determined."

"Yes," Kiran says. "He actually said things, for once," she says, catching Jane's eye, but not elaborating. Finally, as the silence stretches out, she shrugs again and says, to Ravi as much as to Jane, "I'm thinking about the things he said."

"What did he say?" Ravi demands.

"Stuff I'm thinking about," Kiran repeats, stubbornly.

"*What* stuff?"

"Twin, if you haven't figured it out yet, I'm not going to tell you."

"Hmph!" says Ravi. "You're lucky I need to keep you around, in case I ever need a kidney."

"Like I'd ever give you my kidney."

"You would totally give me your kidney."

"There's totally a universe somewhere where I've refused to give you my kidney," says Kiran.

Ravi is smiling. "Let's go get *that* Kiran's kidney, just to spite her. We could keep it on ice until one of us needs it."

"That's a disturbing idea," Kiran says. "But practical." She presses a palm to her forehead. "I guess all three of us are kind of looking at a fresh start."

"What?" says Ravi. "Is this about kidneys?"

"No," says Kiran. "I'm thinking about you, me, and Janie. We're all starting fresh. Janie because she's so young and she's alone. She's got her umbrellas. She could really do anything. Sorry," she adds, glancing at Jane doubtfully.

"For what?" says Jane.

"For reminding you that you're alone."

"It's okay," Jane says. *I might not be,* she thinks. Under the table, Jasper nuzzles his nose against Jane's pants legs. He rests his chin on her boots.

"And you and me," Kiran says to Ravi. "We don't have significant others anymore, or jobs. I guess we could also do anything."

"I do like being single," says Ravi. "We could start a bordello. You could be my madame and find me clients."

"Or something less gross," says Kiran. "Blech."

Grinning, Ravi stands. "I want coffee," he says. "Either of you want anything?"

"A bowl of chocolate ice cream," says Kiran.

"I'd take ice cream too," Jane says.

"Coming right up," Ravi says, then strides away.

In the room's new quiet, Kiran watches Jane take a pawn. Jane has questions for Kiran too, less specific than Ravi's, but, she suspects, just as nosy.

"Kiran," Jane says, after a long silence, not sure how to get to the answer she's seeking. "Are you . . . glad you came home?"

Kiran takes a moment to consider Jane's question. "I'm finding," she says, "that despite everything, I'm glad to live in this universe."

"Huh?"

Kiran moves her knight again, endangering Jane's queen. "If we live in a multiverse," she says, "in which multiple versions of us live alternate lives in an infinite series of universes, I'm glad I live in this one. I think that maybe I'm better off than some other Kirans. In this universe, I found out that Colin was stealing from me *before* I did something stupid, like marry him. Some other version of me somewhere is probably married to a version of him and has no idea. And some other version of me lives with some other, less loving version of Ravi. I like my version of Ravi. I guess I even like my version of Patrick," she admits, "given that he's *mine*. I guess I even like my version of me."

"Well," Jane says. "That's convenient, I guess. If weird."

Kiran laughs. "By the way, you're in check."

"Dammit!"

"What if you'd been born in a universe where there was no rain?" Kiran says.

"Huh?"

"I wonder what you would do," Kiran says. "Would you still find yourself drawn to make umbrellas?"

"Oh," says Jane. "I see. Well, I don't know. Could I make parasols?"

"There's no sun, either," Kiran says. "I wonder if you'd have this irrepressible urge to invent sort of a cloth shield on a stick? Would people think you were nuts?"

"Um," says Jane. "It's true I can't imagine not making umbrellas. But don't you think that's partly because our universe *does* have rain?"

"I wonder if you'd even make them waterproof?" says Kiran. "Despite it being completely unnecessary?"

Her question stirs a memory of the conversation Jane had with Ivy while they were waiting to talk to the police. About the digital camera that makes a shutter sound even though it doesn't have or need a shutter anymore.

"If I did make waterproof umbrellas in a rainless world," Jane says, "would that be one of those things? Those things where a design incorporates a feature a thing used to have but doesn't need anymore?"

"Huh?" says Kiran.

Ravi has stepped back into the room, carrying two bowls of ice cream. He's grinning at Jane. "A skeuomorph?" he says.

"Is that the word?" Jane asks, delighted. "Ivy couldn't remember. I can't wait to tell her."

"I'm pretty sure that's the word," Ravi says, walking to their table and handing each of them a bowl.

"I guess it's a little long for Scrabble," Jane says.

"You could build it onto the word *morph*," Ravi says. "Who's winning, anyway?"

"Me," says Kiran. "Where's your coffee?"

"I've only got two hands. I'll get it on my next trip."

"You're a sweetie," says Kiran. "Checkmate."

"Play chess with me next," Ravi says.

"Which one of us?" Kiran says.

"Either," he says. "Both."

"What, like, as a team?" says Kiran, teasing. "What's wrong with you?"

"Whatever," says Ravi, "I'm bored," then reaches down to put his arms around his sister and pull her into an awkward hug. Ravi has been giving Kiran a lot of hugs these days. Jane has a feeling it's as much for his own benefit as for hers; Ravi seems to need hugs. But it's good for Kiran, Jane thinks, that he needs her.

A noise behind Ravi catches Jane's attention. She leans past him to look. Ivy is in the doorway, in a long, wet coat, with her backpack on her shoulders. Rain plasters strands of hair to her cheeks. She looks at Jane shyly, a question in her face.

"Ivy," Jane says. "Ivy, I have things to tell you."

Ivy's smile starts small, then grows big. She holds out a hand to Jane. "Yeah," she says. "Me too."

A bell rings somewhere in the depths of the house,
sweet and clear, like a wind chime.

Mrs. Vanders, the little girl, Kiran, Ravi, or Jasper?

Aunt Magnolia? Jane thinks. *Where should I go?*

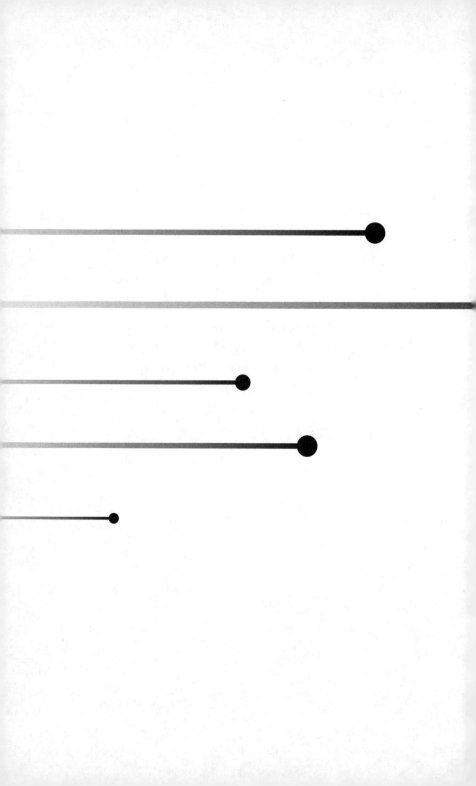

Lies

Without

Borders

Jane decides.

"I'd like to walk with you, Kiran, but can I join you later? I need to check on something."

"Okay," says Kiran, disappointed. "I'll be in the winter garden when you're free."

"I'll find you there," says Jane. "Definitely."

Kiran wanders away.

Jane has to find out the truth about that little girl who looks like Grace Panzavecchia. What if she's in some kind of danger?

Her journey is intercepted on the landing by Jasper, who hops in a circle around her with sharp little barks, as if he's trying to herd her from behind.

"Jasper! I'm not a sheep!" she says, racing down the stairs.

He stays where he is, whining disconsolately.

"You can come with me," says Jane. "I'm on a mission. Aren't dogs supposed to be good at tracking people?"

She turns, descending a few more steps. When she looks back, he's gone. She can't help feeling that it doesn't say much for the likelihood of her finding a little girl if she can't keep track of a dog who was there mere seconds ago. "Jasper, you'd make a terrible sidekick," she says to the air.

Back to the task, Jane weaves through the lilac ladies in the receiving hall and goes to the side table where she saw the girl leave something. Next to a family photo of Kiran, Ravi, Octavian, and a blond, youngish-looking lady who's probably Charlotte is a strange object, itself shaped like a small table. It's a pedestal, with an oak base and a circular mirror top. There's a tiny hole in the center of the mirror. Altogether, it doesn't look particularly significant.

One of the lilac ladies appears beside her. "That's just the sort of stand I need," she says with satisfaction, setting a squat vase of lilacs atop the pedestal.

All right, then. Whatever its purpose was before, it's now a platform for lilacs.

Did the girl leave the pedestal on the table, or the Thrash family photo? And where did she go after that?

Jane crosses into the Venetian courtyard but has no idea which direction to choose next. She's seen some of the rooms to the left— the ballroom, the banquet hall, the kitchen. Curiosity pulls Jane to the right, through the east arcade, then into a room she's never seen before, with old-fashioned, floral green wallpaper, brocaded settees, a fussy green carpet, and no little girl.

Crossing that room, Jane opens a door in the opposite wall and enters another world—for she's found the bowling alley. Not that it's like any bowling alley she's ever seen or imagined; the walls are made of rough stone reinforced with broad wooden beams and the light is low and moody, like something one might find in a cave under a mountain. Two bowling lanes stretch before her, burnished expanses of maple and pine. Pins gleam palely at the end of each lane. *This is where the Pied Piper goes bowling*, she thinks, *by himself, after he's entombed all the children.*

Obscurely concerned now for the missing child, Jane walks straight down the left-hand bowling lane, the only route to a door set in the wall at its end. It feels wrong to her, immoral somehow—surely bowling lanes are not for walking on.

When she opens the door, her world changes again. Heat, light, lapping noises, and the smell of chlorine: the indoor swimming pool. The wall across from her is taken up by an enormous, long fish tank. A fluorescent green eel nestles against the glass, leering at her, and a bull shark—a species of shark known to attack humans—swims lazily from one side to the other.

Uneasily, Jane eyes the water of the pool. No drowned little girl. There's a door in the fish tank though, a normal, wooden door with a brass knob. Jane finds this so peculiar that she opens it, imagining the water, the eel, the bull shark, pouring through the doorway. Instead she discovers a short, dark passage stretching before her, leading through the tank to another door. Opening that door, she finds herself stepping into a patch of crocuses.

Wind whips against stone. Jane can hear the sound of crashing waves somewhere below. It takes her a moment to orient herself: She's at the back of the house.

To the left, some distance along the vast wall, the little girl sits on the ground, nestled against the side of a terrace. She's tucked herself against the house with her arms wrapped around her legs, making herself small.

Jane approaches her stealthily. The girl is crying and shivering. Her hair is short and crooked, a dark shade of blond, her eyes swollen. Her sparkly purple sneakers and her blue jeans are splotchy from the wet grass.

The little girl jumps up as Jane gets closer, glares at Jane, and crouches like a runner about to take off. Jane freezes in her tracks and raises her hands. "It's okay," she says, not certain what she's mollifying the girl about, but doing so instinctively.

"Who are you?" the girl demands.

"I'm Janie."

"Are you with," the girl begins, then spits out a few words in French that sound awfully well-pronounced.

"With *who?*" says Jane.

"Never mind," says the girl. "Why are you here?"

"Did you say 'espions sans frontières'? "

"No," says the girl. "Why are you here?"

"Doesn't that mean 'spies without borders'?"

"I don't speak French," says the girl. "I don't know what you're talking about. *Why are you here?*"

She's not the world's best liar, this little girl. "Because I saw you in the receiving hall and wanted to see where you went," says Jane.

"No." Her tone is shrill. "Why are you in the *house?* What's your *affiliation?*"

Jane finds herself speaking in soothing tones. "My friend Kiran invited me to visit. Kiran's dad owns the house."

"Seriously?" says the girl. "You're just a *person?*"

"Of course. What else would I be?"

"Why should I believe you?"

"Grace?" says Jane. "What's going on?"

"I'm not Grace," says the girl quickly. "My name is Dorothy."

"Okay," says Jane, trying to sound like she believes this. "Nice to meet you, Dorothy. Do you live in the house?"

"I'm related to Mrs. Vanders," says Dorothy. "I'm her great-niece. I'm visiting."

"It's funny, because you look an awful lot like Grace Panzavecchia."

"I don't know who that is."

"She's in the news," says Jane.

"A lot of things are in the news," says Dorothy, wiping her bangs out of her eyes with a damp hand. "A lady got bitten by a bear at a zoo in France. It's raining frogs in Seattle for a record fourteen days in a row. A guy in New York died of smallpox."

"Grace Panzavecchia is a little girl whose parents tried to rob a bank in Manhattan," says Jane. "Then the entire Panzavecchia family disappeared."

"That's preposterous," says Dorothy. "What about their dog?"

"Their dog?" Jane responds in confusion. "What dog?"

"I mean, did they have a dog?"

"Actually," says Jane, remembering something about a dog, spoken by a news anchor who'd looked a little like a St. Bernard (which is why it had stuck in Jane's mind), "it's funny you ask that. I do remember a dog. A German shepherd? The police found it in the Panzavecchias' house after they all disappeared."

"What else?" the girl says.

"About the dog?"

"Yes!" she says. "Who's taking care of the dog?"

"I don't know," says Jane. "The news people aren't talking about the dog. They're talking about the Mafia being involved and the kids disappearing, and the baby being sick with smallpox."

"Smallpox!" the girl says. "The baby doesn't have smallpox!"

"What? No," Jane says, realizing she's misspoken. "Sorry. You're right. You mentioned the guy in New York who died of smallpox and I got mixed up. They're saying the baby has spots, like maybe it's chicken pox or something."

"Smallpox could be used as a biological weapon again," the girl says, "like what the British did to Native Americans at Fort Pitt during the French and Indian War. Did you know that?"

"I—never really thought about it," Jane says. "You seem to know a lot about it."

"Smallpox is supposed to be one of those diseases no one gets anymore," the girl says. "There's supposed to be a stock of it in a lab in Atlanta and one in Russia, just for posterity. But that's only what they say. Microbiologists could alter smallpox so it could be used for modern warfare."

"Okay," says Jane. "They announced on the news a few days ago that the guy who got smallpox had some sort of freak accident. They said he broke into the labs of the CDC in Atlanta and got into something he shouldn't."

"Yeah," says the girl, jutting her jaw with obvious scorn. "That's a likely story."

Jane tries to remember what she's heard from the news. The parents of the Panzavecchia family, Giuseppe and Victoria, are microbiologists. They reportedly walked out of their lab and attempted to rob a Manhattan bank. In the middle of the heist, they panicked, ran from the bank, rounded a corner, and basically disappeared. The bank teller was so startled that she turned to the colleague beside her and asked, "Did that just happen?"

It *had* just happened, and as it was the Panzavecchias' own bank and one they visited frequently on lunch breaks, they were recognized. The police immediately searched their lab (no sign of them); their brownstone (empty except for their German shepherd); and the private academy of their "brilliant eight-year-old daughter, Grace" (who'd asked to use the restroom, then never returned to class).

The search moved on to the section of Central Park where the two younger children, Christopher and Baby Leo, liked to spend their mornings, and where the "distraught au pair" was having hysterics. She'd been walking with the children under one of the arches when "a person of iron strength" had grabbed her from behind and put something to her face. She'd tried to wrap her arms protectively around the children, she'd tried to scream, but darkness had come. The last thing she remembered was her attacker lowering her gently to the ground while a nearby saxophone played the *Godfather* music.

And then at dinner last night, Phoebe brought up the rumors that the Mafia had threatened to harm Giuseppe Panzavecchia's family if he didn't pay his gambling debts. But Lucy St. George, private art investigator, thinks something else must be going on. Giuseppe is too devoted to his kids to risk getting involved with the Mafia; all he ever does is brag about Grace and her amazing mnemonic memory devices.

None of which explains what kind of work the Panzavecchias were doing in their lab. Or if it has anything to do with smallpox. Or why Grace is talking about French spies. Or why she's *here*.

Who even knows she's here, besides Jane? Doctor Philip Okada? He was in the attics yesterday wearing medical gloves, then sneaking around in the middle of the night, saying inscrutable things about a journey and carrying a gun. And a diaper bag. Jane realizes suddenly that the white bag with orange ducks Philip was carrying last night must have been a diaper bag.

Phoebe Okada? Patrick? Mr. Vanders? Jane saw him carrying another small child—little Christopher Panzavecchia?—across the Venetian courtyard only yesterday. What about Ivy, who was with Jane then and didn't give any explanation for the little kid when Jane asked? Ivy was in the attic with Philip too.

What on earth is going on in this house?

"Grace," Jane says. "Are you okay?"

The question seems to trigger the girl's fury. She sits her rump down again, wraps her arms around her legs, and starts crying, but it's angry crying; it's her temper she's trying to contain by holding her own body tight. "I don't even know who you are!" she yells.

"Is someone here hurting you?" says Jane. "Patrick? Or—" She can't get her mouth to say "Ivy." "Phoebe Okada? Are your parents in the house too?"

"I bet you'd like to know! I bet you'd like to ask me a whole lot of questions! I'm not telling you anything!"

"Grace!" says Jane. "I only want to know that you're okay!"

"Stop calling me that! My name is Dorothy!" She rockets to her feet suddenly.

"Where are you going?"

"I bet you'd like to know!" she yells again, then takes off running, around the terrace, along the wall of the west wing and away from Jane. She disappears around the corner of the house.

Jane is standing there, staring numbly after the girl, when the scrape of an opening door spins her around. It's the door Jane came through herself, the one in the fish tank. Patrick emerges, looks to right and left, sees Jane. His face registers nothing. Patrick seems to have a gift for projecting innocent, blue-eyed vacuity. At any rate, his is more convincing than Ivy's.

"Hello," he calls, walking toward Jane. He's swinging a heavy flashlight in one hand, powered off at the moment. "Getting some air?"

"Yes," Jane says shortly. "Clearing my thoughts before I do some work."

"Ivy tells me you make umbrellas," Patrick says, clapping his bright, blank eyes on Jane's face. "Seen anything interesting out here?" he adds, just as if he couldn't care less, and the hair rises on the nape of Jane's neck. She thinks, for some reason, of the leer of that eel in the fish tank.

"Not a thing," says Jane. "What are you doing out here, anyway?"

"Lost something," he says, indicating his flashlight, as if having lost something is a justification for carrying a flashlight in broad daylight. "Thought I might find it here."

"What is it?"

"It's hard to describe."

Does it have crooked blond hair, Jane wants to ask, *a tear-stained face, and a mistrust of all people?* "How enigmatic," she says.

A sudden, staticky noise makes her jump. *"Patrick?"* says a metallic version of Mrs. Vanders's voice. *"Come in, Patrick?"*

Patrick pulls a walkie-talkie from his back pocket. Tucking his flashlight under one arm, he presses a button on the walkie-talkie. "Go ahead."

"Dorothy's come home," says Mrs. Vanders's voice.

Patrick grins brightly. "There's no place like home," he says, then pockets the walkie-talkie, gives Jane a nod, and moves on, taking the same route Grace Panzavecchia took, along the wall and around the western corner of the house.

"Aunt Magnolia," Jane says to the air. "What the actual hell is going on here?"

The air does not respond.

Jane winds her way back through the pool room, the bowling alley, the stuffy green parlor. Her goal is the second-story east wing, where she last saw Mrs. Vanders headed—something about a Vermeer—and where she intends to confront Mrs. Vanders about how she knew Aunt Magnolia, about who Dorothy is, about everything strange going on in this house. But when Jane steps into the Venetian courtyard, Mrs. Vanders is right there, standing beside the fountain, her back to Jane. She's muttering into a walkie-talkie.

"Who's Dorothy?" Jane asks without preamble.

"Oh, hello, Jane," Mrs. Vanders says, lowering the walkie-talkie and turning around smoothly. "Dorothy's my great-niece, visiting from out west. Why? Have you met her?"

"I was with Patrick when you called him on the walkie-talkie and said 'Dorothy's come home.'"

"Yes," says Mrs. Vanders. "She knows she's not supposed to wander around without telling us where she's going, but she does it anyway. I worry, especially since there's a pool in the house. Patrick is fond of her. He was worried too."

"What did you mean by 'Dorothy's come home'? Where's home?"

"Wherever I happen to be when she finds me," says Mrs. Vanders crisply. "I'm her family. Family is home."

"Speaking of family," Jane says, "Mr. Vanders just told me you knew my aunt Magnolia."

Mrs. Vanders grunts, her eyes sweeping the balconies of the courtyard.

"How could that be?" says Jane. "I don't remember Aunt Magnolia ever saying anything about knowing anyone here, besides Kiran."

Mrs. Vanders grunts again, then says nothing, just studies Jane. An odd silence stretches between them. Jane tries again.

"She made me promise once that if I was ever invited to Tu Reviens," she says, "I'd come. Was that so I would meet you?"

"Do you like to travel?" says Mrs. Vanders.

"Yes, I guess," says Jane. "I haven't really traveled much, so I don't really know. Why? Did you travel with her or something?"

"We have one of her travel pictures," Mrs. Vanders says. "A yellow fish peeking out of the mouth of a big gray fish. Your aunt had a talent for . . . uncovering hidden truths."

"Oh," Jane says, amazed, then flushing with pride that Aunt Magnolia's photo should end up on the walls of a fancy house like this. "So, is that how you knew her? Were you in touch about the photo?"

"Do you like Ivy?" responds Mrs. Vanders, peering at Jane.

"Sure," says Jane in confusion. "Why?"

"I may ask for your help at the party," she says. "If I do so, I'll convey the message through Ivy. Now, if you'll excuse me." She turns and walks away.

"I don't work for you, you know," Jane snaps at the empty air.

It's one thing for Mrs. Vanders to lie and evade on the subject of Grace Panzavecchia, who's obviously mixed up in something bad. But why would she need to be cryptic about Aunt Magnolia?

Unsettled, Jane stares into the cheerfully splashing fountain. Somewhere behind her, she hears the approaching voices of Lucy St. George and Colin Mack, and finds herself moving away from them, up the stairs. She needs to think. "I'll be a bit longer," she texts Kiran as she climbs.

Jasper is waiting outside her door. Inside, smoothing her ruffled, red-orange shirt, Jane sits on one of the armchairs before the cold fire. Jasper burrows under the bed and begins snoring, a soft, low, soothing rumble.

For some reason, Jane can't stop picturing the last thing she ever saw Aunt Magnolia wear, the day she left on that final, fateful Antarctic trip. A simple, deep purple dress, flowy, with long sleeves and pockets. Her clunky, sturdy black boots and her long, iridescent purple coat with the silver-gold lining. She'd looked like some sort of fashion warrior set to take on the Antarctic night.

Jane has only just begun the gold-and-brown self-defense umbrella, with its sharp ribs and powerful springs. But what she's imagining now is an iridescent purple umbrella, with a contrasting interior of silver and gold.

Could Jane make an umbrella like that, without it hurting too much?

Probably not. But she gets the feeling she's about to do it anyway.

In her morning room, Jane works, until she becomes aware of the sound of someone yelling. No, not someone; Ravi. Somewhere in the house, Ravi is yelling.

With only half her focus, she goes into the bedroom and sticks her ear out into the corridor. It's coming from the house's middle, quite some distance away.

The trouble is that Jane's stumbled upon an unusual challenge with the curve of this umbrella, and it's asking for her full attention. *Damn Ravi,* she thinks, then comes awake. Wait. If people are yelling, it's got to be about Grace Panzavecchia.

Jane moves quickly down the corridor toward the noise. She steps onto the third-story bridge and finds Ravi in the receiving hall far below, holding that little mirror table she was inspecting earlier, waving it around and screaming. The table's reflective top flashes at Jane as he whirls it about. The checkered floor is strewn with flowers and water, the glass shards of a broken vase.

"Octavian!" Ravi screams. "Octavian!" Cleaners and decorators, interrupted in their work, line the bridges and staircases, staring. Lucy St. George stands beside Ravi, as do Colin Mack, Kiran, Ivy, and Phoebe Okada.

"What's going on?" Jane whispers to the person nearest her, who happens to be the man with the bucket who'd asked directions at breakfast this morning, the apologetic cleaner with salt-and-pepper hair. He's wiping down the banister of the third-story bridge with a wet cloth.

"Don't know," he says, wringing his cloth into his bucket intently. "He just started yelling."

"What's that little table he's holding?" Jane asks. "What's it for?"

"Don't know," the cleaner says again in his unplaceable accent, then freezes for just an instant as Mrs. Vanders sweeps into the receiving hall. She stops before Ravi.

"Be quiet!" bellows Mrs. Vanders. "What in the name of all that's reasonable is the matter with you?"

"This!" Ravi yells, shaking the little table at her. "This is what's the matter with me!"

From where Jane is standing, she can't see Mrs. Vanders's face. She can only observe the housekeeper's silence and the stillness of her stance as she holds a hand out for the little table, inspects it, then passes it to Lucy. White-faced, Lucy inspects it too, especially the small dot in the middle of the mirror. Lucy raises shocked eyes to Colin, who's standing nearby. Lucy doesn't look well; she's a bit shaky.

"Ravi?" Lucy says, clearing her throat. "The sculpture was removed cleanly from the pedestal. Assuming the sculpture itself is unbroken, it should be easy to reattach it."

"Well, that's just wonderful," Ravi says, chewing on sarcasm, "just fantastic, except," he screams, "where is the goddamned sculpture?!"

"Calm down," Mrs. Vanders says. "Take a breath, Ravi, and tell me where you found the pedestal."

"Right there!" Ravi points to a row of side tables. "It was sitting right there—with a vase of lilacs on it—as if it were a party decoration!"

"All right," Mrs. Vanders says. "Breathe."

"It wasn't there last night," says Ravi. "No part of it was there when I got in. Someone took the whole thing away, broke the fish off the pedestal, then put the pedestal back! What kind of lunatic would do that?"

Jane is remembering, now, something about a million-dollar sculpture Ravi was asking Octavian about last night. A fish, a missing sculpture of a fish, by Brancusi. This little mirrored table must be the pedestal for Brancusi's million-dollar fish.

"I don't get it," she whispers to the cleaning man. "Isn't that sculpture worth a fortune? I can see why someone would steal it, but why would someone *break* it?" And why, she doesn't say aloud, would Grace Panzavecchia be carrying the pedestal around, slipping it onto tables in the receiving hall? Are her parents involved in art theft now, since the bank theft failed?

Now Ravi is interrogating Mrs. Vanders, demanding a list of everyone who's recently set foot in the house. Turning suddenly on Phoebe Okada, Ravi spits, "Where's your husband? Where's Philip? He's run off, hasn't he?"

"Good question," Jane whispers, then glances at the cleaner beside her, who's gotten very quiet. It's because he's gone. Only his damp cloth and his bucket of suds remain, and when Jane peeks around in confusion, she catches a glimpse of him stepping off the bridge into the house's east side.

She'd think little of it, except for something odd that happens below. "I'm going to pretend you didn't just imply that my husband stole from you," Phoebe says to Ravi, then strikes out across the floor, heading for the Venetian courtyard. But before she starts moving, she throws her head back and narrows her eyes at Jane, or rather, at the space beside Jane where the cleaner was a moment ago. Something about it seems . . . deliberate. Phoebe's gaze on the empty spot beside Jane is ferocious.

It's enough to turn Jane around and propel her onto the nearest balcony overlooking the Venetian courtyard, to see where Phoebe is going. Behind Jane, Mrs. Vanders is suggesting to Ravi that the broken sculpture might be an accident or a prank. Ravi is responding with bewildered hysterics—"Call the FBI, the CIA, and Interpol!"—while in front of Jane, in her own private world of bewilderment, Phoebe zooms across the courtyard floor to the stairs on its west side. She begins flying up them, two and three at a time, faster than Jane has ever seen anyone move in her life. Phoebe is somehow achieving this astonishing speed in high-heeled boots without making a clatter; Jane hears nothing but the voices in the receiving hall and the splash of the fountain. Who is Phoebe? What is her job? Phoebe shoots desperate glances now and then at the third-floor balconies across from her, and when Jane tracks her gaze, Jane finds the cleaner, slowly rounding the atrium via those balconies. It's as if Phoebe is racing to intercept him somewhere without him knowing, and it's as if everything depends upon it.

"Espions sans frontières," Grace said, or at least, that's what Jane thinks she heard. Espions. Spies.

She's moving before she's even really decided. She catches up with the cleaner as he nears the final turn before the servants' wing. He doesn't hear Jane behind him, just slinks smoothly around the corner and out of her sight again.

As she nears the corner, Jane hears a conversation start up between the cleaner and Phoebe, who seems not only to have beaten him to the servants' quarters but to have done so without getting winded. Their voices stop Jane; suddenly Jane can't think what she imagines she's doing, pursuing the cleaner, spying on Phoebe, eavesdropping. How will she explain herself?

"Hello," Jane hears Phoebe say, in a casual, even tone. "Where are you going?"

The man clears his throat. "To the bathroom."

"So far from where you were a moment ago? There's a toilet beside the main staircase on every floor."

"Why does it matter to you which bathroom I use?"

"When a theft has been discovered," says Phoebe, "everyone's movements become fascinating, don't you think? Interesting that you're sneaking away while a member of the household is making a scene and everyone's distracted."

Jane can't stand there listening anymore. Where does Phoebe come off suggesting that this random guy might be involved in the theft, just because he has to *pee?* She stomps around the corner. "Phoebe!" she says. "What are you doing?"

Neither one seems surprised to see her. "Janie," says Phoebe, raising an eyebrow at her. "Come to play Robin Hood?"

"What does that even mean?" says Jane. "I'm here to tell this guy that he can use the bathroom in my rooms. If that's your idea of Robin Hood, then, yeah."

"All right," says Phoebe. "Go on. Do your 'tired masses yearning to be free' routine, but I've got my eyes on this fellow. I've half a mind to tell Ravi, or Mrs. Vanders."

"Tell them what?" says Jane. "That you can quote the poem on the Statue of Liberty? That you've been stopping people from going to the bathroom? That you hate immigrants?"

"It's 'huddled masses,'" says the man, interrupting.

"What?" say Jane and Phoebe.

"'Yearning to breathe free,'" he says. "'Give me your tired, your poor, / your huddled masses yearning to breathe free, / The wretched refuse of your teeming shore.'"

"Oh," says Jane.

"Whatever," says Phoebe. "I'm British."

"So?" says the cleaner. "I'm South Korean."

"Well, I'm American," says Jane, "and I'm kind of offended by the poem now that I'm hearing it. My ancestors were not wretched refuse!"

"Perhaps the wording was chosen for alliterative purposes," says the man, with a brief, comprehensive look at Jane. His eyes take in her boots, her red-orange ruffled shirt, her striped skinny jeans, her boisterous hair. She feels oddly . . . catalogued.

"I'm getting a headache," says Phoebe. "Are you taking this *cleaner* to your toilet or aren't you?"

"Ugh!" says Jane, disgusted by Phoebe; floored, really, that some people are actually this snobbish. "My rooms are at the other end of the house," she tells the man.

"Thanks," he says.

"What's your name?"

"Ji-hoon."

"Ji-hoon," says Jane, extending a hand. "I'm Janie. Do you know a lot of poetry?"

"I have a remarkable memory," he says. "I use mnemonic devices."

Phoebe watches Jane and Ji-hoon walk away.

* * *

After Ji-hoon uses Jane's bathroom, he takes his leave, bestowing upon her the parting gift of a recitation of "I Hear America Singing" by Walt Whitman. It's a little weird, but by now Jane is beyond expecting anyone to be anything *but* weird. Ji-hoon holds her eyes for a moment, nods briskly, then goes.

Scratching her head, Jane goes back to her Aunt Magnolia Coat umbrella, filling her hands with metallic and iridescent fabrics, letting her work tug at her, and thinking things through. Espions sans frontières. Spies without borders. Jane is no expert on the world of espionage, but she's pretty sure spies wouldn't even exist if there weren't any borders.

Maybe she heard Grace wrong.

Before too long, her stomach informs her it's lunchtime. Jane has no idea if Tu Reviens has an official lunch hour and she decides it doesn't matter. She'll go to the kitchen and bring something back to her rooms. She'll eat while she's working.

"Hungry, Jasper?" she says to the bed as she walks through the bedroom. Jasper pushes an inquisitive nose out into the light and snorts. "I'm going to the kitchen, if you're interested."

He bolts out eagerly, sticking so close to her that Jane feels a bit unsafe on the stairs and holds hard to the banister. On the second-story landing he almost trips her. "Jasper! I need my feet to walk. I can't walk when there's a sixty-pound dog attached to them. I want your company, you banana-head, but we can't actually occupy the same space, do you get that?"

He hops on his front legs once, in a manner heralding an ominous intention to charge. Jane's instinct takes over and she legs it across the bridge. But he doesn't charge. He stays there on the east landing, hopping around in front of that tall umbrella painting, howling delicately, like an opera singer holding herself back before the big climax.

"Fuzzball," Jane calls across to him, "you fit right in with everyone else in this house." Then she continues on into the west wing, because she's just had a thought. If the Thrashes and guests are currently at lunch in the banquet hall, Jane wants nothing to do with it. If there's a back entrance to the kitchen, it might be at the bottom of the staircase at the end of the west wing. She'll try it.

She isn't paying much attention to the art on the walls, until something familiar brings her up short. It's Aunt Magnolia's photograph, blown huge.

Backing away to get a better vantage point, Jane soaks it up.

A tiny yellow goby peeks out from inside the cavelike mouth of a big gray fish. Aunt Magnolia took this photo in the waters near Japan, Jane remembers. And she feels like the little fish right now, bright and determined, but not altogether safe.

Jane is so proud of Aunt Magnolia, she could burst.

Then her perspective shifts and she notices a bulge in the matting behind the photo, as if the matting is way too small for the print. She'll have to mention it to Mrs. Vanders. A framing mistake like that will damage the print, and Aunt Magnolia's work deserves better care.

Jane was right about the back entrance: At the bottom of the staircase is a big metal door that deposits her into the kitchen. The dumbwaiter and a pantry are to her right. Two huge appliances to the left, presumably a refrigerator and a freezer, block her view of the rest of the room. She eases around them, then stops.

Patrick and Mrs. Vanders stand near the stoves with their backs to Jane, blocking her view of the person they're speaking to. But Jane recognizes the voice of Phoebe Okada.

"Yes," says Phoebe. "I think he's the one. He says he's South Korean, but I don't believe him." Then Phoebe hands a distinctive black thing to Mrs. Vanders that Jane also recognizes: Ivy's camera.

Mrs. Vanders peers down at the camera and says crisply, "Yes, I've wondered about him. Patrick, find out what Ivy's learned."

"Now," says Phoebe, "what about my appointment?"

"Mr. Vanders is busy," says Mrs. Vanders. "He's digging holes."

"I saw," says Phoebe. "Why, exactly?"

"He's pretending to garden," says Mrs. Vanders.

"So, my appointment is canceled because Mr. Vanders is playing make-believe?" Phoebe says blandly.

"We got a tip that Grace might've buried it in the garden or the backyard," says Mrs. Vanders. "Mr. Vanders is looking for it."

A tip that Grace buried something? Jane saw Grace herself, digging holes in the rain. Jane mentioned it to Mr. Vanders this morning; she said to him, "I saw a little girl digging in the garden yesterday." Then Mr. Vanders froze in astonishment. So is it Jane, then, who provided this "tip"? About *what?*

"You're kidding," says Phoebe.

"No," says Mrs. Vanders dryly.

"She's a clever pain in the ass, isn't she?" says Phoebe. "How old is she, eight?"

"She's taking years off my life," says Patrick proudly.

"Regardless," says Phoebe, "I scheduled this appointment weeks ago. I need to talk to Mr. Vanders."

"There's nothing we can do," says Mrs. Vanders. "Someone needs to look for that sculpture. If we can't put it back together, our contact isn't going to help us move the children."

"Well, you've made an inconvenient choice as to who's the gardener."

"Mr. Vanders is no happier about it than you are," says Mrs. Vanders. "But he's trying to approach the digging as a meditative activity. He would not otherwise have time to meditate on a day like today. Meditation improves his sessions."

"Well, that's no use to me if my sessions are canceled, is it?" says Phoebe.

"You could go dig with him."

Phoebe makes a scoffing noise. "Sure. No one would think it was out of character with my snob persona if I dropped to my knees in the garden next to the butler and started digging. Why isn't Patrick digging? Are you too pretty to dig, Patrick?"

"Patrick also has his hands full at the moment," says Mrs. Vanders. "It's the day before a gala, Phoebe. I appreciate your needs, but I'm certain you appreciate ours as well. Everyone at Espions Sans Frontières is making sacrifices. Cook has barely had time to touch his saxophone and my yoga has most certainly suffered."

Then Mrs. Vanders shifts to one side and Phoebe and Jane are looking straight into each other's faces.

Phoebe smiles, with a sincerity Jane's never seen in her face before. "You keep popping up," she says, "don't you. You have a talent for sneaking."

Patrick and Mrs. Vanders spin around. Their faces are unsurprised, unreadable.

"I'm not sneaking," Jane says. "I wanted some food. So I came to the *kitchen*."

Patrick glances at Mrs. Vanders, then walks toward Jane, past her, almost brushing against her. "You've got an awfully quiet tread," he says, "for someone your size, and wearing those boots."

"My aunt Magnolia taught me not to push myself onto any environment," Jane says, earning a small chuckle from Phoebe.

"Tell me when Mr. Vanders is free, please, I beg you," Phoebe says to Mrs. Vanders, then turns and exits through the kitchen's main door. Patrick has also made his exit, through the back door.

Jane is alone with Mrs. Vanders. She lifts her chin and holds the housekeeper's steely eyes. There's no more point in pretending.

"I know Grace Panzavecchia is in this house," says Jane. "I know she took the Brancusi sculpture. I know Phoebe and Philip Okada aren't who they're pretending to be, and neither are you."

Mrs. Vanders stares at Jane, with a silence so obstinate that it's somehow aggressive. "Tell me," she says, "how do you feel about it?"

"What does it matter how I feel?" cries Jane. "Is this a therapy session or something?"

Mrs. Vanders smiles, grimly. "It could be, if you wanted it. Mr. Vanders is a licensed psychologist, specializing in these things."

"Specializing in *what* things? People who lie?"

"Specializing in the needs of political agents and government operatives," says Mrs. Vanders.

"Oh, come on," Jane spits out, truly at the end of her patience. "You're all playacting some silly game."

"Well, playacting is part of the job, it's true," says Mrs. Vanders with another grim smile. "Your aunt Magnolia was quite good at it."

"Aunt Magnolia didn't playact," says Jane automatically.

"Your aunt is dead," says Mrs. Vanders. "It's time you knew who she really was. I've meant to get in touch with you for months now, but I guess I've had too much on my plate. Magnolia would be furious at the delay, rest her soul."

Jane has this strange feeling, as if she's in a car, careening in slow motion toward a tree. "Stop it."

"The servants of Tu Reviens are a secret espionage-advocacy group," says Mrs. Vanders. "We provide confidential, non-partisan services for agents, operatives, and assets of all political loyalties, mostly during this house's seasonal galas. We're called Espions Sans Frontières, Spies Without Borders. Your aunt Magnolia—"

"Stop it!" says Jane.

"Your aunt Magnolia was an operative for the American government."

"She wasn't," says Jane. "She was an underwater photographer. She was not a spy!"

"She did underwater photography too," says Mrs. Vanders. "It was the cover for her work as an *operative*. In our circles, *spy* is, in fact, a rather derogatory term."

"Oh, come on! This is preposterous!"

"It may be preposterous," says Mrs. Vanders, "but it's entirely true. It's why I knew Magnolia. ESF helped her from time to time. I'd like to know how you feel about it, because we're always recruiting."

Behind Jane, a door opens and Ivy steps in, tall and easy in her ratty blue sweater. At the sight of Jane, she stops, a stricken look coming to her face. "Janie?"

In Ivy's eyes, Jane sees concern, misery, guilt. She sees the truth. Her heart plummets. *This is real.*

"What is it, Ivy-bean?" says Mrs. Vanders harshly. "You can go ahead and say it in front of Jane."

Ivy clears her throat. "I've looked into that man who's calling himself Ji-hoon," she says. "I'm not sure, but Phoebe could be right."

"Very well," says Mrs. Vanders. "Until we know for certain, we can't do anything extreme, but we can make damn sure he gets nowhere near the children. Please ask Phoebe to come see me at her earliest convenience."

"You can't really ask more of Phoebe, can you?" says Ivy. "She's a British operative. She doesn't work for ESF."

"The Brits benefit if we get the children away," says Mrs. Vanders. "Everyone benefits, and Phoebe knows that. She'll do what I ask."

"All right," says Ivy, then hesitates, looking at Jane.

"Ivy," says Mrs. Vanders, not without a sudden, surprising touch of tenderness. "Go. Ji-hoon and Grace are both in the house; we can't take risks."

Ivy goes.

"You needed food?"

Jane casts about for a grip on what Mrs. Vanders is saying. "What?"

"Come," says Mrs. Vanders. "I'll help you collect some things."

"Okay," Jane says automatically, not caring. As she follows the housekeeper into the pantry, a staticky noise emerges from one of the shelves.

"Sweetie?" says the deep voice of Mr. Vanders.

Mrs. Vanders reaches for a walkie-talkie sitting atop a fruit basket. "Go ahead."

"I found the fish," says her husband's voice. *"I'll bring it up to your studio. It badly needs cleaning."*

Mrs. Vanders releases a breath of air. "Thank heaven for small blessings."

"Are you still worried the Vermeer's been forged?" says Mr. Vanders's voice.

"Ravi hasn't noticed anything wrong with it. We talked for ten minutes standing right in front of it."

"Have you had it out of the frame?"

"Not yet," says Mrs. Vanders. "I'll do it after we've moved the children. If it *has* been forged, it's nothing to do with the children or any of this, so I simply can't spare it a moment's attention right now."

"Don't blame yourself for putting it on the back burner," says Mr. Vanders.

"I do blame myself," says Mrs. Vanders. "If the Vermeer has been forged, it's a calamity. You know how seriously I take my responsibilities to the family. Ravi's already so upset about the Brancusi."

"He'll have his Brancusi back in a week's time, none the wiser," says Mr. Vanders. *"And you'll be able to give the Vermeer your fullest attention after the children are safe. Which will be soon, now that we have the Brancusi in hand. The gala is tomorrow. This is almost over."*

"Thank you, Arthur," says Mrs. Vanders. "I suppose it always gets like this before the galas."

"There is always something," says Mr. Vanders with a chuckle, then a sneeze. Then the static cuts out. Mrs. Vanders shoves the walkie-talkie back onto the fruit bowl and reaches for a cutting board.

"Which cheese do you prefer," she says, "muenster or gruyere?"

"What?" says Jane. "Cheese?"

"I'm making you a sandwich," says Mrs. Vanders. "Do you like chicken liver pâté?"

"Are you—" Jane's head is aching. "Are you using the Brancusi sculpture to pay someone to move the Panzavecchia children out of the house? Because of something to do with smallpox?"

"See now," Mrs. Vanders says, pausing in her swift slicing of thick, dark bread to peer at Jane keenly. "This is what I mean. If you've managed to figure that out, it suggests to me that you have instincts for our kind of work."

"But—it's not your Brancusi," says Jane. "You're stealing the Brancusi?"

"We do not steal the family art," says Mrs. Vanders. "We *borrow* it, to use as collateral while we act as go-betweens. I give a picture or sculpture to Person X. Person X releases an item to me—an agent I'm trying to save, information, goods—and I deliver that item to Person Y. Person Y pays me with the thing Person X needs—again, an agent, information, goods—and I deliver that thing to Person X. Person X gives me the picture or the sculpture back. A masterpiece is an excellent cash alternative. Recognizable, with undeniable value, and harder to trace than cash, which isn't an option anyway, because we don't have it."

Jane feels herself stupidly nodding. She's heard of this strategy. "But Ravi doesn't know," she says.

"No one in the Thrash family knows about ESF," says Mrs. Vanders. "I'll tell Ravi I've taken a picture away to clean it, or that I'm doing some sort of research on it."

"You'll lie," says Jane.

Mrs. Vanders piles cheese and pickles and pâté onto bread. "People want to hurt these children," she says. "There's a woman who's offered to move Grace and Christopher Panzavecchia for us, in return for the brief loan of our Brancusi and also our Rembrandt. She's a peculiar woman. It's not about money or information for her; it's about having various pieces of art in her collection, briefly, from time to time. And she never asks for anything easy. The Rembrandt picture is big and heavy, painted on wood, and the Brancusi sculpture so fragile, but those are the only two pieces that'll do for her this time. We'll have them back in the house within a week."

"Why are the Panzavecchias so important?"

"I can't answer that," says Mrs. Vanders. "ESF provides protection, to political agents who are exploited, kidnapped, left to fend for themselves. If their loyalties come into question, we provide exit strategies, safe passage for them and their families. Often our services require the help of third parties. These third parties don't help us out of the kindness of their hearts. They require payment. We've learned to use whatever's available to us."

"By lying to people in this house who trust you implicitly," says Jane.

"What should I be doing instead?" she says, exasperated. "Should I never lie, which would endanger countless people? Should I not risk the house art, when it can ensure the safety of two children?"

"I need to go now," says Jane.

"Don't say anything to anyone," says Mrs. Vanders. "Grace and Christopher Panzavecchia are only eight and two. You'll endanger their lives if you speak of any of this to the wrong person. Would you like that on your conscience? A dead child?"

"Why should I believe you're trying to help them?" says Jane. "If you're being so helpful, why does Grace keep trying to sneak away? Why did she break the sculpture you need so badly to 'rescue' her?"

"Grace is a traumatized child who's been torn from her family and desperately wants to go home," says Mrs. Vanders. "She doesn't understand that home no longer exists. She's trying to create problems for us, draw attention. She's acting out! But even she knows where the line is!"

"Why does home no longer exist? What happened?"

"That is far more information than you're in need of at this juncture," says Mrs. Vanders.

"Where's Baby Leo?" Jane asks. "Why is no one talking about him?"

"The baby is safe," Mrs. Vanders says. "Here's your sandwich, some grapes, and a kumquat." She shoves a plate at Jane so forcefully that grapes go diving off the edge, rolling into unknown and unreachable parts of the pantry.

"I can't believe you lie to Ravi," says Jane. "And Kiran too. Every single day. How can you do that?"

Mrs. Vanders's face is made of granite. She shoves a doughnut onto Jane's plate, causing more grapes to go flying. "We'll be keeping an eye on you," she says. "We'll know if you start wandering the house. And we have ways of knowing if you're engaging in mobile phone or Internet activity. If we decide that we can't trust you to keep your mouth shut, you'll find yourself deeply regretful."

"Wow," says Jane. "You really make me want to work for you. I want a job where I get to threaten innocent visitors and lie to all the people who trust me most."

"On second thought," says Mrs. Vanders, "you stay right here. I'm getting someone to walk you back to your rooms."

"Kiss my ass," Jane says, then turns and walks out.

As Jane is making her way up the back staircase with her plate, Patrick comes clattering down from the west attics, which doesn't surprise her.

He reaches her, then turns back around to accompany her. Jane doesn't even look at him.

"What would you do if I started screaming something about your stupid organization?" she says. "Wrestle me down and gag me?"

"No," says Patrick calmly. "But I would stop you."

"I'm innocent, you know," Jane says, "and I didn't ask to be involved in all this crap."

"Didn't you?" says Patrick. "Weren't you following Grace around this morning? And weren't you asking everyone questions about your aunt Magnolia?"

"Not because I was hoping to find out she was a spy!"

"She had reasons."

"Do me a favor," says Jane, "and don't flaunt the ways you knew my aunt better than I did."

"Don't be silly," says Patrick. "She was your aunt. You're the one who knew her."

He sounds like he means it, but it's too absurd to be answerable. They're walking back the way Jane came before, through the second story's west wing, past Aunt Magnolia's photograph.

If it's even hers.

"All these years," she says to Patrick, "you've been lying to Kiran about who you really are."

He doesn't speak again for the rest of the walk.

Jane remembers the questions she'd had after Aunt Magnolia's death. One of her aunt's colleagues had called from the Antarctic Peninsula. "A storm came up," he'd said, his voice cutting in and out; the connection on that phone call had been terrible. "She was too far from the base. She never made it back. I'm sorry," he'd said, but Jane hadn't understood what that meant.

So she'd dragged herself to her doctor, Doctor Gordon, and asked what it meant to die in a snowstorm in Antarctica.

Doctor Gordon had sat Jane down gently. "The first thing that happens is that your blood moves from your skin and extremities to your core," she'd said. "This is called vasoconstriction. It helps you conserve what heat you have, rather than lose it to the environment." She'd stopped, waited for Jane's nod. "Then you start shivering," she'd gone on, "all over your body. You become clumsy. It becomes difficult to use your hands or walk." Another nod. "Your thoughts start to get dull, you have some amnesia. Apathy sets in, which is a blessing, really. You might burrow somewhere, like a hibernating bear," she'd said, "before you lose consciousness. Once you do lose consciousness, you might wake now and then to hallucinations, but finally you fall asleep and don't wake up again. Your body can take a long time to die, but during that time, you're not suffering. Do you appreciate that, Janie? That at the end, she wasn't suffering?"

But Jane hadn't been able to bear the idea that Aunt Magnolia had certainly known, in a snowstorm in Antarctica, what her own sleepiness had meant. Jane's sleep had gotten even worse from that day on, because that's how Aunt Magnolia had died. Or so Jane had thought.

Did she ever even go to Antarctica? Or did I drag myself to the doctor and sit through that horrible litany for nothing? She's suddenly hot with shame at the thought, as if Aunt Magnolia has pranked her.

Her eyes find the framed photos she's hung on the morning room walls. The anglerfish in Indonesia. The squid in Peru. The falling frogs in Belize. The Canadian polar bear, suspended underwater. Aunt Magnolia had used to draw Jane a map for every trip she took, with the dates written carefully, so that Jane could have the comfort of following her progress and knowing where to imagine her at any point in time.

All lies. Other people had known where Aunt Magnolia really was. *Ivy* had probably known. Jane crosses to the photo of Aunt Magnolia herself, standing in scuba gear on a New Zealand seafloor, touching a whale. Is that even Aunt Magnolia? In scuba gear, it could be anyone.

Jane reaches into her pocket for her folding knife. She flips the screwdriver extension open, takes the photo down from the wall, and applies the screwdriver to the back. When the backing comes loose, she throws it aside, then grabs the photo and holds it out before her, staring at that person on the ocean floor.

Liar, Jane thinks, and tears it in half, separating the person from the whale. Then, with a growing rage, she tears the person in half, then in fourths, then into as many tiny pieces as she can. She runs to the fireplace in the bedroom, hurls them into the grate, and throws some small pieces of wood in there with them. Finding a box of matches, she lights a few and throws them in there too.

Back in the morning room, she takes the next picture down from the wall, and the next, and the next, tearing the squid in pieces, tearing the anglerfish, the frogs, tearing the polar bear with Aunt Magnolia's writing that says "Sing Ho! For the life of a Bear!"

Lies, she thinks, *all lies!,* stumbling back into the bedroom and throwing the pieces onto the fire. Miraculously, a corner of wood is alight, despite her careless fire-building, and pieces of the first photo are curling and catching fire. She watches them turn black, trying to decide what she's going to do with the huge photo hanging in the second-story west corridor. Bring it back and throw it on the fire? Or smash the whole thing to pieces right there? She runs into the morning room again, lifts the Aunt Magnolia Coat umbrella-in-progress over her head, and crashes it down onto the rug. When nothing breaks, she crashes it again, harder, until she hears the ping of ribs snapping off the runner and small pieces of metal go flying. Crying now, she grabs the purple iridescent fabric and pulls until the seams tear apart with a scream of breaking thread. She traps the silver-gold fabric under her boots and pulls again, ripping it to pieces.

She's reaching for the next umbrella, the pale blue eggshell with brown spots, she's lifting it and raising it high, when Jasper runs into the room, presses against her legs, and starts whining.

Jane is momentarily confused, because she last saw the dog on the second-story landing. How did he get in?

Ravi's voice, rising from her bedroom, answers her question. "Not much of a fire," he's calling to her. "You need to build a sort of chimney out of these smaller pieces of wood."

"What?" Jane drops the eggshell umbrella and grasps her head. *What's going on?*

"Don't worry," Ravi calls, "I'm fixing it."

"You can't just come into my rooms!" she yells back at him.

"I knocked and you didn't answer."

"That means you're supposed to go away and leave me alone."

"The dog wanted in."

Jane glances around. Crumpled on the floor, the Aunt Magnolia Coat umbrella looks like some sort of large insect she's defeated in hand-to-hand combat. And she feels like she's been in a battle. Her face is swollen and her breath short. Mopping her eyes with her sleeves and sniffling hard, she pushes the umbrella's broken pieces into a pile, hoping Ravi won't notice it, or her tears.

Ravi appears in the morning room doorway, wiping his hands on his shirt. He peers at her. "You okay?"

She avoids looking at him directly. "Yeah."

"You look—crazed."

"It's an artist thing," Jane says. "Don't worry about it."

He indicates the mangled umbrella. "What happened to that one?"

"Sometimes they don't work out."

"Okay," he says skeptically, surveying the rest of the room. He wades into the midst of the completed umbrellas and surveys them gloomily, dismal and pathetic, like Hamlet, or maybe Eeyore.

"This is the only room in the house where I feel any peace," he says, gripping his white-streaked hair and sighing.

"If you're hitting on me again—"

"I mean the umbrellas," Ravi says, waving his hand around. He points across the room at one that leans in a corner. It's a simple, understated umbrella, alternating pale yellows with a mahogany rod and handle. "May I open that one?"

"Really?" Jane says tiredly. "Now? I'm working, Ravi."

"I think I want to buy it for Kiran," he says. "It makes me think of Kiran. If I like it when it's open, I'll give you three thousand dollars for it."

"*That is ludicrous,*" Jane says, enunciating each syllable. "Come back when you've recovered your senses."

"No one is taking this seriously," Ravi says. "Have you noticed that?"

"Taking what seriously?"

"The Brancusi!" Ravi says. "Mrs. Vanders still hasn't called the FBI. It's all 'the gala' this, 'the gala' that, as if the gala is more important than the family or the house."

Jane has completely forgotten all about the Brancusi, the gala, everything. She considers, for a moment, what would happen if she told Ravi that his servants are using the Brancusi to pay some woman to protect the missing Panzavecchia children, because Giuseppe and Victoria are mixed up in some sort of espionage, possibly involving weaponized smallpox.

He would flip out. Loudly, and dangerously. That's what would happen.

Jane crosses to the yellow umbrella. Carrying it back to Ravi, she places it into his hands and says, "Take it with you. Open it in your own rooms. Inspect it. If you like it, you can buy it for a hundred dollars."

"Like hell," Ravi says. "That would be theft."

"I'm not taking three thousand dollars from you for one umbrella."

"Twenty-five hundred, then."

"I'm pretty sure this isn't how bargaining is supposed to go."

"I'm not going to stand here while you undervalue your own work," Ravi says. "Don't forget that valuing art is my job."

"You're not going to stand here at all," Jane says. "You're going to leave, and I'm going to lock the door behind you, and then I'm finally going to be alone."

"How about two hundred for the umbrella and twenty-three hundred for me to go away and leave you alone?" he says.

Despite herself, Jane laughs. Ravi has found the only workable angle; her solitude is definitely worth twenty-three hundred dollars. "Take the umbrella," she says, "and we'll talk about it later."

"All right," Ravi says, with a mild twinkle of amusement. "That's acceptable. It's an honor to do business with the artist." He turns to leave.

"Ravi," Jane says.

"Yeah?" he says, turning back. He narrows his eyes on her in curiosity.

Fuck it, Jane thinks. "Have you looked closely at the Vermeer?"

"The Vermeer?" says Ravi. "What about it?"

"Mrs. Vanders mentioned earlier that she thought there was something wrong with it."

"Wrong? What are you talking about?"

"I overheard her talking to Mr. Vanders. I think she might have used the word *forged.*"

Ravi freezes. "Do you have a screwdriver?" he says thickly.

Jane crosses to the place where she threw her little folding knife on the floor, its screwdriver still extended. She tosses it to Ravi, who fails to catch it, scoops it up from the rug, then, without a second glance, leaves the room.

* * *

Alone again, Jane stares at the ruined umbrella. This is her Aunt Magnolia Coat umbrella, and she's lost hold, entirely, of what that means.

She can't quite bring herself to go into the bedroom and check out the state of the photos. She can hear a fire crackling brightly in the fireplace, so she has a feeling she knows what she'll find.

Did Aunt Magnolia even take the pictures?

Did she die because she was a spy?

Outside noises touch Jane's ears: the squeak and rattle of a ladder being placed into position. The wet protest of a cloth against glass. Idly carrying her sandwich and some grapes to the glass wall, she leans, looks down, and can just barely see the edges of Ji-hoon, man of mystery, washing the house's outside windows in preparation for the gala. He too is apparently not what he seems.

Everything around me is a lie.

"Except you, Jasper," she says to the dog, who's watching her anxiously.

After a while, a knock sounds on the bedroom door. The notion of having to talk to someone is exhausting. It'll either be someone she has to lie to or someone who's lied to her. She drags herself through the bedroom and swings the door open.

Ivy stands there rubbing the back of her neck, looking a bit nervous.

"Hi," she says. "Are you okay?"

"Seriously?" Jane says. "You're really asking me that?"

Ivy raises her eyes to Jane's and they're so full of unhappiness that Jane is instantly furious.

"What do *you* have to be so upset about?"

"Plenty, actually," says Ivy, with a touch of sharpness.

"Whatever. What do you want?"

Ivy lets out a short sigh. "Mrs. Vanders says you have to have dinner in your rooms. We'll bring you food."

"She doesn't trust me with the other guests now," says Jane; a statement, not a question.

"She's pretty mad that you told Ravi to go look at the Vermeer."

"It's true, then? It's forged?"

"Yeah," says Ivy with a weary sort of indifference. "Turns out that in the middle of all this other stuff, someone stole the Vermeer."

"So, what, she's not glad to know for sure?"

"Well, yeah. But Ravi's in hysterics, which is pulling Mrs. Vanders away from things she needs to be doing. And now it's even harder to justify not calling in the cops. A lot of cops in the house will make it even more tricky for us to move the kids."

"Oh," Jane says, understanding, with a prick of guilt that makes her mad at herself, and then at Mrs. Vanders, that this would, of course, be true. "Right. It doesn't mean I'm going to start telling people about the Panzavecchias at dinner, though."

"I know," Ivy says miserably. "I'm really sorry." She examines the ratty end of her blue sweater. "I've been trying to imagine what this must be like for you."

Jane finds herself laughing, quickly, once. "Maybe when you figure it out, you can fill me in."

"Look, Janie," Ivy says. "I was born into this work. I've never known anything else. And I've been wanting to get out of it for a couple years now, and finally I'm about to. This is my last op."

"Really?" Jane says, curious, despite herself. "You're allowed to stop?"

"As long as I clear it with headquarters."

"There's a headquarters?"

"Espions Sans Frontières is an international organization," Ivy says. "We're just one of the branches. It's based in Geneva. I'll go there and have an exit interview, then I'll make plans to leave this house. I'll do something else, something that doesn't give me nightmares. This house gives me nightmares!"

Now Jane is trying to imagine what Ivy's life has been like. "Are all the servants here born into this life?"

"Pretty much. I was, and Patrick, and so was the Vanders family," Ivy says. "It's been going on for generations. My parents died doing this work."

"What?" says Jane, startled. "I thought it was some sort of travel accident."

"I guess it was, technically," says Ivy. "It was four years ago. They were trying to help an agent get to—someplace safe, far away from here. The same way we're trying to help the Panzavecchias get someplace safe. That time, we were trying to fake the agent's death. That part worked. But other things went wrong and they were shot."

"My god, Ivy. I'm sorry."

"Well," Ivy says. "You lost your parents unexpectedly, and then the person who was basically your mother too. You know what it's like."

Jane examines her own boots for a moment. "The thing about learning that someone isn't who they said they were," she says, "is that you start to wonder if you ever really had a relationship with them in the first place. You try to picture them, and instead, there's this empty space. The only thing you're sure of is that they were a person who lied."

"Oh," Ivy says with conviction. "You knew your aunt. She was yours more than she was anyone's."

"But I don't even know what she did," Jane says. "In my mind, she was underwater with the animals. She was waiting, and observing, and not pushing herself in."

"I know a little about what she did," says Ivy. "Not a lot. But a little." She pauses. "Do you want me to tell you?"

"What's the point? I should've heard it from her, not someone else. Hearing it from you will just—" *Hurt,* Jane thinks. *It'll just make it even more plain that my life is a lie.*

"I'm sure she didn't mean to hurt you."

"Don't defend her to me," Jane snaps.

"But what if it helps explain things?" says Ivy. "I mean, wouldn't it at least give you a more solid target to be pissed off at?"

"Now you sound like a therapist," Jane says, but she sees Ivy's point. "Okay, fine," she adds. "Tell me."

"Well," Ivy says quietly. "I know she was an underwater nature photographer, for real. But she also salvaged the wreck of a North Korean submarine once, and an Iranian sub, and that Russian aircraft carrier that sank a few years back, remember? And sometimes she tapped undersea cables. Sometimes she cut undersea cables and set it up to look accidental."

This is impossible. Jane is laughing again. There is no way for her to recognize the person Ivy is describing, a person who salvaged submarines full of nuclear missiles, full of secret information, full of the bloated corpses of drowned soldiers. *Aunt Magnolia took pictures of beautiful animals. She was trying to save the oceans.* "That's enough."

"Okay," Ivy says. "I only ever met her a couple times. She had a great wardrobe, and sort of a steady, reassuring temperament. She seemed—eccentric, but also practical, no-nonsense. Kind of like you."

Ivy's words make Jane wish, suddenly, for a mirror. She wants to find the parts of her face that are like Aunt Magnolia's. "Was the Antarctica trip actually a spy trip?"

"As far as we know," Ivy says, "Magnolia was really going to Antarctica to take pictures of penguins and whales."

Is it better or worse, Jane wonders, that she died as a nature photographer, not as a spy?

"You know not to trust anyone in the house, right?" Ivy says. "Especially don't get involved with that guy who's pretending to be a cleaner, the one who calls himself Ji-hoon. He could be dangerous."

"He actually is a cleaner," Jane says. "I mean, he is cleaning things, whatever else he's doing."

Ivy smiles slightly. "I still wouldn't trust him. Even to clean."

"Why is he so dangerous, anyway?" Jane asks. "Who is he?"

"Mrs. Vanders would strangle me if I told you."

"Is he, like, armed?"

"Oh, no question he's armed," Ivy says. "He wants to get to Grace. She has something he wants."

"Grace!" Jane says, thinking of the girl, huddled up and crying, angry. Small. "What could Grace possibly have that armed people want?"

Ivy hesitates. "She's got something in her mind. Information."

In Jane's own mind, something stirs. "Grace has an amazing memory," she says. "She uses mnemonic devices. Her father is very proud of it."

"Yes." Ivy starts to say something more, then stops with a frustrated sigh. Strands of hair have escaped her messy knot and her shoulders seem hunched and tight. "I want to tell you everything," she says. "I'm sorry, Janie. I just can't."

Jane wants to reach out and push a strand of hair out of Ivy's eyes. She wants to touch her shoulder; she wants to understand.

She doesn't touch Ivy, but Ivy's eyes do touch hers once, shyly.

"I have to go," Ivy says. "I'll leave dinner outside your door in a little bit. I'll tell Kiran you're not feeling well, if that would help."

"Okay."

After Ivy leaves, Jane goes back to her morning room.

Tu Reviens is making noises. Hums of water, breaths of heat; settling moans. Jasper wanders blearily into the room and comes to lean against Jane's feet. "This house makes a lot of weird sounds," she says to him. "Don't you think?"

A wail begins, so distant and so faint, so mixed with the strange, metallic banging of the heater that Jane would assume it was just a trick of wind or water if she didn't know it was probably Christopher Panzavecchia, age two, somewhere in the house.

She goes once to the window, peeking down at Ji-hoon. He washes the glass, slowly, like someone giving the house a backrub to help it fall asleep.

Jane tries a deep, jellyfish breath, but she can't do it. Even the jellyfish feels like a lie.

The house wakes her from a dream about—what is it? A man who's stolen Baby Leo Panzavecchia and it's more terrible than even the newscasters realize, because the man is infected with smallpox, and now Baby Leo is too. He'll pass it on to Grace and Christopher, to Espions Sans Frontières, to the Sicilian Mafia, and to the fishes, because Baby Leo sleeps with the fishes.

The dream shifts as Jane leaves it behind, as dreams do. She flails around in a fit of itching, calling for Aunt Magnolia, who saves itchy, underwater babies, it's part of her spy work, and then she's awake, Aunt Magnolia's scratchy wool hat pressed against her sweaty neck.

Jane is in her bed in Tu Reviens. A warm basset hound snoozes at her feet. The clock beside her bed glows the time: 5:08 a.m. She breathes through a spinning panic, remembering that in the weeks before that last Antarctic trip, Aunt Magnolia had been unusually distracted. She'd left a burner on one day after heating some soup, unheard-of for Aunt Magnolia. More than once, Jane had caught her staring into a book she clearly hadn't been reading, because she'd never turned a page. And then there was the night Jane had woken to find her awake, the night Aunt Magnolia had made her promise to come here if invited.

The day Aunt Magnolia had left, Jane went into her own bedroom and discovered the hat sitting in the middle of her bed. Aunt Magnolia always took that hat with her to cold places. But that time she'd left it behind, for Jane to find. Why?

Why do dreams make us wake with questions that have nothing to do with the dreams?

Under the covers, Jasper crawls around until his head is resting against her elbow. Jane listens to his steady breathing, wondering if maybe Jasper breaths are even better than jellyfish breaths.

The day dawns yellow and green. Jane hasn't really succeeded in falling back asleep. Finally she slips out of bed, quietly, so as not to disturb Jasper. She goes to the morning room and peers out the window.

A figure approaches the house from the ramble: Colin Mack, dressed all in black. He seems in a hurry, glancing over his shoulder more than once. It's a little strange; does he think he's being pursued? Why is he out there? Surely not *everyone* in the house is a spy? She watches him enter the house through the door that leads to the swimming pool.

When she turns back to face the room, the ruined umbrella on the floor undoes her. Its broken pieces are angled such that she can see purple fabric with the merest glimpse of a silver-gold interior. It creates a shimmer in her mind, the way a bright light will create a memory of itself that lingers inside a person's eyelids, then fades. A momentary ghost of Aunt Magnolia.

"Aunt Magnolia?" Jane says out loud.

She'd always responded swiftly when Jane had called her, putting aside her own concerns whenever Jane had said her name. Those moments had been real.

Gently, Jane lowers her butt to the floor, her head leaning back against the window glass. The umbrella is a trick, nothing more.

Apparently Jane is allowed to attend breakfast when the time arrives, because no one tries to stop her. The route to the banquet hall passes through the ballroom. She keeps close to the walls and tries to avoid the team of women cleaning the ballroom floor.

No one is at breakfast, and no one seems to be serving, either. A carafe of coffee sits at the far end of the long table next to fruit, cold cereal, milk, sugar, and a pot of congealed oatmeal. She pours herself some cornflakes and eats quickly. Then it's back to the receiving hall, which is swarming with people. She's not sure where to go next, really, until she sees Jasper on the second-story bridge. He's sitting contentedly on his rump, his nose poking through the balusters, and Jane thinks that maybe he has the right idea. She climbs to him. "I guess you've witnessed a lot of gala mornings, haven't you, Jasper?"

The hullabaloo below begins to make more sense. The people resolve themselves into separate currents: cleaners and caterers and musicians. Patrick and Ivy, zooming across the hall or up and down the stairs at random intervals, no doubt doing spy stuff. Do they ever even do any housework at all? Who knows. Mrs. Vanders herself does not zoom. Mrs. Vanders stands like a rock in the center of the receiving hall, the currents swerving gracefully around her. She barely speaks, as if she's controlling the action with her eyeballs.

Kiran comes along the bridge and stops on the other side of Jasper, yawning. Yet another person who has no idea what's going on in her own house. *Don't make me have to lie to you,* thinks Jane.

"Morning," Kiran says with half a smile. Her hair is pulled back into a ponytail and Jane thinks maybe she's not wearing any makeup yet. "Getting the bird's-eye view?"

"It makes more sense from up here," Jane says.

"Are you feeling better?"

"Yeah, I'm lots better today."

Kiran leans her elbows on the railing. "When we were little," she says, "these were our favorite days of the year. I used to love standing here with Patrick, watching all the people. Ivy was tiny then; she would hold my hand and stare, her eyes big as saucers. Ravi loved getting in everyone's way."

"How? What would he do?"

"Mainly he would slow everyone down by insisting on carrying things himself, and having really bad ideas about where everything should go." Kiran flicks her ponytail over her shoulder, half smiling. "I'm sure he thought he was helping."

"And he was allowed to do that?"

Kiran shrugs. "Not if Mr. or Mrs. Vanders or Octavian caught him at it, but they were always running around like crazy themselves. Ravi knew how to avoid them. He was a charming little autocrat. It was . . . educational to watch how people responded to him."

"Educational?"

"A lesson in class," Kiran says. "Probably also sex, and certainly age and race. What does a white, female string quartet do when a little half-Bengali rich boy whose white daddy owns the house tells them to set their stage up someplace really stupid, like the middle of one of the staircases?"

"I don't know," Jane says. "What?"

"It was generally one of three things," Kiran says. "Ignore him; stall until a Vanders or Octavian came through and shut him up; or do what he said while shooting him hateful looks. In that particular case, they ignored him, and when he started howling, they kept ignoring him, and finally Octavian came in and carried him away on one shoulder, kicking and screaming for Mum. Who of course didn't come, because she was working."

"What would Octavian do next?" Jane says. "Spank him?"

"Probably go bowling with him," Kiran says, "while having a man-to-man talk about respect for other people."

Jane supposes it's the sort of approach Aunt Magnolia might have taken, if they'd had a private bowling alley. "That sounds kind of nice."

"Ravi and I have had a lot of character-building conversations while bowling," Kiran says with a wistful sort of amusement. Jane finds herself studying Kiran. Her eyes are too bright and she's blinking. Jane wonders, how much sleep did Kiran get last night? Did Colin share her bed? Has Patrick ever shared Kiran's bed, lying to her when he has to get up suddenly to take care of some spy emergency?

"What about Ivy and Patrick?" Jane ventures. "Would Octavian give them talkings-to too?"

"Oh, no. They got their lectures from their parents, and from Mr. and Mrs. Vanders."

"I see," Jane says. *I'll bet they did.* "Would Patrick tell you about the lectures he got?"

"He used to," Kiran says. "Then he stopped."

"Stopped?"

At that moment, Ravi sweeps into the hall below with wet hair and an air of injured righteousness. Coming to a halt before Mrs. Vanders, he speaks in a voice that booms into all the high spaces.

"I've invited the New York State Police, the FBI, and Interpol to the gala," Ravi announces. "I've given them the run of the house."

Jane's stomach drops. This is her fault. "You've *what?*" cries Mrs. Vanders.

"The New York State police, the FBI, and—"

"To the gala? Have you completely lost your gourd?"

"Why shouldn't I?" says Ravi. "It's my Brancusi and my Vermeer! It's my house! It's my party!"

"It's your father's Brancusi and your father's Vermeer!" says Mrs. Vanders. "It's your father's house and your father's party!"

"My father is a ghost," Ravi says. "He wouldn't care if we built a bonfire in the courtyard with his art. If he's stopped caring, that leaves me to care double."

"I'm already in touch with the police," says Mrs. Vanders. "They are already investigating, *discreetly.*"

"Where? Why haven't I seen them?"

Patrick has walked onto the bridge and is standing beside Kiran. He rests his forearms casually on the banister, as Kiran is doing. Kiran doesn't look at him or even acknowledge him, but Jane senses a new tension in her. Their shoulders are touching.

Jane stiffens when Ivy arrives on the other side and stands beside her.

"What a fun party it'll be for everyone," says Mrs. Vanders acidly, "with the FBI and Interpol asking all the guests rude questions."

"Why should it bother anyone who isn't an art thief?" Ravi demands. "Honestly, Vanny, I could almost think you don't care."

"Damn you, Ravi," says Mrs. Vanders. "You know I care, it's my job to care. I only wish you'd had the consideration to ask me whether inviting law enforcement to the gala might create undue strain for all the people your family has hired to guarantee that the guests of your gala have *fun*. That's our job too, you know. You've made things more difficult for me and Mr. V, Patrick, Ivy, Cook, all the staff, because your single-mindedness makes you thoughtless."

Mrs. Vanders raises her eyes then, to Jane, and pins Jane with the same accusation. Heat suffuses her. Grace Panzavecchia is going to be discovered by someone who shouldn't discover her, and it'll be her doing.

"Hey," Ivy murmurs beside Jane. "Don't worry. You did nothing I wouldn't have done."

"I wasn't looking for reassurance," Jane says, suddenly resentful of Ivy, who has no right to be reading her mind.

"It's our job," Ivy says. "We'll deal with it."

"You do that."

Kiran has been quiet on Jane's other side. Jane has no idea if she's overheard this conversation, or what she'd make of it if she did.

"Good morning, Ivy-bean," Kiran says across Jane, to Ivy, ignoring Patrick.

"Hi, Kir," says Ivy, her eyes bleary behind her glasses.

"Want to go bowling?" Kiran asks.

It takes Jane a moment to realize the question is meant for her, not Ivy. "Me?" she says. "Okay, sure."

Kiran takes Jane's wrist and leads her away, carefully skirting Patrick. "Come on," she says. "The bowling alley will be the only quiet room in the house."

There is, of course, nothing quiet about throwing weighted balls onto a maple floor. But the initial crash, the deep rumble of the rolling ball, and the high-pitched, plasticky explosion of pins are the punctuation to a mostly uninterrupted silence between Jane and Kiran.

Kiran stalks to the foul line, throws a loud strike, and spins back, grim-faced, and Jane registers that she's been angry this entire time. Kiran was angry when she walked into the campus bookstore back home. *Imagine how angry she'd be if she knew the truth,* Jane thinks. *She'd bowl a perfect game.*

Jane slips her fingers into a ball. "The gala's soon," she says, hoping it might get Kiran talking.

"Maybe that'll interrupt the boredom," Kiran says.

"Do you always come home when there's a gala?"

"Pretty often," Kiran says. "I might make three out of four most years. It's sort of a family tradition. Octavian always gives me a special invitation call about it, or anyway, he used to."

"He stopped?"

"I doubt Octavian's raised a phone to his ear since my stepmother left. He's depressed."

Jane strides toward the foul line and releases the ball with a satisfying thud. Idly, she watches its progress toward the pins, six of which go flying. "You did tell me Patrick was the one who invited you this time."

"Right," says Kiran. "With all those vague noises about wanting to confess something."

"He still hasn't confessed anything?"

"Nothing," Kiran says.

Jane's ball pops onto the ball return. "What do you think he wanted to say?"

"Who knows?" Kiran says. "It's typical, really; it's his specialty. He expects the people who love him to be clairvoyant. Can you imagine loving someone like that? Someone who's not going to help you understand him?"

"I—yes," Jane says.

"The problem is," says Kiran, "I've seen a different Patrick. I've seen two or three different Patricks, and they're different from my Patrick."

Jane's next ball misses her remaining pins entirely. "Yes, well, people have many sides."

"My Patrick is secretive," Kiran says. "Pointlessly secretive." Then she flings her ball down the lane, barely waiting for the pins to reset. As her ball eviscerates the pins, she says, "They're not all secretive like that."

"All men?" Jane says, a bit lost.

"All the Patricks," Kiran says. "I've seen a Patrick married to a Kiran. They're happy together. That Patrick isn't secretive. I've asked her."

"I'm confused," Jane says. "Are you talking about ideas of you and Patrick that you've imagined?"

Kiran lets out a short, impatient sigh. "Yeah," she says. "Something like that."

"But the real Patrick is secretive."

"Like you wouldn't believe," Kiran says. "It's ridiculous, the questions he won't answer. 'What did you do last evening, Patrick?' 'Why are you running around the house shining flashlights into all the closets, Patrick?' 'Where were you that time you disappeared for three days,

Patrick?' I mean, I respect his privacy. But it's not like the questions I ask are *nosy*. We grew up together. I'm his *friend*. I don't even need to know! I trust his reasons are good ones, whatever stupid thing he's doing. But it's hard that he doesn't trust me."

This, Jane realizes, is part of what hurts so much about Aunt Magnolia. It's not just that she lied and hid who she really was. It's that she did it because she never trusted Jane enough to tell her.

Kiran, Jane thinks later, *would make a good spy.*

The gala is in full swing. Jane is on the second-story bridge, looking down at all the fancy people, Kiran and Jasper at her side again, except that now Kiran is wearing a strapless crimson gown that probably cost a million dollars. A diamond hangs from a fine gold chain and sits nestled in the hollow of her throat; her ears drip with diamonds. Jane has never seen so many diamonds.

Jane is wearing a gray cashmere sweater dress with long sleeves, unlike anything she's ever worn before in her life. She borrowed it from Kiran. She'd planned to wear a sleeveless gold top over purple jeans to look like a royal gramma, a reef fish found in the Atlantic tropics, and carry the Aunt Magnolia Coat umbrella. She'd planned to keep her tattoo fully visible so people would ask about it. But if Aunt Magnolia pretended to be someone else, well then, she can too.

She's still wearing her big black boots, though. They're what she wears when she's mad.

The scene below is like something out of a movie. Women in flowing gowns of every color and men in black mill about, holding drinks in crystal glasses, smiling and laughing, shifting shoulders and backs now and then to let someone new into their group or squeeze someone out. Lucy St. George is down there, wearing an understated chocolate-colored gown and talking to Phoebe Okada, who's dazzling, actually, in turquoise. It's funny that Lucy goes undercover sometimes as a private investigator, but has no idea about Espions Sans Frontières.

Near them, Ravi, who always looks good in black, has his arm thrown around Colin's shoulder with a sort of affectionate possessiveness and is talking and laughing with a man and a woman Jane doesn't recognize. Among these guests are two New York State Police officers, two FBI special agents, and one Interpol officer. They're formally dressed, like everyone else, except, according to Kiran, who spots them instantly, they're *not* dressed like everyone else.

"Like me?" Jane asks.

Kiran takes a sip of her Pimm's and glances at Jane with an expression that startles Jane, because of the fondness it contains. "You *do* look like the rest of us, sweetie, except for those boots," she says. "It's strange to see you this way. These cops are trying to fit in, but their shoes are cheap and their clothes lack a certain tailored elegance."

Kiran points out the state police officers, the FBI special agents, and the man from Interpol. It's the FBI special agents, in fact, that Ravi's flirting with.

A woman Jane doesn't recognize comes through the front door with Ivy, who, Jane now understands, is the reason black gowns were invented. Her hair is wrapped around her head in a series of complicated twists and braids that must've taken someone ages, and her glasses are the perfect touch. The woman beside her is maybe fiftyish, small and plain, in a simple gray dress, carrying a dripping black umbrella. Ivy leads the woman on a winding route through the crowd, gently taking her hand or her arm, positioning her to left or right.

Jane imagines herself in the woman's place.

"I wonder who that is with Ivy," says Kiran. "I can't tell anything from her clothing. But it's interesting, isn't it, that Ivy's shielding her from the cops?"

"What?" Jane says in instant alarm, less because it's probably true and more because Jane doesn't want Kiran noticing Ivy shielding spy-type people from cops.

"She's doing kind of an amazing job of it," Kiran says.

"What?" Jane says. "She's not!"

"Watch her," Kiran says.

And so Jane watches as Ivy and her charge pass near Colin, Ravi, and the special agents. Not only does Ivy put herself between her companion and them, but she reaches a hand to Colin's arm and gently shifts Colin, hence Ravi as well, to better block the agents' view of the woman she's leading. Colin glances around in absentminded annoyance, but doesn't seem to gather what's happened or who's touched him. Ivy and the woman are already beyond his sight.

Next, Ivy and the woman pass through the doorway that leads into the ballroom. Then, a moment later, the Interpol officer passes primly through the same doorway. Before Jane even realizes what she's doing, she herself is moving across the bridge, propelled by worry for Ivy.

Not missing a beat, Kiran moves with her. "Going somewhere?" she says, too suspicious, too interested.

"Just for a walk," Jane says, beginning to move down the stairs.

"I'll join you," Kiran says, which is stating the obvious, since she's practically glued to Jane's side.

"It's not necessary."

"Isn't it?" Kiran says in a menacing voice, then plunks her Pimm's down onto the tray of a startled serving man who tries to give her a tiny meat pie. "Beautiful party," she tells him with a serene smile, not pausing as she and Jane fly along. The dog thuds from step to step behind them, trying to keep up.

From the ballroom, Jane and Kiran pass into the banquet hall, where guests congregate around mountains of food Jane barely notices, because she's looking for the slightly balding head of the Interpol officer. Kiran grabs Jane's wrist and pulls her into the kitchen, and there he is, striding past the stoves and the long wooden table. An uproar of catering people are preparing tiny English food. None of the regular house staff is present.

"Kiran?" says Jane. "What are we doing?"

The officer disappears into the kitchen's deepest depths, where the dumbwaiter, the door to the back stairs, and the pantry are. Kiran follows him around the refrigerator and freezer, still gripping Jane's wrist, not speaking, her heels clapping across the tile floor like gunshots. Jane feels like she's on a Nantucket sleigh ride.

As they reach him, the Interpol officer opens the door to the dumbwaiter carriage and sticks his head in.

"That seems dangerous," Kiran says to him cheerfully, letting Jane go. "We don't want to be responsible for an injury to an Interpol officer. What if someone sent something down while your head was in there?"

"Up, rather," the officer says, extracting his head from the dumbwaiter doorway, shutting the door, and peering at Kiran and Jane suspiciously. "I can see the mechanism below. What's down there? I heard the voice of a man speaking what may have been Bengali."

"Yes, I heard it too," Kiran says. "That's one of the servants, Patrick. Today's Saturday. Saturdays are Patrick's Bengali days."

"Bengali days?" says the officer dubiously. He's a pale man with puckered lips, French-sounding, and speaks English with a deliberate distinctness, as if he's determined to convey how much he hates speaking it.

"To help him learn," Kiran says. "Patrick has a gift for languages. On Wednesdays he speaks only German. Would you like to meet him?" she says brightly, taking hold of the handle on the back door. "We're headed down to help him carry up some English sparkling wine."

"English wine," says the man, looking mildly offended.

"There's a secret trapdoor in the wine cellar floor that leads to a genuine oubliette," Kiran adds. "You might find that interesting, being French."

"I'm Belgian," says the man stiffly. "And I can think of nothing more silly than an American oubliette in a building barely one hundred years old. This house is a theme park."

"You don't want to see the oubliette, then?" says Kiran. "It's super creepy."

With one last, affronted glance at Jane's boots, the Interpol officer releases a breath of air and stalks from the kitchen.

"Good riddance," Kiran says once he's gone.

"Kiran?" says Jane. "Why did you chase away the Interpol man?"

"This door is locked," Kiran says, tugging at the back door. "Why would it be locked?"

"Does Patrick really speak Bengali and German?"

"He knows some bedroom Bengali," Kiran says, distracted. The dumbwaiter is humming and squawking.

Kiran yanks its door open.

A man sits cross-legged inside, brown-skinned, with thick black hair, dressed in a fine black suit and gaping at Jane and Kiran in sheer amazement as he glides upward in the carriage.

Kiran speaks a few words to him calmly in a language Jane doesn't understand. The dumbwaiter continues its smooth upward climb and the man disappears from sight.

"Did you know that guy?" Jane squeaks.

"Never seen him before in my life," Kiran says, closing the dumbwaiter door, "but that was the guy the Interpol officer thought he heard speaking Bengali in the wine cellars. Because he's an interfering Belgian ignoramus who can't tell Bengali from *Arabic* even though they're nothing alike."

"You speak Arabic?"

"It was one of my majors."

"What did you say to him?"

"'Have no fear,'" Kiran says. "'Your cover isn't blown.'"

Jane is beginning to feel a little hysterical. "What's that supposed to mean? Kiran, why would you say that to him if you don't even know him?"

Kiran shrugs. "It seemed the safest thing to say. I mean, think about it. If he's a bad guy, we don't want him to think we're against him, right? And if he's a good guy, then of course we're not going to blow his cover."

"Kiran," Jane says, enunciating each syllable. "Are you fucking kidding me?"

"Listen," Kiran says, "I don't have the foggiest idea what's going on in this house tonight, but I think you're pretending to be more ignorant about it than you actually are and I don't appreciate being lied to."

The dumbwaiter is making its noises again, and before Jane can contrive to stop her, Kiran swings the door open. The carriage, descending from above this time, passes by containing Patrick, who holds on one arm a toddler with curly dark hair, solemn dark eyes, and southern Italian looks. It's Grace's little brother Christopher Panzavecchia. Jane recognizes him from the news reports.

"Hi!" Christopher cries cheerfully. Patrick, meanwhile, gapes at Kiran in dismay. In his other hand, he holds a gun.

"Hi," Jane says to Christopher, because, wide-eyed and delighted, he seems to be waiting for it.

"I love you," Patrick says to Kiran, almost as if it's a question, as the carriage slowly glides past.

"Go to hell, Patrick," Kiran says, practically spitting.

Once he's gone, she slams the dumbwaiter door, holds on to the handle, and seethes. The groans of the mechanism fade away, then go silent.

"Goddamn him," Kiran says. "Goddamn him to hell. He loves me? He's in my dumbwaiter with a gun and a Panzavecchia baby who's wanted by the Sicilian Mafia and the New York State Police! Goddamn you, Patrick!"

"Oh, god," Jane says, because this is her fault. She's the one who sprang off to follow the Interpol man while Kiran was growing increasingly suspicious beside her. She's the reason Kiran's seen what she's just seen. "Oh, god."

"Oh, brace up," Kiran says, clapping Jane on the shoulder.

"Brace up?" Jane cries, incredulous.

"I mean, really, it's funny," Kiran says. "Isn't it funny? He invited me home. He wanted to confess something! Ha! Ha!" Kiran begins to gasp, then clasps her stomach and roars with laughter, until she's wiping tears from her face with one pinky, trying not to disturb her mascara. "Oh, lordy," she says, hiccupping. "At least now we know the Arabic man is a good guy."

"We do?"

"Well, Patrick is a good guy," Kiran says. "It follows that anyone else riding in the dumbwaiter is a good guy too."

"It does?" Jane cries in utter confusion.

"I mean, I'm furious," Kiran says, drawing herself up straight, dropping all traces of amusement. The dumbwaiter is humming and squeaking again. "I never want to see his face again. The things I've told Patrick, trusting him. And I was right; I always knew there was something off about him. But he'll have a good reason to be in the dumbwaiter with that child and a gun."

"I—think he actually does," Jane says weakly.

The dumbwaiter stops rumbling. Kiran swings the door open. A folded piece of paper is propped inside the carriage with a message written on it. "KIRAN," it says. "GET IN."

"Mrs. Vanders's handwriting," Kiran says, then begins to climb

"You have no idea."

Ivy hesitates again. "I think," she says cautiously, "you should let [M]rs. Vanders tell you whatever she knows. All the details, whatever [th]ey are. It might not help right away. But maybe it'll help eventually."

Jane gives up on her dumbwaiter metaphor. As a tear slides down [he]r face, Ivy takes her hand.

Aunt Magnolia? Jane thinks, then remembers, with a sad tug, that [sh]e's no longer speaking to Aunt Magnolia.

"Come up to the attics," Ivy says. "You'll be safe up there."

[In] the west attics, Jane finds Kiran and Mrs. Vanders standing on [o]pposite sides of a long table, arguing.

"You understand this was over a hundred years ago?" Mrs. Vanders [i]s saying in a voice of exasperation.

"What does that matter?"

"The first housekeeper of Tu Reviens had a son," Mrs. Vanders says. Her son had gotten mixed up in the Spanish-American War some [y]ears before and became an American operative. He'd also fallen in love with a Cuban agent."

"How romantic," says Kiran caustically.

"It ended with both of them dead."

"Of course it did," says Kiran, "or it wouldn't be so romantic."

"They were Mr. Vanders's grandparents," says Mrs. Vanders. "Afterward, Espions Sans Frontières approached his great-grandmother, the housekeeper, about secretly using her employer's house. Given that such an organization might have saved her son, can you really blame her for saying yes?"

"Yes to lying to my great-great-grandfather, who trusted her?" Kiran says. "Yes to endangering everyone in this house, which wasn't hers, for generation upon generation? For making the family *liable*?!"

into the dumbwaiter carriage. "This feels like something out of *Alice in Wonderland*. Where do you suppose this is going?"

"I don't know," Jane says. "The west attics? The servants' wing? The oubliette?"

"There's no oubliette," Kiran says. "I made that up to get rid of the snotty Interpol man."

"You're awfully good at this," Jane says a bit wildly.

"Am I?" Kiran says, sitting there calmly in her crimson gown, clusters of diamonds sparkling in her ears and at her throat, her arms wrapped around her legs. "I guess it's the first time I've had fun since I stepped back onto this goddamned island."

Someone somewhere along the track of the dumbwaiter pounds a wrench—maybe it's a gun—against metal, twice. Kiran checks that her fingers and toes are completely inside the carriage, then knocks twice on one of the walls, impassively, as if everyone knows that's what a person is meant to do in this situation. The carriage begins to rise.

"Meet me above," she says, "if you like. Unless you've got some secret mission you're on too." Then she's gone.

Jane is left in the kitchen, staring at the moving cables in the empty track of the dumbwaiter carriage, trying to fit square pegs into round holes. *Is this why Aunt Magnolia became a spy? Because it was* fun? *How can Kiran see what she's just seen, and laugh, and say it's* fun? *Oh.* Jane clutches her temples, wishing for a way to extract herself from all of this.

Then Jasper leans heavily against her legs.

"Well, Jasper," she says. "I guess, whatever else happened, we succeeded in getting that Interpol man off Ivy's tail. What do you say? Should we return to the party and see if we can undo any more of my damage?"

Back in the ballroom, she finds the Arabic-speaking man from the dumbwaiter drinking Pimm's and being charming with other party guests. She supposes he must be a good guy if Mrs. Vanders is letting him ride in the dumbwaiter, but she gives him a wide berth anyway. Passing into the receiving hall with Jasper, she spots a familiar form: Ji-hoon, the South Korean "cleaner," who's smoothed his hair handsomely back and donned dark-rimmed glasses and black formalwear. Jane almost doesn't recognize him, he's so polished and slick. He's ascending the east staircase calmly, unhurriedly. He doesn't see her.

Abruptly, Jane turns for the west stairs and starts up them, moving as fast as she can without drawing undue attention. *Why do I keep doing this?* she asks herself, exasperated. *Why do I keep involving myself?* Jasper falls behind. Guests drift past now and then as she climbs, seeming to come from all wings of the house. Jane gathers that there must be a tradition, at these parties, of wandering the upper floors to look at the art. No wonder people can sneak all over the place without arousing suspicion.

She's huffing and puffing by the time she reaches the third floor. Stopping outside the door to the servants' wing, she catches her breath, no idea what to do next. Assuming this is even Ji-hoon's destination, she's beaten him, but how will she stop him when he arrives? Start reciting poetry and hope he joins in? Ivy has warned her that he's dangerous, he's armed. Where is Jasper?

Then the door to the servants' wing swings open and Phoebe Okada steps out, her turquoise dress delightfully swishing, her eye makeup smoky and flawless.

"I'd love to know what you think you're doing," she says.

"Phoebe," Jane says. "Ji-hoon is coming."

Casually, Phoebe reaches under her skirt and extracts a gun. "Don't give yourself an aneurysm," she says. "We're tracking him. You need to leave. This is no place for kids. You should go to your rooms and stay there."

The door opens again and Ivy sticks her head out. She grabs Jane's

arm and Jane says, "Wait," irrationally, waiting for the appears on cue, shouldering his way toward them, gaspi Jane is impressed. He must have made a heroic effort stretch of stairs.

"Quick," says Ivy, hustling Jane and Jasper into the ser

"Where are we going?" Jane asks.

"Out of the way."

It's a humiliating answer, coming from Ivy. *I'm like Rav when he was a child, "helping" the gala staff.*

"Is Mrs. Vanders mad about Kiran?" she asks.

Ivy shoots Jane a cautious look, as if trying to gauge w friend or foe at the moment. "Mrs. Vanders has been goir forth about telling Kiran the truth for some time now," sh thinks Kiran would be really good at our work."

"She would," Jane says fervently.

"Personally, I'm relieved she finally knows," says Ivy. "It being around my brother."

For a moment, a wave of dizziness fuzzes Jane's brain. Iv herding her along quickly and it occurs to her that she's bee her breath. "Wait," she says. "Can I have a second?"

"Yes," Ivy says with immediate concern. "Are you okay?"

It's impossible to breathe deeply and deliberately without about a jellyfish. Jane tries to think of a dumbwaiter instead, internal dumbwaiter, air moving up, air moving down. Her microcosm of this house. This corridor is a path toward . . . something. Toward the next step; toward however Jane will get this night.

"Why do I trust you?" Jane asks.

"I don't know," Ivy says. "I trust you too. And I've been tr imagine finding out that my aunt, who was basically my mom, operative. You've been so cool about it. I'd be furious."

Another pitched battle that's been taking place behind Kiran finally erupts into something no one can ignore. It's a quarrel between Patrick and Grace Panzavecchia, who's refusing to get into the dumbwaiter. "Why don't you make me?" the little girl yells. "Why don't you stab me with methohexital, *again?* I hate you!"

"Yeah," responds Patrick reasonably, "I know you do, Grace, but Christopher's down there all alone with Cook."

"Because you brought him down there!"

"Yes. I know it's unfair," says Patrick. "Now, do you want to be awake to look after your little brother, or do you want to be asleep?"

"I hate you!" Grace yells. "You ruined my life! You left Edward Jenner behind!"

Ivy pulls out a chair at the table, then nudges Jane toward it. Numbly, Jane sits, Jasper settling in around her feet. Then Ivy moves to the end of the table and begins wrapping something with long sheets of bubble wrap. Vaguely, Jane recognizes it as the Brancusi sculpture, which is complete again, a flat, oblong piece of marble—the missing fish—attached to the pedestal. Ivy takes great care, as if she's winding sticking plaster around a broken bone. The fish is pale and smooth, bonelike. It soothes Jane to watch.

"It's your decision, Grace," says Patrick calmly. "Awake or asleep?"

"It's not my decision!" Grace says. "I didn't decide to go away from home! I didn't decide to leave Edward Jenner behind!"

"It's true, she didn't," says Ivy quietly. "The least we could've done was collect Edward Jenner."

"Ivy," says Mrs. Vanders sharply, "that's enough."

"Okay," says Kiran, "I give up. Isn't Edward Jenner the guy who developed the smallpox vaccine? Like, two hundred years ago?"

"Edward Jenner—" Patrick begins.

"I was *not* talking to you," says Kiran behind bared teeth, not looking at Patrick.

"It's the dog," Jane realizes.

Mrs. Vanders clears her throat. "Yes," she says, "that's correct. When Ivy, Patrick, and Cook collected the children from school and the park, the dog was at home. They had to leave him behind."

"You left him alone in the house," Grace says. "Now some mean people probably have him. He's living with strangers. He's a German shepherd! That means he's genetically predisposed to degenerative myelopathy! Who's going to take care of him?" Grace's eyes are swollen and crying, her fists are held tight, and her small body is taut with the fury of despair. In Grace's eyes, Jane sees something she recognizes. Grace Panzavecchia has been betrayed.

"Why is this necessary?" Jane hears herself asking, with real indignation. "She's eight years old!"

With a sigh, Mrs. Vanders pulls a chair out and, heavily, sits down. "Because she's in danger and we intend to help her."

"But not my dog!" says Grace. "You don't intend to help my dog! I hate my parents! They drugged me with a diuretic so I'd have to go to the bathroom so you could grab me! What kind of parents drug their kid? You're all kid-snatchers!"

"Christopher is downstairs alone," Patrick reminds her.

"I hate you!"

Jasper has stirred from Jane's feet. He steps out from under the table tentatively. He walks a few steps toward Grace and stands before her.

"That's not my dog!" says Grace. "That's the stupidest dog I've ever seen! What's wrong with his legs!" Then she drops down onto the floor and holds out her arms and Jasper climbs into her lap and she starts yelling "Ow! Ow!" because he's heavy, and then she wraps her arms around him, presses her face into his neck, and starts howling. Jane is proud of Jasper. Possibly he's the most sensible adult in the attics.

"I am never," Ivy mutters from her end of the table, "ever, involving myself in anything like this again." She's now turned her attention to into the dumbwaiter carriage. "This feels like something out of *Alice in Wonderland*. Where do you suppose this is going?"

"I don't know," Jane says. "The west attics? The servants' wing? The oubliette?"

"There's no oubliette," Kiran says. "I made that up to get rid of the snotty Interpol man."

"You're awfully good at this," Jane says a bit wildly.

"Am I?" Kiran says, sitting there calmly in her crimson gown, clusters of diamonds sparkling in her ears and at her throat, her arms wrapped around her legs. "I guess it's the first time I've had fun since I stepped back onto this goddamned island."

Someone somewhere along the track of the dumbwaiter pounds a wrench—maybe it's a gun—against metal, twice. Kiran checks that her fingers and toes are completely inside the carriage, then knocks twice on one of the walls, impassively, as if everyone knows that's what a person is meant to do in this situation. The carriage begins to rise.

"Meet me above," she says, "if you like. Unless you've got some secret mission you're on too." Then she's gone.

Jane is left in the kitchen, staring at the moving cables in the empty track of the dumbwaiter carriage, trying to fit square pegs into round holes. *Is this why Aunt Magnolia became a spy? Because it was* fun? *How can Kiran see what she's just seen, and laugh, and say it's* fun? *Oh.* Jane clutches her temples, wishing for a way to extract herself from all of this.

Then Jasper leans heavily against her legs.

"Well, Jasper," she says. "I guess, whatever else happened, we succeeded in getting that Interpol man off Ivy's tail. What do you say? Should we return to the party and see if we can undo any more of my damage?"

Back in the ballroom, she finds the Arabic-speaking man from the dumbwaiter drinking Pimm's and being charming with other party guests. She supposes he must be a good guy if Mrs. Vanders is letting him ride in the dumbwaiter, but she gives him a wide berth anyway. Passing into the receiving hall with Jasper, she spots a familiar form: Ji-hoon, the South Korean "cleaner," who's smoothed his hair handsomely back and donned dark-rimmed glasses and black formalwear. Jane almost doesn't recognize him, he's so polished and slick. He's ascending the east staircase calmly, unhurriedly. He doesn't see her.

Abruptly, Jane turns for the west stairs and starts up them, moving as fast as she can without drawing undue attention. *Why do I keep doing this?* she asks herself, exasperated. *Why do I keep involving myself!* Jasper falls behind. Guests drift past now and then as she climbs, seeming to come from all wings of the house. Jane gathers that there must be a tradition, at these parties, of wandering the upper floors to look at the art. No wonder people can sneak all over the place without arousing suspicion.

She's huffing and puffing by the time she reaches the third floor. Stopping outside the door to the servants' wing, she catches her breath, no idea what to do next. Assuming this is even Ji-hoon's destination, she's beaten him, but how will she stop him when he arrives? Start reciting poetry and hope he joins in? Ivy has warned her that he's dangerous, he's armed. Where is Jasper?

Then the door to the servants' wing swings open and Phoebe Okada steps out, her turquoise dress delightfully swishing, her eye makeup smoky and flawless.

"I'd love to know what you think you're doing," she says.

"Phoebe," Jane says. "Ji-hoon is coming."

Casually, Phoebe reaches under her skirt and extracts a gun. "Don't give yourself an aneurysm," she says. "We're tracking him. You need to leave. This is no place for kids. You should go to your rooms and stay there."

The door opens again and Ivy sticks her head out. She grabs Jane's arm and Jane says, "Wait," irrationally, waiting for the dog, who then appears on cue, shouldering his way toward them, gasping for breath. Jane is impressed. He must have made a heroic effort on that last stretch of stairs.

"Quick," says Ivy, hustling Jane and Jasper into the servants' wing.

"Where are we going?" Jane asks.

"Out of the way."

It's a humiliating answer, coming from Ivy. *I'm like Ravi,* she thinks, *when he was a child, "helping" the gala staff.*

"Is Mrs. Vanders mad about Kiran?" she asks.

Ivy shoots Jane a cautious look, as if trying to gauge whether she's friend or foe at the moment. "Mrs. Vanders has been going back and forth about telling Kiran the truth for some time now," she says. "She thinks Kiran would be really good at our work."

"She would," Jane says fervently.

"Personally, I'm relieved she finally knows," says Ivy. "It's been hell being around my brother."

For a moment, a wave of dizziness fuzzes Jane's brain. Ivy is shepherding her along quickly and it occurs to her that she's been holding her breath. "Wait," she says. "Can I have a second?"

"Yes," Ivy says with immediate concern. "Are you okay?"

It's impossible to breathe deeply and deliberately without thinking about a jellyfish. Jane tries to think of a dumbwaiter instead, her own internal dumbwaiter, air moving up, air moving down. Her body is a microcosm of this house. This corridor is a path toward . . . toward something. Toward the next step; toward however Jane will get through this night.

"Why do I trust you?" Jane asks.

"I don't know," Ivy says. "I trust you too. And I've been trying to imagine finding out that my aunt, who was basically my mom, was an operative. You've been so cool about it. I'd be furious."

"You have no idea."

Ivy hesitates again. "I think," she says cautiously, "you should let Mrs. Vanders tell you whatever she knows. All the details, whatever they are. It might not help right away. But maybe it'll help eventually."

Jane gives up on her dumbwaiter metaphor. As a tear slides down her face, Ivy takes her hand.

Aunt Magnolia? Jane thinks, then remembers, with a sad tug, that she's no longer speaking to Aunt Magnolia.

"Come up to the attics," Ivy says. "You'll be safe up there."

In the west attics, Jane finds Kiran and Mrs. Vanders standing on opposite sides of a long table, arguing.

"You understand this was over a hundred years ago?" Mrs. Vanders is saying in a voice of exasperation.

"What does that matter?"

"The first housekeeper of Tu Reviens had a son," Mrs. Vanders says. "Her son had gotten mixed up in the Spanish-American War some years before and became an American operative. He'd also fallen in love with a Cuban agent."

"How romantic," says Kiran caustically.

"It ended with both of them dead."

"Of course it did," says Kiran, "or it wouldn't be so romantic."

"They were Mr. Vanders's grandparents," says Mrs. Vanders. "Afterward, Espions Sans Frontières approached his great-grandmother, the housekeeper, about secretly using her employer's house. Given that such an organization might have saved her son, can you really blame her for saying yes?"

"Yes to lying to my great-great-grandfather, who trusted her?" Kiran says. "Yes to endangering everyone in this house, which wasn't hers, for generation upon generation? For making the family *liable*?!"

Another pitched battle that's been taking place behind Kiran finally erupts into something no one can ignore. It's a quarrel between Patrick and Grace Panzavecchia, who's refusing to get into the dumbwaiter. "Why don't you make me?" the little girl yells. "Why don't you stab me with methohexital, *again?* I hate you!"

"Yeah," responds Patrick reasonably, "I know you do, Grace, but Christopher's down there all alone with Cook."

"Because you brought him down there!"

"Yes. I know it's unfair," says Patrick. "Now, do you want to be awake to look after your little brother, or do you want to be asleep?"

"I hate you!" Grace yells. "You ruined my life! You left Edward Jenner behind!"

Ivy pulls out a chair at the table, then nudges Jane toward it. Numbly, Jane sits, Jasper settling in around her feet. Then Ivy moves to the end of the table and begins wrapping something with long sheets of bubble wrap. Vaguely, Jane recognizes it as the Brancusi sculpture, which is complete again, a flat, oblong piece of marble—the missing fish—attached to the pedestal. Ivy takes great care, as if she's winding sticking plaster around a broken bone. The fish is pale and smooth, bonelike. It soothes Jane to watch.

"It's your decision, Grace," says Patrick calmly. "Awake or asleep?"

"It's not my decision!" Grace says. "I didn't decide to go away from home! I didn't decide to leave Edward Jenner behind!"

"It's true, she didn't," says Ivy quietly. "The least we could've done was collect Edward Jenner."

"Ivy," says Mrs. Vanders sharply, "that's enough."

"Okay," says Kiran, "I give up. Isn't Edward Jenner the guy who developed the smallpox vaccine? Like, two hundred years ago?"

"Edward Jenner—" Patrick begins.

"I was *not* talking to you," says Kiran behind bared teeth, not looking at Patrick.

"It's the dog," Jane realizes.

Mrs. Vanders clears her throat. "Yes," she says, "that's correct. When Ivy, Patrick, and Cook collected the children from school and the park, the dog was at home. They had to leave him behind."

"You left him alone in the house," Grace says. "Now some mean people probably have him. He's living with strangers. He's a German shepherd! That means he's genetically predisposed to degenerative myelopathy! Who's going to take care of him?" Grace's eyes are swollen and crying, her fists are held tight, and her small body is taut with the fury of despair. In Grace's eyes, Jane sees something she recognizes. Grace Panzavecchia has been betrayed.

"Why is this necessary?" Jane hears herself asking, with real indignation. "She's eight years old!"

With a sigh, Mrs. Vanders pulls a chair out and, heavily, sits down. "Because she's in danger and we intend to help her."

"But not my dog!" says Grace. "You don't intend to help my dog! I hate my parents! They drugged me with a diuretic so I'd have to go to the bathroom so you could grab me! What kind of parents drug their kid? You're all kid-snatchers!"

"Christopher is downstairs alone," Patrick reminds her.

"I hate you!"

Jasper has stirred from Jane's feet. He steps out from under the table tentatively. He walks a few steps toward Grace and stands before her.

"That's not my dog!" says Grace. "That's the stupidest dog I've ever seen! What's wrong with his legs!" Then she drops down onto the floor and holds out her arms and Jasper climbs into her lap and she starts yelling "Ow! Ow!" because he's heavy, and then she wraps her arms around him, presses her face into his neck, and starts howling. Jane is proud of Jasper. Possibly he's the most sensible adult in the attics.

"I am never," Ivy mutters from her end of the table, "ever, involving myself in anything like this again." She's now turned her attention to a painting. It's the picture of the man in the feathered hat, the Rembrandt Jane saw on her first day in this house, sitting on a table inside Mrs. Vanders's glass restoration room. It's large and seems heavy. Ivy labors to move it around.

Grace throws her head back from Jasper and yells, "Someday I'm going to kill you all!"

"This is the last time I'm asking, Grace," says Patrick. "Awake in the dumbwaiter or asleep in the dumbwaiter?" Patrick remains calm; he might be giving her the choice of broccoli or peas for dinner.

"She's not going to keep quiet," says Ivy. "Do you want a screaming dumbwaiter to slide past the gala guests who are looking at the second-story art?"

"No," says Patrick, "which is why, unless you're silent all the way down, Grace, Cook is going to put you to sleep the moment you reach the cellars, and then Christopher will see you that way."

Grace has grown eerily calm. "Someday I'm going to kill you all," she says, then adds, specially for Patrick, "And I'm going to kill you first."

"Someday," Patrick says with a suppressed sigh, "you're going to look back on this experience and be amazed by how much latitude we allowed you, given the circumstances."

Ivy makes a tiny snorting noise that brings Mrs. Vanders swinging sideways to direct at her the full force of an outraged expression.

"Ivy," says Mrs. Vanders, "we're aware of your dissatisfaction and we're used to your childish tantrums. But HQ will not extend you the same latitude. If you expect fair treatment from them during your exit interview, you're going to have to curb your self-righteousness and your sarcasm long before you get to Geneva."

Ivy doesn't respond to this, only looks down at the Rembrandt as if she'd like to pick it up and smash it on the floor. Instead, she sighs, runs one gentle finger along its top ridge, then eases a soft sack over its form. She follows this with the most enormous sealable plastic bag Jane has ever seen.

"I want my brother," says Grace.

"Have you decided, then?" asks Patrick.

There's a pause. "I'll go if I can take the dog with me in the dumb-waiter," says Grace.

"Quietly?" says Patrick.

"I'll be quiet," says Grace. "I can't help it if the dog starts barking."

"What are you going to do, pinch him?" says Patrick.

"You would think that," says Grace, in a voice of the purest disgust. "You would think I'd pinch the dog, probably because *you* pinch dogs every day for fun."

"All right," says Patrick, with a touch of weariness, gesturing toward the dumbwaiter. "Get in."

"Put the dog in first," says Grace.

"You think I'm going to trick you and send you down without the dog?"

"Yes."

Patrick chuckles once, briefly, then cuts himself off. He crouches down to Jasper. Once Jasper is standing cheerfully in the dumbwaiter carriage, looking like some sort of strange wall ornament, Grace climbs in around him. She grabs on to him and shoots Patrick one last expression of loathing.

"Good luck, Grace," Patrick says, then shuts the dumbwaiter door. He hauls at the cables in the narrow side cabinet for some time, then slows his pulling and stops. Leaning back against the dumbwaiter door, he closes his eyes and releases an enormous sigh.

"I love that kid," he says.

"Do you?" says Kiran, not looking at him. "That explains why you're so awful to her."

An amused bitterness twists Patrick's mouth. "And you've always been so wonderful to me," he says. "How's your fancy boyfriend?"

"Don't you even pretend that this conversation is that conversation," Kiran says. "At least you know all my secrets."

"Kiran," says Mrs. Vanders. "Patrick has wanted to tell you his secrets for some time. Mr. Vanders and I absolutely forbade it, because they aren't just his secrets, they're ours, and many other people's too."

"My mother forbade me to tell anyone *her* secrets too," Kiran says hotly. "Guess who I told anyway? Patrick."

"We're not going to discuss your mother's *secrets,*" says Mrs. Vanders.

"You know why?" says Kiran. "Because I trusted him. Because I wanted him to *know* me and all the places I've been!"

Mrs. Vanders stands so quickly that her chair shudders back across the floor. "I forbid any talk of your mother and her *magic* in this room," she says in a voice that reaches into the roots of Jane's teeth. "We're trying to do good, simple, natural work here!"

"Oh my god," says Kiran, suddenly sounding exhausted. Pulling out a chair, she slumps into it, rubbing her face. "Listen to yourself, Vanny. My mother isn't a witch, she's a scientist."

Jane doesn't understand this turn in the conversation, but she finds she doesn't much care. She's watching Ivy lower the Brancusi, then the Rembrandt, into crates.

Mrs. Vanders sits down again, clasps her hands together, and directs her steely expression at Kiran. "I'll explain everything, as long as you swear there'll be no more talk of your mother."

"All right!" says Kiran, flapping an impatient hand. "I swear! Jeez!"

"Very well," says Mrs. Vanders. "Victoria and Giuseppe Panzavecchia are microbiologists."

"I know that," says Kiran. "Apparently they're also secret agents."

"The Panzavecchias are not agents," Mrs. Vanders says. "They're contractors. They've been working under the auspices of a special CIA research and development grant for the purposes of discovering whether it's possible to develop an immediately contagious strain of smallpox, the indicative symptoms of which manifest late in the course of infection."

Kiran freezes, then speaks in a tone of pure disgust. "You mean a smallpox that wouldn't be recognized as smallpox until it had already spread far and wide."

"Yes," says Mrs. Vanders, "precisely. They've been contracted to experiment with forms of smallpox that could serve as effective biological weapons."

"This is your good, simple, *natural* work? Genetically modified smallpox?"

"In case you're wondering why I want out," Ivy mutters from her end of the table, where she's now pouring an avalanche of packing peanuts into the crate containing the Brancusi. They make a tinkling sound, like ice. Patrick walks over to her and gathers up the ones that hit the floor, plowing them with his boots.

"We don't work with biological weapons ourselves," says Mrs. Vanders. "And our understanding is that the CIA runs these experiments not with the intention of using the weapons themselves, but rather to be better prepared should an enemy to the United States develop the same strain and attack with it."

"Oh, right, I've never heard that one before!" Kiran practically yells.

"Think what you will. Their intentions don't matter to Espions Sans Frontières. We're nonpartisan."

"Another word for complicit."

"A couple of weeks back," Mrs. Vanders continues, ignoring this, "Giuseppe and Victoria had a breakthrough. They discovered something unexpected, I've no idea how. But the fruit of their discovery was pretty much what they'd been directed to develop, a strain of smallpox that's highly contagious long before the carrier can begin to suspect it's smallpox. And then one odd thing and one terrible thing happened. The odd thing is that when they informed their research director at the

CIA of their success, that man became afflicted suddenly with a *different* experimental strain of smallpox, an opposite sort of strain in which the indicative symptoms manifest very quickly. A week or so later, he died, and 'A Smallpox Case in New York' became headline news."

"That's the odd thing?" Jane says numbly. "That's the odd thing? What's the *terrible* thing?"

"No, wait," says Kiran. "I heard about the smallpox guy, of course, but not that it was some sort of experimental strain of smallpox. They said he was a suicidal guy who used to work for the World Health Organization and had broken into the laboratories of the CDC in Atlanta. Which we've all been assured," Kiran says, her voice growing harder, "is one of only two places in the world where the smallpox virus is kept, the other being a closely monitored lab in Russia. Smallpox," she says in a voice now verging on shrill, "is no longer supposed to be a danger anywhere in the world."

"Have your little hissy fit, Kiran," says Mrs. Vanders, "then return yourself to reason. Your brother wears rose-colored glasses, but you've never been naïve."

"How did that guy get smallpox?" Kiran demands.

"We don't know," says Mrs. Vanders. "He certainly never broke into any lab in Atlanta. The Panzavecchias believe he was infected with a strain they kept in their lab in New York, which means that someone got access to a part of that lab no one but they and a few particular people with CIA connections should have had access to. Which suggests a traitor."

"Okay," says Kiran. "*Why* did the guy get smallpox?"

"We don't know that either," says Mrs. Vanders. "But we think it's likely he was infected as a message to the United States from some other state."

"What's the message?" Kiran asks.

"'We know what you're doing,'" says Mrs. Vanders. "'We can get in anywhere. We're one step ahead of you, you can't protect yourself, and by the way, thanks for inventing all this nifty smallpox.'"

"Okay, that's terrifying," says Kiran. "But why infect the guy with some random strain? Why not the new, successful strain?"

"Two reasons," says Mrs. Vanders. "One, the strain they chose was one unlikely to create an epidemic. It's a message, not an act of war, you understand? The man suspected almost immediately what disease he had. He was able to quarantine himself. He called the hospital, sent them pictures of his mouth and skin, and told them his made-up CDC story, so that *only* vaccinated health workers would be sent to care for him. Two, the Panzavecchias' new strain wasn't available, because once they realized what they had, they got scared. They brought it, and all their notes about it, home, where they could control who had access to it. Which leads us to the terrible thing."

"Home!" cries Kiran. "Oh god. Oh god! Please tell me Baby Leo doesn't have smallpox!"

"Of course he doesn't have smallpox," says Mrs. Vanders. "What do you think they did, left vials of it in his crib? Baby Leo has chicken pox."

"How do you know?"

"Because one of the cousins who attended Grace's eighth birthday party two weeks ago had chicken pox. Don't worry about Baby Leo. Espions Sans Frontières has engaged a doctor to care for him personally."

"Philip Okada," Jane says flatly.

"Philip Okada?" Kiran says. "Philip Okada is a spy?"

"He's a *doctor*," says Mrs. Vanders, "and a British asset who's helping us out. Not a spy. You need to stop throwing these words around. In our circles, *spy* is a rather derogatory term."

"Well, forgive me for the gap in my education. You're the one who could've taught me the vocabulary. What's the terrible thing that happened?"

"It relates to Grace," says Mrs. Vanders.

"Grace?" says Kiran. "Obviously she doesn't have smallpox or she wouldn't be in this house."

"Will you get it out of your head that someone has smallpox?" says Mrs. Vanders.

"You've made it clear that anyone could!" Kiran fires back. "We all could tomorrow!"

"Oh, everything could happen tomorrow!" says Mrs. Vanders. "If you can't cope with all the awful things that are always on the verge of happening, then this isn't the work for you!"

"Whoever said it was?" says Kiran. "Fucking hell, Vanny!"

Mrs. Vanders glares at Kiran with her hallmark enigmatic aggression. Kiran glares back. Jane has no idea where everyone's getting all this energy.

"Grace doesn't have smallpox," says Mrs. Vanders. "Her problem is that she's a natural-born snoop with an extraordinary affinity for mnemonic devices."

"Are you going to tell me that Grace found the notes on the weaponized smallpox and now she could make up a batch from memory?"

Mrs. Vanders looks practically pleased. "Very good, Kiran," she says. "Though she couldn't, in fact, create it herself. The notes are ciphered and contain formulas and instructions she couldn't understand. But it's possible she could tell key parts to someone, and maybe that person could figure out how to make sense of it."

"And somehow, people know she got into the notes," Kiran says, "and now they want the information in Grace's head."

"Yes. She might not understand the information she's memorized, but she's plenty smart enough to sense when her parents are worried and lying to her, which makes her angry, so she snoops and disobeys as a kind of leverage. When her parents forbade her to talk about it, she wouldn't stop screaming about it, even when there were ominous-looking strangers in her house. And by this point, the research director was infected and Victoria and Giuseppe were terrified. They began withholding the details of their discovery from everyone, even the CIA people who began showing up at their front door. They destroyed their digital notes, with Ivy's help. They burned their paper notes and destroyed the living strain. They told the CIA they had no intention of sharing the details of the discovery with anyone, ever, because it was no longer possible to know whom to trust."

"And now they're blacklisted by the CIA?" says Kiran. "Considered non-compliant? Rogue assets?"

Mrs. Vanders is pleased again. Jane is kind of starting to hate her. Where is the pleasure in all of this awfulness? "Essentially," says Mrs. Vanders, "yes. The CIA is furious. They've decided to force Victoria and Giuseppe to hand over their research, and treat them as threats if they don't comply. And in the meantime, other states have also taken an interest."

"In Victoria and Giuseppe, and in Grace," Kiran says.

"At this point," says Mrs. Vanders, "it's impossible to know how many people or states they need to be hidden from. Only that they need to be hidden, and that Grace, being a child, is in particular danger."

"I think the lesson here is that when someone offers you a job creating new and exciting strains of smallpox, say no," says Kiran.

"Very funny," says Mrs. Vanders.

"Was I joking?" says Kiran. "Why'd they try to rob a bank?"

"So we could plant the Mafia story," says Mrs. Vanders. "If you take someone with an Italian name, have them break the law, then make them disappear, then add the words *Sicilian Mafia,* everyone loves to talk about it, but no one digs very deep into where they went or why. It's not fair to Italians, but it's effective."

"That's ridiculous. The police must dig deeper than that."

"We have a couple friends in the police," says Mrs. Vanders, "and a couple friends in the press. Most importantly, we have a couple friends in the Sicilian Mafia."

"That's so nice," Kiran says. "How I wish Ravi could hear all this. He'd get such a warm, fuzzy feeling about his Vanny."

"Ravi couldn't handle this," Mrs. Vanders says, "as I think you know."

"He really has no idea?" says Kiran. "Nor does Octavian? Truly nothing?"

"Not Octavian, not Ravi, not your mother," says Mrs. Vanders. "You're the only Thrash who's ever had the slightest inkling, Kiran. This is all yours."

"That's an interesting choice of words."

"Have you ever had anything that's all yours, Kiran?"

Kiran considers Mrs. Vanders. Then she flicks her eyes nastily to Patrick. He makes his mouth hard and insolent.

"Good thing I caught Patrick in the act," Kiran says.

"That forced our hand," says Mrs. Vanders, "but we monitor the dumbwaiter with cameras. We know if the path is clear. I wouldn't have let it happen if I hadn't been willing to risk the consequences. Have you worked out why?"

Another of those silences sits in the space between Kiran and Mrs. Vanders. Finally, Kiran crosses her arms. "What else do you do?"

"A lot of things," says Mrs. Vanders crisply. "This house is a neutral meeting place, during galas usually, for opposing sides. We give representation referrals to agents and operatives under prosecution. Also, Mr. Vanders is a psychologist. The man you saw in the dumbwaiter had just completed a session."

"Spy therapy?" says Kiran incredulously.

"Stop saying 'spy,'" says Mrs. Vanders. "Surely you can see that there might be a need. Our clients have very high-pressure jobs."

"Since when does Mr. Vanders speak Arabic?"

"He speaks Arabic, Farsi, German, French, Spanish, Italian, Mandarin, and Korean," says Mrs. Vanders.

"I don't believe you," says Kiran.

"Why shouldn't he?" says Mrs. Vanders with an affronted air. "He's a very popular therapist."

Kiran begins to giggle.

"I'm rather offended that you find that funny," says Mrs. Vanders.

Now Kiran is shrieking with laughter. Tears are streaming down her face. "I don't," she says. "I can totally see it. He's always talking psychobabble and looking at me like he's diagnosed me with something. It's just—" She pauses for another gale of laughter. "It's funny!" she cries. "I'm dying here! Mr. Vanders is a secret spy therapist! Oh, lordy, maybe I'm having a shock reaction." Taking a deep breath, Kiran wipes her face. "So," she says, "are you going to explain why Ivy has been packing up the house Rembrandt and the famous missing Brancusi?"

Mrs. Vanders sighs. "You're not going to like this part."

"And the rest has been so delightful."

"It's about leverage, power, and payment for services rendered," says Mrs. Vanders.

Kiran's eyebrows rise to her hairline. Jane knows this part. She doesn't need to listen. Over at Ivy's end of the table, Patrick is now engaged in the alarming activity of helping Ivy strap a gun holster over her black dress. Then he helps her into a long black coat. Where is Ivy going?

"You steal the family art!" Kiran says. "Over and over again! Oh, if Ravi only knew!"

"We *borrow* the family art," says Mrs. Vanders, but she's doesn't sound as if she expects anyone to believe her.

"You've lied about your degrees!" Kiran says. "About the cleaning you do and the restoration! I know you told Ravi you needed that Rembrandt so you could clean it. He told me so!"

"I haven't lied!" Mrs. Vanders says. "I do care about the art, deeply! I do clean it, I do study it. I have never failed to recover a piece! I take its well-being and its authenticity very seriously and I'm committed to cultural restitution!"

"Oh, spare me," says Kiran. "If you care so much, why did you break the Brancusi in half?"

"Grace did that," says Patrick proudly.

"Yes," says Mrs. Vanders. "That child has fought us at every turn. We've been moving the family piecemeal, you see, and with the help of different parties. First Victoria, then Giuseppe, then Leo the other night with his doctor. Grace, being a natural snoop, figured out that we needed the Brancusi in order to pay for her transportation. And she's smart as a whip, and she's eight, and all she wants in the world is to go home. So she slipped past Cook one night—Cook has been our child-minder, in addition to arranging all four exchanges. The poor dear is exhausted. Grace stole the sculpture, then hid it. Then, when we reacted with a calm, systematic search rather than the panic she was looking for, she popped the fish off the base, buried the fish in the backyard, waited until poor Cook nodded off again, and stuck the base back in the receiving hall. Which certainly accomplished her purpose. I felt like the top of my head was coming off when Ravi showed me that empty base. I dread to think what she would've done next if Ravi weren't such a drama queen."

"Oh, she would've taken a mallet to it," says Patrick, "and thrown it into the fountain."

"I'm not so sure," says Mrs. Vanders, studying him keenly. "I think she has a well-honed sense of where the line is, and, ultimately, she wants to be with her family. She's just registering her protest."

"What about the Vermeer?" Jane asks.

"Yes, what are you doing with the priceless family Vermeer?" Kiran says.

"The Vermeer has actually been stolen," says Mrs. Vanders.

Kiran lets out a short laugh. "You're kidding."

"I wish it with all my heart," says Mrs. Vanders, "but no, someone in this house has stolen that dear picture and replaced it with an excellent forgery."

"Wow," says Kiran, still laughing. "And Ravi's filled the house with FBI agents, Interpol, and police, on the very night you're trying to get Grace, Christopher, a Rembrandt, and a Brancusi away."

"Yes," says Mrs. Vanders, not sounding particularly troubled. "Even Christopher's given Cook the slip a couple of times, which is quite frightening in a house with a swimming pool. He's two years old!"

"People were starting to notice the crying fits too," says Patrick. "'Is there something wrong with the plumbing in this house? Or the air vents?'"

Kiran is watching them intently. "Is this normal, then?" she asks. "This level of drama?"

Mrs. Vanders purses her mouth and shrugs. "I guess," she says. "Everyone we deal with is a person of great conviction."

Patrick has strapped a cord around the Rembrandt crate and is carrying it to the freight elevator. He props the doors open, then returns for the Brancusi crate. Without meaning to, Jane has locked eyes with Ivy.

"I speak Bengali and a little Hindi," says Kiran. "Also French, Italian, Spanish, Arabic, and some Hebrew. And I can pass as several ethnicities."

"Yes," says Mrs. Vanders. "We're well aware of that."

"This job must give you a stunning comprehensive view of the workings of nations," says Kiran.

"It does," says Mrs. Vanders. "And now it's time for you to return to the gala, Kiran. People will be wondering what's happened to the lady of the house."

Patrick is standing at the freight elevator, sending the two crates down somewhere by themselves. Then he walks to the dumbwaiter and turns to Ivy, who's put on a large backpack. Ivy takes a balaclava out of her coat pocket and pulls it over her head and glasses. It's like she's faceless suddenly.

Jane walks to her. "Where are you going?"

"There's a hidden trapdoor in the cellar," Ivy says. "It opens to a tunnel that leads to a hidden bay in the ramble at the other end of the island. That's where the pickup is happening, of the kids and the art. Cook and the kids are waiting for me downstairs. I'm joining them."

"How far are you going with them?"

"All the way to their parents. Then I'm going to Geneva."

"Will you be okay?"

She considers the question, then nods. "Will you?"

Jane considers the question too, then shrugs.

Ivy grasps her hands tightly, then lets them go and climbs into the dumbwaiter. Jane forces herself back to Kiran. Her arms and legs are made of wet cement. Mrs. Vanders is staring at her.

"When you were very young," Mrs. Vanders says to Jane, "your aunt was just exactly what you thought. She took pictures of animals underwater and studied marine ecology. That was all."

"Her aunt?" says Kiran. "Magnolia? What are you talking about now? Magnolia wasn't—oh," Kiran says. "She was, wasn't she. Jesus."

"Then, one day, she came upon the wreckage of a sunken submarine," says Mrs. Vanders, "hidden in a cavern on the floor of the Pacific."

In Jane's peripheral vision, Patrick closes the dumbwaiter door and starts pulling on the cables.

Kiran touches Jane's arm gently, the place where, under her skin, the jellyfish tentacles reach for her elbow.

"It was a North Korean submarine," says Mrs. Vanders. "The Pentagon, North Korea, and a few other states had their own divers searching for the wreck in various places elsewhere, but they were looking in the wrong area, and in the meantime, Magnolia found it by accident."

Kiran's hand on Jane's tattoo is a comfort.

"She was diving from a Venezuelan vessel with an international crew of divers," says Mrs. Vanders, "and she understood what she'd found. She had a hunch that one of her university colleagues would be able to advise her on what to do about it. So she came back aboard, told no one else in her group what she'd found, and called him. A few days later, she told her diving party she'd been hired for another job, then crossed over onto a highly equipped salvage vessel, American, passing as a mining ship, that came along to pick her up. Magnolia brought them to the wreck and, when they asked her to, helped them salvage it. A nuclear missile. Cryptological information. It was a jackpot."

"Why would she do that?" Jane whispers. "Why would she keep it secret? Why not just tell everyone on the Venezuelan ship what she'd found?"

"She didn't know what to do," says Mrs. Vanders. "She had enough imagination to know it was a political discovery, and relations between the USA and Venezuela were suffering at the time. She did what she thought best."

Mrs. Vanders swipes a small black object—a walkie-talkie—from a nearby table and tosses it to Patrick, who's strapping on his own gun. "Send that down to Ivy-bean," she says, nodding at the dumbwaiter. "Then I think you should take the long way down, Patrick, to give us an extra eye on the party. You'll have to take the aboveground route across the lawn anyway, with the art."

"She wouldn't," Jane says. "My aunt wouldn't have lied to me like that."

"You were seven," Mrs. Vanders says. "She couldn't just come back and tell you all about it, no matter how much she wanted to. It's exciting work, once you've started. It's important work, and those who do it are paid according to the risks they take. Your aunt had bank accounts in the Caymans and in Switzerland that we can help you access, now that you know the truth. This is why I've been wanting to talk to you ever since you came to Tu Reviens. Your aunt made me promise that if anything ever happened to her, I'd help you access her bank accounts."

Jane doesn't care about bank accounts. All she can think of is seven, *seven*. She pushes toward the stairs.

"Magnolia also asked me to pass on a message," Mrs. Vanders says to Jane's back. "'Tell my niece to reach for the umbrella,' she said. She thought of you always, and she wanted to get out. Magnolia was never suited to the work. She came to hate it. She hated to lie; none of us likes to lie. She was going to retire, and we were going to help her."

Kiran has taken Jane into the warm fold of her arm and is helping her to the stairs. Jane is shivering. "Leave her alone, Vanny," Kiran says. "You'd think, the way all of you talk, that no one who's been lied to has any right to feel betrayed."

It's surreal to be spat back into the party. Jane sticks to Kiran, who's in a strange, elated state. It's easy to be her shadow. *I'm not entirely certain I'm awake,* thinks Jane.

Kiran takes Jane's arm as they move around the ballroom, whispering bright, cutting remarks in her ear. "Look at all these people," she says. "I wonder how many of our family friends became our family friends so they could get invitations to the galas and come visit their *real* friends. The servants! Is anyone ever who they seem?"

Yes, Jane thinks. *We are. You and I, Kiran.*

"Think of our guests," Kiran goes on. "Can you believe it about the Okadas?"

"No," Jane says, not really paying attention.

"Colin is too much of a dildo to be a political operative," Kiran says, "but Lucy St. George could have hidden depths, given the whole private investigator thing. Don't you think?"

"Yes."

"Charlotte," Kiran says, stopping to consider.

"Charlotte?" Jane repeats obediently.

"My stepmother. She was redesigning the house."

"Was she?" says Jane, suddenly remembering she never wished Ivy a proper good-bye. Wasn't this the kind of trip that killed Ivy's parents?

"But has anyone told you the details of how Charlotte mysteriously disappeared?" asks Kiran, scanning the dancers in the ballroom as if Charlotte might suddenly appear among them. The music is suffocating. Jane rubs her ears. "Could she have been a spy?" Kiran says. "She vanished into thin air, just like the Panzavecchias seemed to, and just like your aunt."

"My aunt didn't vanish into thin air," says Jane. "She froze to death in a blizzard. Someone called me from the Antarctic Peninsula. And Ivy told me it was real." *Reach for the umbrella. What the hell does that mean, Aunt Magnolia? I've reached for all the stupid, pointless umbrellas. Why?*

"I wonder where they send people," Kiran says. "Where on earth could two infamous adults and three infamous children live and never be found? It would have to be someplace either depressingly isolated or depressingly crowded."

Jasper appears through the shifting crowd then, comes to her, and leans against her feet. Jane wonders if it means Ivy and the kids have departed through the tunnel in the cellar.

"They're right, you know," Kiran goes on, her eyes following her brother, who's managing a sort of half dance, half conversation with both the male and the female FBI agent at the edge of the dance floor. "Ravi isn't suited for the kind of work Espions Sans Frontières does. He'd be livid about the secrets they've been keeping from him. Like the secret trapdoor in the cellar, and the underground tunnel to the ramble. We played hide-and-seek in that cellar. They were always so hard to find. I wonder how young they were when *they* were initiated into the secret of the hidden passage."

Jane rubs Jasper's side, not responding.

"He's too honest," says Kiran, then rolls her eyes as Ravi stoops and whispers something into the ear of one of the FBI agents. "And he'd blow a fuse about the art. He'd never forgive Vanny. I mean literally, never."

"What about you, Kiran?" says Jane. "Are you going to join them?"

Kiran is capable of an impressive range of unpleasant smiles. "It depends on whether I can do so without ever having to talk to Patrick."

"Did you know that this work killed his parents?"

Kiran is stunned. A wave of something—comprehension, horror—passes across her face before she's able to build her wall back up again. "No," she says. "I did not know that."

"Ivy told me."

Ravi appears suddenly, pushes between Jane and Kiran and wraps an arm around each of them. "Hello, beautiful darlings," he says. "Having fun?"

"Not like the fun you're having," Kiran says dryly.

"I'm going for a walk," Ravi says. "You'll have to stay here and be the representative Thrash."

"I don't have to do anything," Kiran says, slurring her words ever so slightly. "I'll go with you if that's what I want to do. You can't boss me around. Where are you going?"

"Bratty twin sister," Ravi says fondly, kissing her on the forehead. "To the bay in the ramble. The lovely FBI special agents have been asking me about alternate places for boats to dock. They want to see if someone could've snuck the art off the island that way."

Instantly, Jane's weariness flares to panic. Ivy! Grace and Christopher! They're waiting for their pickup at that bay. "Kiran?" she squeaks, but Kiran talks over her.

"Both of the FBI agents, Ravi?" she says. "Seriously? Do they know what you're up to? Or do they actually think you guys are going to look for clues in the dark? Do you have a preference between them?"

Kiran is just barely swaying against her brother's chest. Kiran, Jane realizes, is pretending to be drunk.

"The answer to all your questions is, I don't know yet," says Ravi, grinning. "Not knowing is part of the fun."

"I'm going with you," says Kiran.

"Like hell you are," says Ravi.

"I am," says Kiran. "It's fun to ruin your things."

Ravi kisses her forehead again, chuckling. "No more Pimm's for you," he says. Then he releases them both and goes off to find his FBI special agents.

Kiran wraps her hand over Jane's arm and is walking calmly with her toward the banquet hall before Ravi has even taken three steps. "You understand that we need to warn someone," she says, "right?"

"Of course," Jane says, "but how?"

"I know how to get to the bay through the ramble," Kiran says, pulling Jane past the long table in the banquet hall, "so I'll go that way. I'll go after them and try to stall them. You need to find Mrs. Vanders and tell her to warn Ivy and Patrick." She's pulled Jane into the kitchen now. Jane realizes that Kiran intends to send her up to the attics in the dumbwaiter.

She's hardly aware of climbing in. She has a vague sense that Kiran has stuffed her into it like a jack-in-the-box. On the floor, Jasper is hopping and yipping, distressed not to be joining her.

"Good luck," Kiran says, then shuts the door.

The dumbwaiter starts ascending, slowly. The sounds, from inside the carriage, are a cavernous underwater music. *Too slow*, Jane thinks.

Move faster! How do the cameras work? Will Mrs. Vanders know who's arriving in the dumbwaiter? As the carriage comes to a halt, Jane calls out, "It's me! It's me! Don't shoot!"

Someone yanks the door open and Jane is astonished to find herself staring into the face of Ji-hoon, the South Korean "cleaner."

"All right," says Phoebe's voice. "Now get back."

Ji-hoon backs away with his hands raised.

"What's going on?" Jane squeaks. "Don't shoot me!"

"I'm not going to shoot you, Janie," says Phoebe's voice, sounding amused. "What the hell do you want?"

"I need to tell Mrs. Vanders something," Jane says, then sticks her head cautiously into the room. Phoebe is holding Ji-hoon at gunpoint.

"Is Ji-hoon a South Korean spy?" Jane asks, then, with a small shock, "Is he a *North* Korean spy?"

"Ji-hoon's as American as you are. He's the Panzavecchias' research director at the CIA," says Phoebe flatly. "The new one, obviously, not the dead one."

"Oh! What are you going to do with him?"

"Nothing at all," says Phoebe. "Ji-hoon and I are going to stand like this in friendly meditation until various things happen elsewhere, at which point I'm going to escort him from the island."

"Okay," Jane says. "I need Mrs. Vanders. It's urgent."

"I believe she's in a meeting in the wine cellars," says Phoebe. "Ji-hoon will send you down, won't you, Ji-hoon? Go on, move along, and make sure I can see your hands."

Ji-hoon glides carefully to Jane again and reaches for the dumbwaiter door. His eyes bore into hers. "I'm not the bad guy here, you know," he says. "I'm just as committed to protecting those children as any of the rest of you, and *without* breaking the law."

"Hurry up," says Phoebe, bored.

Ji-hoon shoves the door shut with his elbow and a moment later

Jane is slowly descending through darkness and a smell of metal and dust and cold. The smell changes to something like wet wood that's been lying in a pond for a long time. Sweet and sour. Jane recognizes the wine cellars, even though she's never been in a wine cellar before. When the dumbwaiter stops, she fumbles for the door handle and propels the door open. Mr. Vanders is standing ten feet away aiming a pistol at her.

"Don't shoot me!" Jane squeaks again, but he's already returned the gun to the holster at his hip. He comes up to Jane and glares at her.

"Why are you here?" he demands.

"Ravi is bringing the FBI agents to the bay through the ramble," says Jane. "Someone needs to warn Ivy right away."

"Hm," says Mr. Vanders, pursing his lips, thinking this over.

"Call her!" Jane says, frustrated with him for wasting time. "On her walkie-talkie!"

"She doesn't have it," he says, jutting his chin at a nearby table, where the walkie-talkie sits. "She'd left by the time it arrived."

"Call her phone!"

"Phones don't work at the other end of the island," he says. "Mrs. V is in a meeting and I'm with a patient. Phoebe's watching Ji-hoon—not that we could ask any more of the Brits at this point—and Ivy, Patrick, and Cook are already at the bay. I'll have to cancel my session and go myself."

"No," Jane says. "Let me go."

"Absolutely not," says Mr. Vanders. "You are a novice and a civilian."

"I'm not a child," Jane says, pushing herself out of the dumbwaiter one leg at a time. "I can carry a message. I have common sense. I'm my aunt's niece," she says.

Mr. Vanders's eyebrows rise the tiniest smidge.

"Please," Jane says, standing tall to face him. "It's my fault the FBI is here, and there's no time for this. Please, please, let me go."

Mr. Vanders lets out a sigh that's almost a growl. "Come on," he says, grabbing Jane and pulling her down an aisle of wines so abruptly that she almost falls. He eyes her outfit. "Those look like sensible boots. Can you run in them?"

"Yes."

He rounds a corner and launches down another aisle, towing Jane with him, shoving a flashlight at her. He's very strong for a man who seems old. "The door at the bay looks like a rock, but it's got a leather handle on the left that opens toward you," he says, turning another corner. "Turn off the flashlight before you open the door, and open it slowly. Step out slowly and call Ivy's name quietly until you get her attention. She'll still be on lookout while Patrick deals with the kids and the cargo. The water can be noisy but she'll be close. Are you getting all this?"

"Yes."

He reaches for his holster. "Have you ever shot a gun?"

"No!" Jane says. "I don't want it! I wouldn't even know who to shoot!"

"Calm down," says Mr. Vanders. "No one's going to shoot anybody."

"It's not reasonable to assume that when everyone has a gun! I'm not taking it."

Mr. Vanders draws his bushy eyebrows into a fierce V. "You sound like your aunt," he says. Then he moves to a shadowy place where a rug is pushed back and there seems to be a square gap in the brick floor. It's barely big enough to fit a human form.

"There are four steps," Mr. Vanders tells her, "then a pole you'll slide down. Don't miss the pole; the floor beneath is stone. Wrap your legs around the pole as soon as the steps disappear."

Jane stares at him incredulously.

"Come now, do we have time for gawking?" he cries impatiently, taking the flashlight from her and hooking it somehow to the belt of her sweater dress so that it's bumping against her hip. Then he grabs her arm and yanks her toward the opening.

"I'm scared," Jane says.

"That's very sensible of you," he says. "Now go."

It's the stupidest design Jane has ever encountered for the entrance to anything. The four "steps" are impossibly narrow and very deep and wound in a circle, so that she feels as if she's screwing herself into the hole as she clumsily descends them, bending and twisting. Beyond the fourth step is empty space and—yes, she can touch it with her boot—a pole. She hooks her ankle around it, grabs on with her hands, and pushes off the steps with her other foot.

There's a moment of utter lack of control and a scream, then rock comes barreling upward and crashes into her. She tastes blood in her mouth.

Mr. Vanders's voice comes down the hole. "You okay?"

"Just dandy," she says, lying in a heap.

The steps shift; the hole closes. Jane is left in darkness.

Patting around at her middle, she finds the flashlight and flicks the switch. A narrow stone passage stretches before her. It leads downhill and is reasonably straight.

Aching in every bone, hands smarting and bleeding from scrapes, and one of her ankles not feeling entirely trustworthy, Jane pushes herself to her feet and begins to run.

It's just as Mr. Vanders said. The passage ends abruptly at what seems like an impassable boulder, but Jane finds a handle and pulls. With a groan, the enormous heavy door swings open. There's so much noise— the voice of a wailing child, waves crashing, shouts, then the roar of an engine—that she's certain she's too late, the FBI has found the children,

Grace will be tortured, and Ivy and Patrick will spend the rest of their lives in jail for treason and kidnapping.

Then there's a disturbance in the scrub brush to one side, followed by a small, moving circle of light. Ivy shoves her way through branches to Jane, her balaclava pushed back above her glasses so that Jane can see her face.

"Hi," she says calmly. "I heard the door. Is something wrong?"

"Ravi's bringing FBI agents to look at the bay," Jane says, gasping.

Ivy's face sharpens. "When?"

"Now."

Reaching behind Jane, Ivy hauls the door shut. Then she pushes out of the scrub. Jane follows her into a spitting rain, squinting, adjusting to the dim darkness. They're at the edge of a tiny, crescent-shaped patch of beach. In the water bobs a small, wooden boat, attached by a rope to a half-submerged post, its engine running. Patrick stands in the water beside the boat. An adult, presumably Cook, sits in the boat, as does Grace, who's holding Christopher, who's screaming to wake the dead. Ivy's flashlight washes over them irregularly several times and Jane reads the boat's name on the stern: *The Ivy*.

What Ivy's done with the flashlight must be a signal to the people at the boat, because several things happen at once. The boat engine cuts out; Patrick reaches to Christopher and Christopher stops crying; Grace yells something in outrage and Patrick yells something back; then Patrick wades out of the water and begins to run across the sand toward Jane and Ivy.

"I have to go," Ivy says to Jane, grabbing on to her hand roughly. "I'm sorry. I'll be gone at least a week. Will you still be here when I get back?"

"Yes."

"Did Mrs. Vanders tell you the rest of what we know about your aunt's death?"

"Her death? What about it?"

"Ask Patrick," says Ivy, tugging on her hand. "Promise me you'll ask Patrick."

"I promise," Jane says, her breath ragged, almost full of tears.

Ivy pulls her close suddenly, holds her tight, smashes her lips against Jane's. Then in an instant she's gone, flying across the sand. At the water, she unhitches the rope from the post, climbs into the rocking boat. She sits beside Cook and says something to Grace that makes Grace scramble to the floor of the boat with Christopher in her arms, hiding both of them from sight. There's a clatter of wood on wood and Cook has produced oars. He passes one to Ivy and steadily they begin to row the boat toward the open sea.

Patrick grabs Jane's arm and pulls her back into the brush. He pulls her down so that the two of them are crouching with their backs to the rock door. His pants and the bottom of his coat are soaked and the rain is spitting harder. Jane, coatless and bare-legged, shivers violently.

"I'd give you my coat," Patrick whispers, "but it wouldn't warm you."

"It's okay," Jane whispers. "I'm okay."

"What's happening?" Patrick says. "Who's coming?"

"Ravi's bringing FBI agents to look at the bay," Jane says. "Kiran's going to try to stall them."

Somewhere in the ramble, Kiran is shrieking with laughter. A moment later, arcs of light swoop across the sky, then Jane hears the voices of the others. Ravi, quiet, chuckling, and a woman's voice Jane doesn't recognize. A second man shouting in laughter; Kiran, giggling, still emitting the occasional high shriek. Twigs break and leaves rustle as they slide down from the ramble onto the beach. Jane can't see them, but someone is practically putting on a light show with a flashlight.

"What are we looking for, anyway?" Kiran calls. "Footprints? Fin prints! Brancusi fish fin prints!" she yells, then giggles at her own comedy. The FBI man chuckles too, then says something indistinct but cheerful. He sounds drunk.

"We're not likely to find anything at all," says the FBI lady in obvious annoyance, "with you running around in figure eights and trampling everything."

"Ouch! Or shining the light in our eyes!" says Ravi. "Watch it, Kir! I can't see a thing."

"This is not the walk I'd envisioned," says the FBI lady.

"True," says Ravi, "but I like seeing my sister laugh."

"She's drunk," the FBI lady says sharply. "Would you please take that flashlight from her? I'm going blind."

"Kiran," Ravi begins. Whatever he intends to say is drowned out by Kiran's screeches of delight, then splashing sounds as she apparently runs headlong into the water. She turns the light back to shore and shines it deliberately on her companions. Jane can see the brightness swishing back and forth, she can hear Ravi and the FBI man laughing, the FBI lady cursing, and she understands what Kiran is doing. Kiran's making it impossible for them to isolate the silhouette of the rowboat on the water behind her. She's good at this, isn't she?

"Your sister is a child," the female agent says in a scathing voice. "An absolute pollywog. And it's raining."

Ravi's voice is hearty. "Kiran," he shouts, "we're going back now."

"Did I mess up your fun?" Kiran shouts back.

"Yes!"

"I win!" Kiran shouts.

"Congratulations, you pain in the ass!" yells Ravi.

A few more splashes and flashes of light. Then the sound of cracking twigs and shifting leaves as the four of them climb back into the ramble.

Finally, only the roar of the ocean, coming, going, and the patters of rain.

Jane's senses are full of Ivy's kiss. Ivy's mouth was soft, her gun halter palpable through her coat. Nothing is quite how Jane imagined it would be. And it's possible she's never been so tired.

"What now?" she says.

"Now we wait for Cook to come back in the boat with Philip Okada," Patrick says.

"Philip Okada?"

"When the lady who's helping us picks Ivy and the kids up," Patrick says, "she's dropping Philip off. We owe you, you know. Maybe we would've seen Kiran's light in time—well, we probably would've seen Kiran's light in time," Patrick amends, "because Kiran was very smart about it." He stops, looking vague and miserable.

"So you don't owe me after all?"

"Sorry," he says. "No, we do owe you, because even if we'd been able to get the boat away, we wouldn't have gotten Ivy to it in time. I'd probably have had to go in her place, which would've been inconvenient for me, and really inconvenient for Ivy. After she delivers the kids to their parents she's expected in Geneva. Breaking things off with HQ is a long procedure."

"Is it like she's retiring?"

"Yeah," Patrick says, "pretty much, except she'll be in possession of some sensitive secrets when she retires. HQ needs to put her through the wringer about that before they'll let her go. She needs to prove she's trustworthy."

"Will they really let her go?"

"I'm not worried," he says. "You shouldn't worry."

"They're not going to make her move to some horrible, remote place, are they?"

"Nah. She'll be allowed to live wherever she wants. She'll just have to take a trip to Geneva every couple years for follow-up."

"Why does Mrs. Vanders let her have dangerous information?" Jane says indignantly. "Why does Ivy need to know where the Panzavecchias are going?"

"She doesn't know," says Patrick, "and she still won't know when she gets there. I don't know either. Mr. and Mrs. Vanders do a good job of keeping things from us. Even from their son, Cook."

"I bet they do," Jane says, thinking of Aunt Magnolia.

"Hey. Knowing the truth in this business is really dangerous. People *die*." The words are punching themselves out of his mouth.

"Like your parents," Jane says.

"People die," he says simply.

She studies him in the darkness.

"I don't know Kiran very well," Jane says. "But I can relate to how she's feeling. It's . . . confusing. Horribly. It's like having everything ripped away from you and then thrown back at you all sharp and unrecognizable. But I can see you had a not-too-terrible reason for your lies. You didn't do it out of selfishness, or maliciousness, or cowardice."

"I still shouldn't have lied," says Patrick, choking over the words. "She trusted me, and she was always honest with me. She knows me better than anyone, and I lied to her. What was I thinking? If she never forgives me, I don't blame her."

Patrick turns his face from Jane, because he's crying. It takes Jane a moment to realize she's crying too. This is Aunt Magnolia's apology, these words coming out of Patrick's mouth. Aunt Magnolia can't say them herself. She's gone. But she made Jane promise to come to this house.

It was all she'd been able to do.

The rain seems to be clearing away. Clouds push across the sky, revealing stars and obscuring them again. Jane rests a hand on her own shoulder, where the bell of her jellyfish tattoo sits under her sleeve. It's the visible proof that Aunt Magnolia is a part of her. "How long do you think we'll be waiting?" she asks.

Patrick wipes at his face with the back of his hand and squints at the sky above the water. "Not too much longer," he says. "You don't have to wait, you know. There's no reason for you to get pneumonia."

"I'll wait," Jane says, not certain why she doesn't want to leave him. "Will you tell me what happened to Charlotte?"

"Charlotte?"

"Kiran's stepmother."

"I know who she is," Patrick says. "I don't think anyone knows what happened to her."

"So she wasn't tied up in this spy stuff?"

"Oh," he says. "I see why you're asking. No. Charlotte was an interior designer. She had no connection to any of this. Mrs. Vanders even made some serious inquiries—discreetly—after she went away, but nothing came of it. Charlotte's departure is a mystery."

"Okay," Jane says, then swallows. She pushes the words out. "What about my aunt?"

"Your aunt?"

"Ivy told me to ask you for some sort of information about her."

Patrick pauses. "You mean the part where she died?"

Jane breathes in.

"Yeah," she says. "The part where she died." She breathes out.

"You're right to ask," says Patrick. "Just before the Antarctica trip, she came to a gala. At some point during the night, she left us without saying good-bye, which was unusual for Magnolia. We knew she was headed to Antarctica to take pictures of whales and penguins; it wasn't a CIA trip. Then we saw the news about how she got lost in a storm on the peninsula. She was well-regarded as a photographer, so it got picked up, and we pay attention to the news. How did you learn about it? Did you get a call?"

"Yes."

"Do you remember who called you?"

"The connection was terrible," Jane says. "His name was John Something but I couldn't hear straight. Someone from the research station; he didn't really know her. Then we got cut off, and I kept hoping the whole thing was some sort of mistake, until someone from the university came to talk to me. They mailed me her things from Ushuaia. They never found her body."

"Right," says Patrick. "Well, whenever an operative dies, we do some digging as a matter of course. When we dug deeper about Magnolia, our sources in Argentina told us she had the flu when her ship crossed the Drake Passage and she never left her cabin. Our other sources told us that she had the flu in Antarctica at the research station too, and never left her room. Next thing we know, she went out, got caught in the storm, and died."

"But—why would she go out if she had the flu?"

"You're missing my point," says Patrick. "What I'm saying is that none of the people we've talked to ever actually laid eyes on her. No one can confirm seeing her on the ship or on the peninsula. She was always 'in her room,' but we haven't been able to figure out who was initiating that story. And we can't find any records of her flying from any American airport to any airport in South America, either. You see what I'm saying? We're not convinced Magnolia ever went to Antarctica. The CIA has her categorized as a fallen operative, but we haven't been able to confirm how or where she actually died."

Jane's body is an ocean, removed from feeling and from any consciousness of time. *She knew,* Jane thinks. *She had a plan. She left her wool hat behind for me. She made me promise to come to this house. She left me a message.*

Jane sits up straight and stares at Patrick in the dark.

What if . . .

"Oh, for the love of god," Patrick says with sudden violence. He's staring out to sea.

"What is it?"

"That woman is a piece of work," he says, pointing to the sky above the water.

Jane turns to see what he's looking at and is met with the vision of an oblong shape barely visible against the night sky. It's like a whale in the sky, with a few flashing lights where she imagines its belly to be. "Is that . . . a blimp?"

"It's a freaking zeppelin," Patrick says.

"A zeppelin!"

"She owns a helicopter, this lady, and a seaplane, but she decides to pick up the children, the art, and my sister in her zeppelin. That means long ropes, and Ivy having to deal with the stress of not dropping Christopher or Grace or a Brancusi or a Rembrandt into the ocean. It's unnecessary!" he says.

"It's surreal," Jane says.

"It's romantic," Patrick says scornfully, "coming to the rescue in a zeppelin. Poor Philip. He's got to drop *out* of the zeppelin and there's no way he's not going into the drink."

"I didn't know anyone actually said 'the drink,'" Jane says.

"It seemed like the right term to describe the water under a zeppelin," Patrick says, still disgusted.

Jane snorts, and Patrick snickers despite himself.

It's too dark to see what's going on out there. After what feels like a long time, the zeppelin moves off into the clouds. Patrick pushes to his feet. "Stay here," he says, then runs out to the beach with his flashlight and flashes it a few times toward the water in a rhythmic pattern.

Before too long, Jane sees *The Ivy* returning to shore, then hears the purr of its engine. When the boat gets close, someone climbs out, drops into the water, and begins to move toward shore. The boat zips away again, perhaps to be moored on some other part of the island.

Patrick returns to the brush with the new person, who turns out to be Philip Okada, soaked through and shivering.

"Hi," Jane says.

"Hi," says Philip, running a hand through wet hair, not seeming particularly surprised to see her. He's wearing all black with his orange Chuck Taylors.

"Did Ivy and the kids make it into the zeppelin okay?" she asks.

"Yeah."

Patrick pushes through branches, reaches for the big stone door, and hauls it open. Philip ducks through.

"You coming?" says Patrick to Jane.

"I'll catch up," Jane says.

"You sure?"

"Go ahead," she says. "I won't be long."

Jane is left alone, to soak in the night. The clouds are drifting fast and the waves are crashing hard on shore. Her own shivering has calmed.

Jane has things rooting her to the earth. She has her anger; she has her grief. She's awake now, and centered in these things. And she's not alone. There's a friend out there in a zeppelin. There's a dog back in the house. There are people in the house, who have resources. There's an umbrella she intends to rebuild. There's a message from Aunt Magnolia. And there's the seed of a new question—just the seed, which will grow as Jane feels able to nurture it—about whether maybe—just maybe—what was lost could be found.

A bell rings somewhere in the depths of the house, sweet and clear, like a wind chime.

Mrs. Vanders, the little girl, Kiran, Ravi, or Jasper?

Aunt Magnolia? Jane thinks. *Where should I go?*

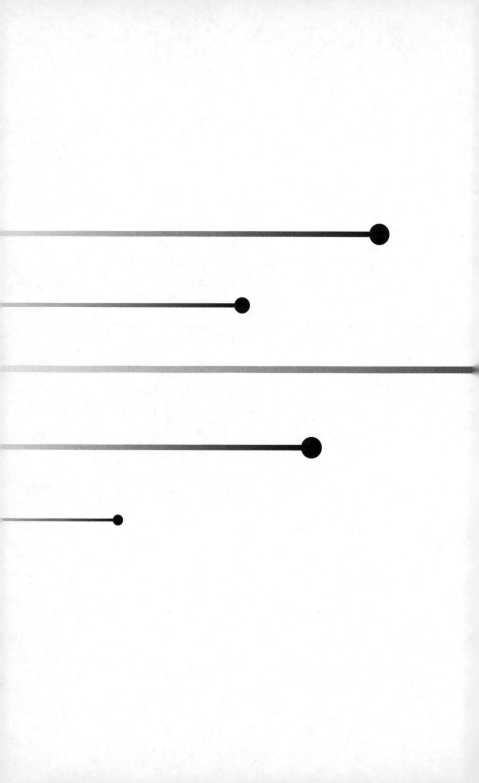

In Which
Someone Loses
a Soul and
Charlotte Finds
One

Jane decides.

What if Charlotte's disappearance is the puzzle piece that will make sense of everything else?

"Okay," Jane says to Kiran, starting down the stairs. "I'll walk with you, and you can tell me about Charlotte."

But Kiran doesn't respond right away. She's cupping her ear and frowning as if she's trying to hear something. "Did you hear that?"

"I can't hear anything but the world's most anxious dog," says Jane, who's reached Jasper's landing. Jasper's now butting his head against her boots, whimpering. She reaches down and rubs his neck in a spot he can't reach with his short legs. He tries to climb into her lap, which nearly topples her.

"Come with us, Jasper," Jane says, disentangling herself. Still whimpering, he follows her down the steps, crowding her feet.

Kiran walks Jane through the Venetian courtyard and the east arcade. "These rooms are all relevant to Charlotte's story," she says. "We'll end up in the winter garden, where we can play chess if we like."

Next she leads Jane into a green room with floral wallpaper, brocaded settees, and a fussy green carpet. "May I present the green parlor," Kiran says. "Charlotte redesigned it in the style of Regency England. Like, Jane Austen," she adds, when Jane crinkles her forehead.

"Ah," says Jane, understanding. Linked arm-in-arm with Kiran, taking a turn about the room, she feels like they could be Elizabeth Bennet and Caroline Bingley. If Mr. Darcy were composing a letter at the elegant writing desk, he'd be aghast at her striped jeans and sea-dragon top. "My favorite parts of the house are the parts where everything seems to fit together," says Jane. "Like this room, or like the Venetian courtyard with its matching tile and marble. You can imagine a whole story here. In the hallways where nothing matches, I just get kind of confused."

"Yeah," says Kiran, pulling Jane across the room toward a door. "The matching parts, that's all Charlotte's doing. She had weird theories that the house is suffering, because it was built from pieces that were torn from other houses."

"What do you mean, suffering?"

"Oh, you know," Kiran says. "From its troubled origin."

"Charlotte thought houses suffer?"

"Charlotte always talked like houses were people," says Kiran. "As if they have souls, or at least, as if they *should* have souls."

"That's kind of nice," Jane says. "But, as an *idea*. Are you saying she actually believed it?"

Kiran shrugs. "She thought that Tu Reviens had been deprived of a soul because of its origin story. 'Its parts are bleeding,' she said. 'Can't you see them bleeding?'"

"Um," Jane says, then pauses. "*Can* you see them bleeding?"

Kiran smiles. "I know how it sounds. But that's just how she talked. You know, I realize I'm not supposed to like the lady who takes my mother's place, especially the blond, skinny, too-young, white lady, but I really do like Charlotte, even if maybe she started to get kind of obsessive about the house. She's from Vegas, but she hated it there. She told me the city had a lost soul. She said she could hear the voices of centuries of suffering."

"So, cities have souls too." Kiran has pulled Jane into a sort of rec room, composed of soft blues, with wraparound couches, built-in media shelves and cabinets, and a gigantic fish tank. A huge painting, taking up an entire wall, shows a scene of an old harbor city at night with two moons glowing in the sky. The double moonlight makes trails across the sea. The painting reminds Jane of Aunt Magnolia's coat, with its purple sky, silver moons, and candles gleaming gold in the windows of towers. Jasper seems to like the painting. He flops onto his stomach, rests his chin on his paws, and sighs up at it with fondness.

"Charlotte is very sensitive," says Kiran. "She suits Octavian so much more than Mum ever did. He's the kind of person who needs a devoted companion, and Charlotte really loved—or loves—being with him. Though it did get to the point where Charlotte seemed more wound up in the house than she was in Octavian, but even then, Charlotte shared all her house thoughts with him. He was even trying to help Charlotte find the house's soul."

"How?" Jane says, then frees her arm from Kiran's, absently, because she needs to touch her ears, and pull at her earlobes, and try to alter some sort of air pressure problem she's having. Her ears feel stuffy, bloated, as if they've eaten too much.

"Charlotte kept saying that the house is made of orphaned pieces," says Kiran.

"Orphaned pieces?" *I'm an orphaned piece, aren't I?*

"Yeah. Charlotte said the only thing unifying all the parts is *pain*. That the house is in constant agony. Charlotte wanted to find another way to unify the house, to bind its pieces. So the house can rest."

"Rest?" Jane says. "What does that even mean?"

"I have no idea," Kiran says, taking Jane's elbow again and pulling her into another, smallish room. This one has showy chairs and tables inlaid with gold filigree and complicated gold-and-garnet fabric on the walls. It's another cohesive little world, a tearoom in the Beaux-Arts style, but Kiran tows Jane on to the next room before Jane can ask more. She's beginning to notice her own disorientation. It's a sort of sleepy distraction. *It's because each room feels like a new world, a new era,* she thinks.

"My impression," says Kiran, "is that Charlotte thought the house needed some kind of glue to unify its parts, something positive and healing, and whatever that thing was could be the house's soul."

"That sounds nice, really," says Jane. "And so she tried to unify each individual room? Or something?"

"That was the start," Kiran says, "but unifying the design of each room does nothing for the unmatching parts of the house's basic structure, you know? The foundations, the skeleton. And Octavian was happy for Charlotte to add things and move things around, but he wasn't okay with Charlotte getting rid of anything. Like, they had an argument about the shelving in the library, because it came from the libraries of lots of different houses around the world. Charlotte wanted to rip out all the shelving and rebuild it with wood sourced from local, sustainable forests. That was too extreme for Octavian. He was trying to convince Charlotte that the house's disparate origins were part of its charm, and therefore part of its soul. Charlotte kept saying, 'It can't be, it can't be,' then finally she stopped talking about it. 'I'll *make* a soul,' Charlotte said."

"Out of what? Duct tape? Or . . . *glass,*" she adds, with wonder, because Kiran has pulled her into a room that seems fashioned out of light. Enormous and L-shaped, this is the winter garden. The base of the L is a greenhouse, unruly and magnificent, while the long part is yet another space with armchairs and card tables, bathed with natural light and the shadows of green leaves. This room, Jane realizes, is where the hanging nasturtiums are cultivated, and the lilacs and daffodils too. A woman is cleaning the moldings with a duster.

"I think she tried to make the soul in a lot of different ways," says Kiran, stopping at a small, square table with a chessboard, its pieces lined up and ready to go.

"Your move," Jane says.

Kiran leans down and advances a pawn. Walking to the other side of the table, Jane does the same, noticing how expansive this board feels, how smoothly the pieces move, compared to the tiny magnetic travel set Aunt Magnolia had owned. The light through the glass walls is warm on her back.

Kiran advances another pawn. A couple of minutes pass while each of them contemplates the board and shifts things around in turn. Kiran is better at chess than Jane is. *Zugzwang,* she thinks suddenly, remembering the word for a situation in which one's obligation to make a move in chess puts one at a serious disadvantage. Ivy will love it; Jane'll have to remember to tell her.

"I guess we should sit," Kiran says, "if we're going to play."

There's something about the feeling of the air against Jane's ears that stops her from wanting to sit. It's an inchoate instinct, to keep moving and find a more comfortable place. "We could," she says doubtfully, advancing one of her knights. "How did Charlotte try to make a soul for the house?"

"Mostly she just got more intense," Kiran says. "She would talk about listening to each room and letting the room tell her what it wanted to be. She was working so hard, day and night; she was letting it run her ragged. And then she disappeared."

"Yes, I heard she disappeared."

Wind pushes at the glass and the house makes a rumbling sound around them, stone pressing back at the wind. Then another noise, a sort of laughter, unstable and faint, like a faraway train whistle. As

Lucy St. George and Phoebe Okada walk into the room, Jane's skin is prickling. She's starting to wonder if she's getting an ear infection. The pressure in her head seems to be growing.

"There," Lucy says, pursing her lips at the walls. "Did you guys hear that?"

"Hear what?" says Phoebe. "I didn't hear anything."

"The house made a noise," says Lucy. "It sounded like a word. 'Disappointed.'"

"I heard 'disappeared,'" Jane responds.

"The two of you are being weird," says Kiran, walloping one of Jane's bishops with her queen. "*I* said 'disappeared,' and then you said it back to me, Janie. Charlotte disappeared one night, about a month ago. She just . . . *left*. Octavian was the last to see her. She was sleeping on the divan in the library. As far as he could judge, she didn't take anything with her, no change of clothes, not even her diary. She left a note behind that said, 'Darling, there's something I need to try. Please don't worry. If it works, I'll come back for you.'"

"What does that mean?" says Jane. "What did she need to try?"

"No clue."

"'If it works, I'll come back for you,'" Jane repeats. "How did she leave? Seeing as it's an island?"

"Someone must've come and picked her up," Kiran says, "because no boats were missing. She must've arranged it beforehand, which I think really hurt Octavian—that she trusted someone else with her plan, but not him."

"People were talking about it at breakfast," says Jane. "Colin told me Octavian hired investigators and everything."

"Yeah," says Kiran. "They were real muckrakers; they dug some stuff up about Charlotte's family, like that her mom had a criminal record, but Octavian said he already knew about that and it was irrelevant. I think he really believes she's coming back for him. I think he's put his life on hold until she does."

Jane thinks of how her aunt died, all alone. Luckily, the people at the research station had known where she'd gone. Because people do disappear sometimes, and if there's no one around to witness it, how can the people left behind, waiting, ever know?

"At the time she went away, she'd remodeled this entire wing," Kiran says, sweeping a hand out. "Green parlor, blue sitting room, tearoom, this room, the bowling alley, the swimming pool, the gun room, and she was almost done with the library. Octavian was definitely worried, but he had no idea she was planning to take off. She wouldn't talk about anything but the cataloging system."

"The cataloging system?"

"Charlotte decided to catalog the library books by color," Kiran says. "Completely impractical. Impossible to find anything."

"What do you mean, by color?"

"Color of the spine," Kiran says. "The library is at the back of the house and it's two stories high. Charlotte started talking about how it was the house's spine, the nerve center, the place of greatest power. Then she started assigning body parts to all the other rooms, like the Venetian courtyard was the heart of the house, and the kitchen was the stomach, and the receiving hall was the mouth, and the east spire where Mum lives was the brain, and the bowling alley was, like, the vagina. It got a little creepy. And it would've looked like the worst kind of Picasso if you'd painted it."

"Well, the library sounds pretty amazing," Jane says. "Organized by the colors of the spines. I've never heard of that before."

"I don't really go in there anymore," Kiran says. "It's Octavian's haunt. It's depressing."

"Don't you want to see it?" Jane says. "I kind of want to see it."

"I've seen it," Lucy says, raising the copy of *The House of Mirth* she holds in one hand. "I got my book from it. It's really pretty in there, like waves of color. It's almost like being underwater. It's an ocean, and we're the fish."

A bead of sadness bursts open inside Jane.

"Let's go to the library," she says.

Someone has scrawled the word *PRIVATE* on a ratty piece of paper and hung it on a fat velvet rope that blocks the entrance to the library.

"That's Octavian's handwriting," says Kiran. "Not to mention his level of craftsmanship. He must be trying to protect his precious haunt from the gala cleaners."

"Does it mean we can't go in?" asks Lucy St. George.

"Of course not," says Kiran. "Only that he doesn't want us to go in."

"Hmm. But it is his house," says Phoebe Okada.

Briefly this strikes Jane as funny, that Phoebe is advocating respect for Octavian's pathetic rope barrier when last night Phoebe was skulking through the servants' quarters with her husband and a gun. But then she loses track of that thought, because it's irrelevant, because she needs to go in and see the ocean of color. If she doesn't go in with Kiran, Lucy, Phoebe, and Jasper now, she intends to sneak in later.

"Someday Octavian will croak. Then it'll be my house," says Kiran. "And it's the freaking library. He can't hold the books ransom. If you want to go in, go in." This last part is directed at Jane, who's craning her neck and gazing with moon eyes.

Jane unhooks one end of the velvet rope and steps into the room.

The color is singing.

The books of any library are colorful. But these books undulate and pulse with color. It's not a straightforward matter of all the blues turning to all the purples turning to all the reds. There's an earthy section, with oranges and greens turning to reds and browns. There's a serene section with cool yellows turning to cool greens to cool blues, and an energetic section with bold, bright tones of every hue. The sections also blend into each other, bright books fading to more muted books, gradually infiltrated by glimmering metallics, and so on. The room feels alive; it's like being inside a living thing. And each book, each colorful spine, is the container of a story. It reminds Jane of Aunt Magnolia's underwater dream worlds, and of her own work too, or of what she wants her umbrellas to be. *Yes,* Jane thinks. *If this house has a soul, its soul is here in this room.*

She finds herself looking around for Octavian, expecting to find him in some corner, but he's nowhere to be seen. Jane remembers Ravi calling him a creature of the night.

French doors look out onto a terrace and Jasper asks to be let out. When Jane opens the doors for him, she can hear the roar of the sea. He shoots outside and turns back to Jane, hopping eagerly, looking longingly into her face, but she's only just arrived in the library. Nothing about the terrace excites her. "Have fun, Jasper-bear," she says, closing the doors in his face and turning back to the room. *Aunt Magnolia? Is this how you felt in your underwater universe? I wish you could see this.*

"What if you don't know the color of the book you're looking for?" she asks.

"Card catalog," Kiran says, pointing to the dark wooden cabinet with little drawers near the entrance. "Like in the days of yore."

Jane goes to the catalog, pulls out the *W* drawer, and looks for the first book that comes to mind, *Winnie-the-Pooh.* "Milne, A.A.," the card reads. "Glimmering Section. Crimson-ginger. Lettering: gold."

"Glimmering Section," Jane says, turning curiously to the room. Across from her is a crimson section that doesn't seem quite mild enough. It's bright and loud, not glimmering. Jane walks to the middle of the room again, turning in circles. A small section of books glows softly crimson, silver, and gold on the second level, above the French doors, on the north wall.

Jane climbs a spiral staircase to the library's upper level. By the time she gets to that glowing patch of books, she's imagining an umbrella that feels like this library. The pressure on her ears is still present, but she's barely noticing it anymore.

It astonishes her how quickly she's able to find the Milne. "Well done, Charlotte," she says, reaching out to it. The book settles into her hand with a pleasurable shiver, like a satisfied cat arching its back against her palm. Once in her hands, it falls open to the story "In Which Pooh Goes Visiting and Gets into a Tight Place." Pooh visits Rabbit, then eats so much honey that he can't fit through the round doorway. He gets stuck, like a plug, and can't leave. On the outdoor side, Christopher Robin sits with Pooh's head and reads him stories. On the indoor side, Rabbit makes the best of it, hanging his washing on Pooh's stubby legs.

Something is strange, though, about this copy of the book. Jane knows, or she thought she knew, how this story is supposed to end. It's one of her favorites, one she read repeatedly, wedged into the armchair with Aunt Magnolia: Pooh stops eating, Pooh grows thinner, and after a week has gone by, Christopher Robin, Rabbit, and Rabbit's friends and relations take hold of him and pop him from the hole.

In this version, something different seems to be happening. As the week goes on, Pooh's body starts to meld with the edge of the dirt hole. It hurts. Pooh is crying.

Jane slams the book shut, alarmed, then angry, actually, at whatever writer thought it would be funny to rewrite it that way. And she's left with the most surreal sensation of being stuck in a hole in a wall, with Mrs. Vanders hanging washing on her legs, oblivious to anything strange about her new drying rack. "Tut-tut," Mrs. Vanders sings. "It looks like rain."

Jane shakes herself. She is not a part of the wall. She's a person, standing on the library's mezzanine. Her ears feel unlike anything she's ever felt before, and she's beginning to realize how wrong this is.

"Charlotte reached a whole new level of obsession with the library," Kiran says, from below. "Octavian practically had to move in here in order to spend any time with her. Seems like he still hasn't moved out."

Looking over the banister, Jane finds Kiran in a darkish corner across the room, behind one of the metal spiral staircases. The books in that section are blacks, browns, and deepest purples. In a room of moving color it's easy to miss the divan there, which is piled with blankets, books, ashtrays containing the detritus of the pipe tobacco Jane now realizes she's been smelling since she came into the room. An ancient-looking record player sits on a low table at the head of the divan.

Jane doesn't care. She wants to leave.

"This must be his nighttime haunt," Kiran says, wrinkling her nose in distaste, then moving an overflowing ashtray from its perch on a rumpled blanket to the edge of the table. "What a way to spend all your waking hours. Ugh. Do you ever feel like there's an inevitability to every version of your life?"

"What does that mean?" asks Phoebe.

"In this version of his life," Kiran says, "was Octavian always going to be depressed? Does it matter what any of us do?"

"I'm not following," says Phoebe. "Of course it matters."

"I don't want to talk about Charlotte anymore," says Jane.

"I'm not talking about Charlotte," says Kiran. "I'm talking about Octavian. Do your ears hurt?"

Jane's head feels like a balloon. "But Octavian haunts this room because he's depressed about Charlotte," she says stubbornly, "right? It's all about Charlotte."

Lucy St. George, still carrying *The House of Mirth*, has crossed to the other side of the room and is gently stroking the burnished wood of the bookcases. Jane finds herself synchronously rubbing the railing of the mezzanine banister. It's an odd compulsion. Snatching her hand away, she says, "Yes, my ears hurt. I have work to do. I'm going back to my rooms."

"What work do you do?" Lucy asks.

"I make umbrellas."

"Really?" Lucy says. "Do you repair them? I've got one that doesn't open right."

"Bring it to me," Jane says impatiently, heading for the spiral staircase, "east wing, third floor, at the end. Come right in. I'll see what I can do."

"Thanks," Lucy says, then cries out and yanks her hand away from the bookcases.

"What's wrong?" asks Phoebe.

"Nothing," says Lucy, inspecting her palm. "Just a splinter, or some kind of—electrical short, or something."

"How could a bookcase have an electrical short?" asks Phoebe.

All the hairs of Jane's body are standing on end. *Get out,* she's telling herself as she moves down the stairs; *Get out.* Jasper presses his nose to the glass of the terrace door, anxiously whining. Jane lets him in, then crosses the room with him as quickly as possible. She's rude. As she passes through the doorway into the Venetian courtyard, she doesn't say good-bye to the others.

"Jasper," Jane says, stopping in the courtyard to take a breath of the sunlit air. "It was weird in there."

Jasper leans his head against the back of her ankles and pushes, whining softly.

"You didn't like it either?" she says. "Let's go."

She's almost to her rooms before she realizes she's still holding tight to *Winnie-the-Pooh.*

* * *

Back in her rooms, the light is bright and warm and Jane thinks maybe work will help clear her mind.

Last time she worked, it was on the self-defense umbrella in brown and gold. She still likes this idea. In fact, she has the nebulous sense of something she'd like to defend herself against, some feeling in the air that's trying to fuzz her brain. *Silly,* she chides herself. *I probably just need some coffee. I'll get some, right after I lie on the floor so I can think about my umbrella.* She uses *Winnie-the-Pooh* as a pillow. The morning sun pours in; the shag rug is soft; Jasper tucks himself lengthwise beside her.

When Lucy St. George pushes through the doorway with a navy umbrella, Jane has just dozed off.

"Wow," Lucy says, surveying the roomful of colorful umbrellas.

"Mrph," Jane says, sitting up, trying to focus. She's lost in a peculiar dream she can't grasp; she's already forgetting it. Jasper is snorting beside her. "Sorry. Patch of sun."

"I'm embarrassed to show you my umbrella now that I've seen yours," Lucy says. "It's positively dull."

Jane has forgotten all about repairing Lucy's umbrella.

"Ow," Lucy says, shaking out her free hand as if it hurts.

"You okay?"

"Yeah, my hand still stings from that splinter or whatever. Here." She passes her umbrella to Jane. "See, it opens funny."

Lucy's umbrella does indeed open funny, but Jane can see that it's just because a metal rib is bent and needs reshaping and reinforcing. "It's a simple fix," she says. "Listen, I don't have the right paints just now, but you can do cute things on this type of nylon with the right kind of glue and the right kind of glitter."

Lucy St. George is pinching her lips together to stop a grin. "Are you saying you want to make my dull umbrella sparkly? Go ahead."

"Really?" Jane says. "It might not be subtle."

"Do your worst," Lucy says. "I'm curious."

"Hey," Jane says, surprised and smiling. "Thanks."

"Do you think this house has moods?" Lucy says.

"Huh?"

"Moods," Lucy says. "You know. Does it have emotions, and intentions, and objectives?"

"The *house?*"

"Yes."

"Um," Jane says. "Isn't that a little bit fantastical?"

"So, that's a no?" Lucy says with a weak smile.

"Yes. It's a no," Jane says, surprised by her own passion. "I mean, I think that's what Charlotte thought, but it sounds like she was kind of . . . an oddball. Have you been talking to Kiran about Charlotte?"

"No, it's just a feeling I get," says Lucy. "Tell me if you change your mind. It's a lonely point of view."

As Lucy leaves, Jane sees the self-defense umbrella, suddenly, that she needs to make. When it's closed, it'll feel like a blade in her hand, good for slicing through bloated air. Then it'll open with a loud crack, good for shoving bad things away. *Yes,* she thinks. *I'll just stay here on the rug and contemplate it,* but when she lies back, her mind keeps picturing Octavian's sad little crumpled corner in the library. What kind of umbrella would that make?

She gets up once to let Jasper out, then lies down again. Air and water push distantly through pipes in an uneven concert of noises like melancholy sighing. Jane finds herself stroking the rug, as if to soothe herself, or someone else.

The house's soft sounds fit themselves as harmonies around Jane's lathe, her drill, her rotary saw, her sewing machine, her own absentminded humming. The glass wall captures heat and light and channels it into

Jane as fuel for her focus. The energy of the room strips everything else away; the umbrella she's building is the entire world.

In fact, it has ribs like Jane. It has one long leg on which its other parts balance; it has moving and bending joints, like Jane, and it has a skin that stretches across its bones. Jane will paint on that skin, just as the tattoo artist marked Jane's skin. How nice, to have a weather-resistant skin and a body that can vibrate with tension or be at rest. How satisfying to have working parts, lovingly crafted. Rain is a musical patter against Jane's imagination. Every umbrella is born knowing that sound, its soul straining for that sound, waiting patiently through rainless day after rainless day for the day when raindrops will thrum against its skin.

Jane shakes herself, confused. She wonders, are those really her thoughts? Why does it feel like she's thinking someone else's thoughts? She's too warm, and, when she tries to remember, she's not certain what she's been doing for the past however-long. She vaguely recalls . . . an intense connection with the umbrella she's making. Her ears still hurt and she becomes aware of her own repetitive humming. It's a Beatles tune, "Eleanor Rigby," about loneliness.

Jane grips the edge of her worktable, takes a jellyfish breath. Then, under her fingers, she discovers a carving of a gentle whale shark swimming with its babies. It runs along the edge in intricate detail. Ivy must've made this table. *Ivy,* Jane thinks, her mind clearing. *Aunt Magnolia. Me.*

Why does Jane smell paint?

Turning suddenly to the work she's been doing, Jane finds a half-painted scene on her umbrella canopy. It looks like the dark brown and black books of the library, and a smudge that's the beginnings of Octavian's divan. This wasn't the plan; this was supposed to be her self-defense umbrella. When did she get so off track?

Jane slaps her paints closed. She needs air, she needs to open a window.

At the wall, she discovers that one of the low panes of glass is designed to crank open. The joint is stiff, but, determined now, she uses her own tools to oil it. Applying all her strength, she manages to budge it slightly. A feeble current of cool air drifts in through the crack.

Jane puts the self-defense umbrella-in-progress aside. It's pulling too hard. It's unnerving. She'll repair and improve Lucy's navy umbrella instead.

The repair to the bent rib is a few minutes' work. As for the embellishments—Lucy, Jane expects, will prefer something on the more quiet and tasteful end of the spectrum. Tiny, glimmering stars in a night sky, maybe—the most obvious approach when one's tools are a navy canopy, glue, and glitter—or maybe something even plainer.

Choosing a gore, Jane spreads an even stripe of glue across it. Simple lines, few in number. She'll start with that, exercise restraint, and see where it leads.

Some unknown length of time later, a noise in the house, like a yell, touches Jane. She misses a high note in the song she's singing and the dissonance jars her out of a haze. It's another Beatles tune, "She's Leaving Home," about a girl who runs away from home, abandoning her well-intentioned but repressive parents, leaving them to dwell in their own heartbreak and confusion. Jane wasn't even aware of knowing the lyrics to that song. She's changed the lyrics too. She's replaced all the names and pronouns with "Charlotte," as if all the people in the song—girl, mother, and father—are named Charlotte. "Charlotte's leaving home, bye-bye."

Jane discovers that she's moved away from Ivy's table, though she doesn't remember picking her supplies up and carrying them across the room. She seems to be working on the tarp on the floor, her legs crossed, her back bent and aching. She straightens herself, stretching her neck. Then she takes a look at what she's done to Lucy's umbrella and is horrified.

The stripes she started with have become the bars of a prison cell. Behind the bars, a woman sits on a cot, one leg propped up, her head thrown back against the wall, eyes staring out, face grim. The whole scene is rich with shadows and depth, composed of various colors and thicknesses of glue and glitter, an impressive artistic feat considering the awkwardness of her media. The woman even wears an orange glitter jumpsuit. A book rests on her thigh.

The smooth curve of her hair makes her look an awful lot like Lucy. *Oh, hell*, Jane thinks. *How did that happen?*

Someone somewhere in the house is shouting, the sharp fury of a male voice somewhere near. Another male voice responds with a roar and Jane recognizes the tone of this argument; she's heard these voices raised against each other before: Ravi and Octavian are at it again. Still holding Lucy's jailbird umbrella open, Jane stumbles into her bedroom, becoming aware that Jasper is whimpering on the other side of the door, scratching to get in. How long has he been out there? Everyone in this house is unhappy. When Jane opens the door, Jasper surges in and runs circles around her, barking too loudly.

Ignoring Jasper as best she can and still carrying the open umbrella, Jane moves down the corridor toward the shouting voices, which seem to be coming from somewhere between her rooms and the Venetian courtyard. "Aye, aye," she says vaguely, almost tripping over Captain Polepants.

The noisy room is Octavian's bedroom. Octavian sits upright in an enormous, tall bed, tangled silk covers pulled to his waist, wearing a T-shirt that says "All You Need Is Love." He's rubbing his pale face wearily, squinting at the light from open curtains.

Ivy stands at the foot of the bed next to Ravi, who is shouting and waving his arms around.

"You don't even care, Dad!" says Ravi. "You're like a shell with nothing inside. You're turning into a ghost. Soon you'll be able to walk through the walls!"

"That may be," says Octavian through steeled teeth, "but I forbid you, positively forbid you, to rifle through the possessions of the staff members *or* the guests of this house in pursuit of the answers to your self-righteous questions."

Ivy's got a small yellow daffodil behind one ear. Lucy St. George is just inside the door, her eyes wide and shocked and focused on Ravi. And Kiran leans against a wall with her arms crossed and an insolent expression on her face, like a mutinying twelve-year-old.

Jane remains in the doorway, holding Lucy's redecorated umbrella out into the corridor behind her, where the wet glue and glitter are less in danger of bashing into a doorframe and making a sparkly mess. Jasper is butting her calves, repeatedly, which is annoying.

Ivy has noticed Jane's arrival. She comes to her, pulling the daffodil from her hair and grinning. Ravi is still yelling at his father.

"Hi Janie," she says, taking in the loony dog, then the open umbrella. Next she glances at Jane's other hand, which is when Jane realizes she's carrying *Winnie-the-Pooh,* which she doesn't remember picking up.

"Look," says Ivy, holding out the slightly crushed daffodil. "They've decorated the suits of armor with jonquils for the gala. Eight letters, with a *j and* a *q.*"

"What?" says Jane, confused.

"Jonquils?" says Ivy. "It's a kind of yellow daffodil."

"Okay," says Jane. "Thanks, but my hands are full. Why are Ravi and Octavian yelling?"

Ivy looks a little deflated. "There's a marble sculpture of a fish," she says, "mounted on a wooden pedestal. It's by a famous sculptor named Brancusi and it sits on a table in the receiving hall. Ravi just found the empty pedestal. The fish is gone. Someone broke the fish off the pedestal and took it away and Ravi doesn't think his father's upset enough about it."

"Oh," Jane says, still not understanding.

Now Ivy's trying to get a closer look at the umbrella behind Jane. She squeezes past Jane into the corridor and Jane holds it out to her. She needs to know what Ivy sees when she looks at it.

"Wait," Ivy says. "Is that Lucy St. George on that umbrella?"

"You think it looks like her?"

"In jail?" Ivy says. "Did you draw a picture of Lucy in jail, using glitter?"

"My fingers slipped."

"It's an amazing glitter drawing," Ivy says, wonder in her voice. "I mean, it's extraordinary. But why did you draw her in jail?"

"I don't know," Jane says. "I didn't mean to."

Ivy's peering into her face. "Janie, are you okay?" she says. "You seem kind of . . . disoriented."

Because Ivy has asked it, Jane realizes it's true. "You know," she says, "I've felt disoriented all day. Sort of like gnats are flitting around in front of my eyes."

Ivy reaches out and wraps a hand around Jane's upper arm, on the jellyfish tentacles there. At Ivy's touch, the corridor comes into sharp focus and the endless pressure in Jane's ears drops away. Ivy smells like chlorine. Her hand is warm, her smile soft. "Oh," Jane says, wondering how strange it would be to give Ivy a full-on hug. "Thank you. Jonquils. I get it. I'm sorry. This has been a really weird day."

Not letting go of her arm, Ivy tucks the daffodil behind Jane's ear. It tickles. Jane flushes.

"Do you think maybe you're working too hard?" Ivy says.

"I don't know," Jane says. "There's something in the air today."

"Well, be careful. Lucy's in there," Ivy says. "You don't want her to see that umbrella."

"No," Jane says, certain. "I didn't mean it to turn out this way. I'm going to have to erase it somehow."

"Oh, man, do you have to?" Ivy says. "Because it's an amazing umbrella. It's just kind of . . . maybe not so nice to Lucy. I mean, do you think of her as a criminal?"

"Of course not!"

"Isn't she even a private art investigator? Like, she puts people in jail herself?"

"I feel awful about it," Jane says.

"Don't. But maybe you should go put it back in your rooms before she sees it. Here, give it to me," Ivy says, reaching for the handle of the umbrella.

The moment Ivy lets go of Jane's arm, confusion washes over her again.

"Lucy's coming," Ivy says quietly. She tugs at the umbrella. "Here, give it to me. I'll put it in your morning room." She has to pry the umbrella from Jane's fingers. With one more puzzled glance, she carries the umbrella away, down the corridor toward Jane's rooms.

Lucy St. George speaks behind Jane. "Excuse me."

"Sorry," Jane says, moving out of the way.

Lucy bumps against Jane as she passes into the corridor, her face blank and panicked.

"What's wrong?" asks Jane.

"Nothing," Lucy responds, rushing away.

"Do you feel weird today?" Jane calls to her back. "I feel weird today."

Lucy halts her mad rush. She turns back to Jane with an expression of great and pale strain. Like Jane, she's clutching her book in one hand.

"Did you ever love someone," Lucy says, "and know they love you, and you're attracted to them, and you know they're attracted to you, and so many things are exactly right, but it doesn't matter, because the few things that are wrong are completely, totally fucked?"

"Are you talking about Ravi?" Jane says.

"I've made some unfortunate decisions," Lucy says, then clutches her temples. "My head feels like it's splitting open. Does yours?"

"What do you mean, unfortunate decisions? Like Ravi?"

"Oh," Lucy says, "like a hundred things. Ravi is impossible. I can't believe I'm talking to you about it. Never mind."

"Have you made *criminal* decisions?" Jane says, thinking about the umbrella.

Lucy's eyes widen. "Why on earth would you ask me that?"

"Sorry," Jane says, confused. "I don't know where that came from. I just feel really weird today."

At that moment, Ravi pushes out of Octavian's bedroom, putting a hot hand on either side of Jane's waist and shifting her out of his way, not gently. He strides on down the hall toward his rooms at the corridor's end, his face wet with tears. He doesn't even glance at Lucy, who watches him go, folding the hard angles of herself up inside a disappointment she can't hide.

Lucy's phone starts ringing, but she doesn't react. She's still staring after Ravi.

"Your phone is ringing," Jane says.

"What? Oh," Lucy says, patting her front pockets, her back pockets, then producing a phone. She walks away, toward the house's center, saying, "Yeah, what is it, Dad?"

Jane is left alone in Octavian's doorway with the world's most agitated dog. He's gone back to head-butting Jane, as if he's trying to knock himself unconscious against her shin.

Inside the bedroom, Octavian and Kiran are having a stare-down.

"Is this what it takes for you to visit your old dad?" says Octavian, passing a weary hand across his eyes. "Someone steals a sculpture?"

"You haven't exactly come looking for me, either, Dad," says Kiran. "You know I've been home."

"Why would I push myself on you when I'm unwanted?"

"If Charlotte came home after all this time away," Kiran says, "you wouldn't sit back waiting for her to come to you."

"That's different," says Octavian. "Charlotte left without any warning. I have no idea where she went, or why."

"If I left without any warning," says Kiran, "you'd accuse me of being selfish and immature. When Charlotte does it, you mope, and smoke too much, and stop taking showers, and oversleep. You knew I was coming yesterday and you didn't even stay awake."

"Kiran," says Octavian. "Are you suggesting that I love my wife more than I love my daughter? That I wouldn't be distraught with worry if you disappeared? Do you really believe that?"

"I'm saying you need to snap out of it," says Kiran, suddenly angry. "Since when do you sleep all day, or not care if a major piece of art is missing?"

"So," says Octavian, his voice rising too, "you're mad at me because I'm depressed? Should I be mad at you because you're depressed?"

"Yes!" Kiran cries. "You should! You should be subjecting me to long, boring talks about how I need a job, and how you think I've chosen the wrong man and I'm ruining my life!"

"You *have* chosen the wrong man!" says Octavian, almost shouting now. "You *are* ruining your life!"

"Then tell me so!" Kiran cries. "Don't just shuffle around in your slippers mooning after Charlotte and acting indifferent to everything else!"

"I'm not indifferent!" says Octavian. "I'm just . . ." He stops, passing another hand over his eyes. "I'm tired."

"So go for a walk!" says Kiran. "Go for a swim! Go to New York and buy a painting! Of course you're tired! You never do anything!"

"I haven't been able to think clearly," Octavian says. "Not since Charlotte left."

"I understand you're hurt, Dad!"

"No," says Octavian. "No! It's not just that. It's like she took some part of my brain with her when she left. I get confused, and I only want to be in the library. I get sleepy, and I lose track of time."

"That's not normal, Dad," says Kiran. "You should go to the city and see your doctor."

"I can't leave."

"What are you talking about? Of course you can leave."

"Charlotte needs me, she wants me," says Octavian.

"Charlotte isn't *here.*"

"She's close," says Octavian. "If I stay here, and keep reaching, I can bring her back."

"Dad," says Kiran. "You're not making sense. Bring her back from where? The underworld? Like Orpheus and Eurydice? Charlotte left! She went away!"

"She talks to me," says Octavian. "She sings. She wants me to join her."

"Okay," says Kiran sharply, "that's it. You're delusional. After the gala, Ravi and I are putting you on a boat and taking you to the doctor and you don't get to have an opinion about it."

Jane is noticing something about the room, about the way the air seems buzzy and strange, as if there's an extra energy to it. The buzziness is focused on Octavian. *If the thing I'm sensing were visible,* Jane thinks, *Octavian would be blurry. As if he were existing partly in some other dimension.*

"I bet you almost disappear when you're in the library," Jane says out loud to Octavian.

Kiran and Octavian both turn to stare at Jane, startled by her interruption. Below, Jasper nips Jane. Then he opens his mouth, clamps it around her calf, and bites, hard.

"Ow!" cries Jane. The room comes sharply into focus again and the buzzing drops away. "Jasper! You sadist!" He's punctured a hole in her black-and-white-striped jeans. She wants suddenly to go outside and get some air. She needs some air. It's a desperate, pressing need.

"I'm going for a walk," Jane says to Kiran and Octavian. "Bye."

Jasper turns and sprints into the corridor, hopping in anxious excitement. Jane follows him.

Jasper leads Jane down the stairs. For once, he doesn't try to trip her. In the receiving hall, he herds her around a woman who's picking pieces of lilac and glass from the floor. Jane doesn't even notice the woman at first, which upsets her, that she's so out of it, she almost steps on another human being. *Aunt Magnolia,* she finds herself repeating. *Aunt Magnolia, Aunt Magnolia.*

A framed photo on a side table catches her eye. It's a portrait of a youngish blond woman with some other people and when Jane tries to go to it, Jasper herds her away with enthusiasm. The woman has a maniacal smile on her face. Jane knows it's Charlotte. She cranes her neck to keep looking at it while Jasper shuffles her out the front door.

The moment she passes into the outside world, she begins to come awake again. She feels the straining sunlight on her skin and hears the pounding sea, the pushing wind. The sounds are normal, natural; there's no strange pressure on her ears. Standing in the front yard, buffeted by wind and light, she takes a deep, jellyfish breath. *Aunt Magnolia.*

Jane thinks, suddenly, of the way her aunt died. Aunt Magnolia froze to death, in a blizzard. Hypothermia. Jane has learned, since then, from her doctor, some of the details of what it would have been like. Aunt Magnolia would have struggled with a mental fog like the one Jane has been experiencing today. An inability to remember things, to feel coherent and whole. She would have fought for clarity, but found it impossible, and finally given in to the fog. She would have had no choice. *Aunt Magnolia? Why did you send me to this strange, strange house? Did you know it would make me feel this way?* She looks up. Tu Reviens stretches before her, huge and cold, pockmarked with windows and unmatching stones. It makes her think of an old dragon with missing scales and multiple beady glass eyes, protecting its treasure. *It feels . . . lonely,* she thinks. *And hungry.*

An instinct tells her that in future it might be wise to stay out of the library.

Jasper's forging a path across the front yard through grass up to his neck, aiming for the east side of the house, where Jane can just make out the edges of the garden. Jane follows, pushing herself through the soggy grass, taking slow breaths.

Rounding the house's corner to the garden, she's bombarded by the smell of fresh, cold dirt and the sight of tulips and daffodils—jonquils, she thinks, touching the one at her ear—and a magnolia tree that looks like it's ready to explode into flower.

Near the edge of the east lawn, Mr. Vanders sits on a funny, crooked bench that looks more like it's made for meditation than for gardening. Or maybe it's just the slow, contemplative manner in which he's digging. The garden and yard are covered with uneven, random holes and piles of dirt.

"Hello there," Jane says, not wanting to interrupt, but wanting him to know he's not alone.

He attempts to speak but instead begins sneezing.

"Bless you," says Jane.

"Thank you," he says, pulling a handkerchief from his pocket. "Forgive me. I'm allergic to spring. Going for a walk, are you?"

"I needed to clear my mind," Jane says, gesturing with her book hand. "I've been feeling muddleheaded. So I came outside for some air. Should you be gardening if you have allergies?"

"We mustn't neglect the gardening," says Mr. Vanders. He sneezes again, explosively, then sighs, stretching his back.

The damp chill is doing wonders for Jane's mental clarity. Jasper sniffs happily at the holes Mr. Vanders has made, then starts digging one of his own. Jane feels an urge to go for a jog across the yard and toss her book like a javelin.

Mr. Vanders closes his watering eyes and turns his dark face to the sun. Jane can see every fine line crisscrossing his skin and wonders if the day will come when sudden little details will stop being about Aunt Magnolia, when the lines in the face of an old person won't make her think, *Aunt Magnolia will never be that old.*

She remembers, with a start, that Mr. Vanders knew Aunt Magnolia. Before she started feeling so foggy, she meant to investigate. "I haven't managed to talk to Mrs. Vanders yet," she says, "about my aunt."

"Mm-hmph," says Mr. Vanders, not opening his eyes. "Maybe after the gala. She'll find you once it's all over with."

The gala, Jane remembers. The gala is tomorrow. The details of this day are trickling back. She takes one great, big breath and decides that never again will she go into the library. "Apparently something happened with a Brancusi sculpture?" she says. "Of a fish?"

Mr. Vanders opens his eyes, blows his nose. "Apparently."

"We're lucky Lucy St. George is visiting, since she's an art investigator," Jane says, with a sudden flash of the jailbird umbrella. "It's scary, actually, isn't it?" she says. "If someone in the house stole a piece of art?"

"Yep," Mr. Vanders says, not sounding scared, or even particularly interested. Jane considers his messy garden. It's unclear what he's doing besides creating craters.

"Do you like gardening, then?"

"I wouldn't say so," he says, grasping his back. "My lumbar region is in agonies and I couldn't tell a flower from a weed if my life depended on it. But I'm trying to approach it as an exercise in mindfulness."

"Is it working?"

"Not particularly," he says wearily.

Jane watches Jasper root happily around in his hole. Then she anchors her eyes on Tu Reviens again.

"Have you always lived here?"

"Aside from college and grad school and some travel," says Mr. Vanders, "yes. My parents worked for the Thrashes. I grew up here, and have watched Octavian, then my own son, then Kiran and Ravi and Patrick and Ivy, grow up in this odd, wonderful house."

Jane considers the winter garden. "Even the glass of that wall is a patchwork," she says, indicating the panels.

"Just part of the house's lopsided charm," says Mr. Vanders.

"Is it? Kiran says that Charlotte thought the house was suffering from its origins."

"Well," says Mr. Vanders. "We all suffer from our origins in one way or another, don't you think?"

Jane thinks of her own story. Her father had been a high school science teacher. Her mother had been near the end of her dissertation on a new meteorological explanation for why it rains frogs. She'd been invited to speak at a weekend conference on Frog-Inspired Architecture in Barcelona and Jane's parents, in love with their eighteen-month-old baby but exhausted, had decided to make a thing of it. They'd left Jane with her mother's younger sister, Magnolia. This had been difficult for them, and for Jane's mother in particular, who'd just weaned Jane. She'd almost canceled the trip at the last moment; she'd almost contrived to take Jane along. But Magnolia had told them, *No, go, see the churches, eat paella, get some sun, spend some time alone.* The plane, hit by lightning, had lost an engine, then crashed during landing. Jane didn't remember them; she only remembered Aunt Magnolia, who had used to cry, sometimes, when it rained frogs.

It's hard for Jane to miss something she can't remember. Or does some part of her miss it? Might it be buried and unseen, but something on which the whole of her life rests, like the foundations of a building?

"What about a house?" Jane says to Mr. Vanders. "Can a house suffer from its origins?"

Mr. Vanders purses his lips at the house. "I guess if this house were a person, it'd be a reasonable candidate for an identity crisis. Poor house!" Mr. Vanders cries, holding his arms out suddenly, as if he'd like to embrace the house. He intones in a hearty voice, "You are our Tu Reviens!"

"Do you think that helped the house?" Jane asks, amused.

"Well," says Mr. Vanders, "the more we accept our lack of cohesion, the better off we are."

"Oh?"

"Let go of the illusion of containment and control!" he says, flinging out his arms.

"Good lord," says Jane, trying to imagine Mr. and Mrs. Vanders having conversations like this at night while sitting in bed.

"If the house is distressed by its lack of cohesion," says Mr. Vanders, "it's because of society's unreasonable expectations for integration."

"I see," says Jane, not seeing.

"The house could also be suffering from a diagnosable psychological disorder," he says. "Why shouldn't a house have dissociative disorder or even a severe narcissistic disorder? In a different universe, we would call in a house psychologist and get it the help it needs. Though presumably the house, being a house, isn't suffering at all, except from clogged gutters."

"What did you study at school, anyway?" asks Jane.

"Oh, this and that," says Mr. Vanders.

The French doors of the back terrace distantly open and Kiran comes out. She wades toward Jane through tallish grass, then skirts the dirt piles at the north edge of the gardens. She seems distracted, her face closed and trapped someplace far away. Jasper, meanwhile, is bounding around in his now very deep hole, licking something and making frenzied yipping noises at Jane. He seems to be trying to get her attention. Jane crouches down, tucks her book into her lap, and attempts to wipe mud from his fur with her hands.

"Hey, Mr. V," says Kiran vaguely. "How are you?"

"Decimated by pollen," says Mr. Vanders, appraising her with a quick glance. "How are you feeling, Kiran, sweetheart?"

"Marvelous," Kiran says, an obvious lie. "Come play bridge," she says to Jane.

"I don't know how to play bridge," Jane tells Kiran, still making dubious attempts at wiping mud from Jasper. "And my hands are dirty."

"I'll teach you," Kiran says. "Come on. Phoebe needs a partner."

Phoebe. Jane saw Phoebe in the servants' wing last night, with Patrick and Philip and a gun. She keeps forgetting about that. Should she tell someone? What if Phoebe stole the fish sculpture?

Jasper shoots out of his hole and rolls around in the grass, barking. He pops up again, shaking himself out, surprisingly clean. "All right," Jane says, wiping her hands on the damp grass. "I'll try bridge."

She grasps *Winnie-the-Pooh* carefully between her wet thumb and forefinger and pushes herself to her feet. Maybe spending some time with Phoebe will clarify things.

Glancing into Jasper's hole as she passes it, Jane notices something long, pale, and opalescent inside. "Nice talking to you, Mr. Vanders," she says. "By the way, Jasper seems to have unearthed an interesting long, white rock."

Mr. Vanders's eyebrows rise slowly to his hairline. He watches Kiran, Jane, and Jasper as they pick their way across the gardens to the house.

* * *

Kiran leads Jane to a small door in the house's back wall, through a dark corridor, then into a space flooded with moving light. Jane's never seen this room before. It's the indoor swimming pool, with gold tile floors and massive glass walls, one of which is an enormous fish tank. A lime-green eel stares straight through the glass at Jane with an almost human leer stretched across its face.

"Shark tank," says Kiran in a bored voice, then heads along the edge of the pool toward a couple of doors at the room's far end. "One of Charlotte's design choices."

"Sharks?" Jane says, then barely suppresses a gasp as a gigantic bull shark swims by. Bull sharks are predators. Jane used to have nightmares of Aunt Magnolia being eaten by one. The shark reaches the end of the tank, turns, and swims back the other way. The eel is still leering at Jane like some sort of terrible, crazed clown, but the shark neither knows nor cares that Jane exists.

Jasper nudges Jane's leg to get her moving. As she follows Kiran, she's certain the eel has its eyes on her back. It reminds her of the woman in the photo in the receiving hall; its expression is the same. Charlotte. Jane decides she's not going to talk, or think, about Charlotte anymore. It makes the air feel charged.

Kiran rounds the pool, chooses a door in the narrow wall at the pool's end, and leads Jane through a small, teak-paneled changing room that glows with the quality of its varnished wood. Teak is not cheap. Jane has made only one umbrella with a teak rod. Of course, maybe the first Octavian Thrash stole the teak from a monastery in Burma, which would've made it quite economical.

Another door brings Jane, without warning, into the library.

At the library's west end, Jane sits at a card table facing her partner, the mysterious Phoebe Okada. Jasper's tucked against Jane's feet. Kiran and

Colin make up the other team and Lucy St. George has curled herself up in a nearby armchair. Jane has lost her daffodil somewhere; it's not behind her ear.

"I can't stay long," she says, because she's promised herself not to spend time in the library. The problem is that the waves of color soothe her anxieties. When she entered, the blues and greens and golds swept her gently across the room. If the room is like being underwater, surely it can't be the wrong place for Jane to be?

Phoebe, to her surprise, is an intuitive teacher. She can anticipate Jane's bridge questions, then answers them so that she understands, and with no particular snobbishness. "It's an elegant game once you get into the rhythm. Good," she says as Jane trumps the ace of spades with the three of hearts. "You're catching on."

At the other end of the room, a toddler bolts through a doorway suddenly, then disappears through the door to the changing room. Jane can't see the child's face or skin, only a mop of dark hair and fast, sturdy little legs. A middle-aged, light-skinned black man bolts after the child, slowing only to look over a shoulder and assess the occupants of the library. He catches eyes, briefly, with Phoebe Okada, exchanging a significant, mysterious expression. He's wearing a chef's hat and checkered pants. Then he's gone.

"Does your cook have a child?" Jane asks Kiran.

"Come on," Phoebe says to Jane, with some impatience. "Focus on the game."

"What?" says Kiran. "Cook? My head hurts. Does your head hurt?"

"Your cook," Jane says. "That's the guy who wears checkered pants and a chef's hat, right?"

"Cook dresses like that sometimes," Kiran says. "Though I always get the feeling he's doing it to be ironic."

"Ironic?" Jane says. "What do you mean?"

"How should I know?" Kiran says, then sighs. "What does it matter? It's like his name. His name is Cook, that's why we call him Cook. Corcoran, actually, but he's always gone by Cook, and I think he does, in fact, like to cook, but I don't think he ever cooks. He's always busy doing god-knows-what instead. Playing his damn saxophone. Caring for his parents. Cook is Mr. and Mrs. V's son. Patrick does most of the cooking. Everyone in the world has fulfilling work but me."

This is such a striking thing for a bored millionairess to say—especially about her own servants—that Jane is momentarily stunned into silence.

"Kiran," says Colin gently, not taking his eyes from his cards, "you speak half a dozen languages fluently and have as keen a political mind as anyone I've ever known. You'll find a job, when the time is right. Don't rush yourself."

There's a particular quality to Kiran's silence. Jane is beginning to recognize it: a kind of irritable resentment at the expectation of her gratitude. As if his niceness is oily and self-serving.

Nearby, in her armchair, Lucy St. George sighs over *The House of Mirth*. "I thought I remembered the plot of this book," she says, "but I guess I don't."

Jane glances at Lucy uneasily. Lucy's wrapped her hand in a bandage, which seems extreme, for a splinter. There's a bruised look to the skin around her eyes, a fragility Jane sees in her own mirror after nights when she's not slept well. "What do you mean?" she asks. "Is the plot different from what you remember?"

"Everyone is playing more bridge than I remember," says Lucy. "Lily Bart is sitting in an armchair in a library, reading a book and watching her friends play bridge, endlessly, which I don't remember. Didn't she usually play bridge herself? Isn't that what got her into financial trouble? And wasn't she always having clever conversations with gentlemen?"

"I don't remember the plot either," Jane says. "I just remember thinking there wasn't much mirth. Is your hand okay?"

"She's getting awfully sleepy as her friends play bridge," says Lucy. "It's making me sleepy."

Jane's own bridge game is stalled, because Kiran is staring into space. "Charlotte chose something interesting for the ceiling of this room," Kiran says.

"I don't want to talk about her," Jane says, automatically.

"Doesn't it look like an open book?" Kiran says. "The way Charlotte designed the ceiling?"

"Don't say her name," says Jane. "She can hear her own name. It wakes her up."

"What?" says Kiran. "What are you talking about, Janie? Just look at it!"

Jane cranes her neck. The ceiling has two halves, painted white, that, ever-so-slightly vaulted, meet in the middle. The effect is accentuated by what seem to be small images, like miniature ceiling frescoes, arranged in neat lines across each "page." Jane finds it difficult to decipher the images. This difficulty contributes to the ease of imagining them as letters, or words. Yet, they're regularly shaped, aren't they? Not letters of the alphabet, but rows of rectangles and squares. Little windows or doors, painted on the ceiling? Little book covers?

Lucy, now dozing in her armchair, makes a loud snorting noise through her nose. It sends a shock through Jane's body, like the sound of a gunshot would, and Jane sucks in air.

"Lucy!" she cries. "We should wake up. We should have a clever conversation."

"Huh?" Lucy says, half-asleep. "Lily Bart is sleeping."

"You're not Lily Bart." Propelled by a sudden sense of urgency—she doesn't know where it comes from, and even Jasper is startled by it— Jane gets up and grabs on to Lucy's arm, hard, shaking her. "Wake up."

"I want to know more about Charlotte and the ceiling," Lucy says blearily.

"No," Jane says. "We don't want to talk any more about—"

Jane means to end with the word *that*. Her mouth forms the shape of the word *that*, then somehow the word *Charlotte*, awkward and full of spit, shapes itself around her intentions and pushes itself out of her mouth. "Charlotte," Jane says. Frightened, she tries again, but again, her mouth won't take the form she wants it to take. Her lips purse forward and her breath pushes through. "Char—" she says, struggling against it. "Char—!"

"Shark!" cries Phoebe, who holds her cards in tight hands and stares at Jane, eyes wide and frightened. "Shark," Phoebe says again, with some triumph. "Try it. You can turn it into the word *shark*."

Jane thinks of the bull shark in the fish tank. She imagines the creature pulling the word *shark* out of her mouth as it swims back and forth. "Charlotte," Jane says, almost weeping with frustration.

"Shark!" says Phoebe. "Try harder!"

Jane reaches for something more powerful: the gentle whale shark Ivy carved into the edge of her worktable. Jane holds her hand up and imagines touching it.

Jane is underwater, touching the underbelly of a benevolent shark. It glides above her and moves on. Everything is quiet and slow. Jane is herself. "Shark," she says, feeling the compulsion sink away, down into the darkness. "Shark! Oh, I've never been more happy to say the word *shark*."

"That was strange," says Phoebe. "Wasn't it?"

"What's wrong with you guys?" asks Colin, squinting at each of them in turn. "You're being really weird. You're making the strangest faces too. And what's wrong with the dog?" he adds, for Jasper is tugging on Jane's bootlaces with his teeth.

"I don't know," Jane says. "But I want to leave."

"You're all acting funny," says Colin.

A phone bursts into song, Lucy's phone. "My phone!" Lucy cries, then begins patting her body until she finds it. "Hello!" she cries. "Dad!" she cries. "No. Not yet. Don't worry! It's safe! It's behind—"

"Lucy!" says Colin, interrupting hastily. "No one wants to hear you yelling at Uncle Buckley."

"Never mind!" Lucy cries into the phone. "I'm not telling you where I'm keeping it! I'm not telling Colin, either!"

"All right," says Colin, shooting to his feet. He shuffles Lucy toward the doorway urgently, shushing her like she's a child, or a dog.

"Well," says Phoebe. "We can't play without Colin and I have things I could be doing." She stands slowly, as if she's not entirely sure her limbs are going to behave as usual. But then she crosses the room and strides out.

Jane is left alone with Kiran. Kiran's not staring at the library ceiling anymore, which is a vast relief, because Jane has no intention of looking at the ceiling again. She wants to pretend there is no ceiling, which is difficult, because she can feel it above her, pressing down. It's humming some note that makes her own nerves jangle discordantly and she feels that if she looks up, it will sound infinitely worse. *Aunt Magnolia? Aunt . . . what?*

"Kiran," she says. "Let's get out of here."

"Okay," says Kiran, still holding her cards, but not really looking at them.

Lucy has left *The House of Mirth* behind; it's sitting, facedown, on the seat of her armchair.

With a sudden, certain compulsion, Jane grabs *The House of Mirth*, carries it to the French doors overlooking the terrace, opens the doors, and flings it as far as she can into the yard. When she returns to Kiran, Kiran raises quizzical eyebrows at her.

"That was weird," Kiran says. "What do you have against Lucy?"

"I don't have anything against Lucy," Jane says firmly. "Quite the opposite. I'm trying to help Lucy. That book felt bad to me."

"You're an oddball," Kiran says, "did you know that?"

The dog is whimpering softly at Jane's feet. "Yeah," Jane says. "I know. Let's go, okay?"

"Okay."

She's thrown Lucy's book into the great outdoors, but without a second thought, she picks up her own book and carries it back to her rooms.

Ivy has kindly returned the jailbird umbrella to Jane's worktable. When Jane walks into her morning room, Glitter Lucy catches the hot light in a pleasant, humming sort of way.

The umbrella wants Jane to go to it. It's singing to her. She feels this, and she wants this too. She goes and presses her palm flat over Glitter Lucy's image. Song shoots up her arm to the top of her spine. The glue is dry, but when Jane looks into her palm, small particles of glitter stick to her skin like jewels.

She lifts the umbrella by its handle and carries it to the sofa where Ravi slept only this morning. Propping the umbrella up, Jane sits under it and opens her book. Jasper whines, so she lifts him onto the sofa, where he nestles against her leg, still whining.

This time, Jane opens to the story "In Which Eeyore Loses a Tail and Pooh Finds One." Eeyore, the gray donkey, misplaces his tail in the forest. Pooh goes to Owl for help brainstorming what to do. As usual, Owl turns out to have little to contribute besides bluster, but he does have a new bellpull, which captures Pooh's attention. *Oh, that? I came across it in the Forest,* Owl says. In a moment of cleverness, Pooh realizes that Owl's new bellpull is Eeyore's missing tail.

In the story Jane remembers reading with Aunt Magnolia, Pooh brings Eeyore's tail victoriously back to Eeyore. Christopher Robin, with great gentleness, fixes it back in place on Eeyore's rump. End of story.

In the story Jane is reading, Owl pops Pooh's nose off his face and hangs it up as a doorbell. Then he takes Rabbit's ears and makes sashes for the curtains. Then he takes Piglet's head and hangs it on his wall and instructs it to call out the time regularly like a cuckoo clock, though mostly Piglet just cries, because he's frightened and wants his body back. This story fascinates Jane. But Jasper keeps trying to climb into her lap and knock the book out of her hands or knock the umbrella out from behind her. He's flailing around like a basset hound who's drowning, actually, and when he starts trying to close his teeth around Jane's arm, she shouts his name. "Jasper! If you make any more holes in me, I'm going to lock you in the closet!"

Jasper keeps his mouth wrapped around Jane's arm, but doesn't bite. He stares up at her with reproachful eyes. Then, with an expression of tremulous hurt, he plunks down, goes into the bedroom, and finds some corner in which to whimper in solitude.

Something about this pricks Jane. She's just spoken cruelly to the dog. *Shame,* she thinks. Pushing to her feet, she sways, unbalanced. She can hear the dog crying. My goodness, how sleepy she is.

She manages to make it to her bed, still clutching her book. Patches of the pale red paint on the wall behind the headboard are peeling, the wall beneath it, purple and wounded-looking. "Gross," says Jane. Jasper comes out of his corner and dances around her feet, wanting to be picked up. She reaches down, scoops the dog up, and deposits him on the blankets.

"I'm sorry I said that thing about the closet, fuzzball," she says.

Then her head touches the pillows and she's asleep.

* * *

She's dreaming of a house with an internal gash, like a circus performer who's swallowed a sword and punctured his own stomach. The gash is an opening to another world. Whenever anyone passes through, stretching the opening, tearing its edges, the house screams in agony.

The screams of the house wake her. There are words to the screams, but she's sweating and shaking and too trapped in the space between sleeping and waking to make them out. She kicks Jasper by accident—he's under the covers at her feet. He grumbles and crawls up to where she can hold him.

"Jasper," she whispers, having a moment of pure clarity. "I don't like this house."

Well. She's awake now. The clock reads 5:08 a.m., but there's no point trying to fall back to sleep. Lying in bed shivering until the sun rises doesn't strike her as an appealing alternative, because the house is laughing all around her. Someone, somewhere, is laughing in the walls, and something needs to be done.

"I hate this house," Jane tells Jasper, steel in her voice. Damn Aunt Magnolia and the promise she'd exacted from Jane to come to this house. *Why would she do that?* Jane wonders. Damn Aunt Magnolia for her easy courage, for the things that had never scared her. Not bull sharks, not poisonous squids, not giant clams. Not the weight of the ocean's water pressing down on her, not the numbing cold. Damn Aunt Magnolia for going out into the cold, for not knowing, for not being more scared. *Who in their right mind ever goes to Antarctica?* Jane scrabbles around in the bed for Aunt Magnolia's scratchy wool hat and holds it to her face, willing herself not to cry. Her knee touches the awful book. She pushes it over the edge so it thuds to the floor.

After a number of deep, jellyfish breaths, Jane pulls Aunt Magnolia's hat onto her own head. "Jasper?" she says. "Come for a walk?"

Jane steps into the cold corridor, wearing a hoodie over her *Doctor Who* pajamas, happy for her slippers and Aunt Magnolia's hat. She clutches its long tassels for security. The tiny lights on the walls that illuminate each painting flash on and off again as she walks, throwing Jasper and her into grotesque, shifting shadow. Of course she forgets Captain Polepants and almost breaks her neck.

She wishes the house would stop making breathy noises. Then she questions her logic and wishes it were easier to tell where the breathy noises are coming from. She expects they're coming from herself.

Jasper gives Jane anxious, exhausted looks, but she doesn't notice. Her feet take her down to the second story, then around the atrium and through an entrance that leads straight onto the library's second-story level.

Jane is startled to hear the quiet voices of Octavian and Ravi just below. She can't see them, because they're under the balcony she's on, but she can tell from their easy tone that they've stopped arguing. She breathes the smell of Octavian's pipe. A strange, scratchy noise is hard to place, until Jane realizes it's the record player, which has finished its record and been left to turn, endlessly playing nothing.

"I think the books change color while I'm not looking," Octavian is saying.

"I think you need to get out of this house once a day and take a walk in the sun while breathing fresh air," Ravi says, trying to sound amused, but only sounding tired, Jane thinks. "Remember when you used to travel, Dad? You loved to travel."

"I'll ask Ivy-bean to take pictures of the books from hour to hour," says Octavian. "I'll show you. You'll see. The shapes on the ceiling change too."

"Yeah, okay," says Ravi. "I never thought I'd hear myself saying this, but right now I feel like Mum is the only member of the family with a grip on reality."

"Shall we listen to it again?"

"Are you trying to kill me?"

"I'm trying to bring Charlotte back," says Octavian.

"Explain to me how playing her favorite music will bring her back."

"I can't explain it," says Octavian. "Haven't you ever felt something in your gut?"

"Kiran's friend Janie makes me feel something in my gut."

"That's not your gut," Octavian says sharply. "And don't be crude, boy."

"Jesus, Dad," says Ravi, sighing. "You always were a sanctimonious asshole."

"Language!"

"Mm-hm. Sanctimonious."

The scratchy noise stops. A moment later, Jane hears the guitar intro to the Beatles song "You've Got to Hide Your Love Away."

Soundlessly, Phoebe Okada appears at Jane's side. Jane's body flies into a panic. She spends thirty seconds gripping the banister and trying to catch her breath.

"Did I scare you?" Phoebe whispers. "Sorry."

Her face, free of makeup, is tired, unguarded, pretty. She's wearing a silk robe tied tightly at the middle and is barefoot. Her toenails are turquoise and cute.

"Why are you here?" Jane whispers back.

"I heard the music," Phoebe whispers.

"Charlotte's music?" Jane whispers. "You heard Charlotte's music all the way from your room?"

"Charlotte's music," Phoebe says. "I was walking and I heard Charlotte's music. I sleep badly when my husband's away. I worry about him."

Jane remembers that one night, a long time ago—no! It was only last night, which seems amazing—Jane saw Phoebe and her husband, Philip, who's a doctor, sneaking around with Patrick and a gun. Then Philip left the house. "Why do you worry?" says Jane. "Is your husband's medical practice dangerous?"

"I program ciphers normally," Phoebe says. "For Britain. Ciphers are my specialty. I'm a bit of a genius. God save the queen."

Jane is pretty sure she hasn't asked Phoebe anything about her profession, her level of intelligence, or the queen, but she can't really remember. After "You've Got to Hide Your Love Away," Octavian switches records and plays "I'm Looking Through You," then "Norwegian Wood." Then he mutters something about Charlotte and *Abbey Road* and Jane hears the opening strains of "Come Together."

Jane pulls on the tassels of her hat. "I think I was meaning to go back to bed, but I can't remember," she whispers to Phoebe.

Phoebe also seems to be thinking hard. "My husband and I are British, but we're helping keep the missing children safe. Remember? The little kid with Cook?" she says, then looks confused. "I mean, no. Never mind."

"What are you talking about?"

Before Phoebe can go on, Octavian speaks again. His voice comes rough and raspy through the music.

"Charlotte was reading *Frankenstein* when she left," says Octavian. "I'm keeping it here, still marking her place."

"I know," says Ravi.

"I've read Charlotte's journals back to front," Octavian says. "I can't find any explanation for where she went."

"I know, Dad," says Ravi gently. "You've told me."

"Charlotte wrote here that the house, with the unmatching origins of its parts, is a microcosm of the world. Do you think living on an island, in this big old house, made Charlotte pine for the world?"

"I don't know, Dad. Could we talk about Kiran? She's *here*. We can do something about her. She seems depressed. I'm worried."

"I'd never have held Charlotte here if she wanted to travel," Octavian says. "We could've traveled anywhere."

Their voices go silent again. A good many songs go by. Jane thinks about the house being a microcosm of the world. She turns it over and over in her mind, she flips it back and forth, because it reminds her of something. It takes her a long time to place the memory.

"My aunt used to say," she whispers to Phoebe, "that my body was a microcosm of the sea."

"My massage therapist always says," Phoebe whispers back, "that my body is a microcosm of the universe."

"Or the multiverse," whispers Lucy St. George, appearing beside them and causing Jane to jump a foot in the air. "Sorry," she whispers. "Did I scare you? I was out walking. When I came in, I heard the music."

"Charlotte's music," Jane whispers. "Charlotte. Oh, fuck," she whispers, rubbing her ears hard, because now she notices that it's happening again, that weird compulsion to say Charlotte's name. Lucy St. George is dressed all in black, from her black knit hat down to her black sneakers, and smells like the cold. She's tight and pale and ready as a bullet in the chamber of a gun; Jane can feel it. Jane studies Lucy, trying to focus on Lucy instead of on the choking colors of the library, instead of on Charlotte. Trying to process what Lucy said. Jane realizes Lucy has just come in from outside. Lucy is less muddled and bumbling than she, because Lucy's been outside the house, breathing fresh air.

"What's a multiverse?" Jane asks her.

"Oh," Lucy whispers, pulling off her hat. Her smooth hair tumbles down around her shoulders. "It's this theory Ravi likes to talk about. His mom is a theoretical physicist, you know. His real mom, not Charlotte."

"Charlotte," whispers Phoebe.

"Yes," Lucy whispers, "Charlotte."

"Multiverse?" Jane whispers, stubbornly not saying "Charlotte." It makes her head ache, sharply.

"The concept of the multiverse," Lucy whispers, "comes from the idea that every time something happens, everything else that could have happened in that moment also happens, causing new universes to break off from the old universe and come into being. So there are multiple versions of us, living different lives than the ones we live, across multiple universes, making every decision we could possibly make. There are versions of us we wouldn't even like, and some we'd barely recognize."

This stirs at something in Jane's memory, but she can't place it. Conversations about various realities and versions of lives. Things Kiran has said, and Ravi. It didn't make sense then and it's very confusing now. Jane feels like her own muddled and overstretched brain could be a microcosm of the multiverse. The ceiling is pressing down.

"God, I feel all over the place," whispers Phoebe. "Like all my parts are spinning away."

"Yes," Jane says passionately.

"I'm dying to talk to Mr. Vanders," says Phoebe. "He could help."

"I talked to him today," Jane says, remembering. "He says that the more we embrace our lack of cohesion, the better off we are."

"That sounds like Mr. Vanders," says Phoebe wistfully.

"But this is different, isn't it?" Jane says. "This weird feeling? Don't you feel like it's coming from outside us? Like, from the walls and the ceiling?"

Lucy St. George is winding and unwinding the bandage around her hand. "You know," she whispers, "I get the feeling this house doesn't like me."

"Hm," says Phoebe. "Do you get the feeling it can see everything we do?"

Lucy pauses. "If that's true," she says quietly, "I'm in trouble."

"Why?" says Phoebe. "Did you do something the house wouldn't like?"

Making no answer, Lucy continues to wind and unwind her bandage. Perhaps Octavian has reached the end of his playlist, because the next song Jane hears is the first song she heard, "You've Got to Hide Your Love Away."

"Listen, Dad," says Ravi, in a voice that's patient, but pleading. "I know you love her, and it's awful she left. I get it, and I'm sorry. But I'm done talking about it. I want to talk about finding some way to get through to Kiran. Some work she might like that we could hook her up with, maybe?"

"What about your own problems, son?" says Octavian. "Why aren't you in the bed of your supposed girlfriend right now?"

Ravi releases a short sigh. "Lucy broke it off with me again," he says, "and anyway, how'll I ever see my father if I sleep at night? I'm worried about you too, you know. I wish you'd get dressed, go outside, go for a walk. Will you come for one now?"

"You're a good boy, Ravi," says Octavian. "You're always trying to hide it. I'm sorry about Lucy."

"Well," says Ravi glumly. "I'm sure I'm too young to be in a serious relationship anyway."

"Have you learned anything about the missing Brancusi?"

"No, and Vanny's being so aggravating," says Ravi. "It's all 'the gala' this, 'the gala' that. I'm not even sure she's notified the police."

"Then notify them yourself," Octavian says, "in the morning. It's your house, and Kiran's."

"It's your house, Dad."

"It'll be yours," says Octavian, "after I disappear."

Ravi groans. "You depressed people are so melodramatic. It's tedious. Come for a walk."

Lucy is staring at her bare hand. What Jane sees when she follows Lucy's gaze makes the back of her throat thrum. The splinter, or whatever injury she sustained earlier, is bruised and festering, green, yellow, gray, and it's taken on a vague shape. In the dim light, at Jane's indirect angle, it's a shape that evokes a familiar scene: an abstract sort of person, sitting on what looks like a cot. Thin veins stand out blackly across the person, like the bars of a prison cell. The person has strange, bruise-colored hair, oversized shoes, and a fresh drop of blood for a nose.

Lucy turns her face to Jane. Her expression is a mask of sadness. She sings along to the song playing below: "Gather round, all you clowns."

Jane returns to her rooms in search of the Lucy umbrella.

Dawn has broken. She walks past her bed, hearing the hum of *Winnie-the-Pooh* lying on the floor. The peeling paint on her bedroom wall has spread, continuing to uncover patches of something red and moist underneath. She pushes on to the morning room and stops in the room's hot center, contemplating the Lucy umbrella, still propped on the sofa.

The canopy is angled away from Jane, so she can't see sparkly Lucy sitting behind bars. The umbrella is asking Jane to come to it. She can feel the pull. The umbrella wants her to pick it up and appreciate its artistry, which is interesting, because it's *her* artistry, really, isn't it? Jane made the umbrella what it is. It came from some part of her. Jane wonders: If she's admiring it, isn't she really admiring herself? She wonders: Might it even be a kind of mirror? If she looks at it, will she see a version of herself?

When Jane begins to move toward the umbrella, Jasper pushes against her legs, whining. "Jasper," she says, "remember what I said about the closet." Jasper sits down and stops pushing.

Jane lifts the umbrella gently by the canopy and gazes at her own work. It's beautiful. It's exquisite. *Lucy must have done something very bad,* she thinks.

Then a flicker of doubt touches Jane. The thought seems wrong somehow, it seems uncharitable. She likes Lucy. She threw Lucy's book into the yard to protect her from her weird book that was making her sleepy, like Lily Bart. Jane likes the dog too, she loves Jasper, and now, when she looks at the poor little guy, he's shivering and miserable and pleading at Jane with his eyes.

"Jasper," she says cheerfully, "want to come with me while I bring this umbrella to Lucy?"

By some instinct she doesn't examine, Jane knows which rooms in the west corridor of the second story are Lucy's. To her astonishment, directly on the wall outside Lucy's rooms hangs a blown-up and framed photo, taken by Aunt Magnolia.

Immediately, the photo raises Jane to a higher state of wakefulness. It isn't just the surprise. It's Jane's pride, that Aunt Magnolia's art hangs with the other masterpieces on the walls of this house.

A small yellow fish peeks out from inside the open mouth of a huge gray fish. Aunt Magnolia took this photo in Japan. It's exactly the impossible-seeming sort of photograph Aunt Magnolia was known for taking, because she had an extraordinary patience and a kind of natural serendipity when she was underwater with her camera. She would, very simply, wait for the amazing thing to happen. And it would.

Jane backs away to the opposite wall to get a better view, breathing slow and deep, the way a jellyfish moves. Someone has framed this photograph badly, or else there's some other, smaller piece of art in the frame too, behind Aunt Magnolia's print. Jane can see its rectangular outline. She'll have to say something to Mrs. Vanders. It's liable to create creases in Aunt Magnolia's print.

Jane's head rests against the wall behind her and she clasps Lucy's open umbrella at her side. Gradually she notices that on the other side of that wall, a conversation is taking place. She rests her ear against the wall like a stethoscope. It's a muffled conversation between two voices she recognizes. Two cousins: Lucy St. George and Colin Mack. The yellow fish and the big gray fish stare at Jane as she spies.

"It's exactly the sort of thing you would do," says Lucy.

"It's not," says Colin.

"Then why was the first word out of Dad's mouth when I told him about it, *Colin*?"

"Because you're both assholes," Colin says.

"Oh, trust me," says Lucy. "Dad can be an epic asshole, but I, as an asshole, am legendary. I'm sick to death of how hard you make my job. It's over now."

"Over?" says Colin. "What exactly do you imagine you're going to do?"

"You'll see."

"Oh, give it up, Luce."

"You'll see!"

"And when you realize I'm not the one who took the damn sculpture? Will your little rebellion have been worth it?"

"Oh," Lucy says with her familiar laughter. "Dear Colin. This rebellion will be worth more than you can possibly imagine."

"That can only mean the Vermeer," Colin says. "What've you done with the Vermeer?"

"Nothing you need to know about."

"Mm-hm," says Colin. "You're bluffing. You wouldn't turn against the family."

"You're leaving my rooms right now. Go be fake and insincere to your girlfriend. Not to me."

"Ha," says Colin. "What I'm doing with that stupid bitch is no different from what you're doing with Ravi. We're exactly the same."

"Fuck off, Colin," says Lucy with sudden passion. "Stay away from me."

"I love you too, fair cuz," says Colin.

A door opens and shuts. Colin comes into the corridor and sees Jane, standing there, staring dazedly at the photograph, accompanied by the world's most haggard dog.

"Oh. Hello," he says, trying to find a natural tone for his voice, but looking distinctly alarmed. "Why are you lurking in the hallway?"

"I fixed Lucy's umbrella," says Jane.

"Oh, right," Colin says, barely glancing at it. "I'm sure she'll be thrilled." He marches away.

A moment later, Lucy St. George steps into the corridor, then starts in surprise at the sight of Jane. She looks terrible. She holds her bandaged hand to her side. Her eyes shoot anxiously to Aunt Magnolia's photograph, then back to Jane.

"It's just me," Jane says, "and Jasper. Sorry to startle you. I brought your umbrella." She holds the umbrella out to Lucy, like a gentle offering.

The glitter drawing faces Lucy so that she can see it. Lucy's lips part in wonder, then in a sort of revulsion. "You made that just now?" she says.

"I made it yesterday."

"You can't have."

"That's true," Jane says, "but I did. It's for you. You're meant to take it."

"Yes," Lucy says. "I know."

Such a strange, resigned voice Lucy speaks with. She holds out both hands, reaches for the umbrella's handle, and takes it gently from Jane. Then she carries the umbrella away, down the corridor, holding it firmly, but far removed from her body.

She will fall in. Somewhere, out of Jane's sight, Lucy will fall into the scene in the umbrella, enter that story, and become that umbrella's soul. And Charlotte will have had her revenge on Lucy. Part of Jane knows this somehow, and wonders, with a morbid curiosity, what it will look like, because really, it doesn't make sense. How can a person fall into a story?

Feeding someone to Charlotte, personally delivering someone the way Jane has, bonds Jane to Charlotte in a whole new way. Jane feels it. It's probably why, when she gets back to her rooms, she loses patience with the whining dog and closes him in the closet.

All day long, currents and waves of people move through the house, preparing it for the gala. Cleaners, decorators, caterers, musicians. Occasionally Jane sees Ivy, or Patrick, or one or another Vanders, from a distance, doing what she supposes are any number of Important Gala Things.

She glides down to the receiving hall at one point, weeds among the people, and picks up the photo of Charlotte. Charlotte seems bigger than she did before; the other people in the photo are cast into shadow. Her face gleams with triumph, which Jane knows is about Lucy. It aches with hunger, which Jane knows is about anybody, everybody.

A wave of warmth rushes through Jane suddenly and she knows, without looking, that Ivy is touching her. She also knows Charlotte doesn't like it, Charlotte wants her to lie to Ivy and get away from her.

"Janie? Are you okay?" says Ivy. "You've got the weirdest expression on your face."

"I'm fine," Jane lies, turning to face Ivy, who's holding her tattooed arm. She's all light and color, dark hair and blue eyes, jasmine and chlorine, and some part of Jane shakes into clarity. She hugs Ivy unhesitatingly, body to body, startling Ivy, who hugs her back with awkward surprise.

"Are you sure you're okay?" Ivy says in her ear.

"Yes," Jane says, meaning it, for she *is* okay in Ivy's arms.

But then, before too long, Ivy disentangles herself apologetically, explaining that Mrs. Vanders is calling her name, but that she's worried about Janie, she's going to come check on her later, as soon as she can, okay?

"Okay."

As Jane watches Ivy disappear into the throngs of gala workers, she's touched by a sense of having lost her chance at something. She lost it when Ivy left. Ivy is a sorceress, a good witch, a priest, Jane thinks. But Ivy is gone.

Jane seeks out the room with the indoor pool and sits in a deck chair across from the shark tank, inhaling the smell of chlorine.

Eventually, Kiran joins her, then, shortly thereafter, Phoebe. Jane, Kiran, and Phoebe sit together, for hours. It's warm and moist. There's little to say. They all understand, on some level, that they're having a different experience of gala day than the others in the house, but part of that experience is a lack of curiosity. The bull shark swims steadily back and forth, back and forth. It's mesmerizing. Bull sharks will eat anything they see, so Jane wonders at the other, colorful fish darting about. Is that their purpose? To be eaten? The eel, lime-green and horrible, leers at Jane, stretched along the tank's bottom, barely moving. Jane understands that Charlotte can embody any part of her house, she can look through that eel's eyes. The eel grins, slightly flicking its tail.

Jane's book rests on her knee, unopened, but humming to her pleasantly.

"I'm worried about Octavian," says Kiran.

"Why?" asks Jane.

"He's being so weird and mopey," Kiran says. "I told him he needs to go see his doctor. Maybe he should also see a psychologist."

"He could talk to Mr. Vanders," says Phoebe. "Mr. Vanders could give him therapy."

"Mr. Vanders?" Kiran says.

Phoebe sits up straight in her deck chair, a confused sort of expression on her face. "Wait," she says. "Holy crap. I have to go." She slides her legs onto the gold tiles and pushes herself to her feet, then runs out of the pool room.

Jane and Kiran remain together, silent and sitting.

Sometime later, Ravi sticks his head into the room.

"There you are!" he says. "Sweetheart, are you paying any attention to the time?"

Kiran turns her face numbly to him. "Huh?"

"The gala's started," Ravi says. "You need to get ready! Twin," he says, standing before Kiran's deck chair and peering at her, then crouching, scrunching his eyes in concern. He's dressed all in black. As usual, he sweeps and moves like a storm of light. The streaks in his hair shine. Interested, Jane stirs.

"Are you okay?" Ravi says. "People are asking after you."

"I'm worried about Octavian," says Kiran.

"Yeah," says Ravi. "Tell me about it. Come on, I'll walk with you up to your rooms. Do you know what you're going to wear? Wait till you meet the hot FBI agents."

"FBI agents?" says Kiran vaguely as her brother practically lifts her to her feet.

"FBI *special* agents," says Ravi. "*Special* means they're armed, apparently. I invited all kinds of cops to the party, to investigate the Brancusi theft. Vanny is furious with me and you have to help me keep everyone else entertained so it doesn't feel like a party full of cops."

"Okay," says Kiran doubtfully.

Ravi chatters as he pulls Kiran out of the room. "You're being weird," he says. "Like you're half-asleep. Come on, let's go outside and look at the water first."

"Outside?" says Kiran in puzzlement.

"It's cold, and spitting rain," Ravi says. "The waves are high. You won't like it, but it'll wake you up." He's always trying to get his depressed people outside, isn't he? Jane senses that Ravi doesn't have the first idea about Charlotte; he merely has the instincts of a person who's more alive than everyone else. Maybe Jane just missed another chance there, with Ravi. Unfortunately, Ravi has chosen his twin.

Jane is left alone, staring into the eyes of the lime-green eel. She wants her underwater world, where she feels close to Aunt Magnolia. Eventually, she gets up, walks to the west end of the room, and enters the changing room that leads to the library.

Someone, presumably Octavian, has set more rope barriers and private signs up at every library entrance. Sounds filter from the other parts of the house, musical, tinkling, joy-and-laughter sounds, party sounds. The library is empty, dimly lit, glowing softly with color. Humming with energy. Jane steps over a rope.

The library has a few plush armchairs, a few hard-backed chairs around the card table, but the most comfortable-looking seat, and the one from which Jane can best observe the ceiling, is Octavian's divan. The blankets are rumpled and smell like pipe smoke. Jane smoothes them out and lies down. The ceiling feels closer than it did before and she can better make out the designs running across its "pages." They are—bird cages? Some of them look like bird cages. Jane can see Hansel, trapped in a cage while the witch fattens him up. Nana, the dog from *Peter Pan,* in her kennel. A rat in a cage that's attached to a man's face: *1984,* by Orwell. Juliet, waking on a stone bed, behind the bars of a tomb. A man walling up another man alive: That's an Edgar Allan Poe story. A wild woman behind a barred window, in an attic: *Jane Eyre.*

There are also scenes of freedom. In fact, there's Christopher Robin, Winnie-the-Pooh, Piglet, Eeyore, Kanga, Roo, and all the others walking together alongside a stream.

Jane opens her book.

It's the story "In Which Christopher Robin Leads an Expotition to the North Pole." Jane remembers reading this one with Aunt Magnolia. It was one of Aunt Magnolia's personal favorites, fond as she was of *expotitions* of her own. In it, the group sets out to discover the North Pole, but then little Roo falls into the stream. Pooh finds a long pole, drapes it across the stream, and rescues Roo. Afterward, Christopher Robin considers Pooh's pole thoughtfully. "The Expedition is over," he tells Pooh solemnly. "You have found the North Pole!"

By now Jane knows to expect, of course, that Charlotte is telling the story.

The group sets out, walking in a line. First comes Christopher Robin and Rabbit, then Piglet and Pooh; then Kanga, with Roo in her pocket, and Owl; then Eeyore; and, at the end, in a long line, Rabbit's friends-and-relations. Behind them, someone else.

"I didn't want to come on this Expotition," says Eeyore. "I only came to oblige. My tail's getting cold. I don't want to complain but there it is. My tail's cold."

Rabbit's ears are cold. Pooh's belly is cold. Piglet begins to squeak because the cold is burning his feet and his nose.

"Cold can burn," says the person at the end of the line. "But don't worry."

"Why shouldn't we worry?" asks Piglet.

"After you burn," says the person at the end of the line, "you'll shake. After you shake, you'll stop shaking, and then you'll start to feel warm and sleepy and wonderful."

"How do you know that?" chatters Piglet, who is beginning to shake.

"It happened to my aunt Magnolia," says the person at the end of the line.

"Did Aunt Magnolia come back and tell you about it?" chatters Piglet, who's shaking harder now.

"Not exactly," says Jane.

"How did you learn about it, then?" asks Piglet, who yawns.

"It's called hypothermia," says Jane. "It happens to people who set out for the North Pole without the appropriate supplies."

"Did Aunt Magnolia do that?" asks Piglet.

"No," says Jane. "She set out for the *South* Pole, *with* the appropriate supplies. Isn't it nice to be doing the parallel and opposite thing? Just like Aunt Magnolia, but different."

"But, why did she get hypothermia if she had the appropriate supplies?" asks Piglet.

"She got caught in a blizzard."

It begins to snow, steadily. The wind picks up and the snow blows harder. The snow looks an awful lot like cherry blossoms, soft and delicate and sweet-smelling, but when it hits Jane's skin, it's like being poked with pins.

"Ow!" cries Piglet. "Ow! Ow! It stings!"

"Hold on, Piglet," says Jane as the stinging snow piles around Jane's feet, her ankles, her shins. Her jellyfish tattoo begins to burn, a jellyfish-shaped fire stinging her arm. "This is how it's supposed to happen," says Jane, beginning to be alarmed. "Soon you'll feel warm and sleepy and wonderful."

The cherry-blossom snow has a way of finding the crevices in Jane's clothing, and sticking to her skin. There, it's like acid; it eats her top layer away. It lays her bare. It happens very fast. Christopher Robin is screaming. *How strange,* Jane thinks, watching him as he screams. *He's skinless.* The cherry-blossom snow has eaten the skin of his face and arms and of the legs above his expedition boots. He's red and oozing, his outside is visceral, he is the scene in the movie we turn away from because it's horrible. But it's how our bodies look, under our skin. Pooh is screaming. Piglet is screaming. Rabbit is screaming.

Jane is also screaming, but she makes no noise. Lying on the divan in the library, *Winnie-the-Pooh* open on her lap, her back is arched and her mouth forms a perfect silent scream. Jane is struggling with Octavian, who's puttered in wearing his robe and found Jane there, flailing around like a person being skinned. Jane doesn't look like a person being skinned, but she feels it, and Octavian understands.

"She's taking you," Octavian says. "Why is she taking you instead of me?"

Jane knows why, because Charlotte knows why, and there's no boundary between them anymore.

Charlotte is taking Jane because Jane got here first, to this room, on this night when Charlotte is more powerful than she has been before. Charlotte's more powerful because not just Octavian, but Jane, Lucy, Phoebe, and Kiran have been giving her power, by talking about her, saying her name, dwelling in her library. Jane got here first because Octavian was still asleep. She got here first because she closed Jasper in the closet. She got here first because Phoebe is elsewhere, trying to hold it together in her job, Kiran is elsewhere, trying to hold it together at the party, and Jane is the one who fed Lucy to Charlotte.

The moment Jane first entered the library, she gave Charlotte so many openings. An orphaned part, looking for where she belonged. Jane's wounds were openings.

Jane entered the library because Kiran and Lucy described it in a way that made it sound like Aunt Magnolia's underwater world. Kiran and Lucy described the library because they were talking about Charlotte, because, at the moment when Jane could have followed Mrs. Vanders, or the child, or Ravi, or Jasper the dog, Jane chose to go with Kiran.

None of this, incidentally, has helped Kiran. As it happens, Kiran is about to have the worst night of her life. Not because of what's happening to Jane—though this would hurt her too—but because of a scene playing out elsewhere on the island. Kiran doesn't know about it yet, but Jane does. At the moment, Kiran is shuffling around the ball-room, trying to keep the guests amused, while Ravi takes the two FBI special agents outside for a walk. A walk to a hidden bay, where they've stumbled upon a strange scene with Ivy, Patrick, Cook, and the missing Panzavecchia children. Remember the famous missing Panzavecchia children? FBI special agents are, by definition, armed, and so are Patrick, Ivy, and Cook. And it's dark outside, and bad things happen when armed people get confused. And Patrick is the type to jump in the line of fire in order to protect children, when shots are being fired.

If things had gone differently, Jane, or Kiran, or both, might have been there to prevent it. Instead, Kiran will get some terrible news, and Ivy is on her knees, shaking over her brother, who's bleeding into the sand of the island's secret bay. It's the worst night of Ivy's life too.

But, back in the library.

Earlier, Jane wondered what it would look like when Lucy fell into the umbrella.

She knows now. Not just what it looks like, but what it feels like. Yes?

It looks like—almost nothing, really. It looks like Jane: bright, living, fighting, fabulous Jane, writhing, in solitary, silent pain that no one but Charlotte has the power to ease, on a divan, while Octavian tries to hold on to her. And then, instantly, she's not there. She's gone. Octavian is left with empty hands and a lingering chord, a note that vibrates his throat and his teeth and makes him look up at the ceiling, where he knows to seek out the image of Christopher Robin, Pooh, and the other creatures of the forest, walking together alongside a stream. He sees that a tall figure has joined the end of the line.

* * *

What does it feel like?

The acid snow is skinning Jane alive. The snow isn't just warm, it's burning; freezing to death feels like burning. Where's the numbness Jane was promised? Where's the sleepiness, and the lack of pain? Jane understands now how scared Aunt Magnolia must have been.

Aunt Magnolia?

Aunt Magnolia can't hear Jane. And Jane isn't going where Aunt Magnolia went.

Jane's final scream is the discordant strum that Octavian hears in some part of his being, causing him to look up at the ceiling.

Jane is stuck in the ceiling, at the end of a procession, in a cherry-blossom blizzard of acid snow. Jane's physical vision is limited. With part of one eye, she can see some distant edges of the library. But she knows everything Charlotte knows. It's dark, but she's not numb. It's silent, but she still feels pain. Jane is on fire. She understands that she is the house now. Except, not really: Charlotte is the house, and Jane is a smothered part of her structure. Charlotte is the jail and Jane is her prisoner.

Charlotte is trying to use Jane like glue.

It will not be painless, and it will not work. It won't satiate Charlotte's bottomless need to feel whole. What will happen then? It will depend on whether Kiran and Octavian and Phoebe and so on keep talking about her, keep saying her name, sitting in her library, giving her power. If they do, Charlotte will pick them off, one by one.

How much time has gone by? Days? Weeks?

The gala is still happening.

Jane thinks, *Octavian will tell people what he saw, and someone will rescue me.* Or will Octavian keep his mouth shut, and wait his turn?

Or Ivy will find my book open on the divan. But will Ivy know to look up? If she does, could she ever understand what she saw, and is her magic, her power, strong enough? Would she even care, now that her brother is dead? Deceased, departed, perished, quenched. Eight letters, with a *q*.

Charlotte worries sometimes about Ivy. Ivy might get in the way. She worries about Jasper too, and Ravi, and Ravi's mother, and Mr. Vanders. These are Charlotte's least favorite people. She's less worried about Jasper now, though, because he's giving himself a massive brain injury trying to break out of the closet.

Charlotte worries, but not too much. She knows she's doing well so far. She's only just begun.

A bell rings somewhere in the depths of the house, sweet and clear, like a wind chime.

Mrs. Vanders, the little girl, Kiran, Ravi, or Jasper?

Aunt Magnolia? Jane thinks. *Where should I go?*

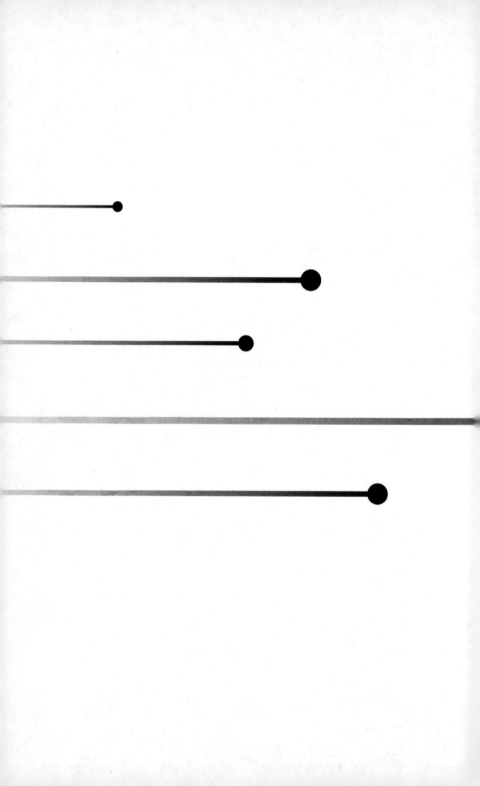

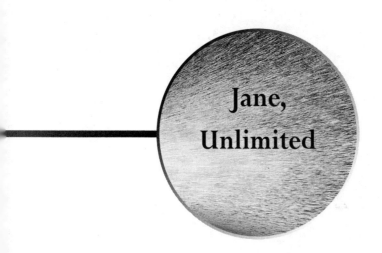

Jane,
Unlimited

Jane decides.

"Oh, hell," she says.

"What is it?" says Kiran.

The thing that worries Jane most about choosing Ravi is that it feels . . . a little *too* tempting. And distracting, from other things in the house that are certainly more important. But, "There's something I need to check on," she tells Kiran. "I'll join up with you later, okay?"

Kiran shrugs, disappointed. "Okay. I'll be in the winter garden." She wanders off.

As Jane steps onto the landing, Jasper blocks her path, clambering around her feet as if he thinks they're a portal to his home planet.

"Fuzzball!" she says. "Desist!"

She rushes past him up the stairs but he's utterly determined to follow her. It's too pathetic. She slows down to let him catch up. "Jasper," she says. "You're breaking my heart."

When she gets to the third-floor east wing, Ravi is standing right there, a little way down the corridor, his back to her. He's bent over his phone, balancing his fruit and toast in one hand. Jane stops and waits, unseen.

Ravi pockets his phone, redistributes his food, and starts moving. Then, inexplicably, Jasper sneaks past Ravi, runs farther down the corridor, and begins frolicking and larking about in a manner that seems designed to distract Ravi, dancing and hopping in a way Jane wouldn't have thought possible.

"Dog of little brain," Ravi tells him fondly.

The runner muffles Jane's footsteps as she follows them. When Ravi reaches the door with the doormat that says WELCOME TO MY WORLDS, he unlocks the door with a key from his pocket.

Jane hotfoots it forward, sticks her foot in the door before it closes, and applies her eye to the crack. Jasper joins her. She catches a glimpse of Ravi's torso, legs, feet before he disappears up a squeaky spiral staircase.

A woman with a deep voice says something cheerful-sounding in a language Jane doesn't understand. Ravi responds in kind. The woman says something else, at length.

"Thanks," Ravi responds in English. "Here, I brought you some fruit, courtesy of Patrick."

"Oh, thank you, darling," the woman says, with a British accent that perhaps contains a hint of the Indian subcontinent. "I'd expected to eat in UD17, but my counterpart there is in no state for hospitality."

"You sound worried," says Ravi. "Did something go wrong?"

"The UD17 house is in danger of being boarded by pirates."

"Pirates!" says Ravi. "What kind of pirates? Are they after the art?"

"Oh, Ravi, you always think everything's about the art. No. They're UD17 pirates, looking for the portal in the tower. Everyone's very stressed out about it."

"Oh," Ravi says. "How do they know about the portal?"

"Unclear. The existence of the multiverse is common knowledge in UD17, but we've kept this particular portal hidden. They have it in their pea-sized brains that they'll be able to use it to travel to alternate dimensions, locate alternate versions of themselves, then bring them back through, into UD17, to bulk up their numbers."

At the foot of the steps, Jane is incredulous. "What on earth is UD17?" she whispers to Jasper. "And how can a house be boarded by pirates?" *And how can pirates have alternate-dimension versions of themselves? And, seriously, just, what the hell?*

"Why is that a pea-sized idea?" asks Ravi. "Wouldn't that work?"

"Of course it would work!" the voice exclaims. "That's why I'm so worried! Here, have your stupid UD17 Monet and stop pestering me with questions!"

"Oh, come on, Mum," says Ravi. "Don't take it out on me. It's your own fault; you opened those portals. You and all the alternate versions of you."

"I've never told anyone outside the family about the portals. You can't blame me if alternate-dimension versions of me are indiscreet within their own dimensions. I am not they!"

"And yet I have an idea of what most of them are like," says Ravi wearily.

"Be respectful," says the first Mrs. Thrash. "We're your mother." There is a pause. "Well?" she says, rather aggressively. "How are you?"

"I'm fine, Mum," says Ravi, an edge to his voice. "Worried about Kiran. She still seems low."

"Still blaming me for that, are you?"

"Ma," says Ravi sharply, while Jane wonders if maybe Kiran's depressed because her mother is delusional.

"What Kiran needs is a job," says the first Mrs. Thrash. "Such a brilliant child, and she's wasting it, mooning about with no direction. I've noticed quite a motivational range across the spectrum of Kirans I've met, have I told you? I never know what Kiran to expect. Some of them are dynamos. The Kiran in Unlimited Dimension 17 is now—"

"Oh my god!" Ravi says. "I don't want to know! Haven't we done enough damage with that already?"

"Oh, don't be silly. How's Ivy? You could bring Ivy to visit me, you know. I could hide my little pets upstairs."

"Ivy knows all about your pets. Kiran told Patrick everything; you know that. Patrick told the Vanders family and Ivy."

"And you criticize *me* for being indiscreet."

"It won't go any further if Vanny has anything to say about it," says Ravi. "Anyway, she's decided it's a fairy tale. You know how Vanny is."

"She doesn't understand it, therefore she thinks it's magic, eh?"

"Precisely."

"What do you tell Vanny when you bring her the paintings from UD17?"

"She makes a point of not asking," Ravi says.

"Just like you make a point of not asking Vanny why she knows so many out-of-the-way collectors who want to buy your weird art for their personal collections."

"It's her field. Of course she has contacts."

"I think there's something fishy going on there. She's mixed up in the art black market or something."

"Oh, Mum," says Ravi, sighing. "Mrs. Vanders is the world's most respectable person. She helps me out of kindness. First she convinces herself that the pictures are normal, then she passes them on to collectors she met in grad school. It's that simple. Are you going to show me what you brought me?"

There's another pause. Then the first Mrs. Thrash says, "Well? Is it the sort of picture you hoped for?"

"Better than," says Ravi. "You've done well. Buckley's going to love the animatronic frogs on the lily pads."

"There's a Limited Dimension I've visited," says Mrs. Thrash. "LD387. Their Monet didn't paint frogs on his lily pads at all. In fact, I don't think a single art movement in that world has ever focused on frogs, with the possible exception of their Muppets. Which makes me wonder, where did the Kermit of *their* world come from?"

"Is he any different?"

"Well, he's not blue. He's pea green."

"Pea green!"

"And he's in love with Miss Piggy."

"Oh, just stop it," Ravi says.

"Would you like a frogless lily pad Monet in your inventory? I'll see what I can do next time I'm there. It's trickier in a Limited Dimension because—well—we're dealing with smaller-minded versions of ourselves, of course. Less imaginative. They may not want to sell."

"I thought our own dimension was a Limited Dimension."

"Well, yes, we've categorized it as one, for the moment. But the categorization is an ongoing process, and the more we learn about what's commonplace across dimensions and what isn't, the more our categorizations change. I won't be at all surprised if our dimension is recategorized as Unlimited someday. There could be transnormal phenomena here we haven't discovered yet."

"Ha. You just don't like to imagine yourself as limited," says Ravi dryly.

"Oh, pah," she says. "I'm a scientist. Transnormal phenomena are simply phenomena that we do not yet understand. Even now the scientific community in our dimension is dissatisfied with our explanations for, oh, I don't know, why humans need sleep, or why it rains frogs. But everything everywhere has a scientific explanation, whether or not we know what it is. We'll have to come up with better labels than 'Limited' and 'Unlimited' eventually. But—there's Limited and there's limited, my dear. When I appeared through the portal belonging to LD387's me, where they have these frogless Monets, she actually fainted. She'd left her portal open, so she had to have known one of us might show up, but even *she,* it turns out, doesn't entirely believe in the multiverse, or in transdimensional travel. Even now that I've met her! I gather her family considers her some sort of madwoman in the attic, to the extent that she almost believes it herself. She's not certain I wasn't a hallucination. They've got her taking medication."

"Hm," says Ravi. "Well. Is the frogless art any good?"

"It's simple, but sublime. I think it's lovely."

"Then yes, if you can. Get me anything. I like making Buckley's head spin."

"I don't see why you have to lie to him about where all these paintings come from," the first Mrs. Thrash says. "You who can be so snotty about the provenance of the art in your own house. It's not like they're stolen, or pillaged in a war. You're spending a fortune of your own money to import them and it's only going to mislead the art historians of the future. Not to mention the dimensional archaeologists. Someday there will be dimensional archaeologists, you know."

"First of all, *I'm* keeping records," says Ravi in a scoffing tone. "Secondly, how can you suggest I reveal the secret just moments after you criticized others for revealing the secret? It could cause a lot of trouble if I told Buckley. What if he was indiscreet? We've got plenty of people in this dimension who'd take advantage."

"Well, I don't understand what you get out of it, Ravi."

"It's a game," Ravi says, "and I'm winning. I get to plant transdimensional art all over the world and no one knows its provenance, except for you and me. And Kiran's friend, who's listening at the bottom of the steps."

Oh *hell*.

"Ravi!" says the first Mrs. Thrash. "Is that why the door never slammed?"

"My best guess, anyway," says Ravi.

"And presumably why you switched me to English. You *wanted* this person to overhear. Honestly, Ravi. Is this one male or female? I assume this is another of your conquests?"

"Oh, don't be so haughty," says Ravi. "You know it's not like that."

"You could be doing more with your time and your talents," says the first Mrs. Thrash. "When's the last time you picked up a paintbrush? You were so talented."

"Mum," says Ravi impatiently, like the word is a small explosion. Then he finds his pleasant voice again. "You'd like her. What do you say? Want to meet a new friend who probably thinks we're both delusional?"

"Or," says the first Mrs. Thrash, "that I'm the delusional one and you just come up here to keep me company and humor my delusions."

These are exactly the two possible conclusions Jane has come to. Transdimensional art-dealing. Alternate versions of house-boarding pirates. Kermit in love with *Miss Piggy*?

Jane takes a panicked step back from the door and immediately encounters Jasper, because he's standing behind her feet. "Blaaaaaaaa!" she whispers frantically, windmilling her arms to prevent herself from stepping on him or falling on her back. "Jasper," she whispers. "Stick your head in the door and pretend it's all your doing!"

Jasper looks down his long nose at her in contempt.

And Jane supposes that when it comes down to it, she does want to know whether Ravi is delusional, or simply loves his mother that much. She stays in the doorway.

Ravi descends the stairs most of the way and sticks his head down to look at her. His grin, when he spots her, is triumphant. "I waited forever in the corridor for you to catch up," he says. "Well?" His face contains both amusement and a kind of warning. "Care to meet my mother?"

"Fine," Jane says, trying not to show how flustered she is.

"Let the dog in," Ravi says.

Jane does so, then allows the heavy door to swing shut behind her. Ravi comes the rest of the way down the steps, saying, "Silly old dog." He picks Jasper up and carries him, indignant and squirming, back up the stairs. Jasper is not made for carrying and he glares at Jane over Ravi's shoulder. "Come see your pals," Ravi tells him.

Jane follows, trying not to find Ravi attractive. It's probably why he picked up the dog in the first place. Ravi is the type to know that his Adorable Quotient increases steeply when Carrying a Dog.

"I know you won't tell anyone what you're about to see," Ravi tells Jane quietly as they climb. "Except for Kiran and Octavian. They already know, and Patrick and Ivy, and the Vanders family knows some of it too, though Mrs. Vanders wants as little to do with it as possible. She thinks my mother is upsetting the natural balance of the universe."

"I won't tell anyone."

"I've been wanting you to meet my mother," Ravi says.

"Why?"

He's not facing her, but she knows the sound of his grin. "You remind me of her. You say what you think, without apology."

"I remind you of your mother, and you've been hitting on me since you met me. That's lovely, Ravi."

"I assure you, that's for other reasons."

"That's what Oedipus said too."

"Mum," says Ravi in a voice suddenly resonant and strong, stepping off the stairs into the room above her. "Allow me to introduce our eavesdropper. Janie, this is my mum."

Jane emerges into a room tall and square, full of dappled light from small windows in every wall. With a stove, fridge, cabinets, and counters, it appears to be a kitchen. On a table lies Ravi's bowl of fruit and a Monet lily pad painting both familiar and unusual.

The first Mrs. Thrash is a tall, dark-skinned woman, stately, with smooth black hair neatly tucked into a knot at the nape of her neck. She wears simple black slacks, a fuzzy gray turtleneck sweater, and an aspect of utter normality.

"It's impertinent to listen at doors," she says, even as she shakes Jane's hand firmly.

"I'm sorry," Jane says.

"Are you? I wouldn't be," says the first Mrs. Thrash. "Some of my most rewarding experiences have come from sticking my nose where it didn't belong."

Jane is standing near a window. Enormous wind chimes hang on a bracket outside, and it occurs to her that she's been hearing their sweet tinkling ever since she stuck her foot in the door. Looking out, she can see into the west attics, quite a distance away. Then a soft yipping noise comes from the floor above them.

"I apologize for my miniature velociraptors," says the first Mrs. Thrash. "It's time for their second breakfast. Maybe you'd like to come up and meet them? It might help you accept the existence of the multiverse."

"Er," Jane says, with a quick confused glance at Ravi, who seems amused. "Okay."

The first Mrs. Thrash begins a march up a second metal spiral staircase. "Don't be frightened of them," she says. "They're from an Unlimited Dimension that's bred them to be quite small and friendly to humans, and anyway, their portrayal in that dreadful movie was entirely unrealistic. Pinky likes to comb my hair gently with his enlarged claw."

"I see," Jane says, coughing.

"Ravi doesn't like it when I import animals," adds the first Mrs. Thrash. "He doesn't like me to import anything but art."

"With good reason," Ravi says, starting up the stairs and motioning for Jane to follow.

"It's because of the time I tried to bring him and Kiran two sparkle ponies from a high-level Unlimited Dimension and the poor things went mad and exploded."

"I can still hear them screaming," Ravi says.

"Well, I hadn't come to appreciate yet the dangers of moving highly Unlimited creatures into uncorrelated Limited Dimensions. I've since refined my calculations. Of course it would upset a small boy. But honestly, Ravi, that was so long ago. Your tenth birthday!"

"Twelfth," says Ravi.

"Eons ago," says Mrs. Thrash. "Anyway, Janie, I'll explain everything. Basically, what we've discovered is a thermodynamically reversible quantum boundary that allows for local recoherence. Boom! Inter-dimensional portals."

"Oh my god, Mum," says Ravi. "No one understands what you just said."

"Too technical?"

"At least offer her an analogy first!"

"Schrödinger's frog? Quantum superposition?"

"Oh, for god's sake," says Ravi, turning to Jane. "Do you know much quantum physics?"

"Not much beyond the basics," says Jane.

"Well, all you really need to know is that everything that could conceivably happen does happen, somewhere, in alternate universes across the multiverse. So, you can imagine the possibilities. And Mum—together with a bunch of alternate Mums—has found a portal to cross from one to another. I mean, plenty of other universes have had portals before this, but this is the first known portal that allows travel to and from *our* universe."

"If I'm being honest," says the first Mrs. Thrash as she reaches the next level of the tower, "we can't entirely explain how the portals work. But, observably, they do."

Jane has decided to stop listening to all the nonsense. She's focusing hard on her surroundings instead. This level of the tower is much like the one below, square with small windows and another spiral staircase leading up to yet another level, though that level is closed off by a bright red trapdoor in the ceiling that has an impressive number of locks. There's a largish bed positioned against one wall. Next to it is a bedside table piled with dozens of haphazardly balanced paperback books. Romance novels. A pair of doors beyond the bed probably leads to a bathroom, or a closet, or both.

An animal is moving under the deep red bedcovers, a large cat or a small dog. It wriggles its way to the edge, slides down the side, and emerges into the light head-first. It scuttles forward on all fours, then balances itself on its hind legs. It stares at Jane suspiciously, with a canted face and blinking eyes. It's got a lizard head, a tail fully as long as its body, and a coat of fine feathers. Jane has been to the museums, she's seen the TV shows. She understands that she's looking at a miniature velociraptor.

Jane wakes to find herself staring at the red door in the ceiling, the one with all the locks. She's lying on the first Mrs. Thrash's bed. She's woozy, but otherwise unhurt.

She remembers now: She saw a velociraptor and suddenly had no legs. Ravi and Mrs. Thrash caught her. Fainting, while dramatic in stories, turns out to be deeply unpleasant in real life.

There's a warm presence nestled against her left side. It quietly yips as it breathes. Jane has only just woken; she doesn't have the fortitude yet to cope with the fact that she's being snuggled by a velociraptor.

"Ravi?" she says.

His voice rises absently from the armchair in the corner of the room. "Mm?" He pushes himself up and comes to Jane, eyebrows deeply furrowed. In one hand, he holds an open romance novel. "You're awake," he says. "Feeling okay?"

"What the hell, Ravi," Jane says. "What's going on?"

"It's just what we told you. Would it help if you pretend you're inside a *Doctor Who* episode? It'll take a minute, but just go with it," Ravi says. "Listen to this passage, does this sound realistic to you? The main character, her name is Delphine, says, 'I wouldn't have you if you were the last man in East Riordan,' and this man named Lord Enderby says, 'You are the only woman in East Riordan. My darling, you're the only woman in my world. We were meant for each other, can't you see?' Then Delphine is overcome and starts kissing him and shrieking."

"Does she?" Jane says, becoming conscious of another warm, yipping presence resting against her ankles. Also a larger, warmer, silent presence against one knee. That one is Jasper.

"Why does my mother read this stuff?" says Ravi.

"You're reading it."

"Critically!" Ravi says.

"Maybe she reads it critically too."

"I wonder if other versions of my mother read this crap," Ravi says in annoyance. "I suppose there are versions of her that do *every* kind of thing. Like, there must be versions of her that aren't even scientists and versions who don't even know they have portals, just as there must be infinite universes where she doesn't exist at all. There's so much we don't know about the multiverse yet. And you'll notice I'm focusing on my mother, not me. I'm extremely uninterested in thinking about all the multiple versions of me."

"Ravi." Jane's chest is tightening. Her eyes are tearing up; she can't breathe. "Ravi," she whispers. "Just stop."

The first Mrs. Thrash has it in her head that she needs to send Jane to an alternate-dimension Tu Reviens in order to prove to Jane that there are alternate dimensions. She promises to send Jane to one of the more similar dimensions, where the house and its inhabitants correspond closely enough that she'll be able to communicate, but not so closely that she doesn't feel like she's left.

"Though of course," says the first Mrs. Thrash, "*most* of the universes I'm able to visit correspond rather well. My portal, as far as I've experienced, will only send me through to dimensions that have a correlating Tu Reviens with a correlating portal in their tower. And for this house to have been created elsewhere in recognizable form, nearly an infinite number of correlations between universes needed to have occurred across time. Add to that the necessity of my own existence— a theoretical physicist with the time, means, and necessary genius to discover and activate the portal—at any rate, you'll see, my dear. You'll be very comfortable in UD17. Despite the alien invasion."

"Alien invasion?" Jane is still in bed. "It's really not necessary. I'm happy to believe in alternate dimensions from the comfort of my own dimension."

An hour of resting and breathing has gone by and Jane is feeling somewhat calmer. She's even taken to petting the velociraptors, cautiously. Their names are Pinky and Spotty, they're still nestled against her side, and they like to yip gently at Jasper and touch him with their snouts.

But when Mrs. Thrash talks, it brings on that airless feeling again.

"I can see you're afraid," says Mrs. Thrash. "Exposure is an excellent tool for learning to overcome fear. If you're afraid of spiders, jump into a pit of spiders. If you're afraid of the existence of alternate dimensions, go on a tour of alternate dimensions."

Slightly hysterical, Jane decides that the best way to defend herself from Mrs. Thrash's designs is to act like she accepts everything and isn't afraid of anything. She sits up in bed. The velociraptors, disturbed in their sleep, yip in confusion. Jane directs the calmest expression she can muster at Mrs. Thrash and also at Ravi, who has, in fact, been arguing with his mother to leave Jane in her own dimension, with a quiet steel in his manner.

"I see your point," Jane says, "but really, I'm not afraid. It just took me by surprise, is all, but now I'm one hundred percent on board.

Of course there are alternate dimensions. Unfortunately, I don't have time for any travel right now, because I need to be building umbrellas. You're not an artist, so you might not understand artistic inspiration, but believe me, I've got no choice but to answer the call."

"Umbrellas," says Mrs. Thrash, sounding intrigued. "It's true I'm not an artist. But I am a scientist, which may, in fact, be similar in spirit. I'm an inventor and an explorer. I understand the compulsion to follow where one is called." The first Mrs. Thrash seems to make a decision. "Well then. I won't stand in your way."

Jane finds it unsettling that the first Mrs. Thrash imagines she could stand in her way. She suspects she'd be a fool to waste this reprieve. "Allons-y," she says, then jumps up from the bed. At the resulting head rush, she steadies her hand on Ravi's shoulder. Then she gives him a farewell pat and heads for the spiral stairs. Jasper thumps onto the floor and follows. Together, Jane and Jasper make their way down to the tower's base.

The door to the tower is heavy and the threshold slightly raised. Jane stumbles a little as she enters the corridor, then feels a sturdy hand, strong on her arm. It's Ivy, who's holding her camera and looking upon Jane with concern.

"You okay?" says Ivy. She's wearing black leggings and a ratty blue sweater and the ceiling lights burnish the edges of her hair to gold. She's solid, real.

"Yeah," says Jane. "Thanks. I'm a little disoriented," she says, waving vaguely in the direction of the first Mrs. Thrash's door.

"Oh," says Ivy, in a different tone of voice. "Oh, god. Did she—did you—"

"What?" says Jane. "No. No! I just met her, that's all. And her—pets."

"I've heard about the pets," Ivy says.

"I'm trying not to think about them," Jane says.

"Oh, right. Sorry."

"No, I mean, the fact is that I'd like to talk to you about it," Jane says, realizing this to be true. Telling Ivy all about it would be a great comfort. "I'd love to, later, when my head is clear. I kind of—passed out when I saw the pets," she says, pushing at her own forehead, "and I don't feel like I've reassembled all my parts yet."

"Can I bring you anything?" Ivy says. "Soup? Tea? Kumquats?"

"Kumquats?" says Jane in confusion. "You really have kumquats?"

"Mr. Vanders has a soft spot for them, so we keep some around when we can. But mostly I just wanted to tell you the word," Ivy says, grinning.

Understanding, Jane counts the letters. "Plus, it has a *q* and a *k*," she says. "High points."

"Yep."

Jane doesn't want Ivy to feel like her servant. "I don't need anything," she says. "How's the gala prep going? Need help?"

Ivy frowns down at the camera in her hands and Jane remembers the weird pictures she's been taking. Ivy has secrets. Is there anyone in this house who *doesn't* have secrets?

"You can come rescue me from it," Ivy says, "later. We could go bowling or something, and talk about stuff."

"Sure," Jane says, just as the tower door opens again. Ravi emerges, the Monet under his arm.

"Hello, darling children," he says.

"Don't be a douche, Ravi," says Ivy, with no malice.

Chuckling, he plants a kiss on her forehead. "Ivy-bean," he says, "it's nice to see the two of you getting acquainted. And you," he says, leaning toward Jane. "You know where to find me if you decide you want company."

Jane's face is blazing with heat as he walks away. "Sorry," she says to Ivy, not sure what she's apologizing for.

"Don't worry," Ivy says. "I'm used to it."

"Why doesn't he hit on you?" Jane says. "You're gorgeous."

Ivy turns away before Jane can fully appreciate the wattage of her sudden smile. "He knows better," she says. "See you later, Janie."

Back in her morning room, the umbrella Jane was working on previously—the self-defense umbrella in brown and gold—no longer calls to her. She's sure it matters to someone that Philip was lurking around with a gun and Phoebe was making allusions to the Panza-vecchias and Patrick seemed in on it, et cetera, et cetera, but who cares? Ravi's mother has velociraptors.

This circumstance calls either for a project so dull that she forgets everything, or so weird and complicated that all her anxiety can flow straight out of her and into it.

What, she wonders, would a transdimensional umbrella be like?

It would need to be able to blend into any scenario, in any kind of world, without drawing attention to itself.

Jane has never made a plain black umbrella before.

The canopy would need to be perfectly curved, the tips at the end of each rib and the ferrule on top perfectly straight. A plain black umbrella won't have any frills or furbelows to distract from her mistakes. All her umbrellas have mistakes.

It's going to be a disaster.

What would Aunt Magnolia say to that? *It might. But you'll learn something from it, sweetheart. Why not try?*

All right then.

As Jane trims the shaft with her lathe, the world starts to make sense again. Explanations offer themselves. Pinky and Spotty are obviously not velociraptors. After all, since when is Jane familiar with every species of animal currently living on Earth? Why shouldn't there be a small, lizardlike sort of animal that the first Mrs. Thrash, being delusional, found in the Sahara, or the Amazon, or the great desert of Rajasthan, then convinced herself are transdimensional velociraptors? Earth lizards, yes. With feathers.

And what had she said? Something about the house in the other dimension being in danger of being "boarded by pirates." Ridiculous. Pirates attack ships, Jane thinks, not houses, and houses aren't things to be boarded like ships. Anyway, pirates are something out of a bad fantasy story. The pirates offer the most solid proof that the first Mrs. Thrash is making everything up.

"Someone should help that woman," Jane mutters to herself. It's funny the way crazy people can cause you to start losing your own grasp on reality. Stunning, really, the things Jane had almost begun to believe. It's so nice to be back in her morning room, surrounded by familiar things, with Jasper, a completely normal basset hound of Earth, snoozing under the bed in the other room. How wonderful to be making a deadly boring black umbrella. Her fingers move smoothly through her collection of runners.

Tu Reviens is making noises around her, pulling her out of herself. "Is someone shouting?" Jane says aloud, because it's hard to distinguish the house's moans, watery hums, and breaths of heat from other kinds of noises, and she thinks she might hear someone shouting.

When the shouting gets closer and resolves itself into Ravi's voice, raised in anger, Jane goes to her gold-tiled bathroom, rifles through her toiletries, and unearths a pair of earplugs.

In her new, underwater sort of silence, Jane chooses a runner for the umbrella's shaft. She threads ribs onto tying wire; she slices and sews gores together. It's slow, focused work.

It should be meditative work, but Jane's mind keeps spinning off. Had Aunt Magnolia ever stood in a boat, looking down at a deep, cold, unexplored stretch of ocean, and been terrified? Had she ever stood there, wrestling with herself over whether to stay in the boat or drop herself in?

As far as Jane knows, Aunt Magnolia had always eventually decided to drop herself in. Face what scared her and open herself to whatever she might learn.

Why not try, Janie?

Dammit, Jane thinks to herself, dropping her unfinished umbrella on the worktable. She covers her face with her hands and thinks to herself repeatedly, *Dammit.* She grips the table. When her fingertips find a rough patch, she opens her eyes to the discovery of a carving, a blue whale and its calf. Next, along the top edge of the table, she finds a carving of a peaceful whale shark and its babies. Ivy must've made this strong, beautiful table.

Jane takes a jellyfish breath.

Aunt Magnolia? Is this why you wanted me to come to this house? Is this what you wanted me to try?

Removing her earplugs and choosing two umbrellas, Jane leaves her rooms.

Ravi is in the corridor, headed in her direction. His face is stormy. "Where are you going?" he asks in an accusatory tone.

"I haven't decided," Jane says, which is true.

"Really?" says Ravi, his voice milder. He stops before her, too close again. Her body responds, moving until her back is to the wall and Ravi is almost up against her. He's so close that she has to bend her head back a little to see into his face.

"Ravi," Jane says, uncertain what's happening, and alarmed. "What are you doing?"

He brings his mouth near to hers. Then, slowly, he takes her upper lip between his lips, lightly. Her breath catches; her lips part. His skin is scratchy, his mouth curious and insistent, and her mouth responds. His hands are on her, his body pressing her against the wall. She wants Ravi to press harder and fix her to the earth, and this terrifies her, because she knows, Jane *knows,* that Ravi is not someone she should do this with. It might be casual for him, but it would not be casual for her.

Maybe her hands are more intelligent than the rest of her body, or maybe the intelligence is in her umbrellas. Jane wedges both of them between her body and Ravi's and pushes him off.

He backs away, unprotesting. He tilts his head, studying her face. "Okay," he says. "Are you angry at me?"

"No," she says. "But please don't do it again."

"All right," he says. "I won't." He's speaking plainly, sincerely. But if he's the kind of person who understands so easily, then is she so sure she doesn't want him to kiss her again? A feeling touches Jane, a feather touch. What is it? Resentment? No. Envy. Jane wishes she could be that casual about kissing, about sex. She thinks it must be nice to have kissed so much that it's no big deal. As she continues down the hall, she hears his door shutting.

It strikes her as funny, what she's just said no to, considering what she's willingly walking toward.

Then Jane sees the figure up ahead, standing at the top of the corridor near the courtyard, watching her. It's Ivy. Ivy is standing there in her ratty blue sweater, a daffodil behind her ear, tall and still, as if she's been standing there watching for some time. Ivy saw the kiss.

What had it looked like to her?

Ivy pushes her glasses higher on her face, then raises a hand in greeting. It's a friendly gesture. It tips Jane's panic into immediate relief, then, just as quickly, into despair. Doesn't Ivy care that Jane was just kissing Ravi? Is it completely irrelevant to her?

Jane's own hands are again behaving intelligently, one hand passing its umbrella to the other, then raising itself in response. Jane hopes Ivy can't read her face, because she has no idea what expression she's wearing. When Ivy turns and walks out of sight, Jane stands there for a moment, wondering how a tiny, earthbound thing like the question of whom to kiss can possibly be as confusing as transdimensional velociraptors.

The first Mrs. Thrash responds to the bellpull so quickly that Jane wonders if she's been waiting for her inside the door. Mrs. Thrash peeks surreptitiously up and down the hall, then says, "Come up, Janie dear, come up."

Jane's black umbrella is still uncompleted, the canopy unfixed to the ribs, flapping around like the robes of an absentminded professor in a high wind. It's missing its finishings too, like the curved handle and the metal tips. Nonetheless, the first Mrs. Thrash is appreciative. "The elegance radiates," she says. "I can see that it will be as graceful as a clean transdimensional jump."

Jane grunts a skeptical thanks to this.

She's brought the brown-copper-rose satin too, the one she used yesterday on the yacht to make herself feel better, the heroic-journey umbrella, just to keep from feeling misrepresented by her own work. "I don't usually make plain black umbrellas," she says. "But you inspired me to try something that'd be appropriate in multiple dimensions." She adds, cautiously, "Metaphorically speaking, of course," because while it's true that she's brought herself here, it doesn't mean she's decided anything.

"An honorable objective," says the first Mrs. Thrash. "Come up and visit the velociraptors. They're very fond of you."

As Jane climbs the stairs to the next level, she thinks of Jasper longingly, Jasper, the plain old dog, who she now remembers is sleeping under the bed in her rooms. "I need to get back soon," she says. "The dog is closed in my rooms."

"I understand," says the first Mrs. Thrash.

The red trapdoor in the ceiling is ajar. Its many locks line the edges of the opening like teeth in the square mouth of a living house.

"Of course," the first Mrs. Thrash adds, "there's no rain in UD17."

"What?" Jane says. "Rain?"

"They don't have umbrellas," she says. "But every invention is likely to find some use there, especially anything that might be classed as historical costume. Imagination and fashion are both valued in UD17."

"No kidding," Jane says, wishing someone, anyone, were here to share incredulous glances with. "Why is there no rain?"

"Because there's no planet," says the first Mrs. Thrash. "After the UD17 earthlings lost their Earth, they fled to the edges of their solar system and built a huge number of ships and space stations, arranged in a sphere, to mimic Earth's surface, but much smaller, of course. It's like an empty eggshell, or a beach ball—nothing in the middle. Some of the space stations are truly gargantuan—Mexico City, Beijing, Los Angeles, Bombay—but even they aren't large enough to have much in the way of atmospheric phenomena. Anyway, water reclamation is far too important for them to indulge in the whimsy of letting it rain."

"Lost their Earth?" Jane says. "How did that happen?"

"Alien attack," she says, her attention still on the umbrellas, which she's opening and closing in succession, admiring the smoothness of their operation and their fine, sharp ferrules. "The planet was blown apart. Hadn't I mentioned the alien invasion?"

"Sure," Jane says.

"Consequently," she says, "when you cross through the portal into my counterpart's tower on the Tu Reviens of UD17, you find yourself aboard a cleverly representational spaceship-castle on its own island dock."

"Uh-huh." Then Jane understands. "The house is a ship, in danger of being boarded by pirates."

The first Mrs. Thrash's face grows grim. "So *very* worrisome," she says. "We simply cannot have criminals doing what they like with the portals. What sort of havoc will ensue?" Then she peers at Jane with an intent expression that makes Jane nervous. "I don't suppose you have any experience with pirates?"

"None whatsoever," Jane says firmly.

"You might distract them," she says, handing the umbrellas back abruptly. "You're young, but you're rather intriguing, with your umbrella-making and all. Funny I haven't run across your counterpart in any other Tu Reviens, isn't it? We could use you to create a distraction somehow, while UD17 Ravi and UD17 I rough the pirates up a bit."

This is patently absurd, even for a delusion. "And how is UD17 you at roughing people up?"

"You're right, of course," says the first Mrs. Thrash with an enormous, gloomy sigh. "It's an appalling plan. I'm no good at fisticuffs. I like an antagonist I can verbally manipulate or trick into performing my will, or, as a final resort, jab with a bit of live electrical wire. Here, come up and see the portal, it'll help you stop presuming I'm crazy."

"I don't presume you're crazy," Jane protests with rising panic as the first Mrs. Thrash herds her toward the staircase to the level above. It's like the woman can shove people along with the force of her will. Jane is halfway up before she realizes she's acquiesced.

"It's very sweet of you to say so, Janie dear," says the first Mrs. Thrash. "The pirates fly these tiny little ships, you see. They're much stealthier than the chappies in *Treasure Island*. They can dock themselves on the roofs and walls of the house. If they're determined enough, and if the house is in a mild enough mood, the pirates will board."

"I see," Jane says as she passes through the red trapdoor in the ceiling. "The house has moods, does it?"

The room beyond is empty of furnishings and decoration. There's not even a rug or a folding chair. Jane steps in cautiously, then sidles toward the wall. For some reason, the emptiness of the room makes her jumpy. Wouldn't a delusional woman with an imaginary transdimensional portal have something set up in this room, some sort of silver capsule with seats and a steering wheel, and a sign on it that says CAUTION: TRANSDIMENSIONAL PORTAL?

"Good heavens, my dear. Don't go that way," says the first Mrs. Thrash in alarm, hastily grabbing Jane's arm and swinging her toward the center of the room. "You'll step right through the portal."

"Oh! Thank you—" Jane begins to say, then loses her voice and her grip on the umbrellas. Jane loses her hands. She loses her breath, her need to breathe, her vision and her memory. The feeling of being in her body. Jane loses her everything, except for a frozen and stunningly focused sense of just exactly who she is.

When it all comes back again, Jane sees that the first Mrs. Thrash has changed her clothing. And her hair, and the décor, and the lighting. She is standing before Jane in a very odd hat, wearing an indignant expression.

"Who in the dazzle dance are you?" she says. "And where did you come from?"

Oh, *hell.*

Her green, leafy hat, part scarf and part necklace, is wrapped all around her upper half. With her brown shirt and pants, she looks like a tree. The room is familiarly shaped, but made of metal, not stone.

Jane searches for the words her own first Mrs. Thrash would use. "Your counterpart sent me through her portal," she says. "I'm Jane. Janie."

"Which counterpart?" says this first Mrs. Thrash. "You do realize I could have as many as infinitely many?"

"Oh, god," Jane says. "I feel sick."

"Aha!" she says. "A god-worshiping dimension. Likely a Limited Dimension, then. And you're carrying—what are those artifacts? Are those what are known as umbrellas?"

"Yes," Jane says, holding her stomach. "She tricked me. I can't believe it. Is this UD17?"

"Yes," says UD17 first Mrs. Thrash. "Remind me. What is an umbrella for? Self-defense?"

"It's for shielding yourself from the rain. Here," Jane says, handing her the unfinished one, opening the other numbly as a demonstration. "Some people think it's bad luck to open one inside."

"Superstition! A severely Limited Dimension, then," says UD17 first Mrs. Thrash. "And rain. An atmospheric Earth with sufficient surface water. What has my counterpart from your world been visiting me for?"

"Art, I think."

"Ah!" she says. "Now we're getting somewhere. Did she recently buy a froggybank I got in UD33 for her android daughter?"

"No."

"A Dali of melting clocks from LD107 for her son, Rudolfo?"

"No!"

"A Monet of speculative lily pads and frogs for her son, Ravi?"

"Yes," Jane says, "that's the one."

"Yes," she repeats. "That's our own painting. My own Ravi hasn't let me hear the end of it. Never said a word to me about that Monet, until I made an intelligent business decision. Now suddenly it's his favorite painting in the house and all I hear is the foulest bile. My children!"

"I need to go back," Jane says, trying to breathe. "I need to go home."

"Why did she send you?"

"I have no idea. She tricked me."

"Well then," says UD17 first Mrs. Thrash, scrutinizing Jane with an aspect that makes Jane nervous, in quite a familiar way. "She must've had a reason."

"I think she just wanted to prove to me that she wasn't out of her mind."

"Doubtful. I have not met many counterparts of myself who care if other people think they're out of their minds," she says with convincing finality. It's impressive that she can be so convincing in that silly hat. The leaves bounce around as she talks, as if she's a maple tree on a pogo stick. "She sent you here for some purpose. I wonder. You're young, and the young are inspiring. Do you approach life with above-average gusto?"

"Um, I don't know," Jane says. "Probably my gusto is about average?"

"Did she mean you as a friend and influence for my Karen? Or as a lover? Oh, forgive me—you'll know her as Kiran."

"She hasn't said much about Kiran," Jane says in confusion. "I mean, her own Kiran. She hasn't mentioned anything about anyone named Karen, I don't think."

"My Karen is a brilliant girl who should be engaged in a brilliant career, but lacks gusto. Hm," she says, peering at Jane closely. "Do you have any experience with pirates?"

"No!" Jane exclaims. "Why does everyone think I have experience with pirates?"

"Aha!" she says. "So she *did* send you through about the pirates. How thoughtful of her. We need someone who can delve into the deepest depths of the mind of a criminal and anticipate his every move. Are you some sort of psychic, my dear?"

"Of course not."

"Telepathic?"

Jane draws herself up tall. "No!"

"Right," she says, seeming embarrassed by Jane's outrage, though

Jane senses she's not embarrassed for herself, she's embarrassed for Jane. "Silly of me. Sad little Limited Dimension."

"My dimension is not sad!"

"No," she says, patting Jane's shoulder sympathetically, "of course it isn't, dear. Are you, perhaps, a very young psychologist? A criminal behavioralist?"

"No!"

"A criminal yourself?" she asks hopefully.

"I'm an umbrella-maker," Jane says.

"An umbrella-maker," she says, sounding defeated. "How mystifying of LD42 Anita."

"Is that her first name?" Jane says. "I mean, your first name? Anita?"

"Yes," she says. "Both. Nice to meet you. We don't even have rain here."

This woman is a dizzying conversationalist. "Well, then, I may as well be going," Jane says.

"Maybe LD42 Anita means you to serve as a distraction while I rough the pirates up," she suggests brightly.

"Listen," Jane says sternly, really rather tired of this. "You've got a problem with pirates. You're afraid they're going to pass through your portal and search for their own pirate counterparts in other dimensions, to strengthen their numbers. They fly little ships and have clever ways of getting on board. Couldn't you just focus your energies on fortifying this room so that the pirates can't reach the portal? And what is this, anyway, a lawless dimension? Don't you have police?"

"Of course we have police," she says, sniffing in indignation. "But why should I trust *them* around the portal?"

"If you don't trust anyone," Jane exclaims, "all the more reason to fortify the portal! What are your security measures?"

Jane begins to march to one of the windows—portholes?—then remembers the purpose of this room. "Where's the portal exactly?" she asks, not wanting to step into it by accident and transport herself god-knows-where. UD17 first Mrs. Thrash points to a chalk square on the floor, right at the edge of Jane's big black boots.

"At least yours is marked," Jane says in a chilly voice. Then she crosses the room to a window, wanting to assess its potential for break-in by pirates.

The view from the window confuses Jane. She's been informed that this house is a spaceship, but the view here is much like the view from a window in her own Tu Reviens. A green yard, and beyond that, an ocean. A sunny day.

"It's not a real window, my dear," says UD17 first Mrs. Thrash. "It's merely a projection of what we imagine we might see, had we not lost our planet."

This seems pointless to Jane. Surely the actual view must be spectacular. "Come down into the house," UD17 first Mrs. Thrash continues, "to the command center. We have some real windows, and I'll show you a model of the defenses we have in place for the ship."

Walking through UD17's Tu Reviens is like an off-kilter dream version of walking through Jane's usual Tu Reviens. She recognizes rooms and staircases; the atrium; even the art, in some cases—with differences that give Jane the chills. The polar bear rug, for example, is not a polar bear rug. It's a gruesome, grimacing, Abominable Snowman rug. Presumably made of synthetic materials, since there's no snow here and monsters aren't real. Are they?

The lighting is harsh, the oval-shaped doorways raised a few inches from the ground. Oddly dressed people pass Jane occasionally. Some of them wear small wheels on their shoes. One is dressed like the guards at Buckingham Palace, complete with a beefeater on her head. Another wears butterfly wings. A third carries a bucket and is dressed like a milkmaid. Are there cows in the house? There's no milk in the bucket. The bucket seems to be full of . . . kittens? Jane wonders if when these people lost their planet, they lost their history too, and are trying to pull it back somehow, with the way they dress. Trying to recapture lost things. She touches the ruffles on her own sea-dragon shirt.

"This ship is constructed from the cannibalized parts of other ships," UD17 first Mrs. Thrash tells Jane as Jane follows her toward the stairs. "Octavian Thrash the First had an eye for a bargain, and was a pushy bastard too. He lifted our atrium from an Italian pleasure cruiser."

The atrium is eerily similar to the Venetian courtyard Jane knows, with marble floors, terraced gardens, tinkling fountains, even hanging flowers. Except that it's shinier, more perfect. Of course: It's fake. The marble is fake, the flowers are fake. It's an imitation of something that no longer exists in this world. It's soulless, like the atrium you might find in a Roman Empire–themed casino in Vegas.

"Is that real sunlight?" Jane asks, pointing at the light flowing through the ceiling.

"Dear child," UD17 first Mrs. Thrash says. "We're at the farthest reaches of the solar system. New Earth has no access to that kind of sunlight."

Aunt Magnolia, Jane thinks, *if you could see this.* It's frightening, somehow, to contemplate Aunt Magnolia while in this other universe. Jane's been trying not to think about her too directly. "Do you know if there's a version of me in UD17?" she asks UD17 first Mrs. Thrash, even though the question makes her breathless.

"Not that I know of," says UD17 first Mrs. Thrash. "Come."

She leads Jane to the east staircase—companionway?—which clanks hollowly under Jane's boots as she descends. Instead of a tall painting of a room with an umbrella on the second-story landing, Jane finds herself looking through a doorway into an actual room, which contains . . . what looks like a crumpled spacesuit made for a horse, lying on the floor. People are walking in and out of the doorway. Crew of the ship? Guests of the family? "Is there a gala going on?" she asks.

"No," says UD17 first Mrs. Thrash. "Why?"

"So many people."

"Most houseships of New Earth house hundreds, if not thousands of people, my dear. It's not like we have a planet to spread out across."

Most of these people are strangers, but Jane could swear that a little girl who bolts into the room, glancing over her shoulder, is Grace Panzavecchia. She's so fast, it's impossible to be sure. Moments later, a version of Mr. Vanders hurries up the stairs and crosses in after her. He's wearing chartreuse sequin suspenders and looks a bit fed up.

It's the strangest thing, though: Once people pass through the doorway, they change. Jane notices it when the Panzavecchia kid glances back. She looks, weirdly, like some other little girl. As someone else steps out of the room onto the landing, Jane cries out in surprise, because she recognizes the person.

"Lucy St. George!" she says, amazed, really, that she can tell it's Lucy. It must be something about the way Lucy's carrying herself, because her face is made up as a sad clown, complete with a red clown nose and dripping black tears, and she's wearing baggy pants and suspenders, floppy shoes, a white tank top, an oversized bow tie, and pigtails.

"Lucy!" Jane says again. "Is it Halloween?"

"Oh, it's you," UD17 Lucy says gloomily. "Of course it's you. Who else would it be?"

"Me?" Jane says. "You know me?"

"Are you sure you know her, Lavender?" UD17 first Mrs. Thrash asks, surprised. "Janie's a visitor from another dimension. Have you seen our dimension's version of her here?"

"Oh," says Lucy. "Then you're not that Janie? Yes. I saw another version of her just today, in Ravi's bed."

"Ravi's bed!" Jane says, but Lucy has already turned her shoulder. She tromps toward the east corridor, her big shoes requiring large, awkward steps, as if she's walking in water. She turns back to look at Jane once. Her clown face burns itself into Jane's soul, sad and reproachful.

"Ravi's bed!" Jane repeats. She has no idea what to do with that information.

"Move along now, dear," says UD17 first Mrs. Thrash.

"Why was she dressed like that?"

"Like what?" says UD17 first Mrs. Thrash, nudging Jane forward down the stairs.

"Like a sad clown," Jane says, continuing on.

"A sad clown?" says UD17 first Mrs. Thrash. "Why on earth shouldn't she be dressed like a sad clown?"

"But why—" Jane begins, then stops as a pirate—a pirate!—comes exploding up the stairs toward her. Instinctively, Jane adopts a blocking stance and rams herself into him, which sends him tumbling down the steps again with a high-pitched scream.

"Ow!" he yells once he's arrived at the bottom. Lying on the floor in a heap, he presses his own head, his hip, his knee, inspects his elbows. Glares up at Jane in disbelief, and, *Good god*, it's Colin Mack. Colin, with an eye patch, a skull-and-crossbones bandana over long, scraggly hair, and a tight silk vest with a puffy-sleeved shirt beneath.

"Colin!" Jane cries out.

"What did I ever do to you?" Colin calls up the steps. "You could've killed me!"

"Colin!" Jane says again. "You're one of the pirates?"

"Who the flying flotsam are you?" Colin says. "Anita, where did you get this snollygoster?"

"Really," UD17 first Mrs. Thrash says to Jane, chiding. "You need to remember, dear, that you're in a different dimension. If you have a bone to pick with your own Colin, it's hardly just to take it out on our Colin."

"I didn't knock him over because he's Colin!" Jane says. "I didn't know he was Colin! I knocked him over because he's one of the pirates!"

"Oh, don't be ridiculous," says UD17 first Mrs. Thrash. "Colin is an art dealer."

"Then why is he dressed like that?"

"Oh, and now you insult my appearance," Colin says indignantly.

"Don't take it personally, dear," UD17 first Mrs. Thrash calls down to Colin, the leaves on her head swinging about. "Janie here is a visitor from a Limited Dimension. As such, she can't help having a narrow conception of the multi-world."

"Neanderthal! Go back where you came from," Colin says, then picks himself up, brushes himself off, and marches away in a huff. His pants are ratty and unhemmed and he's got a couple of pistols in holsters on either hip.

"So, he's not a pirate?" Jane asks in confusion, then sees her Jasper, dear Jasper the dog, plodding his way up the stairs toward her. She's never been happier to see a dog in her life. He looks like himself. He's struggling with the climb just exactly the way Jasper does. She crouches down and holds out an eager hand.

Jasper pauses briefly, swings his nose around to her hand, gives an indifferent sniff, and continues on. He doesn't even look her in the face.

Jane wants to sit on the steps and howl.

"Poor dear," says UD17 first Mrs. Thrash. She leans over Jane, her hat giving her the aspect of a weeping willow. "It takes all of us that way, you know. You need to remember that even though this world is familiar, you don't belong here. You'll never feel like you do."

The ship's command center has floor-to-ceiling windows, and Jane was right: The views are extraordinary. A vast purple ocean of space, across which tiny, bright spaceships zip now and then, twinkling like silver and gold fireflies. Beyond, a faint metallic line that must be the "mainland" in this planetless, floating, human community. Far, far beyond that, a single point of light, tiny, but so bright that it's painful to look at.

"Do you recognize that star?" says UD17 first Mrs. Thrash. "It's the sun."

"The sun!" Jane says in astonishment. "But it's so small!"

"We're much, much farther from ours than you are from yours, my dear."

How is it possible that this morning Jane woke up in her ordinary life, yet now she's experiencing what the sun would look like from the edges of the solar system?

"Come," says UD17 first Mrs. Thrash. "I'll show you the house's security measures."

She brings Jane to a holographic projection of the house that spins, or splits open, or magnifies its parts, based on the voice command of the ship's captain, who is, unsurprisingly, Mrs. Vanders. Or, Captain Vanders, here. She's got wheels on her feet and is zipping around the holograph, while wearing a chartreuse ball gown replete with shimmering sequins.

Captain Vanders and UD17 first Mrs. Thrash have a rapid exchange about the details of the ship's current defense system, the majority of which Jane can hardly believe. It seems the ship can sense when a person has ill intentions toward one of its parts, and, like some sort of haunted fairy-tale forest, can turn parts of its floors to strange, boglike mouths, or twist the walls so that doors are inaccessible, or push books off the library shelves.

"You realize you're suggesting that the ship is *conscious?*" Jane says, interrupting Captain Vanders, who has just predicted the ship's willingness and ability to pitch a pirate over a balustrade into the atrium.

"Indeed," says Captain Vanders grimly. "It's a recent development, regrettably inconsistent, but observable as a phenomenon. Patrick and Ravi got into some sort of scuffle the other day. We found them both snagged on light fixtures in the Mercury Sitting Room."

"Aren't Patrick and Ravi friends here?"

"Oh, they're wonderful friends," says UD17 first Mrs. Thrash. "But Karen and Patrick are newly married, and Karen's pregnant with twins, and Ravi's planned some off-world adventure that coincides with the expected birth, and Patrick got all indignant and protective of Karen. He thinks Ravi should want to be around when his sister's babies are born."

"Of course he should!" Jane says. "Ravi isn't that selfish, is he? And Kiran is married to Patrick here? How did that happen?"

"You keep forgetting," says UD17 first Mrs. Thrash. "This is not your world. You can't know what any of us are bound to be like."

"Can't I? When there are so many similarities?"

"The tiniest stone dropped in the water ripples far in every direction," she says. "You should like that metaphor, coming from an Earth with water covering seventy percent of its surface."

"Wait," Jane says. "Kiran—Karen—is pregnant with twins, yet you're criticizing her for not having *gusto*? And a brilliant career?"

"Oh, she's only eleven weeks," says UD17 first Mrs. Thrash. "She just sits around. Ravi makes appalling decisions, don't mistake me, but at least he has gusto!"

"I see," Jane says, feeling very sorry indeed for UD17 Karen, whose body is creating two brand-new humans with what some people consider to be insufficient gusto. Or is she *happy* for UD17 Karen? Isn't it a good thing that this Kiran/Karen is married to her Patrick? Especially a Patrick who gets indignant on her behalf?

"Oh, honestly," says Captain Vanders. "Could we please focus on the matter at hand?"

"Yes," Jane says. "How can a ship change into a conscious entity?"

"She's from a Limited Dimension, Captain Vandy," says UD17 first Mrs. Thrash apologetically.

"Nevertheless," Captain Vanders says bleakly, "it's a valid question. I'm afraid I don't understand it myself; it's caught all of us unawares. I'm of the strong opinion that Anita should be looking to other dimensions for the explanation—and the solution."

"Do you think there *is* a solution?" Jane asks.

"The universe is infinitely vast," says UD17 first Mrs. Thrash huffily. "Of course there's a solution. Maybe we need an architectural psychologist, or someone who specializes in imbuing inanimate objects with power. I've wondered if our own Ivy might have some potential on that front."

"Ivy!" Jane says.

"I'm just not convinced the ship has a problem that needs solving," UD17 first Mrs. Thrash adds.

"Because you've traveled so much that you've lost perspective on what's normal in your *own* world," says Captain Vanders. "And I'll ask you to leave Ivy be, she has enough on her plate. You'd make more progress consulting the *second* Mrs. Thrash. Though unfortunately," Captain Vanders tells Jane, "the second Mrs. Thrash left us just around the time the phenomenon began. She is a spaceship whisperer."

"A spacesh—" Jane begins, then stops as a new person enters the command center. It's Ivy, instantly recognizable, but also obviously not the same. Jane can't put a finger on the difference but feels that it's something to do with the particular balance of tension in this Ivy's face. Jane's Ivy *could* look like that. But she doesn't.

Immediately UD17 Ivy notices Jane, begins to grin, then stops. Puzzlement furrows her brow. "Sorry," says UD17 Ivy. "Have we met?"

"No," Jane says. "I'm from Limited Dimension something-or-other."

"Ah!" she says. "That explains it." Her smile is warm and extremely

Ivy-like. Her dark hair is streaked with ice-blue highlights, shortish and wispy, spiked like a star around her head. It probably should have been the first thing Jane noticed about her, but it wasn't, maybe because it feels right somehow. Jane finds herself smiling back.

"Do you—" Jane begins, suddenly wanting to ask if *this* Ivy knows, or knew, an Aunt Magnolia. Then she stops. She's not ready for the answer, whatever it is.

Suddenly the house holograph goes haywire and everyone in the room is crowding around it. The holographic roof of the east wing is flashing, bulging, and wrinkling. Captain Vanders runs to a nearby console and reads the words and symbols flying across it.

"Two intruders!" she cries out. "In two separate ships. They've landed, 02 level portside! They're cutting through the hull!"

"Pirates!" says UD17 first Mrs. Thrash. "Pirates with a nefarious transdimensional scheme! I'm sure of it!"

"Well then," says Captain Vanders, "get going! Intercept them!" She takes Jane by the shoulders and gazes earnestly into her face. "Stab them with those pointy things you're carrying!" she says, which is a reference, of course, to Jane's umbrellas.

As Jane is running back down the eastern third-floor corridor with UD17 first Mrs. Thrash, feeling utterly unprepared to intercept pirates, a version of Ravi comes whizzing toward her on sparkly blue roller skates with red stars.

The version I'm sleeping with, Jane thinks to herself, then understands that there is no way to prepare herself for such a Ravi. Her face burns. She hopes he'll pass her by. Instead, he rolls right up to her, grabs her arms, and says, "Hey. Are you okay?"

"I'm not who you think I am," Jane says.

"What? But you're dressed exactly the same," he says, stepping back and examining Jane from top to bottom. He's very tall, perched on those skates. "You're carrying those same umbrellas. My mother didn't send you through? She told me she tricked you so she could prove the existence of the multiverse!"

"Aren't you UD17 Ravi?" Jane asks, then notices that aside from the roller skates, he's also dressed the same as the last time she saw him, in addition to having the identical white streaks in his hair.

"I'm the home Ravi!" he says. "LD42 Ravi! I came to get you. Come on. I hate this dimension."

"Ravi? Why the hell are you wearing roller skates?"

"My mother used to do roller derby," he says with an impatient wave of the hand. "I wanted to get in, find you quickly, and get out, and I've been here before. I know how it is."

"But don't imagine for a moment that you blend in, Other Ravi dear," says UD17 first Mrs. Thrash, pityingly. "Come along now, we're after the pirates."

The house is so conclusively punishing of the pirates that Jane wonders why everyone's been so worried. One of them, the tallest man she's ever seen, comes shooting through the seam where the wall meets the ceiling as they approach. The seam widens and spits him out, its edges rough and splintery, like teeth. Then it emits a cavernous burp and resettles back into place. The pirate lies in a heap at Jane's feet. He's not dressed like a pirate. He's dressed like a sad clown, which confuses Jane thoroughly.

UD17 first Mrs. Thrash rolls him up in the Abominable Snowman rug. Ravi—Jane's Ravi—is making anxious noises around first Mrs. Thrash, uncertain whether she might be destroying a priceless work of art or whether the snowman rug really is as awful as it seems.

"Why are you dressed like that?" Jane asks the pirate, crouching down at his head.

"For the love of a woman who hardly knows I exist," the sad-clown pirate says gloomily, his floppy shoes sticking out of one end of the rug and his curly rainbow wig out of the other. He resembles a sad-clown hot dog.

"Do people always dress up like sad clowns here when they're heartbroken?" Jane asks, trying to find patterns. Patterns are comforting.

"I don't know what you're talking about. I'm dressed like this because it's how she dresses," the pirate says as UD17 first Mrs. Thrash rolls him to the side of the corridor, then presses a button on the wall that allows her to communicate with Captain Vanders.

"I'm so confused," says Jane. "Are you in cahoots with Lucy? I mean, Lavender?"

A bit farther along the corridor, the ceiling spits out an orange. It falls to the floor, bounces, and rolls toward Jane.

"Oh! Well! That's just insulting," the sad-clown pirate says from his rug roll.

"What?" says Ravi. "The orange? An orange is insulting? What's wrong with you? God, I hate this dimension."

"It's my friend's orange," the sad-clown pirate says mournfully. "My friend has become part of the hull of this ship. After he cut through it, I mean. The hull shook his ship off, but hung on to him. It stuck his body into the opening to plug it up."

"Like a finger in the dam?" Jane asks.

"The damn what?" he says.

"Your friend's ship is gone?" says UD17 first Mrs. Thrash with rising alarm. "What do you mean? Does he have any air?"

"No," says the pirate. "I watched him turn blue."

UD17 first Mrs. Thrash stares at the pirate in disbelief. "Are you telling me that the house has killed him?"

"But decided to spare the orange," says the sad-clown pirate. "It's a bizarre ship you call home, if you don't mind my saying so. Has some peculiar defensive capabilities. We weren't warned of this. Judging by how summarily we were defeated, I feel that perhaps I have been used."

"By whom?" Jane says. "For what?"

"By her, of course," he says. "To create a distraction. Is it pathetic if I hope she gets away with it?"

"Huh?" Jane says. "What are you talking about? You're not here for the portal?"

"Porthole?" he says. "What porthole?"

"Wait—are you even really a pirate?" says Jane. "*Are* you here for the art?"

"It's true I am a painter of great talent," the pirate says. "But I think I've said enough. Don't you?"

"I—don't know," Jane says, trying to understand. Is *Lavender* after the art?

A number of staffpersons Jane doesn't recognize have arrived with a gurney and are surrounding the rolled-up pirate. They lift him and the Abominable Snowman rug directly onto the gurney, then strap him in. UD17 first Mrs. Thrash is telling the staffpersons something chilly and grave about the dead man who's currently plugging up the hole he himself cut in the roof. The staff doesn't believe her. The house has never killed anyone before. Jane wonders if Captain Vanders will be surprised. She has a feeling she won't.

Jane has been trying to remember where Lucy—Lavender—was headed the last time Jane saw her. "Ravi," she says quietly. "Come with me."

With perfect manners, Ravi offers to carry one of Jane's umbrellas and makes no reference to how he kissed her in the halls of their own Tu Reviens that morning. He also takes off the roller skates to match himself to the clomping pace of her boots. Jane finds him easy company, really, when he's not flirting all the time. It's strange that her relief is mixed with wistfulness.

"Where are we going?" he asks, the skates dangling from his hand by the laces. When Jane was little, Aunt Magnolia used to walk with her to the park, then sit on a bench and wait for her, offering words of encouragement while she skated. On the way there and back, Jane would tie her laces together and carry her skates the way Ravi is carrying his.

"Well?" says Ravi impatiently.

"Huh? Oh. Second story, east wing," Jane says. "Or 01 level portside, I think they say here. I have a theory."

"What is it?"

"I'm not ready to say yet. But I don't think those guys were pirates after the portal."

"Great," he says. "Another mystery." Ravi is not comfortable walking the corridors of this Tu Reviens. Jane can tell from his voice, and from the way he keeps glancing over his shoulders.

The lights in the second-story east wing are flickering wildly. They hold steady as Ravi and Jane arrive, as if they've been trying to get someone's attention, and these two people will do. Jane supposes she's not entirely surprised to find Lucy—Lavender—alone in the corridor. She's standing there, whimpering, because her hand has been sucked up by the wall. It's happened right at the edge of a small painting— really, almost behind the painting—of a woman writing a letter at a table while her frog stands peacefully nearby. It's nighttime in the painting. The scene is softly lit by a swirling galaxy of stars.

"Lucy-Bear!" cries Ravi. "Clown Lucy! What happened?" Then, "Holy shit. Look at that Vermeer."

"Vermeer?" Jane says.

"That gorgeous picture," Ravi says. "*A Lady Writing a Letter with Her Frog*—or at least, that's what it's called in our dimension."

"Oh, right," says Jane, remembering. "Mrs. Vanders actually mentioned your Vermeer this morning."

"She did?"

"She was worried about it, possibly?" says Jane. "She wanted you to look at it."

"Worried? Hang on, what's this?"

Ravi bends down to get a better look at a small canvas lying flat on the floor beside Lavender's oversized clown shoes. Then he freezes. Putting his skates down carefully, handing Jane the umbrella he's carrying, Ravi picks the canvas up and holds it at arm's length. It's a painting of a woman writing a letter while her frog stands nearby. It's identical to the painting on the wall.

He turns to Lavender. Ravi, suddenly, is almost crying. "Lucy," he says. "What are you doing?"

"My name is Lavender," says Lavender, gasping. "And you're not even my real Ravi."

"All this time," Ravi says, "you've been pretending?"

"It's none of your business if I've been pretending!" Lucy—Lavender— cries out. "You're not you. I shouldn't have to explain myself to you! To *any* of you!"

"You told me you loved me."

"Oh, listen to yourself. That wasn't me and you, it was you and someone else, me and someone else. Anyway, you don't even know what the word means!"

"Which painting is the real one?" Ravi asks, his voice choked.

"Figure it out," Lavender says, "if you care so much! You don't care who's in your bed, but *ohhh,* it matters what painting is on your wall!"

"I will figure it out," says Ravi. "I assure you. And I'll tell your father and your cousin what you did. I'll tell everyone!"

Lavender begins to laugh, a disgusted laugh that turns into a short scream as the wall sucks harder on her hand.

"I'm calling the police," says Ravi, placing the canvas carefully on the floor where he found it. "Or the captain. Whatever it is you've got in this goddamn dimension for dealing with clown-nosed, lowlife art thieves. Guard the paintings," he says to Jane stiffly. "I'll be back."

"All right," Jane says. Then she waits, patient and still, an umbrella in each hand, until, swearing quietly, Ravi has retrieved his skates and rolled off down the corridor.

Jane turns back to Lavender. The wall, it seems, is steadily consuming Lavender's hand. She's in deeper now, almost to her elbow, and she's gasping in pain. Tears are running oily tracks through her makeup; black is dripping onto her white shirt.

"Did you pay those two men to distract the house while you stole the painting?" Jane asks.

"I assure you," Lavender says with a weak rush of fury, "you're the last person in the multiverse I would ever explain myself to." Her eyes go bright and flash at Jane. "The second-to-last person," she cries out. "You're just a copy! Of a nobody! Of Ravi's latest in a string of nobodies!"

"What are you stealing it for?"

"Why does anyone steal anything?"

"Money?" Jane says, disgusted.

"It's a painting," Lavender spits at Jane. "It's a thing. It doesn't hurt anyone for me to take it. Other than Ravi, maybe, and he deserves it!"

"One of your associates died," Jane says. "The house killed him."

Lavender cries out as the wall slurps her arm in past the elbow. She's lost the strength of her legs and is hanging from her trapped arm like a sad-clown ragdoll. Jane tries not to think about the state of her hand, her forearm, inside that wall. Jane tries not to wonder how far the wall is going to take this punishment.

"Is there anywhere you can run?" Jane asks her.

"What?" Lavender gasps, confused.

"Do you have an exit plan?"

Lavender swings her head up to look at Jane briefly, exhausted, her eyes glazed with pain. "I wasn't supposed to get caught," she says. "But yes. There are places I could go."

Jane has the feeling that deliberation will only convince her of the impossibility of her plan. So, without deliberation, she jams her unfinished, flapping black umbrella into the wall, right at the edge of the spot where Lavender's arm is being eaten. The wall shudders, growls, and squeezes. Lavender screams.

Jane grips her brown-rose-copper umbrella hard and jams it into the wall on the other side of Lavender's arm. It's hard to know what's happening, exactly, as the wall shrieks and balks and drips a strange, glutinous, snotty substance around Jane's stabbing places, but instinct causes her to use the umbrellas as crowbars, to pry open the hole that's sucking Lavender in. The wall roars, then screams. Lavender pulls. Lavender screams.

Then her arm, bloody, mangled, and limp, slips out of the wall like some sluggish creature being born. Lavender falls.

"Run!" Jane yells. "Run!"

Lavender staggers, then, bent over her arm, runs. Alone in the corridor, Jane yanks the umbrellas out of the wall and jams them back in, stab, stab, stab, trying to keep the house distracted while Lavender runs. The wall buckles; it forms fingers that grab at the umbrellas; Jane stabs, keeps stabbing.

But then the floor beneath her boots begins to rumble and shift and she decides she's risked enough. She lets go of the umbrellas, leaving them stuck in the wall. "Nice house," she says. "Wonderful house. I would never hurt this dear, lovely house." Jane breathes jellyfish-deep through her very sincere intention not to do a single thing to cross this horrifying house.

Lavender, when she ran, left behind both paintings. Jane leaves them where they are too, and backs away. The wall still seems to be having a bit of a tussle with the umbrellas, which jerk back and forth, but the floor is calming itself.

"I want to go home," Jane says. "Please, god, let me go home." It's funny to find herself speaking words that sound like prayer. She's never been religious, she doesn't know what she believes, and she doesn't really know what she means by *home,* either.

She does, however, give herself a second to mourn the brown-rose-copper umbrella with the brass handle. Her heroic-journey umbrella; she realizes she's going to have to leave it behind. She thanks it for the important job it's done.

As she leaves the second-story east wing, she understands that there's one more thing she needs to do before she departs this dimension.

When she reaches the third-story east corridor, Jane finds that the mess has been cleaned up. No pirates, no paramedics. Even the Abominable Snowman rug is back in place. Judging by the thunks from above, it sounds like a team of people on the roof, or the hull, is retrieving the dead man and repairing the breach. Jane wonders if the house is giving the man's body up willingly.

At the sound of skates, she turns to find Ravi gliding toward her from the direction of the atrium, looking like a stormcloud. "We got to the painting and Lucy was gone," he says testily. "You let her go, didn't you?"

"That wall was going to kill her," Jane says. "And her name is Lavender."

"The wall wasn't going to kill her!"

"You didn't see what it did to her arm," Jane says.

Ravi swallows. He looks uncomfortable. "What did it do to her arm?"

"Maybe it's better you don't ask."

"Well?" he says, anxious now. "Will she be okay?"

"I have no idea! But you know as well as I do that this house kills people!"
Ravi is fighting with some thought inside his head. "Okay," he says.
"Well, there's nothing we can do about it at this point, and given what
we saw, I'd like to get back home now. I need to have a chat with *my*
Lucy about a Brancusi. Maybe also take a closer look at our Vermeer."

"One more stop first," Jane says.

When Ravi raises questioning eyebrows, Jane holds out her hand.
He takes it, puzzled, and Jane pulls him down the corridor.

"No," Ravi says, when he sees where they're going. "No way."

"Oh, come on."

"No," he insists, breaking out of Jane's grip. "I'll meet you at the portal."

"What are you afraid of?" Jane snaps at him. "The truth?"

"No," he snaps back, finally, thoroughly losing his temper. "I'm
afraid of exactly the opposite, of believing things of myself that aren't
true. You don't get it, do you? UD17 Ravi is a prick. I know. I've met
him. He's like me, but without any—" Ravi waves his hands around in
frustration, reaching for the words. "He's cold. He has no compunc-
tions. And he's *so much like me*. It screws with my head. He's not the
only Ravi I've met and not liked, either. Kiran too. You know when Kiran started moping around all depressed, and pushing Patrick away? It
was after she met UD17 Karen and Patrick, who're so disgustingly moti-
vated and happy and in love, and made her feel like her own Patrick was
holding back, keeping secrets, being dishonest somehow. She's decided
something's wrong with her, and she doesn't trust her Patrick, and she
feels like she's stuck in the wrong world. This place will screw you up!"

"UD17 Ravi isn't you," Jane says. "Don't you know who you are?"

"Yeah," he says, "and I intend to keep it that way." Then he turns
and leaves her.

He has not left her alone. UD17 Ivy is walking calmly down the
corridor toward Jane.

"Hi," she says. Her grin is so much like the Ivy Jane knows that Jane flushes, remembering that other Ivy—*real* Ivy—saw her kissing Ravi earlier today. Though this Ivy, Jane realizes, doesn't wear glasses. Her eyes are less brightly blue too.

"Captain Vanders sent me to do a last check of this passageway," UD17 Ivy says.

"Is she your boss?"

"Yes. One of my bosses."

"Wait," Jane says. "If she's a captain, does that mean you're some kind of soldier?"

"It's not a military ship," she says. "But as it happens, I've been getting some pressure to train as a military officer."

"Really!"

"My brother is one," she says. "He's in intelligence. Karen's thinking about it too, after she weans the babies."

Now Jane is trying to imagine the Ivy of her world as a military officer, involved in intelligence. "Do you want to be in the military?"

"Not particularly," UD17 Ivy says, another smile transforming her face. "I have other interests."

Jane is feeling a sudden urgency not to know this Ivy's interests. She doesn't want this Ivy to overlay her Ivy, whom she only met yesterday. Her Ivy does beautiful carpentry and this world probably doesn't even have forests. And what carvings would a carpenter in this oceanless world carve, in lieu of Ivy's whales, sharks, and girls in rowboats?

"Well," Jane says. "I've got one more visit to make before I go home."

"Here?" says UD17 Ivy, indicating the door behind Jane. "You know that's Ravi's cabin, right?"

"Yeah."

"I don't think you're going to catch him alone," she says. "You know who's in there?"

"Yeah," Jane says. "Someone told me. I was—surprised," she says, leaving it at that. "It's not Ravi I'm wanting to see."

"Oh," UD17 Ivy says, her eyes widening. "Do you think that's a good idea?"

Jane pauses, swallowing. "There's a question I need to ask."

UD17 Ivy bites her lip. *She's trying,* Jane thinks, *to stop herself from telling me not to go in there.*

Instead, UD17 Ivy says, "Would you like me to wait here for you?"

Jane's breath comes out in a rush of relief. "Really?" she says. "Do you have time for that?"

"Sure," says Ivy. "I could stand outside the door, if you want? You could knock if you need me."

"Yes," Jane says. "Please. That's awfully kind. I won't be long."

Jane doesn't knock. She pushes right in, takes one look, and perceives, immediately, why everyone's been warning her.

It's not because there's anything wrong with the appearance of the person in Ravi's bed. It's something else, something more primal.

UD17 Jane and UD17 Ravi are in the massive bed together. He's on the far side, asleep, turned away from both Janes. There's some sort of metallic gold dye streaking his otherwise dark hair. One bare arm is visible above the sheets and he's got the most gorgeous sleeve of tattoos. Jane sees Earth things curving and looping around his muscles. Trees. Poppies. Valleys. Cities of stone stretching away to the sea.

Jane had, of course, realized that she might walk in on sex happening, but it's only now that she appreciates how strange and overwhelming that would have been. To see herself doing something so intensely private, something she hasn't even ever done, and discover what she looks like doing it. To see it, but not be feeling it.

Instead, UD17 Jane is sitting up in bed, wrapped in a sheet as if cold, or shy of nakedness. The first thing that rocks Jane is how vulnerable she looks, how young, her expression uncertain, her hands twisted together. The second is how alone.

Startled at Jane's entrance, this other Jane yelps, then makes an indignant noise. Then, finally, seeing who Jane is, sits wide-eyed and stunned.

"Hi," Jane says. Real Jane.

"Hi," UD17 Jane responds automatically, then, glancing over at UD17 Ravi, shifts to the edge of the bed, farther away from him. "I don't want him to wake up yet," she whispers. "Let's keep our voices down."

Is that how she looks when her face is moving, talking? Jane knows it is; it's fundamentally familiar. But it's also not quite what she's imagined her own face doing. With a shock, Jane realizes it reminds her of Aunt Magnolia.

Something else: Why does she find herself sharp with immediate . . . *resentment* toward this person?

"You know about the multiverse, right?" she says quietly.

"Yeah, of course," says UD17 Jane, a little breathless. "We all do here."

"Do you—"

Jane had almost been about to ask, ridiculously, if UD17 Jane knows how to breathe the way a jellyfish moves. Then she remembers that in addition to this being a weird question to ask after bursting in on someone, there are no oceans in this world. "Are there jellyfish here?" she asks quietly, then presses her palm to her forehead. "I'm sorry," she says. "I'm overwhelmed. I can only think of stupid questions."

"It's okay," says UD17 Jane. "Really. I'm overwhelmed too."

Yes, Jane can see this. Her own feelings are reflected in the short breaths and guarded eyes, the baffled expression of this other Jane.

"But I don't know what you mean," UD17 Jane goes on. "Are you asking me about an extinct fish?"

Jane begins to roll up her sleeve. "It's an invertebrate, jellylike, marine animal," she says, hearing herself describing jellyfish to herself and resisting the urge to laugh hysterically. "Not a fish, actually. Look."

Jane turns her shoulder so that UD17 Jane can see the golden bell, trailing arms, and tentacles of her tattoo.

"Wow," says UD17 Jane. "That's beautiful."

"They've lived in the oceans for over five hundred million years," Jane says. "They're the world's oldest multi-organ animal."

"I think I remember hearing about them," says UD17 Jane. "An Old Earth monster. They're extinct now."

Jellyfish extinct? When they've lived for over five hundred million years?

Jane begins to comprehend what it means that these people's Earth was blown apart. How can she conceive of the loss of oceans? The loss of dirt, solid under her feet? True sunlight, warmth, rain? How would Aunt Magnolia have taught Jane to breathe in this world, if not like a jellyfish?

Jane doesn't hate this dimension the way Ravi does. But it's sad, and impossible, and scary.

And at least now she understands her resentment for this alternate version of herself. She understands it as it fades. Jane has felt as if faced with a person who's stolen her identity. Stolen, even, her facial resemblance to Aunt Magnolia. Mocked her decision not to sleep with Ravi by sleeping with him anyway. As if everything special and unique about her has been appropriated by this person, whose existence, sitting there like a mirror, dilutes Jane somehow.

But Jane is not diluted. Jane is Jane and it doesn't matter who this person is. Jane is a person who lives on Earth, in a world where jellyfish have floated in the oceans for five hundred million years. Jane has a home. This place is not her home.

Also, Jane is a person who decided not to sleep with Ravi. She decided to let Lavender escape. She sacrificed her umbrellas. She knows how to breathe the way a jellyfish moves. She has a girl named Ivy, whom she barely knows and whose counterpart is standing like an anchor outside this room. UD17 Ivy is doing that for Jane, not for *this* person, and Jane has no idea what will or won't come of her feelings. She had a father who taught high school science, a mother who studied the science of falling frogs, and an aunt who swam with whales. Jane makes umbrellas. She can't bear the thought of a world where there are no ailing oceans for Aunt Magnolia to try to save.

She is her own aunt Magnolia's child.

"Are you happy?" Jane blurts out, because suddenly, despite all she's just been thinking, she cares.

That face grows quiet, in a cellularly familiar way. Jane knows that UD17 Jane is considering the question hard. "Not really," she finally responds. "Not since my aunt Magnolia died."

It's the answer to the question Jane came here to ask. The answer, now that Jane has it, is both crushing and not as crushing as she thought it would be. Would Jane really want to know a UD17 Aunt Magnolia? Would she really want to pile so much hope and expectation onto that person?

Jane realizes she's been wondering if this, the multiverse, is why Aunt Magnolia made her promise to visit Tu Reviens. So that if anything ever happened to her aunt, Jane could surround herself with other, different Aunt Magnolias. But no, Aunt Magnolia would have known that *she* was the one Jane had, and the one Jane lost. The only one she wanted.

"I'm sorry about your aunt Magnolia," Jane says to UD17 Jane quietly. "My aunt Magnolia died too. In Antarctica. She was an underwater photographer."

A look of comprehension crosses the face of this other Jane. "Is your tattoo based on one of her photos?"

"Yeah," Jane says, surprised. "How did you know that?"

UD17 Jane turns to show Jane her other shoulder. A comet tattoo streaks up the arm of this other Jane, reaching all the way to her neck. "My aunt Magnolia was a galactic photographer."

Jane is speechless. The tattoo is so like hers.

"And a spy," continues UD17 Jane. "She died on a mission."

"Aunt Magnolia a spy?" Jane says, surprised.

"Yeah. I never knew it, until she died."

"Wow," Jane says, trying to imagine what that would be like. "Did that feel like a betrayal?"

"Not nearly as much as her dying," UD17 Jane says with a quiet bitterness.

Jane feels the pressure of her own rising tears. Some instinct causes her to reach out, curiously, to touch the other Jane, to touch that familiar grief. The other Jane understands and reaches back. The two Janes grasp hands, warm, alive, and a perfect fit.

Behind the other Jane, UD17 Ravi shifts, snores. Their grip on each other tightens in a strange sort of instinctive, mutual self-defense. Jane has a feeling that if UD17 Ravi wakes up and sees her, he's going to invite her into bed. And she realizes, suddenly, why her own Ravi, home Ravi, who's a better Ravi than this Ravi, is not for her. Ravi makes Jane feel excited, delighted, but he does not make her feel anchored in herself. Ivy makes Jane feel excited, delighted, and anchored in who she is.

"Will you be okay?" UD17 Jane asks her.

"I don't know," Jane says. "But this has been a helpful visit."

"For me too. I think you've inspired me, actually," other Jane says, "with the jellyfish."

"Are you an artist?"

"I'd like to be," says UD17 Jane. "I've been designing some pretty wild lampshades lately."

Jane's mind flashes with images. Adornments for lights; jellyfish that glow in a world of no jellyfish. She lets out a laugh, surprised to recognize that she likes this Jane. Her next umbrella, she decides, will be a lampshade umbrella.

"I make umbrellas," Jane says. "I'll have to make a lampshade-inspired one next."

The other Jane scrunches her face. "I think I know what an umbrella is."

"Look it up, if you like," Jane says. "Umbrellas might be inspiring too. I could totally see them coming into fashion here."

"Thanks," says other Jane. "I will."

"I hope you'll be okay," Jane says.

"You too."

"I really mean it."

"Yeah. I do too. I feel like I have a vested interest."

This makes Jane laugh again. "I have to go back now. But a word of advice for you?"

"Yeah?"

"Don't piss off the house."

UD17 Jane raises an eyebrow. "Okay. And one for you?"

"Yeah?"

"Don't sleep with Ravi."

Jane grins, then nods, not mentioning that she's already figured that one out. Something is tugging at her throat. It's a conversation she wants to have with Ivy. A few conversations, really; she wonders if Ivy will want to have them with her. She has no idea. Anything can happen. She'll find out.

Holding the hand of this different version of her, Jane takes a deep, jellyfish breath. When a quietness suffuses her, she lets go and turns for home.

A bell rings somewhere in the depths of the house, sweet and clear, like a wind chime.

Mrs. Vanders, the little girl, Kiran, Ravi, or Jasper?

Aunt Magnolia?

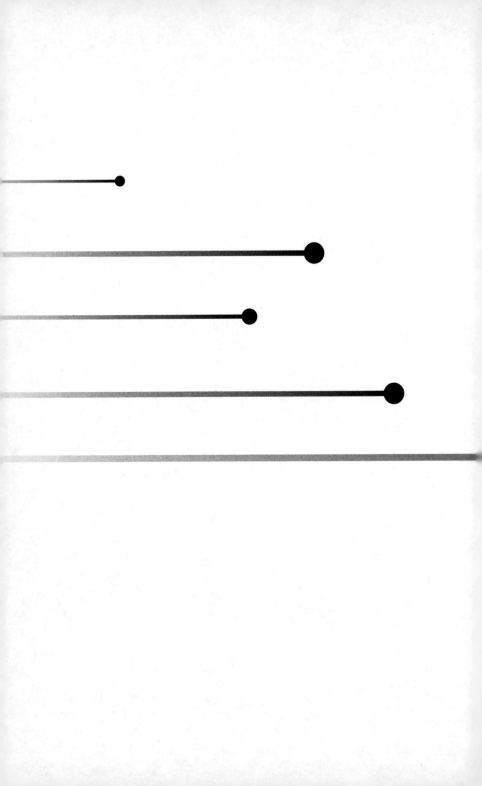

The Strayhound,
the Girl
and the Painting

Jasper is now sprawled on his stomach in front of the tall painting, his chin on the floor, his expression bleak, like a basset hound who's finally given in.

Jane decides.

"Kiran," she says, "I'll catch up with you soon, but first I'm going to try to help this dog, okay?"

"Yeah," says Kiran, wrinkling her nose at Jasper, "what's his problem?"

"I don't know," says Jane, "but I'll see if I can find out."

"It's not your job," says Kiran. "The staff feeds him."

"I know," says Jane. "I don't mind."

"Okay," Kiran says, moving away. "I'll be in the winter garden."

Jane turns to face the dog. "Jasper," she says, "dear Jasper."

He jumps up eagerly, wagging his tail.

When she reaches the landing, there's something of a face-off. She tries to move toward him, but he dodges her, circles her, then runs straight at her from behind.

"Jasper!" she says, trying an evasive maneuver. "How am I supposed to pet you if you're running at me?" He shifts himself and slams into her calves.

It's no use; her balance lost, Jane begins an inexorable topple into the tall umbrella painting. Literally *into* the umbrella painting: She doesn't come up against its surface, it doesn't stop her. She falls on through. Crashing onto a hard horizontal surface, she scrabbles around in bewilderment. She's flat on a checkerboard floor, in a lantern-lit room, in what looks like a fancy house. An unusual umbrella of greens and reds is drying on the floor beside her.

Certain she's just fallen through a crack in her own sanity, Jane scrambles to her feet and spins around to face the way she's come. There's a wall, on which hangs an enormous woven hanging. It shows the landing of a staircase in a big, grand house. A suit of armor, holding daffodils, stands on the landing, as does a basset hound. Across a great hall, another staircase is visible, rising from the ground to the third floor.

As Jane watches, the basset hound in the hanging moves toward her. Suddenly he comes stepping into the room with her, through the hanging, a real dog, but—no longer Jasper. He pants excitedly just like Jasper. But his ears are small and pointy, his snout pert, and his body more proportional to his legs. His markings are similar to Jasper's, but the whites are whiter, the blacks blacker, the browns softer.

"Jasper," Jane says, scaring herself when her voice comes out in a shriek.

"My real name is Steen," the dog says to Jane, somehow conveying even the spelling to her, *S-T-E-E-N*, and causing her to fall backward onto the floor in utter confusion.

"I'm losing my mind!" Jane says to the ceiling, shaking her head from side to side.

"Not your mind," he says, trotting around to her head. "Your narrow and fragile conception of the world. Oh, I'm so happy to have found you!" he says, hopping and jumping like a puppy experiencing snow for the first time.

"Dogs don't talk," Jane says to the ceiling.

"I'm not actually talking!" he says. "Pay more attention. You're understanding me with your mind, not your ears."

"What?" Jane says. "Do it again."

I'm communing with your mind, he says. His mouth doesn't move. No sounds come out of him.

"I guess that makes sense," Jane says, then hears herself, and despairs of her reason.

We need to move out of this room, Jasper says, *before someone in Tu Reviens notices a difference in the painting.*

"What?" Jane says in her shrieky voice.

We need to move, Jasper says. *Look. There's someone coming.*

And indeed, the hanging on the wall has changed again; not only has the basset hound disappeared, but there's now a dark-haired person in a blue sweater, standing on the landing across the receiving hall, holding a small black box. It looks an awful lot like Ivy, with her camera.

"Ivy!" cries Jane.

Shh! She'll hear you! Jasper says.

"Good! She can rescue me!"

Shhhhhh! She'll see us in the painting if she bothers to look. Move. And stop thinking of me as Jasper! My name is Steen.

"Help!"

I'm going to bite you if you don't move.

"Go ahead! None of this is real!"

Jasper takes her earlobe between his teeth, chomps down hard, and tugs in the direction of the doorway. The pain is real, and excruciating.

"Ow! Jasper!" Jane cries out, pushing him away and scrambling to her feet. She runs—past the umbrella, through the doorway, into another room, a dark room, where she crouches against a wall, shaking and weeping. Her ear is bleeding and hurts terribly. Would her ear be bleeding if this weren't real?

Jasper comes beside her and leans against her. He's warm and steady. Her arm goes around him. *I know you're inconsolable right now,* he tells her. *But I want you to know that I do know how you feel. The first time I went through the hanging from my world into your world, I felt the same way. And I was very young, and there was no one I could talk to. I had no idea where I was. I'm sorry about your ear. Are you okay?*

She pulls him into her lap and grips the silky fur at his neck, petting it hard. "Is this real?" she whispers.

Yes, he says, snuggling against her happily.

"Can I go back?"

Anytime, he says, *through the hanging. But only do it when no one's in sight.*

"Where are we?"

The land I come from, he says. *It's called Zorsted.*

Jane understands the spelling of that one too, pronounced ZOR-sted.

We don't actually have the same letters as you, he adds. *I'm transliterating.*

"You can spell?" Jane says in her shrieky voice.

Is that so surprising, considering I can also commune with your mind?

"Dogs can't spell," Jane says weakly.

I'm not a dog. I'm a strayhound. I'm an excellent speller. I was first in my class, he says, *what you would call the valedictorian. We don't have to go anywhere today. We can sit here until you feel strong enough to go back through the hanging. You can think things over and not come back here until you're ready.*

"Ready for what?" Jane says. "Why are we here?"

I'm here because Zorsted is my homeland, he says. *I brought you here because you're my person.*

"Your person?"

Every strayhound can commune with one person, he says. *Some never find their person. I thought I never would. Then you came along. I knew you right away, even in your Other Land form. I could barely believe it. My person, in the Other Land! Did you recognize me?*

"Recognize you as *what*? I've never heard of a—*strayhound*. I don't recognize you now!"

You're still in shock, he says. *I'm going to stop asking you questions.*

He curls into a tight ball and snuggles deeper in her lap. Jane closes her eyes, leans back against the wall, and tries to stop her spinning mind.

When she opens her eyes sometime later, she's still in Zorsted with a strayhound in her lap, but now she's come to a conclusion: Either this *is* real, or she's having hallucinations. And if she's having hallucinations, she might as well collect more information to bring back to her doctor, Doctor Gordon, who always asks for details.

She tries the name out cautiously. "Steen?"

Yes! he says. *Very good.*

"I'd like to go back," Jane says. "But first, I'd like a small peek."

At Zorsted?

"Yes. At Zorsted."

All right, he says. *Let's find a window.*

"Are we in someone's house?"

We're in the servants' quarters of the duchess's mansion. The duchess takes in strayhounds who haven't found their person, he explains. *Come along,* he says, leading Jane to a different doorway from the one she came through. The room they pass into is also dimly lit, by candles.

"Is there electricity in Zorsted?"

Not the way you understand it, but there's something else, which you might perceive to be . . . legerdemain. Conjury. Wizardry.

"Wizardry?"

Magic, says Steen. *Those candles won't go out for a very long time.*

"Are we going to meet wizards? Like, with wands? *Like in Harry Potter?*"

It's not like that, he says soothingly, *and anyway, we're not going far.*

"Okay," says Jane, flustered. "Is it night right now?"

Yes, says Steen, *the sun has just set. That's why that bell rang, did you hear it?*

"Bell?"

When we were in Tu Reviens and you were deciding whether to go with Kiran or not. Remember? A bell rang?

"I thought it was wind chimes."

Yes, that's what Tu Reviens people tend to think, because there are wind chimes in the east spire. They ring bells here in Zorsted, at sunrise and sunset. But these rooms are often dark. The duchess's spy network operates from the servants' quarters, which is where we are. These particular rooms are unknown to most people. They're used for secret meetings.

"Spy network! What if someone sees me?"

I'll bite them while you make a run for it, he says.

"Seriously? That's your plan?"

Well, you don't need to be making all that noise, he says. *Stop talking. I'll understand you even if you think your thoughts at me.*

This is too much. "Are you telling me that you can read my *mind?*"

Only the things you mean to tell me.

"How can I know that's true?"

Steen doesn't answer. Then he says in a small, dejected voice, *Because I told you so. You're my person. I'm not going to lie to you, especially not on the same day I finally get to commune with you.* He starts making wet, slurpy noises.

"Are you crying?" she asks.

I'm extremely sensitive, he says. *It's just how I am. And this has been an overwhelming day.*

"I'm—sorry," Jane says in utter confusion. "Jasper, I'm sorry. I didn't mean to make you upset. There's just a lot to take in, you know?"

You're the only person in Zorsted for me. You're the only person in either land, Steen says. *We were meant for each other, don't you see?*

"But Jasper, don't *you* see? It's like I discovered my long-lost twin, except I never even knew I was missing a twin, plus he's clairvoyant and always wants to sit in my lap! I'm sorry, Jasper—Steen," Jane says hurriedly, worried she's making things worse. "It's just—" She stops when Steen starts to make a snorting noise. "Are you *laughing*?"

It is a little funny, he says.

Jane gives up. There's a window in this room, hidden behind heavy curtains. She pushes the fabric aside. What she sees stuns her into silence.

It's a dark city lit with pinpricks of flame, set against the backdrop of a vast purple sky. She's high above the landscape; she looks across roofs and through windows into rooms lit with candles. She looks down thoroughfares, lit by street lanterns, that end abruptly at a darkness that puzzles her, until she sees water moving with the flashes of stars. This is a city on the shore of a great sea.

Reflected on the water are two enormous round moons.

"Two moons," Jane says. "Two moons! Reflected like that, it's four moons!"

Yes, says Steen. *What's the Other Land expression?*

"For what? Multiple moons?"

We're not in Kansas anymore, says Steen.

A strange instrument is playing wisps of music, somewhere so distant that Jane can barely hear it. It sounds like a piccolo, but even higher. Then laughter rings out, faint and far away.

"Jasper?" Jane says, overwhelmed by the moons, but comforted by the way he's pressing himself against her feet. "I mean, Steen? Should I pick you up? Do you want to see the view?"

No, he says. *I just want to look at you.*

"Oh, don't be such a dip," Jane says. "You've seen plenty of me."

Ahem-hem, he says. *You know how when I stepped through the hanging into Zorsted, I became a different dog?*

"Yes."

Well, he says. *You know what, never mind, it's a lot to absorb, we'll talk later, yes, please, pick me up so I can see out the window.*

Jane has been standing with her face pressed to the glass. Now, looking down at Steen, puzzled by his sudden evasion, an impossible thought touches her. Backing away from the window so that she can see the reflection, she looks into her own face. Someone else's face looks back at her.

Jane can't get herself through the hanging into Tu Reviens fast enough. She's so desperate that she's careless about it and bursts onto the landing without checking to see if anyone's there who might witness her appearance. There is, in fact, a man on one of the bridges, the cleaner who interrupted breakfast because he was lost. He's washing the banisters, wringing a cloth out repeatedly into a bucket of water. Luckily, he's mostly turned away from her.

Steen—Jasper?—is more circumspect. He waits until the man has completely turned his back, then steps out of the painting, a basset hound again.

Jane has collapsed onto the landing. She sits next to the painting with her back to the wall and legs spread out before her in a V. Jasper—Steen?—takes the long route around her legs, then nudges her thigh with his nose, gently, in a gesture clearly meant to encourage her to get up and step back into the painting.

"No," she whispers. "Forget it. Never again."

He burrows his head under her arm and rests his chin on her lap. A moment later, apparently deciding that's not good enough, he climbs over her leg and rests his chin on the other side of her lap, then, when perhaps that strikes him as no improvement, he tries to perch himself lengthwise on top of one of her legs. Basset hounds are ridiculous. She crisscrosses her legs to give him more room and he manages to nestle awkwardly on top of her lap. Laying his head on her arm, he stares up at her fondly. He weighs a ton.

With tears rising to her eyes, she pets the short hair on the back of his head, gently. Then she strokes his long ears. His basset hound ears are much longer than his strayhound ears.

She both wants his comfort and doesn't want it. She wants his dog comfort; she doesn't want his strayhound comfort. "Can we communicate with our minds on this side of the painting?" she whispers to him.

Jasper shakes his head.

That, at least, is relieving. Closing her eyes again, Jane sits there for a long time.

Soothing noises surround her: the man wringing his cloth out into his bucket. The voices of Lucy and Phoebe below, moving across the receiving hall. The sucking of air when gala people open and close the doors. Sometime later, the voice of Colin, speaking to someone who's not answering—probably Kiran. Jane breathes slowly and pretends her lungs are a jellyfish. She is as vast and deep and heavy as the sea.

Then a new sound: the distinctive shutter slide and clap of Ivy's digital camera. Opening her eyes, Jane finds Ivy on the opposite landing, seeming to take a picture of the cleaner with the bucket. She remembers, not much caring, that Ivy's been lying to her about something, or at any rate, been evasive; that Patrick and Philip and Phoebe were up to something sneaky last night. That Grace Panzavecchia might be in the house.

Across the landing, Ivy watches Jane curiously. "Hi again," she says. When Jane is unable to stretch her face into anything pleasant or friendly, Ivy's own face goes guarded, almost a little hurt. Then, as she continues to watch Jane, she begins to look concerned.

"Hey, are you all right?" she asks, walking across the bridge toward Jane.

No, Jane thinks. *I stepped into a painting and turned into someone else.* "Take a picture of me?"

Ivy pauses, surprised by this, then brings her camera to her face and clicks. Then she comes to Jane's landing and crouches beside her, pressing a few buttons and handing Jane the camera so she can see her own image on the screen. It's nicely framed. Jasper is adorable in her lap. And the person in the picture looks just exactly like Jane: Jane's facial features, her hair, her clothing, her body, and an expression of distress on her face that mirrors exactly how Jane feels. *That's me. That's me. Right, Aunt Magnolia?* Jane resists the urge to touch her own face for further confirmation.

"Thanks," Jane says.

"You're welcome," Ivy says. "You seem . . . upset. Did something happen?"

Did something happen? Laughter rises into Jane's throat, bursts out of her mouth. Ivy tilts her head, puzzled. There's nothing Jane would rather do than tell Ivy all about it. She'd like to send Ivy through the painting to *show* her, as long as she doesn't have to go in again herself. "Yes," Jane says, then swallows. "Something happened. I want to tell you what it is, but I don't think I can just now. I'm sorry."

Ivy seems unfazed by this. She's comfortable, crouched beside Jane, her arms resting on her knees and her camera perched in one hand. "It's funny you say that," she says, "because there are things I'd like to tell you too."

Footsteps sound very close. Coming from the direction of the east wing, Mrs. Vanders appears on the landing, then stops short.

"This is not a convenient assembly point," she says. "Especially on the day before a gala."

"I'm just leaving," Jane says, despite not having any intention of ever going anywhere again.

Mrs. Vanders grunts. "Have neither of you located Ravi?"

Right. Jane remembers that once, long ago, in a time before Zorsted, Mrs. Vanders was looking for Ravi, because of something somehow related to a Vermeer painting. It doesn't matter now, at all. "I saw him," Jane says. "With fruit and toast. He went up to the third floor to visit someone."

Mrs. Vanders grunts again. She's begun to peer at Jane suspiciously. "What's wrong with you, girl?"

Jane remembers she's got some questions for Mrs. Vanders about Aunt Magnolia. She was shocked to learn that Mrs. Vanders knew Aunt Magnolia. Since then, Jane's threshold for what qualifies as shocking has risen. Opening her mouth to form some sort of Aunt Magnolia–ish question, Jane discovers that Mrs. Vanders, who's apparently not a woman blessed with patience, has grunted yet again and marched on down the stairs. "Ivy," the housekeeper calls sharply over her shoulder, "I expect Cook could use an extra hand or two today, if you're quite done with your camera."

Ivy doesn't move. "Maybe we can talk later," she says to Jane.

"I'd like that," Jane says, "very much."

"Are you going to be okay?"

One of her legs is falling asleep under Jasper's weight. "Yeah," she lies, shifting him incrementally.

"It's good you've got the basset for company," Ivy says. "Jasper's never been so obsessed with anyone." She makes a move to stand up.

"Take my hand?" Jane says.

For the merest, surprised second, Ivy hesitates. Then she reaches out and takes Jane's hand. Her hand is warm, strong. She holds Jane's tightly.

"Thanks," Jane says.

"You're welcome."

Somewhere in the house, Mrs. Vanders shouts Ivy's name.

"Sorry," says Ivy with a sigh.

"It's okay. Go ahead," says Jane.

So Ivy lets Jane go and turns away, leaving behind a faint whiff of chlorine. Closing her eyes again, Jane can't stop seeing that *wrong* face that looked back at her in the window reflection.

Suddenly Jane is clambering to her feet while Jasper yelps and trips and fights for his footing. He fixes Jane with an indignant expression.

"Sorry!" she says, already on her way up the stairs. "Sorry, Jasper! But I need a mirror."

The thing that upset Jane about the face in the Zorsted window reflection wasn't that it was a terrible, ugly face, because it wasn't. If someone walked through the door of Tu Reviens wearing that face, Jane would think, *Wow, that person has an interesting face. I can't begin to guess what part of our Earth that person gets her genes from.* But she wouldn't be bothered.

The thing was, Jane could feel herself underneath that unfamiliar face. She had looked out of her *own* eyes, into those unfamiliar eyes. This is more disturbing than she ever would have anticipated. It's as if a total stranger broke in and stole her insides.

In her gold-tiled bathroom, Jane stands before the mirror above the sink, Jasper at her feet.

When it comes down to it, there's little to see: just the old, familiar Jane. *I take my face for granted,* she thinks, noticing, remembering, that she shares Aunt Magnolia's cheekbones, her nose. She runs a gentle finger along them. If Aunt Magnolia saw Jane wearing that other face, would she even recognize her? If the people who love you can't recognize you, *are* you you?

Jasper follows her into the morning room. The brown-and-gold self-defense umbrella she's been working on holds no interest for her now. How can she defend herself against herself?

Jasper is quiet beside Jane as she stands in the middle of the room, surrounded by her creations. He seems determined not to desert her today. She wonders if maybe it's making her claustrophobic. Would it hurt his feelings if she asked him for some time to herself?

"Jasper," she says, then realizes, when he twists his neck up to look at her with an eager expression, that she doesn't want him to go. He's the only one who gets what she's going through.

Jane makes a frustrated noise. "You recognized me as your person the day I arrived at Tu Reviens, looking like this," she says. "Right?"

Solemnly, he nods.

"Did you recognize me as your person in the other form too?" Jane asks. "Once we were inside the painting? Did I look . . . *right* to you?"

Again, he nods.

Jasper, at least, knows who she is.

A bubble of laughter rises into her throat. Once she starts laughing, a growing hysteria propels her to continue laughing, finally so hard that tears stream down her face. Jasper watches her with his front paws held primly together and his head cocked quizzically. She doesn't speak it aloud for fear of hurting his feelings, and she hopes he can't read her thoughts: that she will allow her shaky sense of self to be held together by the faith of a dog.

"Except," Jane says, wiping tears from her face, "you're not a dog, are you, Jasper? You're a Zorsteddan strayhound."

She drops to her knees. Jasper rests his head on her thigh.

"You're *my* Zorsteddan strayhound," Jane says with wonderment, "whatever that means. And I'm your person."

Jasper sighs happily.

After a few minutes of scratching him behind the ears, Jane rises and begins to search her fabrics for reds and greens that match the umbrella that sits on the floor inside the painting. She wants to work. And this is the only umbrella design she feels capable of focusing on.

Work helps.

The umbrella inside the painting, Jane recalls, has six ribs, rather than the standard eight, and the ribs are straight, rather than curved. She's never built an umbrella like that; she'll have to figure out how. Color is also a challenge. She wishes she could reach for the umbrella in the painting, pull it out, bring it up here, and see how the colors look in this light, but she expects there would be an outcry in the house if someone noticed that the painting had lost its umbrella. They would assume—quite rationally—that it was an art heist; that someone had stolen the original painting and replaced it with a sloppy, unconvincing forgery. People would start poking at the painting and falling through, the FBI would come, it would be like a real-life version of *The X-Files,* and Zorsted would be swarming with confused, disoriented, gun-toting invaders.

"Where did the painting come from?" Jane asks Jasper.

He's lying on the floor. At the question, he lowers his chin to his crossed paws. It doesn't feel like a yes or a no. Jane gets the sense that this is his way of saying he doesn't know.

"Does anyone else in the house know it's possible to enter the painting?"

He shakes his head.

"Why not? How has no one ever discovered it?"

Jasper's head pops up at this, then he labors to his feet and runs into her bedroom. Jane hears him whimpering. When she pokes her head in after him, he's at her bedroom door, looking at her over his shoulder and whining.

"You know the answer," Jane says, "but you can't tell me unless we're inside the painting, where you can talk?"

He nods.

"No way," she says firmly.

Jasper stomps his two front feet, as if he's kneading bread dough, but madder. With a grim shake of the head, Jane returns to her work, because it's not happening. After a moment, he rejoins her in the morning room.

"Something else," Jane says. "You're from Zorsted, right? You were born there? It's home? And I was born here?"

He nods. He's plopped himself on the floor again, this time with his chin propped on one paw.

"How can I be your person if we're not even from the same side of the painting? How can you be my strayhound if people where I'm from don't have strayhounds?"

He whines again, looking at the doorway. That question will have to wait.

"Does anyone else in this house know that you understand human speech?" Jane asks.

He shakes his head.

"Does anyone else in Zorsted know it's possible to step through the hanging into Tu Reviens?"

He pauses, then thumps his tail on the floor once.

"One other person in Zorsted knows?"

A vigorous nod of the head.

Jane has an alarming thought. "Is someone in this house actually Zorsteddan?!"

Jasper shakes his head. This is a relief. She doesn't like to imagine the people around her being so dramatically different from what they pretend.

Returning to her worktable, Jane slices fabric and sews gores together, breathing through the work of her hands. After a moment, she notices the carvings on the table: whales and sharks, peacefully swimming. Ivy made this table, then. She traces a shark baby with her finger, breathing. Then she gets back to work.

She's just thinking it's time to take a break when the shouting begins. It's coming from some distant part of the house, far enough away that it takes a moment for her to be certain it's a person noise rather than a house noise.

"What's that about?" Jane asks Jasper as she examines her six-part canopy.

He looks back at her evenly. Jane susses that he knows but can't tell her.

"Is it about us," Jane asks, "or anything to do with Zorsted?"

He shakes his head.

"Okay," Jane says. "Then I don't really care. But how are you doing? Don't dogs need to go outside now and then? Want to go stretch our legs?"

He jumps up and runs for the door.

As they walk down the corridor together, the volume of the yelling increases, sounding like it's coming from the house's center. It's Ravi's voice.

By the time Jane and Jasper reach the stairs, Ravi's yelling has become sufficiently interesting that Jane can't help her curiosity. She descends one level and walks onto the second-story bridge. Jasper follows.

In the receiving hall below, Ravi is having a temper tantrum while Mrs. Vanders tries to calm him down with words like *proper authorities* and *in due time*. Practically the entire household is standing in the room with them. The stairs and bridges are lined with gala staff. Lucy St. George hugs a small wooden pedestal with a mirrored top to her chest, looking ill. Jane gathers from the hullabaloo that the sculpture of a fish has been stolen. She remembers Ravi asking Octavian about it last night in the courtyard, some Brancusi sculpture that was missing.

Whatever. Jasper seems to be crossing the bridge to the west side of the house. "Jasper," Jane whispers, skipping to catch up, "why aren't we going downstairs? What do you do, pee off the balcony into the courtyard?"

The look Jasper shoots her could burn a hole into another dimension. When he leads her into the west wing, she's puzzled enough that she steels herself, just in case he's about to run at her again and topple her through some other piece of art into some other realm he hasn't told her about. Instead, he continues down the hall. She follows until a photograph hanging about halfway down the corridor stuns her. She stops in her tracks.

It's one of Aunt Magnolia's most famous photographs, enlarged and framed. A tiny yellow fish, a goby, peeks out of the open mouth of a huge gray fish with a bulbous nose. Jane remembers when Aunt Magnolia came back from Japan with this photograph, and how amazed she'd been at her own serendipity. The little fish had darted into the mouth of the big fish, then out again, all in the space of a couple of seconds, yet somehow Aunt Magnolia had managed to immortalize it.

Jane can't catch her breath. *This* is why Mrs. Vanders knew her aunt: Mrs. Vanders respects art. It makes her chest hurt that one of Aunt Magnolia's photos should hang in a house containing Rembrandts and Vermeers. She moves closer to the photograph until her nose is almost touching it and she can see her reflection in the glass. *Aunt Magnolia,* Jane thinks. *The things I could tell you about. Would you even believe it?*

She'll have to remember, next time she sees Mrs. Vanders, to tell her that the photograph needs to be reframed. Now that she's looking super close, she can see a faint rectangular bulge behind the photo, as if it's been badly matted. Aunt Magnolia's work should not be carelessly framed.

Jasper is gazing up at Jane with a calm question in his face.

"Walk?" she says to him.

He continues along the corridor toward the door at the end. Jane follows.

He's brought her to the freight elevator.

"Of course," Jane says, pressing the call button. "Because steps are hard for a basset hound. I wonder why you turn into a basset, instead of a Lab or a husky or something."

Jasper—unable to answer, of course—walks into the elevator, which has another set of doors at its back. When they reach the ground floor, both sets of doors open, one to a landing inside the house, the other to sunlight, shadow, and gusts of wind.

Jasper shoots out into the sun.

Jane holds a hand up against the brightness. The sound of the sea, crashing on rocks far below, startles her; she'd practically forgotten where this house is. She follows him around some scratchy, unkempt shrubberies, onto grassy ground.

Jasper seems shy about peeing. Every time she glances at him, he slams his leg down and runs off behind a shrubbery or hillock of grass to try again where she can't see him. Finally, he sprints toward the northwest corner of the house, stops, glares at her, then disappears around the corner. Jane supposes she'd rather not do her business in his sight, either, given how the relationship has progressed. She stands in place, tactfully waiting, until he reappears, gives her another inexplicable look, then sets off again toward the yard in a high-stepping, carefree manner.

Mr. Vanders is on his knees in the gardens, applying a trowel to the dirt with graceful movements. The terrain nearest the house is riddled with holes so large, she's surprised Jasper doesn't disappear into one altogether. Jasper pushes toward a patch of scrub pines. She crosses the lawn with him.

Once in the trees, Jasper leads her down a steep incline. She follows, sliding on dirt and stones and dead leaves, swearing under her breath about the unfair advantages of four-legged creatures. When she finally lands on what appears to be solid ground, she finds he's brought her to a tiny inlet, shaped like a crescent moon, with smooth, dark sand. A crooked wooden post juts out of the water. Jane wonders if small boats are sometimes moored here, like the one Ivy built with her brother.

The wind is strong, and chilly; Jane shivers. Seeing this, Jasper trots to an outcropping of stone and shrubbery that serves as a wind break. He drops down, whining for her to join him. Jane sits beside him.

Something about wind, water, sand, and Jasper's kindness propels Jane to pull him closer so she can scritch his neck. His tongue hangs out in what seems like classic canine happiness. It's very peculiar in someone she's been having intelligent conversations with all day. It's also extremely cute.

She speaks one more overwhelming question out loud.

"How do you know I'm from this world, Jasper? How do you know I'm not from yours?"

He tilts his head thoughtfully.

"You can't say?" Jane says.

Jasper nods. Then he raises his quivering nose to the air and howls, quiet and melodious, at the sky.

They sit together, watching the water, for a long time.

Later, as they cross the lawn again to the house, Jane sees that Mrs. Vanders has joined her husband. She's kneeling beside him, muttering grimly into his ear. He nods, frowning, then sneezes. The wind blows bits of her conversation across the grass to Jane. "Of all the days to [incomprehensible]" and "You know I can't bring it to his attention now, with [incomprehensible]" and "I'd like to wring the neck of whoever dared [incomprehensible]."

Jane has no idea what this is about—the Brancusi sculpture? Philip and the gun? Grace Panzavecchia? But on the chance that she's the one who dared, she approaches warily.

"You," Mrs. Vanders says, breaking off her muttering and turning her eyes on Jane.

"Yes," Jane says. "Hi there. How is everything?"

"Ha," says Mrs. Vanders. "Wonderful. Fabulous. Grand."

"Okay," Jane says doubtfully.

"My husband tells me you have a question for me," says Mrs. Vanders.

"I do?" Jane says, confused. "Oh, right. Okay. That painting on the second-story landing, the tall one with an umbrella. Where did it come from?"

"Where did the umbrella painting come from?" says Mrs. Vanders, incredulous. "That's your question? It was painted by a friend of the first Octavian Thrash, Horst Mallow, over a hundred years ago. An average talent and a very odd man. Octavian asked him for a painting of underwater creatures seeking solace in a forest of anemones, and instead, Mallow painted an umbrella in a room. Then Mallow disappeared. Vanished!" she says. "Vamoosed!"

"Eight letters," Jane says wearily, "with a *v*."

"What?"

"Never mind."

"Is that all you wanted to ask me?" says Mrs. Vanders. "I thought you were curious about your aunt!"

"Oh, right," Jane says, remembering. "Of course. I *am* curious about my aunt. You knew her?"

Mrs. Vanders fixes Jane with those unreadable eyes. "Were you aware, before today, that I knew your aunt?"

"No, but I just saw her photo on your wall."

"Were you aware," says Mrs. Vanders, "that she came, on occasion, to the galas at this house?"

Jane blinks. "When did that happen? Who invited her? And why?"

"She would come to a gala," Mrs. Vanders says, "then take off from here on one of her trips."

"No," Jane says. "That can't be. She always told me her itineraries. She never said anything about island galas."

"I'm sure she had her reasons," says Mrs. Vanders.

"She would've told me," Jane repeats, sure of it. The glamor of a fancy dress ball in a house like this, of imagining Aunt Magnolia taking part in such an event, would have enthralled and comforted Jane, especially in the times when her aunt was gone. And Jane is quite certain Aunt Magnolia would have told her about visiting a house as strange as Tu Reviens.

Though, she supposes Aunt Magnolia *did*, in fact, tell her about Tu Reviens. Aunt Magnolia made her promise never, ever to decline an invitation here.

"I'll tell you more about your aunt after the gala," says Mrs. Vanders gruffly, then picks up a trowel and begins whacking at the ground.

"I'd rather hear it now," Jane says.

Mrs. Vanders ignores her, doesn't even look at her. It's a clear dismissal. In the meantime, Jasper moves on, high-stepping through the grass, looking back at Jane over his shoulder.

Fine, she thinks. She'll return to her umbrella-making. It's okay, really. Zorsted is enough to think about.

When, early that night, Jane gets ready for bed, Jasper seems a little droopier than usual. She tries to focus on buttoning her *Doctor Who* pajamas rather than on his disappointment. She wants to tell him, *There's no point in crossing through the painting now anyway, because it's night in Zorsted,* but she can't even make herself ask him if that's true.

Has she really spent the entire day discussing complex topics with a basset hound who understands English?

Which is more likely, a psychotic break with lingering hallucinations, or Zorsted inside a painting?

A person who's hallucinating needs her sleep, Jane wants to say to Jasper, but doesn't, because her very desire to make excuses to him is the proof that she's hallucinating.

The house wakes her from a dream in which Mrs. Vanders is trying to shove children into the mouth of an enormous fish sculpture in order to keep them safe, but it's not working, because she can't figure out which end of the fish is the tail and which is the mouth.

The clock on her bedside table reads 5:08. The house is yelling something, except that houses don't yell, so the yelling must be part of the dream too. Regardless, she's awake now. She gets up and drags herself into the morning room, where she stares groggily out the window.

Jasper joins her, leaning against her leg. It's not yet dawn and there are two figures crossing the lawn, heading to the forest. The moon is visible. A single moon. In Jane's world, there is only one moon.

Aunt Magnolia made her promise to come here if invited. Fearless Aunt Magnolia, who always traveled to new places, who dropped herself into the water, and explored unknown worlds.

Aunt Magnolia? I'm scared.

But I don't want to disappoint you.

"Jasper?" Jane says. "Steen?"

Tiny moons shine in the eager eyes he raises to her.

"Can a person wear *Doctor Who* pajamas into Zorsted?"

* * *

Someone in some distant part of the house is listening to Beatles music as Jasper and Jane step into the painting. If she focuses on it, Jane can hear the faraway, surreal strains of "You've Got to Hide Your Love Away."

She's still in her *Doctor Who* pajamas because Jasper considers her other clothing no less conspicuous. Inside the duchess's house, he leads her to a nearby room with a wardrobe that contains a large quantity of plain, dark clothing in many sizes.

Her Zorsteddan body is shaped differently from her real-world body. Her pajamas fit oddly, tighter in the shoulders and too long below. And her hands, the more she thinks about it, feel large and swollen, and her Zorsteddan legs and feet feel . . . bouncy. As if perhaps she's likely to be able to jump higher in this body.

"Which clothes should I choose?" she whispers, trying not to think about it, then noticing that the timbre of her voice is slightly different too.

Whatever you like, he says. *Though you'll draw the least attention in a tunic, loose pants, and cloak. It's early autumn,* he says, *and still dark out. Zorsted has a colder climate than the one you're used to. The sun will rise in a few*—he says a strange word—*but we may be walking near the sea, where it's windy. Choose sturdy boots and consider a scarf for your head.* Steen is trying to contain his happiness, but he's practically prancing around her, his toenails clapping on the tile floor as he zooms back and forth excitedly.

"Steen," she says. "You're making me dizzy."

Sorry! he says, stopping in place, but still hopping. *Sorry!*

Once Jane has pulled them on, the pants are comfortable and warm. "I understand that word you said about when the sun'll rise," she says, repeating the strange word aloud. "It's a unit of time, more like minutes than like hours. I've never heard the word before, though."

We speak a different language in Zorsted, he says. *And our days and nights are longer, and we measure our time in different units.*

Her hands pause in their rapid perusal of tunics. "Steen! How will I ever pass as Zorsteddan if I can't speak the language?"

You're speaking it right now, he says.

"What?"

You're speaking it perfectly, he says. *You have been since the first moment you stepped through the painting.*

This is a dizzying piece of information. *Boots,* Jane thinks, focusing on something concrete. *I'll try on boots instead.* But as she does so, she repeats to herself, silently, the words she's been speaking aloud. They are not English words. And the words she's thinking *in* aren't English words, either. These tall, sturdy foot-coverings are not *boots. English* is suddenly the only English word she can remember.

In time, Steen says to her gently, *you'll be able to access both languages in both places. Until then, you'll always have the one you need. That's how it was for me. I expect you'll find you can even read our letters.*

"But how can I know a language I've never learned?"

I don't know, he says. *It's one of the mysteries.*

Dressed in her Zorsteddan clothing, Jane crouches on the floor of a dimly lit Zorsteddan room, her arms wrapped tightly around her legs. Across the room is a wide, full-length mirror. There's just enough light in this room for her to see the angular cheekbones, the pointy chin of the face that feels like a betrayal.

Steen props his paw on her knee and licks her strange face. It pulls Jane out of herself.

"Ick," she says, wiping away his spit. "I'll have you know that I'm not a fan of being licked by Zorsteddan strayhounds."

Let's go, he says. *The sun is rising.*

The duchess's mansion is extensive and has a great many stairs. Steen's strayhound legs are much longer than his basset legs and he scrambles down them easily.

As Jane approaches what must be the seventh staircase leading down, she hears herself speaking a Zorsteddan expletive. "How many stories does the duchess's mansion have?"

Fifteen, says Steen. *Zorsteddans build tall.*

"Tall and elegant," Jane says, for the stairways and occasional halls through which they move are simple and graceful, composed of a white stone that doesn't shine like polished marble, but rather, seems to catch the light gently and hold it softly, like the inside of a shell. "Is there— magic in the walls?"

I guess it depends on what you mean by magic. The mansion responds to the sun, and partially lights itself. But so do all stone buildings in Zorsted.

Through glass windows in a stairway Jane catches glimpses of a pinkening sky, flashes of a silver sea. Distantly, that sweet bell starts ringing, the one that means the sun is rising.

"How do you know I'm not from here?" Jane asks again. "How do you know I'm not Zorsteddan?"

I just know, he says, trotting beside her. *The same way I knew you were my person.*

"But, how did you know that?"

I recognized your soul.

"Oh, please."

I did! says Steen. *I can see your soul! But you're not from here. You are from the Other Land.*

"Then *why* am I your person?"

I don't know, he says. *Many Zorsteddan strayhounds never find their person. Maybe it's because their person is in the Other Land.*

"Can you commune with other people besides me?"

No, he says. *Only you, because you're my person. But I can commune with other strayhounds.*

"Why has no one else in Tu Reviens ever discovered it's possible to step into the painting? Surely in a hundred-some years, someone would've"—Jane gestures vaguely—"stuck an elbow in by accident, or something."

Not everyone can get through, Steen says.

She almost misses a step. "Really!"

I saw Mrs. Vanders touch it once, Steen says. *Nothing. And Colin Mack has had his hands all over it.*

"Really?"

Colin touches all the paintings, Steen says smugly. *There's a lot about the house that I could tell you.*

"But why me and not them?"

I'm not sure, Steen says, *but I have theories. I've wondered if it might only be open to seekers.*

"Seekers?" Jane says, wondering what she's seeking.

Or maybe just artists.

"Really?" Jane says. "Artists!"

I've watched Zorsteddan people touch the hanging on this side too, and find it to be just like any other hanging, he says. *But never anyone I know to be an artist or a seeker.*

"Are you an artist or a seeker, Steen?"

I'm a strayhound, he says simply.

"Can all strayhounds get through?"

I don't know. I've never told anyone about it. Tu Reviens is my house, he says, with a possessiveness that Jane finds endearingly doglike, but also pretty human.

"Hasn't anyone in Tu Reviens ever seen the painting changing?" she asks. "Like when we could see Ivy in the hanging from the Zorsted side? Doesn't anyone Zorsteddan come looking for their red-and-green umbrella?"

It's a painting of an unused corner in a dimly lit room, Steen says, *in the part of the duchess's mansion used by her spy network, as you know. The* umbrella *was placed in that corner ages ago to serve as a sign to Zorsteddan spies that they've come to the right place. It's never been moved in over a hundred years.*

"Hm," says Jane. "And I guess if the umbrella painting briefly changed, then went back to normal, you'd assume you were just seeing things. You'd doubt your own eyes."

Yes. And as for any changes in the hanging on the Zorsted side, Steen adds, then pauses. *Again, it's a dimly lit room. But also, a hanging with a scene that changes wouldn't be considered so remarkable in Zorsted.*

"I see," Jane says. Their descent has finally brought them to a long, enclosed corridor with a series of doors. Steen leads her to a wooden door that's larger and more sturdy-looking than the others.

"Who made the Zorsteddan hanging?" Jane asks.

An artist named Morstlow, says Steen. *And it sounds like he did so around the time your Horst Mallow was painting, if Mrs. Vanders is correct.*

A lamp on the wall by the door gutters. Yellow light dances across Steen's fur.

"Did this Morstlow also have a reputation for being eccentric? Like Horst Mallow? The names are awfully similar."

The Zorsteddan attitude toward . . . people who see things differently *is not the same as the Other Land attitude,* he says. *I don't think Morstlow had any particular reputation.*

"Is he the one person you told me about?" Jane says. "The one person in Zorsted who knows about the passage into Tu Reviens?"

No, says Steen. *Morstlow's been dead a long time. I have no idea what he knew.*

"Who is the person, then? Is it the duchess?"

It's not the duchess.

"Then who?"

Steen's neck is craned back so that he can look into Jane's face. She can feel him begin words, touch her mind with the edges of words, then pull them back. It tickles oddly, like a feather in her brain. She recognizes this as the feeling of his indecision.

He breaks eye contact, turning to the door. *This door leads to the outside,* he tells her. *Don't be scared; you look just like everyone else. Are you ready?*

There's a distinct feeling to being up and about at dawn. This is one of the first things Jane notices: Zorsted feels surprisingly as other places feel at dawn. People communicate not in words but in glances. A number of people on the streets, opening the doors of shops, leading recalcitrant horses, or simply standing in windows, look pleasantly into Jane's face and say nothing.

Jane tries not to stare. She stays close to Steen, who trots along with his head held high.

The buildings, tall, with steep roofs, are wooden and shingled, the streets made of paving stones. No matter where Steen leads her, she can always see a few stone towers, rose-colored against a gray-pink sky; and always, between buildings, the sea.

Slowly, that magnificent pink wash fades and Jane sees the true colors of the towers: whites and grays and browns. They glow slightly.

"Do the wooden houses respond to the sun and glow too?"

To some extent, says Steen, *but not like stone. Stone is older. It contains more power.*

"Do all stone things create light? Would you want that to happen with a stone chair, or a bowl, or a tomb?"

The dead of Zorsted are buried at sea, not in tombs, says Steen. *But regardless, the stone has an intelligence. It generally won't light an unpopulated room, and it knows what it's being used for. It knows if it's been made into a thing that shouldn't glow.*

"What do you mean? How can it know?"

There's a consciousness to the world here.

"To the *stone?*"

To everything, Janie, Steen says simply. *The earth, the ground, the clouds.*

"The *clouds?*"

Not an extreme consciousness. Consciousness might be too strong a word, really. But things have awareness.

Jane thinks this through. "But—if the stone has awareness, is it wise to cut into it? Like, to make bricks?"

The wise builder is careful, Steen says, *and respectful.*

"Or?"

Or the stone is unhappy, says Steen. *And then the building is unhappy, and everyone can feel it.*

"And then what happens?"

Nothing happens, says Steen. *That's all.*

"The building doesn't do anything? Like, drop rocks on people or something?"

No! says Steen. *It's nothing like that. It's more like, you might find yourself depressed whenever you enter the building. And it might be bad for business. The owners might eventually decide to renovate, in a way that the stone might like better.*

"How would they know what it would like better?"

Some people have sensitivities to stuff like that, says Steen. *But this doesn't happen often, really, Janie. It's not as strange as it sounds.*

"I think maybe you don't realize how strange it sounds," Jane says.

More people are on the streets now, and some of them are dressed colorfully, in purples, reds, golds. Jane sees people with dark skin, light skin. She studies the back of her hand. She's already noticed that her skin here is pretty much the same color it is at home.

Steen notices her examination. *Zorsted is an international hub,* he tells her. *Zorsteddan citizens have roots from all over, including across the sea.*

"Across the sea," Jane says, startled. "How big is Zorsted?"

Zorsted is a small island. It's only one of the nations of this earth, Steen says, *which is an entire planet, just like yours.*

She's too overwhelmed. Tu Reviens is a gateway to an entire other planet? Of conscious rocks, trees, and clouds? "What's wrong with this place that you haven't discovered electricity?" she says, distress making her want to be antagonistic. "Is it the dark ages here? Do I have to pee in the gutter?"

Steen makes a small, hurt noise, and Jane is ashamed of herself. "I'm sorry, Steen," she says. "It's just a lot to take in."

He draws himself up tall (for a strayhound). *We have plumbing, and toilets, and infrastructure,* he says with dignity, *and a brilliant and just duchess. We've made advances in science and medicine that would astound the quacks in the Other Land. We have technology that* doesn't *destroy our environment. If you pee in the gutter, you'll probably be arrested for public drunkenness and indecency.*

"I'm sure I would," Jane says penitently.

He walks beside her with a stiffness that feels like a cold shoulder in her brain. No, in her heart. She knows how much she's hurt his feelings.

"Steen," she says gently. "If I were arrested, would you speak up on my behalf? Do strayhounds ever testify in court?"

Why shouldn't they? he responds huffily. *Every court employs an unbiased human reporter who has a strayhound, to assist with translation of witness strayhounds. It's entirely civilized.*

"Can strayhounds be arrested for crimes too?"

Of course, he says. *We have free will. What do you think, we're pets?*

"Do you have jobs?"

Most of us choose to work alongside our person, but we can do what we like.

She watches the prim, careful steps he's taking. A few other people in the streets have had strayhounds trotting beside them, but the vast majority don't. And it occurs to her that Zorsteddan strayhounds may, in fact, pee in the gutter. She sighs. It's complicated to be bound to a telepathic dog.

"Steen?" she says. "I'm sorry."

He ignores her.

She's seen some of the people petting their strayhounds, so this must be acceptable public behavior. "Hold on," she says, stopping, squatting down to Steen. He glares at her.

She touches the soft, silky fur at the side of his face. "I'm sorry," she says. "Forgive me. The truth is, I've never been so scared in my life. If you weren't here to take care of me, I'd be crying my eyes out."

He transfers his glare to his feet. Then his manner softens. *I remember the first time I stepped through the hanging,* he says.

"It's a lot to get used to," Jane says.

I'm just so happy, he says. *I've been looking for you for so long. No matter what happens, you're my person.*

"No matter what happens," she repeats carefully. "What's going to happen?"

I don't know, he says, too quickly.

Jane stays on one knee for a few more minutes, stroking his fur, thinking things through. She's noticed that the people, all of them, have the same angular, pointy-chinned look to their faces that she has in her present form. Taken individually, no person here would alarm her. But taken together, as the society filling the streets, they are evidence that she's far, far away from home.

Steen has been leading her down sloping streets that turn back on each other, distorting her sense of direction. But she knows she's some distance from the duchess's tall mansion now, and lower. Something brackish stings the air that she breathes.

"Who's the one person in Zorsted who knows about the painting in Tu Reviens?" Jane asks.

Steen has taken an interest in his own front paws. He lifts one and stares at it. *I'm bringing you to that person now.*

"Oh?" Jane says. "It'll be nice to be able to talk to someone who understands."

He glances into her face, then inspects his paw again. *The animals here are different from the animals in the Other Land,* he says. *We have sea creatures here that don't live in the seas of your land.*

"Is the person who knows about the painting a sea creature?"

No, he says. *It's a human who's helping to care for our sea creatures. Our sea creatures are sick,* he says. *I'm taking you to the sea. That's usually where to find her.*

"All right," Jane says. "Let's go then, shall we?"

It's only once she's walking again, on a road very near the sea, that a kind of impossible understanding touches her, so lightly, she almost can't feel it. It's a tiny flame trying to catch hold inside her. A hope. Suddenly frightened, she glances at Steen, who does not look back at her.

At the end of a dock at the bottom of a staircase that hangs over the crashing waves sits a woman in a purple coat, her feet dangling above the water. As Jane's boots clap along the dock, the woman twists around, turning her face to the sound. Jane has never seen that curious face before, she's never seen that configuration of eyes, nose, mouth; but of course, Jane was expecting that.

The woman smiles at Jane and Steen, pleasantly. "Good morning," she says in Zorsteddan, in a voice that Jane doesn't recognize. Then the woman focuses on Steen. "Why, hello, my friend," she says in hearty tones. "Don't tell me you've finally found your person? Sing Ho! for the life of a strayhound!"

Disbelief has dropped Jane to her knees. Tears trickle down her face. The woman clambers up and comes to Jane, distressed at her pain. Her coat is open; the lining, silver and gold, shimmers in the light. "What's wrong?" she says. "Can I help you?"

"Aunt Magnolia," Jane says. "Aunt Magnolia. Aunt Magnolia."

Once the interlude of hugging and weeping has passed, Jane seems to be capable of only two words. One of them is *How?* and the other is *Why?*

"I used to attend the galas now and then at Tu Reviens," Aunt Magnolia says quietly.

The three of them are sitting together at the edge of the dock with Jane in the middle. Aunt Magnolia's arm around Jane's shoulder is jarring, while Steen's warmth grounds her in normalcy. Jane is too overwhelmed to appreciate the irony of this.

"I knew the day was coming when I was going to have to plot an escape," says Aunt Magnolia.

"Escape from what?" Jane asks hoarsely. "Why would you need to escape? And why would you go to the galas? Why did you never tell me? Some man called me from Antarctica and told me you were dead!"

Aunt Magnolia squeezes Jane's shoulder more tightly. "One night," she says, "very, very late—the gala was nearly over—I was making my way up to the third floor, when some drunken party guest jostled me and I found my arm going right through that painting. Going *through* it, and not harming the painting one bit. I managed not to scream. But I knew I hadn't imagined it, and it left me shaken. I contrived an excuse to delay my departure that night. That was the trip to the Black Sea, do you remember the Black Sea trip?"

"The last trip before Antarctica," Jane says weakly.

"Yes," says Aunt Magnolia. "I found the bedroom of someone I knew to be spending the night with Ravi Thrash. I hid there. When the guests had all gone and the house was settling in to sleep, I went back to investigate. I touched the painting and my finger sank in. I reached deeper and fell right through."

I saw her do it, Steen tells Jane, *from the landing above. I followed her in and watched her explore. I've kept close tabs on her, but she doesn't know I'm the basset hound from the house.*

"I explored," says Aunt Magnolia, "and found—well, I found what you've also found. A world where no one was likely ever to follow me, and where I'd be unrecognizable even if they did."

"But why did you need a world where no one was likely to find you?"

Aunt Magnolia pauses. Jane notices that she does this every time Jane asks her a question, as if the pause counts as some sort of answer, which it doesn't. The Aunt Magnolia Jane remembers never hesitated to answer her questions.

"I returned to Tu Reviens and caught up with my colleagues going to the Black Sea," says Aunt Magnolia. "After I got back from that trip, I sat you down and made you promise to come to Tu Reviens. Then, next time I was able to get to a Tu Reviens gala, I asked Mrs. Vanders to please pass you a special message. Did she pass you the message?"

"What?" Jane says. "No! I didn't get any message!"

"I told Mrs. Vanders to tell you to 'Reach for the umbrella,'" says Aunt Magnolia. "Then, when no one was watching, I passed into Zorsted, intending to stay here and wait for you."

She didn't have a strayhound to explain anything to her, Steen tells Jane. *She was completely alone.*

"How can you say you made me promise to come to Tu Reviens?" Jane says. "That's not what you did. You only made me promise never to turn down an invitation."

"I also made Mrs. Vanders promise to invite you, should anything ever happen to me. Didn't she invite you?"

"No! Kiran invited me! You were dead! Why would I look for you if you were dead? And how can you imagine the message 'Reach for the umbrella' would make me think to try jumping into a *painting*? And even if it *did*, how would you expect me to find you in a *strange city*?"

Jane finds herself shaking Aunt Magnolia's arm from her shoulder. Something is wrong here. The story is grievously lacking sense, and no one is telling her why. Why did Aunt Magnolia need to leave in the first place?

When Aunt Magnolia puts her hands in her lap, clasps them together, and studies them, Jane studies them too. They're not the hands Jane remembers. They're larger, the fingernails more blunt. The irises of this woman's eyes are clear too, unblemished; this Aunt Magnolia has no starry splotch of color in one eye. *Maybe this isn't Aunt Magnolia.*

Then Jane sees that her own Zorsteddan hands are very much like Aunt Magnolia's Zorsteddan hands.

"I've wanted to tell you the truth about my life for so long," Aunt Magnolia says. "Now that I finally can, I'm scared to pieces."

"The truth about your life?" Jane says. "Aunt Magnolia, what are you talking about?"

"The truth about my work."

"Your work! The pictures? What are you telling me? Didn't you take the pictures?"

"I took the pictures," she says. "I always took the pictures."

"Then *what*?"

Aunt Magnolia is staring unhappily into her hands. "One day," she says, "when I was taking the pictures, I discovered, by chance, a sunken nuclear submarine. A foreign submarine."

"You never told me that."

"I was forbidden by the United States government to tell anyone," she says. "We salvaged it secretly."

"You helped the US government salvage a nuclear submarine?"

"And then they asked me to help them with other things," says Aunt Magnolia. "They offered me money. You were a child. We had no money and I was raising you alone, on the paycheck of an adjunct. I didn't know what was ahead for either of us. I said yes."

"Aunt Magnolia," Jane says, piecing this out. "Are you telling me that you became some sort of underwater . . . spy?"

"Yes," she says.

"Oh," Jane says, flabbergasted. "What does that even mean?"

"There are underwater operatives," says Aunt Magnolia. "There are people who salvage sensitive military wrecks like that submarine, and people who tap underwater cables. There are exchanges of goods and information that take place at the bottom of the sea. At first, I didn't understand the extent of it. I got mixed up in things I now wish I hadn't. Bad things can happen underwater, in the dark, where no one else can see."

What Aunt Magnolia is describing is somehow more absurd to Jane than the existence of a fantasy world inside a painting where dogs can talk and rocks have feelings. "You never told me," Jane says. "You never told me."

"I wanted to stop," says Aunt Magnolia. "They started to ask me to do things I hated to do. Bombs are disposed of underwater sometimes, did you know that? And eventually there began to be some confusion about my allegiances."

"I don't understand anything you're saying," Jane says.

"In time, I'll tell you every detail," she says. "I'll confess every lie. It'll be a great relief to me."

"Not to me."

"That's my greatest regret," she says. "I only ever wanted you to be safe. Did Mrs. Vanders tell you about the money? It's yours to access, whenever you want it."

Jane doesn't want to hear about money. "Who called me from Antarctica?"

"A colleague," says Aunt Magnolia. "A diving friend, another operative, who agreed to help me disappear, though I never told him where I was going."

"You let me believe you were dead," Jane says. "You were dead."

"Darling," Aunt Magnolia starts, reaching for Jane, but Jane is standing, Jane is pushing away from her.

"You were dead," Jane says, tears running down her face.

"I'm sorry," Aunt Magnolia says. "I didn't have a lot of time to plan and maybe I did it badly. But I'm not dead. I came here. I've been waiting for you. I've looked for you every day."

"I might never have found you." Jane's voice is rising with hysteria. "I wouldn't have," she says, pointing to Steen, "if that dog weren't nuts. I had a gravestone put up for you. Your friend sent me your things, your supposed Antarctica things. I've been sleeping with your fucking hat!"

Aunt Magnolia has always been the type to rush to soothe a person who's upset. It's instinct for her, she can't help herself. Jane can see it now in the unfamiliar face and reaching arms of this strange but undeniable Aunt Magnolia.

The water bulges then under the dock at Aunt Magnolia's feet. The head of a gray creature rises above the surface of the water, vaguely bear-like in appearance, round-faced with a long nose. It's as big as a beluga whale and has flippers, whiskers, and a blow hole on the top of its head. In amazement, Jane stares into its face.

The animal's mouth is set in an even line that gives it an aspect of patience and serenity. Its dark eyes are large and deep with pain. Jane knows as well as anyone that creatures who live in the depths of the ocean are sometimes bizarre to the point of challenging credulity; Aunt

Magnolia's work has taught her so. But just as Jane knows by looking at the people of this earth that they're not from her Earth, she knows that this animal belongs only to this world.

It doesn't speak, but gazes intently at Aunt Magnolia. Aunt Magnolia lies down on the dock on her stomach, her trousered legs sticking out behind her and her arms and head hanging over the edge. Her coat lies open, purple with flashes of silver and gold, like a nebula. She reaches out and places a hand on the bear-like creature's forehead. She says nothing, and Jane doesn't entirely understand what's happening. But she recognizes that Aunt Magnolia has found a willing recipient for her soothing. With her touch, Aunt Magnolia is soothing this animal, which now has big tears rolling down its face.

Aunt Magnolia and the sea animal stay in that position for several minutes. Jane stands on the dock, tears dripping onto her cloak. Steen is pressing himself hard against her legs and glancing up at her frequently. Like Aunt Magnolia and the sea animal, he is silent.

The sea animal moves its head so that it's looking into Jane's eyes. Jane is locked in its gaze, lost in the well of its feeling. *This animal has power,* she finds herself thinking, though she has no idea what that power is.

The sea animal sinks away. The water closes silently above it.

Aunt Magnolia shifts to a sitting position again, her feet dangling over the edge. She doesn't look at Jane. Jane interprets her shoulders. Aunt Magnolia is depleted from soothing someone else, and she's ashamed for having hurt Jane.

Jane can't quite get herself to sit next to her, but she sits a few feet removed. She dangles her legs again over the water.

"Steen," Jane says, "that's my strayhound's name, Steen. He tells me the sea creatures are sick."

Aunt Magnolia's head dips, slowly, in agreement. "They're called sea bears."

"Were you talking to it?"

"Not exactly."

"Were you giving it—some kind of medicine?"

"It was something much more elemental than that," she says, "and less fantastical. They're sick because they're traumatized and grieving. A huge number of their population were killed by Zorsteddan hunters. Their meat came into fashion and for a period of time, they were massacred. The hunters convinced the government that the sea bears were dumb brutes—though how anyone could think such a thing of a creature like the one we just saw—"

Her voice breaks off, rough and choked with disgust. Jane watches her take one even breath.

"It was a long time ago," Aunt Magnolia says. "Hunting them is illegal now. But they live a very long time, and Zorsteddan scientists believe their memory goes deep and heals slowly. I'm in a program organized by the scientists. I come out here in the morning and I wait. If one of the sea bears visits, and one usually does, I sit with it, and touch it with kindness."

"What does that mean?" says Jane.

"I think you know what it means, sweetheart," says Aunt Magnolia. When Jane doesn't answer, she looks into her hands and says quietly, "Just *being* with the sea bear. Not trying to impress anything upon it. And just letting the sea bear be too. They have what we would probably call a . . . psychic ability. If I have the intention of simply *being* beside it, it will know that's my intention. That they allow our company in this way now—for they haven't always allowed it—is a sign that they might come to trust humans again. Until they do, and until the pain of their grief subsides, it's as if the ocean here has a sickness in its soul. I can feel it, Janie."

It's hard for Jane to know how to respond. "This is your job here?" she says.

"Yes," says Aunt Magnolia. "The government pays the scientists."

"Are you in charge of the operation?"

"Good heavens, no," she says. "My position is very junior. I'm receiving training, but I've only been in Zorsted a short while. There's a program. Anyone with an affinity for animals can apply. You could apply."

Jane blinks at this; she can't answer. "How did you convince them you were from here? Weren't they suspicious?"

"I keep to myself, and I pretend that I don't want to talk about my past. There've been moments when I've gotten odd looks, sure, but there's a high tolerance for oddness here. People seem to expect not to understand everything they see. Anyway, if you met someone who didn't seem to know your customs, would you assume they came from an alternate reality?"

"I guess not," says Jane. "Do you miss our technologies? Could you solve the problem faster with scuba gear?"

She flashes Jane a quiet, sideways smile. "Even in the absence of compressed air," she says, "diving techniques here are pretty sophisticated. They have a sort of diving bell, with air tubes that extend up to the surface. Regardless, even if we had scuba gear, I doubt we'd use it. It does not help the healing of the animals for us humans to push ourselves into their homes."

It's a particular kind of confusion to be angry with the person who taught her about gentleness, respect; who taught her how to soothe herself. Jane watches the water dancing beneath her feet, conscious of Steen beside her. Carefully, she leans out until she can see her own reflection. Something about that strange face strikes her. Jane turns to study Aunt Magnolia and realizes that even in this world, she has Aunt Magnolia's cheekbones and her nose.

"How are your umbrellas," Aunt Magnolia says, "my darling?"

Jane's lungs are a jellyfish, moving silently through a great sorrow. "I don't know why I'm here," she says. "I don't know why I should have a strayhound if I'm from the other side. I don't know why I came to Tu Reviens in the first place."

Aunt Magnolia takes a minute to answer. "I don't see why creatures from different worlds shouldn't fit together," she says. "Zorsted is full of strayhounds who haven't found their people. Maybe it's because those people are in different worlds."

"Steen said the same thing," Jane says. "But what do you mean, different worlds? Do you think there are more than two?"

"Well," Aunt Magnolia says, "I used to think there was only one. Once there were two, I guess I began to feel there may as well be a thousand. You know?"

Jane smells the brackish air and hears the water slap against the posts of the dock.

Aunt Magnolia left Jane alone. Orphaned, with no money Jane knew of. Her plan to reunite with her niece obscure and unspoken, balanced on a pin.

"I need to think," Jane says.

When I need to think, says Steen, *I walk.*

"Will you come with me?" Jane asks him.

Of course I will, if you want me.

"Of course I do," Jane says, touching the place between his ears, then standing. "You're my strayhound, aren't you?"

Watching Jane, Aunt Magnolia rises to her own feet anxiously.

"We're going for a walk," Jane says carefully.

"All right," Aunt Magnolia says, swallowing. "I'll see you again, won't I, darling? Please?"

"I don't know," Jane says. *You're not who I thought you were,* Jane doesn't say. *You're not who you pretended to be.*

Aunt Magnolia's eyes are bright with tears. She holds Jane in a long hug and kisses her forehead. She tells Jane she loves her. "Come back," she says. Jane holds her tightly before letting her go.

"Where are we going?" Jane asks Steen.

Where would you like to go?

"Someplace that isn't challenging," Jane says, "for either of us."

Steen walks her back up the staircase, then along a road crowded with small houses. A snaggle of children runs past. Someone is frying something that smells like bacon.

"I'm hungry," Jane says. "Are you hungry?"

We could go back to your aunt, he says. *She'll have money.*

"I'll survive," Jane says, "if you will."

I know where there's fruit, he says.

"Do strayhounds like fruit?"

This one does.

The street bends sharply to the right but Steen continues straight, into a patch of gnarled trees. He leads her through thick grass and fallen branches. Eventually the land begins to slope downward and they end up in a grove of stocky trees heavy with a rose-colored fruit that looks somewhat like, but decidedly isn't, apples.

The Zorsteddan word for it comes to her. She speaks it aloud.

Yes, says Steen contentedly. *The duchess owns the orchard.*

"Are we stealing?"

Not with me here, he says. *I live in the duchess's mansion. She takes care of us. Her food is mine.*

"Are you sure you're still welcome in the duchess's mansion, now that you've found your person?"

You don't have a residence here, he says significantly, *so I'll still live with the duchess. If you establish a residence here, that will change.*

He doesn't look at her, and Jane carefully doesn't look at him. She fills her deep trouser pockets with fruit and continues to follow him down the slope, which grows steeper. Stepping out of the orchard, she finds herself on a small, crescent-shaped beach of pale sand. The sun is strong and her Zorsteddan clothing blocks the chill of the wind. Steen trots to an outcropping of rock and shrubbery and settles in beside it. She joins him there; she sits beside him, watching the water rush onto the sand, then pull itself back. The fruit is crisp like an apple, but sweet, like a pear.

"It's such a strange feeling, being in Zorsted," Jane says. "I feel like I've died and been reincarnated in a different body, a different life, except they forgot to wipe my memory of the life that came before."

I don't believe in reincarnation, says Steen.

"Don't you? If there's more than one world, why shouldn't there be more than one life?"

There are *many lives in every life,* he says.

"You and Aunt Magnolia are both very fond of obscure philosophical pronouncements," Jane says. "Tell me, is there a market in Zorsted for umbrellas?"

It certainly rains. Though it never rains frogs.

"Another oddity," Jane says. "Where would umbrellas be sold?"

In the public market, he says. *If you sold enough umbrellas, you might be able to open a shop. Might I ask why you're asking these questions?*

"I don't know," Jane says. "Maybe because umbrellas are less scary than existential philosophy."

Steen passes her a prim look. *I saw a strayhound once with a curious umbrella hat,* he says. *I thought it was quite fetching.*

Jane tries not to smile. "Would you like me to make you an umbrella hat, Steen?"

That's entirely up to you, he says with dignity.

"Would I be making it to fit Jasper the basset hound, or Steen the strayhound?"

He hesitates. *I guess that's also up to you.*

Yes. I guess that's one of the big questions of the day, isn't it? Tu Reviens or Zorsted?

See? he says. *I told you you could talk to me without speaking out loud.*

Yes, I see.

Do you— He hesitates, and she feels his eagerness. His vulnerability. *Do you like it?*

She lets out a breath. *I can't say yet, Steen.*

He burrows his nose in the sand, as if it's a way to stop himself from saying what he wants to say.

This inlet is an awful lot like the one you took me to at Tu Reviens, Jane says, after a pause.

I like to come here, he says.

Do you go to the inlet at Tu Reviens because it reminds you of this one?

I found the one at Tu Reviens first, he says. *I guess I like this one because it reminds me of that one.*

That's confusing.

Yes, he says. *Home is. After all, it's one's headquarters, one's backdrop, one's framework. One's history, and also one's haven.*

Are you good at Scrabble, Steen? Jane asks, smiling.

Steen sniffs. *We have a much superior game here. It's like Scrabble. You win by putting the highest-value words down. But the words you put down also tell a story, and you have to take care, because that story will play out somehow in your day.*

Seriously? The game changes your day? *That sounds dangerous!*

You're interpreting it too extremely. No one has ever been seriously hurt.

Oh! Just minor injuries, then!

The story plays out metaphorically, usually in some harmless and amusing manner, he says soothingly. *I can see it sounds strange. But I promise you, Janie, this world is no more dangerous than yours.*

It's so different here, she says. *Do both Zorsted and Tu Reviens feel like home to you?*

Yes. And no. In Tu Reviens, I'm mute, and no one understands me, or anyway, no one did before now. In Zorsted, I'm lonely, or, I was before now. He pauses. *Don't you think it's the people that make a place feel like home?*

This does make sense to Jane. It explains why nowhere has felt like home, ever since she got that phone call—*fake* phone call—from Antarctica.

On the distant horizon, a tall ship with brilliant white sails comes into view. It's too far away to guess if it's coming or going.

If I'm a seeker, Steen, I don't know what I'm seeking, Jane says.

Steen hesitates again. *Well,* he says, *I'll keep you company while you figure it out.*

The long, difficult morning is tugging at her limbs. Her unfamiliar body is asking for the sleep it missed in the night. *Yes, please,* Jane says.

She curls on her side in the sand with an arm around Steen, and allows her Zorsteddan self to rest.

She wakes to a night lit by two enormous yellow moons. Both are bigger than her moon. Together, they cast far more light. The sky is streaked with stars.

Steen is nowhere to be found.

"Steen?"

There's no answer. She pushes to her feet groggily, turning in circles, then suddenly wakes with a violent shiver, thinking about Zorsteddan hunters, or predators, or stones that decide they don't like you. "Steen!"

I'm coming, he says, the message faint in her mind. Turning, she sees his dark form trotting toward her, across wet sand that's bright with reflected moonlight.

"I got scared!"

I wouldn't leave you to find your way around alone.

"I mean I got scared *for you!*"

When he reaches her, she drops down and puts her arms around him. He smells like wet fur and tries to lick her hands. "Ick!" she says. "No licking!"

No hugging, he says. *Strayhounds like to be petted, not hugged.*

She lets him go. "If you don't lick, I won't hug."

Deal. But you don't need to be scared for me, Janie, he says. *People here pretty much leave strayhounds alone.*

"Okay," Jane says thickly.

Are you cold?

"Yes, and hungry."

You slept for a very long time. I did too, when I was first adjusting to your world. Crossing over is tiring. Let's go someplace warm.

"How far are we from the hanging in the duchess's mansion?"

Your aunt's home is closer. She won't mind if we wake her.

"No. Tu Reviens."

All right, then, he says. *The long, uphill climb will warm us.*

An orchard on a steep hill is treacherous at night, even in the light of two moons. Jane keeps tripping, and whacking her head on low branches. She pulls her scarf tight around her ears and mutters to Steen that it'd be nice if the orchard would light itself for their convenience.

On the streets high above the water, the silence of the Zorsteddan night is striking. Zorsteddan buildings don't hum or buzz. Zorsteddan streetlamps make the tiniest sizzling sounds as flames eat away at wicks.

Light and sound spill from the occasional building down the occasional street, but Steen leads her away from those streets. *Drunken revelers are the plague of every harbor town,* he says fastidiously.

Crumpled and cold from sleep, Jane is content enough to stay out of the way of drunken revelers. They climb quite a distance before the duchess's mansion looms, and Steen is right. The long walk is warming.

I'll have to get the attention of one of the few strayhounds in the castle who has a person, he tells her, *to let us in.*

"How will you do that?"

Strayhounds can communicate with each other mentally, remember?

"How will you explain why I deserve to be let in?"

Hopefully my brother will be awake.

"You have a brother?"

I have twelve brothers, seven sisters, and two hundred and forty-two cousins.

Jane speaks a Zorsteddan expletive. "Does your brother know about Tu Reviens?"

No. I told you, I haven't told anyone. But he's my brother. He trusts me, and his person trusts him. His person will open the door for us.

"It all sounds kind of complicated. Your brother trusts you, but you're not actually telling him the truth."

Well, it's hard to know what to do sometimes, says Steen. *If I tell my brother, should I tell my other eighteen siblings? What if I tell my brother and he tells his person? It's not a small thing, a hanging that leads to another world. I have to be careful. You understand that, don't you?*

As she climbs into a garden on some obscure, high-walled side of the duchess's mansion, Jane feels tired, and old. "I'm not a big fan of deception at the moment."

Steen glances at her. *I know. But you'll see. It's your secret now too. You'll have to decide who to tell. Now, stop talking out loud. You'll wake the entire ground-floor staff, and anyway, I'm trying to focus on communicating with my brother.*

A minute later, a gruff man in a nightshirt opens a wooden door in the high wall, grunts, then steps back inside without even looking at them. A strayhound moves at his feet, shorter and stockier than Steen. He and Steen briefly stand in the doorway together, sniffing and snuggling each other.

Then Steen sets off with purpose. *This path will take us through the kitchens,* he tells Jane.

Jane follows. They climb all fifteen stories of the duchess's mansion, gorging on bread, cheese, more Zorsteddan fruit with names Jane magically knows, and a long strip of what tastes like the most delicious beef jerky in any world, all pilfered from the kitchens. She has the sense that her Zorsteddan body finds fifteen stories of steps far less arduous than her real-world body would.

As she changes back into her *Doctor Who* pajamas, a faraway city clock tolls, and Jane understands the current time in Zorsted. It suddenly occurs to her to wonder what time it is at home. She speaks a Zorsteddan expletive. *It's gala day!*

Not anymore, Steen responds. *We missed the gala.*

Another expletive. *What if someone noticed my absence?*

Just say you weren't feeling well. If anyone gives you a hard time, I'll bite them.

Steen! You can't start biting people for no reason! My world does very mean things to dogs who bite! Just do something distracting that humans love. Put out your paw for them to shake.

Oh, that's dignified, says Steen. *Next you'll tell me to roll over.*

Jane laughs.

Don't worry, says Steen. *After all, if anything ever happens, I have a safe place I can disappear to.*

Jane doesn't answer, because she's not ready to tell him that she doesn't like the idea of him disappearing somewhere without her. When she moves into the room with the hanging, Steen follows. The view of Tu Reviens is dim and unpeopled, so Jane takes a moment to examine the umbrella on the floor. The ferrule and the handle are a bit different in shape and color from her own work and the workmanship is finer, but overall, the umbrella is gratifyingly like the one she's just built. Picking it up, carrying it to the lantern in the far corner, scrutinizing it under the light, she's pleased to think that she's chosen appropriate shades of red and green for hers.

What do you think you're doing! Steen says. *That umbrella hasn't been moved in over a hundred years!*

The workmanship is gorgeous, really, Jane says, smoothing the dark, varnished shaft with her fingers. *And someone dusts it regularly.*

With the most delicate of feather dusters! Steen says. *I wish you would put it down.*

You're one of those strayhounds who never got sent to the principal's office, aren't you? Jane says. *All right, all right,* she adds as he begins to stomp his feet again like bread kneading. *Calm down.*

But as she sets it down on the floor, the ancient material of one of the gores begins to tear along the seam. As Steen screams bloody horror in her mind, the gore falls out of the umbrella and collapses limply to the floor.

Look what you've done! Look what you've done!

Steen, Jane says calmly. *I've got a nearly identical umbrella sitting in my morning room this very moment. It's well-built enough. It'll last another hundred-plus years.*

Steen is breathing like a husky who's just finished the Iditarod. *Oh, thank goodness,* he says. *Thank goodness. Let's go get it. This very instant. Right now!*

Steen goes through first. Jane follows.

She needs a minute. It's amazing, somehow, to be standing on the second-story landing of Tu Reviens; she almost feels as if she's never been here before. There's a slight scent to the receiving hall. Sweat, perfume, spilled alcohol, people: a post-party smell. Also, those lilacs, bringing Aunt Magnolia back to her. Hurting differently now, with a whole new confusion.

Someone in a faraway room is listening to the Beatles again. Jasper the basset hound maneuvers himself behind her and head-butts her ankles urgently.

"I'm going!" Jane whispers, obediently climbing to the third-story landing. "Calm down!"

Then Kiran and Ivy appear on the third-story bridge, crossing toward Jane from the west side of the house.

"Janie!" says Kiran. "Where on earth have you been? I looked for you at the party but I never saw you."

Kiran's wearing a lovely strapless gown in scarlet. Her mood, her expression are odd: both cheerful and hard. Triumphantly brittle. Also, the bottom edge of her skirt is damp-looking and crusty. Something's happened.

Jane wants to ask Kiran about it, but she's afraid it'll encourage Kiran to ask her questions too, questions Jane can't answer. "What time is it?" she squeaks.

"Nearly four in the morning," Kiran says. "Ivy and I have been talking."

"Actually," Ivy says to Jane, "I wanted to talk to you too."

"Right," Jane says, trying not to gawk at Ivy. Her dress is long and black and so elegant that Jane's *Doctor Who* pajamas make her feel twelve years old.

"I'm going to bed," Kiran says smartly, then sets off down the steps.

"You were magnificent tonight," Ivy calls after Kiran. "We're really grateful. We couldn't have pulled it off without you."

"I didn't do it for Patrick's sake," Kiran says.

"Yeah, okay," Ivy says, "whatever. *I'm* really grateful."

Kiran turns and gives Ivy a broad, warm smile before walking away. Jane has never seen Kiran smile like that before.

Jane turns to Ivy. "I'm awfully tired. Can I talk to you tomorrow too?"

"Sure," Ivy says.

"G'night, then," Jane says. Then she stands there looking at Ivy for another moment, until Jasper head-butts her. "Damn demented dog!" She turns away toward her rooms.

But when Jane and Jasper return to the stairs a few minutes later, carrying the umbrella Jane has made, Ivy is still on the second-story landing, staring intently at the umbrella in the painting. Her nose is probably two inches from the paint, her glasses pushed to her forehead and her eyes focused on the gore that lies limply on the checkerboard floor.

It's too late to turn back; Ivy hears them. She stands straight and raises her eyes to Jane. Loose wisps of dark hair swing around her face.

And so Jane continues bravely down the stairs, umbrella in hand.

Ivy's steady blue gaze takes in Jane, Jasper, and, with interest, the red-and-green umbrella in Jane's hand.

"Going for a walk?" Ivy says, glancing at Jane's pajamas.

"Possibly," Jane says.

"Do you want company?"

"Yes," Jane says. "I mean, yes. I do, very much. But I should probably go alone."

"Okay," says Ivy. "I looked for you during the gala. Weren't you feeling up to it?"

The excuse is on the tip of her tongue. She ate something that disagreed with her, she slept through the gala. She hates parties, she hid in the west attics. She spent the night in a bedroom with one of the guests. "I don't want to lie to you," Jane says. "I want to tell you the truth."

In her long black dress, with her hair up, Ivy looks like a woman in a portrait by Renoir, or John Singer Sargent. She studies Jane. "I want to tell you the truth too," she says.

Another silence fills the space between them. It's not an awkward silence. It's full of something like hope, and curiosity.

Jane knows, finally, what she wants.

She speaks in a whisper. "Ivy?"

"Yes?"

"Can you keep a secret?"

"Hell, yes."

Jane thinks through her words before she says them. "Would you please touch that painting?"

"This one?" Ivy says, pointing to the painting, then wrinkling her nose in puzzlement. "Mrs. Vanders would crucify me."

"Please?"

"Okay," she says, and stretches her finger to the painting. When she touches it, her finger sinks in. Her entire hand falls through. With a cry of alarm, she snatches it back. She inspects her own recovered hand, carefully, closely. Satisfied that she still has all her fingers, she raises amazed eyes to Jane.

"I can't wait to hear what you ask me to do next," she says.

"I'd like to bring you to meet a woman who communes with sea bears," says Jane.

Ivy blinks. "Sea bears?"

"I want to show you. Will you come?"

Ivy cocks her head at the painting. "Are the sea bears through there?"

"Yes."

Ivy blinks again. "Will you be with me the whole time?"

"Yes."

"Promise?"

"I swear it."

"Okay, then," says Ivy.

"What do you think, Steen?" Jane says, looking down at him. "Can a strayhound and his human make a home in two different worlds, with an aunt and a friend?"

Jasper holds Jane's eyes and cants his head to the side, as if considering. Then he walks into the painting.

Jane turns to Ivy, whose mouth has dropped open. "Do you trust me?" Jane says.

Ivy's eyes on Jane are wide and deep. She nods.

Jane takes Ivy's hand and leads her into another world.

hand spring

handle

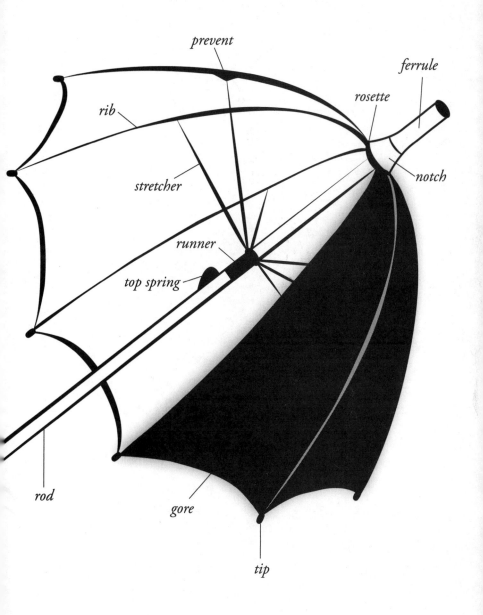

prevent

ferrule

rosette

rib

notch

stretcher

runner

top spring

rod

gore

tip

Author's Note

This book is an homage to a number of my best-loved books. A lot of my names, for example, come directly or indirectly from Daphne duMaurier's *Rebecca,* one of the classic "orphan comes to a house of mystery" texts. DuMaurier's strange, scary housekeeper is named Mrs. Danvers; my housekeeper and butler are Mr. and Mrs. Vanders. The dog in *Rebecca* is named Jasper; mine is too. An important boat in *Rebecca* is named *Je Reviens,* French for "I return"; my house is named Tu Reviens, French for "you return." I also gave Ivy and Patrick the last name "Yellan," which is the last name of the heroine of another wonderful duMaurier novel, *Jamaica Inn.*

In the first part of *Jane, Unlimited,* I describe a writing desk Jane finds in her morning room. This is essentially the writing desk from Rebecca's morning room, right down to the labels Jane finds on the docketed drawers. There are other connections, deliberate and otherwise, but I'll let you find them yourself. I've always considered *Rebecca* to be one of the most extraordinary books I've ever read. Writers breathe in books, mix them up with whatever else we've got going on in there, then breathe out.

I also had that other great "orphan comes to a house of mystery" text in mind, *Jane Eyre,* by Charlotte Brontë—the most obvious reference being Jane's name, though Jane is really named after my childhood cat! I suppose Charlotte Thrash's name is also a partial reference to Brontë, though I actually named my Charlotte after Charlotte Perkins Gilman, because of her creepy novella "The Yellow Wallpaper." Also, my house has a "madwoman" in the attic, so to speak. As in *Jane Eyre,* my madwoman is the first wife of the man of the house. In my case, though, she's not actually mad, she's just a theoretical physicist.

Edith Wharton's beautiful but depressing *The House of Mirth* also plays a part in this book. *The House of Mirth* stars a poor orphaned woman named Lily Bart who lives in turn-of-the-century New York, uses her looks to cling to her place in high society, and . . . well, as Jane remarks to Lucy St. George, there's not much mirth. I suppose it was impossible for me to write about wealthy Kiran inviting her poor friend to her fancy house without thinking of Lily Bart and the age of lady companions.

I pulled the initial wording and dialogue of Jane's *expotition* to the North Pole directly from "Chapter VIII: In Which Christopher Robin Leads an Expotition to the North Pole" in *Winnie-the-Pooh.* Sorry, Pooh-Bear. Despite appearances, I really do love you and you have always been my #1 go-to comfort read. I guess that's why my mind reached for you when I asked myself, "What would be horrifying?"

Of course, it isn't just books that inspire books. Constantin Brâncuşi's sculpture *Fish* is real. Brâncuşi, a Romanian artist and one of the pioneers of modernism, created several fish sculptures. The version in my story actually lives at the Philadelphia Museum of Art. When I e-mailed the restoration department to ask them how the fish was attached to its pedestal and whether removing it would damage the sculpture, they e-mailed back that they weren't going to answer that question. Probably a wise policy. Writers ask a lot of weirdly specific questions. It's because we are up to no good.

Johannes Vermeer's *Lady Writing a Letter with her Maid* is also real. In 1974, this painting was stolen from a private house in Ireland by members of the IRA, then recovered soon after. In 1984 it was stolen again by a Dublin gangster, and this time it wasn't recovered until 1993. After its recovery, a Danish conservator named Jørgen Wadum, anxiously examining it for damage, noticed a pinprick in the lady's eye, which led to the discovery that Vermeer attached a string to the canvas to work out his perspective. The painting is now in the National Gallery of Ireland. I have two books to thank for my art theft knowledge: *Museum of the Missing* by Simon Houpt and *The Irish Game: A True Story of Crime and Art* by Matthew Hart.

Speaking of art theft . . . I've essentially lifted Tu Reviens's Venetian courtyard from the Isabella Stewart Gardner Museum in Boston, especially the nasturtiums, which are famously displayed in the courtyard every spring. It's not identical—the courtyard at the Gardner does not have interior steps that climb all the way to the top, for example. But it's pretty similar, and Gardner visitors probably recognize it (especially if they've seen the nasturtiums). The Gardner has a greenhouse where all the courtyard flowers are cultivated; similarly, Tu Reviens has the winter garden where its flowers are cultivated. The Rembrandt self-portrait that lives in Tu Reviens actually lives at the Gardner (*Self-portrait, Aged 23*). And in 1990, the largest art heist in history took place at the Gardner; thieves stole thirteen works of art valued at $500 million, including Rembrandt's *The Storm on the Sea of Galilee* and Vermeer's *The Concert.* The works have never been recovered and no arrests have ever been made. When you visit the museum today, the frames of the stolen pictures hang empty on the walls. It's heartbreaking.

I used these two books to ensure that Aunt Magnolia was photographing realistic things in the correct locations: *Ocean Soul* by Brian Skerry and *Oceanic Wilderness* by Roger Steene. Both books are full of gorgeous underwater photography. Skerry has a photo of a southern right whale and a diver facing each other on the ocean floor that directly inspired Jane's underwater photo of Aunt Magnolia touching the nose of a southern right whale. I'm embarrassed to admit that I can't remember whether I ever saw a photo somewhere of a yellow goby peeking out of the mouth of a big gray fish, or made that up. I've been scrambling to find this image, so that I can credit it to the correct photographer, but so far I've got nothing. In *Ocean Soul,* Brian Skerry has a stunning photo of a yellow goby peeking out of the opening of a soda can, and a stunning photo of a bluefin tuna opening its mouth to capture a smaller fish. Maybe I combined the two in my imagination?

British science-fiction writer Arthur C. Clarke famously wrote that "Any sufficiently advanced technology is indistinguishable from magic." I play around with this quote in some of my dialogue, but never cite Clarke—so I'm doing so here.

A lot of research goes into the writing of fiction. Two sources I've not yet mentioned are *Bioterrorism: Guidelines for Medical and Public Health Management,* edited by Donald A. Henderson, Thomas V. Inglesby, and Tara O'Toole; and the article "Parallel Universes," by Max Tegmark, in the May 2003 issue of *Scientific American.*

Acknowledgments

I wrote the first draft of this book as a choose-your-own-adventure, in the second-person POV, with numerous diverging paths from which the reader was to choose. Then, over the course of four years, I revised it over and over, gradually shifting it into a third-person POV story intended to be read from beginning to end. Sometimes it takes many attempts (and a lot of frustration) to figure out what a book is asking you to do!

Did I figure it out alone? Hell no.

The early drafts of this book were pretty headache-inducing reading. I am endlessly grateful to my early readers, who waded in, sorted out what I was aiming for, and gave me the feedback I needed in order to achieve it. Thank you to Marie Rutkoski, Rebecca Rabinowitz, and my agent Faye Bender (all of whom read it more than once); thank you to Catherine Cashore, Claire Evans, Deborah Kaplan, Amanda Mac-Gregor, Marc Moskowitz, JD Paul, Cindy Pon, Jessica Quilty, Anindita Basu Sempere, Rebecca Stead, and Tui Sutherland. Thank you to my partial readers who gave feedback on their particular areas of expertise: Dorothy Cashore, Joe Flowers, Kevin Lin, and Kate Marquis.

Thank you to Aunt Mary Previtera, Aunt Rose Luscan, Sarah Manchanda, and Nikhil Manchanda for answering nitpicky questions about things like how bridge is played and what kinds of names are given to pets in Indian cultures. Thank you to Deborah Kaplan, Marc

Moskowitz, Lance Nathan, Michelle Dunnewind Nathan, and JD Paul for helping with questions about stuff like what sorts of things governments do underwater, who has police jurisdiction over private islands, and what basset hounds are like. Thank you to Stephanie Smith, David Kroll, Meg Curley, Eric Idsvoog, Case Kerns, Kevin Birmingham, and Scott Hirst for horror-story brainstorming sessions over dinner. Thank you to Eve Goldfarb for her strength, support, and kindness.

Special thanks to JD Paul, who answered (nearly) infinitely many questions, on numerous topics but especially things science-related, quickly, tirelessly, and completely. JD went above and beyond this time, for real. Special thanks to Marie Rutkoski and Kevin Lin, for talking me through plot points over and over, brainstorming, living the book with me, and keeping me company while the book beat me over the head for a very long time.

Thank you to my warm, enthusiastic, tireless, crackerjack team at Penguin, which includes Elyse Marshall, Jen Loja, Jocelyn Schmidt, Emily Romero, Carmela Iaria, Rachel Cone-Gorham, Shanta Newlin, Felicia Frazier, Erin Berger, Todd Jones, Mary McGrath, Cristi Navarro, Claire Evans, Debra Polansky, Regina Castillo, Alan Winebarger, Mary Raymond, Ev Taylor, Nicole White, Nicole Davies, John Dennany, Sheila Hennessey, Steve Kent, Biff Donovan, Colleen Conway, Doni Kay, Jill Nadeau, Jill Bailey, Judy Samuels, Tina Deniker, Christina Colangelo, Erin Toller, Alexis Watts, Venessa Carson, Kathryn Bhirud, Madison Killen, Theresa Evangelista, Dana Li, Deborah Kaplan, Jenny Kelly, Lily Malcom, and Vanessa Robles. There's no way to express it without sounding trite and clichéd, but I *really actually am* the luckiest writer to have this group of people in my life, along with all the Penguin folks, each of whom plays such an important role in the process of getting a book out into the world. Thank you.

Thank you, as always, to my parents and sisters, without whom I would be lost. My father in particular caught a lot of little errors before this thing went to press. I dedicated this book to my many aunts and great-aunts, whom I've always considered to be models of all the wonderful things I could decide to be, if I chose. My aunts are kind, adventurous, creative, funny, accepting, and full of love. (Uncles, you're not so bad, either.)

Faye Bender, I don't even know what to say. You are my rock, and my friend. Thank you.

Do you notice I haven't mentioned my editor yet? It's because every time I try, I tear up.

If this book is any good, my editor, Kathy Dawson, is the reason why. I thrive on the difficult work Kathy and I do together, and this book was the most difficult one yet. Kathy took my hand and led me through, sometimes gently, sometimes firmly, always patient when I insisted on a circuitous path, and always aiming me toward my vision. Kathy, my books and I would follow you into another dimension, if that's what we needed to do in order to be with you.

About the Author

Kristin Cashore grew up in northeast Pennsylvania and has a master's degree from the Center for the Study of Children's Literature at Simmons College. She lives in the Boston area. Her epic fantasy novels set in the Graceling Realm—*Graceling, Fire,* and *Bitterblue*—are all *New York Times* best sellers and have won many awards and much high praise, including picks as ALA Best Books for Young Adults, *School Library Journal* Best Book of the Year, *Booklist* Editors' Choice, and *Publishers Weekly* Best Book of the Year. In addition, *Graceling* was shortlisted for the William C. Morris Debut Award and *Fire* is an Amelia Elizabeth Walden Book Award Winner.

You can find Kristin online at
kristincashore.blogspot.com.